PRAISE FOR

Louder Than Love

"An emotional ride with a to-die-for hero and with a sparkling ending. Topper is an author to watch!"

—Laura Drake, author of *Nothing Sweeter* and *Her Road Home*

"I was absolutely blown away . . . A wonderful story [and] amazing characters." —*The Book Pushers*

"I can't begin to say all the reasons that I loved this book . . . I just found myself enraptured and so caught up with the story that I was talking to Adrian and hugging Kat in my mind."

—*Nocturne Romance Reads*

"A beautiful and engaging story that will melt your heart . . . Absolutely an emotional whirlwind and well worth the buildup! I don't want to say too much about the story itself because as I've said before, there is such a raw human element to this book that you need to experience it as it happens. My final words would be to read *Louder Than Love*. Allow yourself to be open to a new experience and reap the rewards! You will not be disappointed." —*Open Book Society*

Dictatorship *of the* Dress

JESSICA TOPPER

BERKLEY SENSATION, NEW YORK

THE BERKLEY PUBLISHING GROUP
Published by the Penguin Group
Penguin Group (USA) LLC
375 Hudson Street, New York, New York 10014

USA • Canada • UK • Ireland • Australia • New Zealand • India • South Africa • China

penguin.com

A Penguin Random House Company

This book is an original publication of The Berkley Publishing Group.

Library of Congress Cataloging-in-Publication Data

Topper, Jessica.
Dictatorship of the dress / Jessica Topper.—Berkley Sensation trade paperback edition.
p.   cm.
ISBN 978-0-425-27625-9
1. Mothers and daughters—Fiction.   2. Wedding costume—Fiction.
3. Responsibility—Fiction.   4. Domestic fiction.   I. Title.
PS3620.O587464D53 2015
813'.6—dc23
2014038153

PUBLISHING HISTORY
Berkley Sensation trade paperback edition / January 2015

PRINTED IN THE UNITED STATES OF AMERICA

10 9 8 7 6 5 4 3 2 1

Cover design by Lesley Worrell.
Cover photo by Ilina Simeonova / ImageBrief.com.
Interior text design by Laura K. Corless.

For my mother, Helen.
No cape necessary—you are my ultimate superhero.

ACKNOWLEDGMENTS

Every dress has a story.

I'll never forget asking my mother if she still had her wedding dress. I must've been in my teens or twenties at the time. "Sure," my mom had said, and went to fetch it. I don't know why I wanted to see it; maybe I harbored some illusion that I would someday wear it myself. She came down the stairs, carrying a short, sleeveless dress. It was navy blue worsted wool, with a thick stripe in burnt orange around the bottom of it. I'm sure it was very mod in the late 1960s, back when she and my father tied the knot. I knew the history: It was her second marriage, and his first. But I remembered being shocked and confused. Where was the white? The poufs? The lace? No beads? Not even a veil? Shouldn't it be preserved in some box, somewhere, for all time?

"Oh, I had a dress like that when I married Mr. G.," she replied, waving her hand to dismiss all my questions. "I donated it to the Salvation Army." Then she proceeded, with eyes shining and excitement in her voice, to tell me about the day she married my dad. They got married on his lunch hour, went for coffee in the courthouse cafeteria, and he returned to work.

It's the perfect, quirky nutshell of a story that I love to tell about my parents and their happily-ever-after, now forty-seven years strong and counting. The dress is just an accessory, sold separately. It's the love and whom we share it with that is custom, couture-fit, and fabulous. And the memories are the cherished heirlooms, preserved for all time.

Recently, I asked her to tell me the story again. She added more detail this time, recalling their trip to B. Forman's department store to pick out the dress together. Of putting it on that day, and walking down to meet him at his office, which happened to be in the courthouse. It had been a beautiful, sunny September day, and she remembered how happy she was as she walked back home on her own, the newly minted Mrs. R.

Every dress has a story. And every bride deserves her day in the sun.

As for *this* story, I've dedicated it to my amazing mother, whose superpowers of love, support, strength, and unwavering belief inspire me every single day. Love you, Mom.

I'd also like to express my heartfelt gratitude to those who helped make this novel shine:

My critique partner, Pat O'Dea Rosen, deserves full credit for planting the story seed. Like Laney's snowflake of a white lie avalanching, Pat's mention of her daughter once being mistaken for a bride on an airplane snowballed into a series of "what if" questions in my brain that set me on the path to writing Laney and Noah. I owe thanks to Pat and her daughter, Amy, for the kernel of inspiration, and double thanks to Pat and our other critique-partner-in-crime, Kristin Contino, for reading many chapters and versions of this tale!

Kickass kudos to my tireless agent, Nalini Akolekar. When I can't see the forest for the trees, she's always there to hand me a compass. Endless thanks to my editor, Leis Pederson, for taking my "Much 'I Do' About Nothing" concept to the next level, and to the amazing team at Berkley: production editors Andromeda Macri and Lynsey Griswold for keeping me honest, art director Lesley Worrell for gracing my book with a cover so perfect it brings me to tears, and publicist Jessica Brock for getting the word out.

Hugs and high fives to fellow authors Amanda Usen, Alison Stone, and Natasha Moore, and the entire WNY chapter of RWA for their wisdom, guidance, good humor, and the amazing words they put down, page after page. You remind me that this brass ring dream of writing *is* within reach, but it's more fun having others on the merry-go-round with you! Long-distance shout-outs to my cousin Liz for her flight attendant's knowledge, my sister-in-law Dawn for her nursing expertise, and to Mindy Reznik for her Chicago street smarts.

A double fist-bump to both my mom and dad for their unconditional love, kisses to Selma and Wes for their encouragement . . . and an endless supply of comic books to Jon and Millie, from their biggest fan.

And last but not least, virtual hugs to all the readers out there who decided to jump on the plane with Laney and Noah for their grand adventure.

Terminal C Departures

Really, LaGuardia? One of the busiest airports in the country, and you couldn't come up with a better name? You could've skipped *C* altogether, like some hotels do when they omit the unlucky thirteenth floor. You know, Terminals A, B, D, E . . .

I'm sure there would still be some clueless tourists in life, scratching their heads, consulting their maps. Pointing and asking, *Whatever happened to Terminal C? Where's Terminal C?*

"It's in my bones, Laney Jane." I could still hear Allen's throaty whisper and feel his long, strong drummer's fingers tangle through my hair. "It's not going away this time."

If I were an airport architect, I would've come up with something better. Because only 25 percent of people make it five years through Allen's type of Terminal C.

I pushed on, eager to check my luggage: the crappy soft-sided Samsonite I'd had since college, and the invisible, matched "his and hers" mental baggage I had solely inherited two years back. Perhaps Hawaii would be good for something.

The lame heel on my favorite pair of boots finally gave out, sending me sprawling right foot over left. The heavy garment bag I carried twirled with me as I pirouetted like a demented ballerina across the concourse to the closest bench.

Freakin' A, talk about adding insult to injury. I rubbed my ankle in quick consolation before yanking the boot zipper down the length of my entire calf. They were cheap 8th Street boots, not even worth the fix if it could be made. But they had been my first Big-Girl Paycheck purchase when I moved to the city, and their soles had carried not only me, but also miles of memories. *Va-va-voom boots*, Allen had christened them upon first sight.

There was no time to mourn them; into the trash they went. I plucked my flip-flops from my carry-on and slipped my freshly pedicured feet into them. Onward.

"Hi, one bag to check, two carry-on items."

The Windwest Airways desk attendant threw a skeptical glance at the bulky garment bag as she reached for my license and boarding pass. "Are you sure you don't want to check that now?"

I could hear my mother's words echoing in my head louder than the PA speakers booming last call for Flight 105 to Miami. *Whatever you do, do not let them check it, Laney. Do not hand it off.*

"No, thanks."

Rebel on the outside, mouse on the inside, Allen always used to say. *Do you always do what your mother tells you to do, Laney Jane?* Only Allen Burnside had the cojones to call me out on that.

"We can't guarantee there will be room in the overhead. You may have to gate-check it anyway." The attendant slapped a tag onto my Samsonite and sent it hurling onto the rolling belt, where it was quickly swallowed by two rubber flaps in the wall. She fixed a stare on me that made me wonder whether she got paid a commission per checked bag.

I contemplated the huge midnight blue bag with *Bichonné Bridal Couture* emblazoned across the front in frosty silver lettering. The metal hook of the hanger was cutting into the skin between my thumb and index finger. It would be so easy just to let it go. I imagined it getting chewed up through the luggage shoot, mangled in the greasy, mechanical gears. Stepped on by the handlers' dirty boots. Run over on the tarmac by a baggage cart. Left behind in the dust.

I smiled.

"My mother called ahead. The airline told her a wedding dress could be carried on if the bag was under fifty-one inches."

I watched as the attendant's demeanor did a complete one-eighty; I'm talking ollie-on-the-half-pipe-at-the-skate-park one-eighty. "Oh, true!" Her left hand fluttered up near her name tag—April R.—and a lone carat of promise on her ring finger glittered in solidarity. Apparently I had said the two magic words. "I would die if anything happened to my dress. I'm June."

"I'm Laney," I said slowly. "But your name tag says April."

She laughed. "I mean my wedding! I'm a June bride."

And you're an oversharer, but that's okay. "Cool, congrats." I hefted the bag's bulk to my shoulder and used my free, noncrippled hand to grab my carry-on. Out of available limbs, I had no choice but to pop my boarding pass between my lips. April the June bride was still smiling at me expectantly, so I offered my raised brow as valediction and lumbered on.

People talk about a monkey on your back; well, mine was eggshell white silk and taffeta, beaded and sequined and weighing in around ten pounds. About as heavy as my regret, but nowhere near as heavy as my grief.

And it belonged to my mother, the blushing bride.

Third time's the charm, or so they say.

"Shoes in a separate bin, handbags, too. Any metal, loose change . . . take laptops out of their carrying cases," droned the TSA worker. "Separate bins for everything, keep moving."

Strangers around me in various stages of undress—belts whipped off, shoes untied and loosened—shuffled toward security. Oh, crap. I instantly regretted my sock and boot toss as I was forced to kick my flip-flops off. *Think happy thoughts. Clean thoughts. Sanitary thoughts.* My toes curled as my bare feet touched the cold airport floor. In less than twelve hours, I could buff my feet in Kauai sand and let the Pacific wash away the East Coast grime. *Happy thoughts, happy thoughts . . .*

"Is that yours?"

"Yep, that's one of my two allowed personal items." *Personally, though, I wouldn't be caught dead in it.*

"Ain't no bin big enough for that, girl." TSA and I both watched as the garment bag went down the conveyor belt, followed by my bag and my cell phone, chirping happily. It was probably Danica texting, loopy on the time change. I wasn't going to need an alarm clock in Hawaii, not when I had a best friend who was an extreme morning person under normal circumstances. I couldn't imagine Dani on Hawaii-Aleutian Standard Time. I was going to have to slip an Ambien into her mai tai.

Although as heavy as chain mail, the dress made it through the X-ray and metal detector with flying colors. Me, on the other hand . . .

"Anything in your pockets, miss? Belt on?" I shook my head. "Jewelry?"

Allen's class ring.

I hadn't removed the chunky platinum band with its peridot stone since the weekend of our ten-year high school reunion, except to replace the string knotted on the back keeping it snug.

"But it's so small." And LaGuardia Airport was so, so big.

My heart vibrated in my chest like Allen's sticks on the snare drum when he sound-checked to an empty room.

Mr. TSA wasn't backing down. And there was a pileup of travelers in their stocking feet, holding up their trousers and grumbling, behind me. "All right, all right." I plunked the ring into the little gray dog dish, held my breath, and crossed over to the other side.

East Concourse, Gate C15

Nothing a grande latte and a lemon poppy seed muffin wouldn't fix. Ring? *Check.* Dress? *Check.* Phone? Useless, but I had time to power up before boarding. Boarding pass: nowhere to be found.

Are you kidding me?

I could practically hear my mother's voice as I retraced my steps, back through Starbucks and over to the newsstand. "I swear, Laney, you'd lose your *tuchus* if it wasn't stamped on the back of you!" No boarding pass tucked between the trashy novels I had contemplated buying for a beach read. I checked the perfume counter where I had impulse-purchased Aquolina Pink Sugar because no one was around to judge me . . . no sign of it. Nor was it in the restroom, first stall on the right.

I was a ticketed passenger without a ticket.

"Not a problem, we can certainly print a new one up for you, Ms. Hudson." The attendant at the gate clacked manically at her keyboard. "I may even have an upgrade for you. That way you'll be closer to your gown if there's room for it in the first-class closet."

"It's my—" I paused. If I had to be the dress bearer while my mother globe-trotted around with her sugar daddy fiancé, shouldn't I at least milk it for all it was worth? I had lost a boot heel and a boarding pass, but gaining a first-class seat would more than make up for it. "It's my first time on a plane," I finished, flashing pearly whites to go along with my little white lie. "That would be terrific, thank you."

"Oh, then you definitely deserve a bumping up, Miss Bride-to-Be!" she enthused. "I won't know until boarding time, so I'll call you to the desk then, okay?"

"Sounds good."

I made a beeline into the waiting area, in search of my favorite comfy seat and a power source. Between touring on the road with Allen's band and escorting him down to that medical trial in Philadelphia, I was actually a frequent traveler through this particular waiting lounge.

The airline had pairs of great square chairs near the windows, in padded black leather with electrical outlets built right into the armrests. Unfortunately, the only free one was next to a guy in a matchy-match gray suit, draining half the tristate's electric grid. Not only was he hogging both armrest outlets, with his fancy phone and his tablet charging, he was also typing one-handed on a laptop balanced on his knee, its power cord like a tightrope that I had to maneuver past just to get close to the empty seat. At close range, his cologne was a force field I had to skirt around. A hands-free device winked from behind a lock of his thick jet-black hair like a glowing blue locust. This guy was wired to the gills and completely self-absorbed within his sensory-overload bubble.

I made a production of carefully draping the garment bag across the chair before plopping myself down on the floor near the one wall outlet he wasn't zapping power from. New text messages from Danica lit up the minute I plugged in.

Where are you!?!?! TEXT ME.

Sorry, needed to find a plug. Evil supervillain is harnessing all airport energy at his superbase to fuel his death ray.

Tech-Boy had stopped typing. I stole a glance. Maybe that was no ordinary Bluetooth device in his ear: could it read my thoughts? *Or my texts?*

English, please?

Dude totally hogging the outlets at my gate. And now he is staring at me.

Oh. :-) Is he cute?

I flicked my eyes up nonchalantly. He now had his cell phone in his hand and was frowning at the screen as he loosened his tie.

A little like Keanu.

Pre-Matrix or post-Matrix?

Pre-Matrix. But with more technology. And more hair.

LOL. Take a pic!

Are you THAT bored in Hawaii already? What time is it there, anyway?

Laney! Come on. Pic or I don't believe you.

The stuff I do to amuse you, Dani.

I nonchalantly angled my phone and pretended to admire my toes, freshly shellacked in a blue the color of sea glass, and stealthily captured him still in frowning mode. Three button pushes later, his picture was in Hawaii, in my best friend's waiting hand. Gotta love technology.

Pretty hot. I like the scruff.

I snuck another peek. I liked it, too. It was a nice contrast to his high cheekbones.

Maybe I should go buy him an electric razor so he can have one more thing to plug in.

Ha! Maybe he'll be sitting next to you.

Just what I don't need. Thanks.

Come on. Live a little. Think WWDD.

What Would Dani Do? You'd probably be joining the Mile-High Club with some sexy pilot.

LOVE a man in uniform! LOL. But no, not exactly . . . I would keep my eyes open, tho. And you should, too. You're one bad sweater away from becoming a crazy cat lady, you know.

I frowned, glancing down at the long, gray, belted cardigan I had picked for my traveling ensemble. After a day of criminal-butt-whooping badassery, I could totally picture Wonder Woman or Super-girl kicking back to relax in such a thing. It was comfy and hip when paired with my black leggings and high black leather boots . . . although my boots were no more. True, I had picked the sweater's neutral color with the thought in mind that it wouldn't show cat hair as much as black would.

One cat does not a crazy cat lady make, Dan.

Wait, I thought you had three cats.

No, Sister Frances Tappan Zee Got Milk just has a really long name.

LOL. Whatevs. You're about to board a jet for a grand adventure, Laney. At least take off Allen's stupid ring.

I bit the raised stone on the ring guiltily. Even from the middle of the Pacific Ocean, my best friend knew me all too well. The peridot was warm against my lips, but the metal was cold. It was a subject I really didn't feel like talking—or texting—about. I deleted her last comment and changed topics.

They want to upgrade me AND the dress to first class. Isn't that a scream?

Cool. Will it get you here any faster? Cuz your mom is already driving me crazy! Tell me again why she didn't just have her wedding on Long Island. There's a perfectly good beach, like, a mile from your house.

You know my mom . . . she was worried people would get stuck in traffic on the L.I.E.

I sent the last text and smiled, picturing Danica laughing at the absurdity of Hawaii being an easier commute than the Long Island Expressway.

A half hour till boarding time. Reaching into my bag, I pulled out my sketchpad, a fresh Faber-Castell 2B, and my earbuds. Music was essential when I worked, especially with Tech-Boy keeping up his staccato one-hand typing trick just inches away from my eardrums. Using my legging-clad knees as my easel, I began to flesh out an elaborate throne. Coils of wire and tubing emanated from every crack and crevice; if I had my colors handy, I would ink them in neon yellow or toxic green, perfect for the supervillain siphoning all the world's energy for his death ray.

I bit my lip into a smile as I sketched, my lines becoming looser and freer with every stroke of the pencil. Tech-Boy was sprawled spineless in his airport lounge chair now, barking short responses at someone on the other end of his Bluetooth. Funny how one tiny piece of technology was the fine line between socially acceptable and looking like a crazy person ranting into thin air.

In my drawing, he was rod straight in the chair, long fingers gripping the armrests in evil victory. A large *T* was emblazoned across his muscled chest in classic superhero style. I added Bluetooth devices to both ears—why not?—and, for added effect, a metal band around his head like a crown, connecting with bolts to all the tubes. May as well wire his brainpan. With simple wavy lines and a few bursts, I achieved a glow effect in a halo around him.

I was totally lost in my process now, not even aware that I was staring as I studied his facial features. Those cheekbones could cut glass, they were so sharp. His dark eyes were almond shaped, but I could see the curling fan of perfect, lush lashes. I had eyelashes like that, too, but mine came out of a mascara tube. His brow was thick and straight. He was actually a dream to draw. I smudged in his five o'clock shadow with the tip of my pinky, softening his strong jawline.

Allowing myself one last look to make sure I had captured the length and wave of his hair, I was met with a stony, irritated stare. I quickly dropped my eyes and slammed my sketchbook shut. Since leaving my job at Marvel, drawing was a guilty luxury, an escape.

Since losing Allen, I had a hard time being on board with the whole justice-prevailing-over-evil thing. Turns out, the good guys don't always win.

Noah

CHOOSE YOUR BATTLES

From: Manhattan Paperie <service@manhattanpaperie.com>
Subject: Bidwell-Ridgewood wedding PROOF
Date: March 5, 2013 8:00 AM EST
To: Noah Ridgewood <noah.ridgewood@bidwellbutler.com>,
Sloane Bidwell <sloanerose@me.com>

Dear Sloane and Noah,

Thank you for letting Manhattan Paperie help commemorate your special day!

Attached please find your revised invitation proof. Your approval is required to complete the order, so please let us know at your earliest convenience if it meets your satisfaction.

It is a pleasure to be of service to you at this joyful and important time in your lives.

Mr. and Mrs. Christopher Bidwell
request the honor of your presence
at the marriage of their daughter

Sloane Rose
to
Mr. Noah L. Ridgewood

Saturday, the eighth of June
two thousand and thirteen
at half after five in the evening
Grace Church
New York, New York

Dinner and dancing
immediately following
The Altman Building
135 West Eighteenth Street, Manhattan

From: Kewana Jones <kewana.jones@bidwellbutler.com>
Subject: Fwd: Fwd: Wedding flowers
Date: March 5, 2013 8:28 AM EST
To: Noah Ridgewood <noah.ridgewood@bidwellbutler.com>

Is she STILL not speaking to you?

P.S. Don't shoot the messenger . . .

K

Begin forwarded message:

From: Sloane Bidwell <sloanerose@me.com>
Subject: Fwd: Wedding flowers
Date: March 5, 2013 8:25 AM EST
To: Kewana Jones <kewana.jones@bidwellbutler.com>

Tell him if we change date, lily of the valley go out of season. Imported from Holland $9/stem. Revised estimate attached. Remy's shooting schedule is tight and he leaves for Paris on June 20th. Also, band now booked up for the entire month of July. HIS CHOICE.

From: Noah Ridgewood <noah.ridgewood@bidwellbutler.com>
Subject: Sorry . . .
Date: March 5, 2013 8:31 AM EST
To: Kewana Jones <kewana.jones@bidwellbutler.com>

Kiwi,

I bet you didn't think handling the boss's daughter's rebel fiancé would be in your job description when Bidwell-Butler hired you to be

my secretary, did you? Sorry you are caught in the middle of this . . .
I will deal with her.

Thanks, N.

From: Kewana Jones <kewana.jones@bidwellbutler.com>
Subject: Re: Sorry . . .
Date: March 5, 2013 8:32 AM EST
To: Noah Ridgewood <noah.ridgewood@bidwellbutler.com>

Noah,

Don't apologize. You know I would follow you to the ends of the earth.
If only you could pay me half as well as B-B does.

Kiwi

From: Noah Ridgewood <noah.ridgewood@bidwellbutler.com>
Subject: Re: Re: Sorry . . .
Date: March 5, 2013 8:33 AM EST
To: Kewana Jones <kewana.jones@bidwellbutler.com>

LOL someday. Meanwhile, you would NOT have wanted to follow me
into 7am mtg. w/ Bidwell today. Was basically handed my balls in a
sling. Told to go "get it out of my system" in Vegas, then come back
and make things right. As if it were that simple . . .

From: Kewana Jones <kewana.jones@bidwellbutler.com>
Subject: Re: Re: Re: Sorry . . .
Date: March 4, 2013 8:35 AM EST
To: Noah Ridgewood <noah.ridgewood@bidwellbutler.com>

Mama always told me to keep my eggs out of the same basket. You should never have put all your balls in that one basket, if you know what I mean.

Safe travels, boss. What happens in Vegas . . . ain't none of my business!

My father had always told me to choose my battles wisely, but with a fiancée on the wedding warpath, no topic was safe these days. Sloane had accused me of not caring enough about the details, but then she had thrown a fit when I suggested dove gray ink for our invitations might be a nice alternative to the traditional black. She sulked for days after I chose my groomsmen (they're more IQ than *GQ*), but couldn't understand why I might have a slight problem with her inviting not one, not two, but a whopping three of her ex-boyfriends to the wedding. She turned that tug-of-war into an exchange as complex as the Dix-Hill Cartel: my five buds for her three exes. I would hardly put them in the same category, since I had never slept with any of my groomsmen.

I hit speed-dial and announced my name and account. "I'd like to order two dozen long-stemmed roses, please. Um, cool water lavender and white. She likes a fuller petal in white, is that the Vendela? Perfect. Yes, to the usual address. No, no card needed. Thanks."

Chi non ha denaro in borsa, abbia miele in bocca, my mother liked to remind me. He who has no money in his purse, should have honey in his mouth. But when it came to girls like Sloane, bribing with sweetness didn't really impress. You'll catch less hell with the push of a button to Sloane's favorite West Side florist, over more flies with honey, any day of the week.

Last month we were fighting over honeymooning in Belize or Sardinia (as if either were a losing proposition) and this month: the date. She changed it while I was out of town on a business trip last week. And by changed it, I mean she changed it with the church, the caterer, and the venue before even consulting me. I got a "BTW," courtesy of a Post-it waiting on my pillow when I got home. Since when does the groom rank a "by the way" level of importance on the ball-and-chain food chain?

Sounds petty, but out of the three hundred and sixty-five days in the year, she had to pick the one day that I'd rather have wiped from the calendar altogether.

I frowned as I scanned over the proof from the printer once more, my eyes going out of focus as they stared at the details I had not agreed to. "Can we not make any other changes until I'm back from Vegas?" I had specifically asked her. "And what about all the Save the Date e-mails that went out earlier?" Sloane had dismissed my concerns with a blanket "Oh, nothing's set in stone" comment, but seeing it there in the printer's proof felt pretty damn concrete.

My thumb worked its way into the tight Windsor knot of my tie while I waited for her voice mail. "Sloane. I saw the bill you forwarded to Kiwi. So import the flowers from Holland if you have to, that's fine. I'm all right with choosing another band if it comes to that. And I'm sorry, but there are other photographers in the world besides Remy Georges. Just . . . please. Don't sign off on that invitation proof until we've had time to figure this out, okay? Just . . . just call me back." I slumped back in the chair and let out a gusty sigh, remembering the power struggle over the Post-it Note.

As usual, she had had the last word: "I get that the day sucks for you. It's a lemon. So why not turn that day into lemonade?"

Because that's not how my brain works.

And I thought she'd know that about me by now.

I'm not a game changer. Slow and steady wins the race. Not that I'm winning at much lately. Especially not the game of Marital Monopoly. In that game, Sloane's father is the top hat piece. Mr. Moneybags. He's also my boss in real life. And he's controlling the bank; he rolls the dice first. Sloane, she's like the iron token. She gives off the impression of being sweetly domestic, but when no one's looking, she whacks me upside the head and leaves a scalding burn mark. Me? I've been the Scottie dog. Trotting along behind them, loyal to a fault. Trying to keep the peace. Trying to please everyone.

But lately, it's all been Do Not Pass Go. Do Not Collect Your Prize. Sloane and I had been fighting like crazy. Plus, there was not even the bonus of amazing makeup sex, because even when we agreed to disagree, there was still the no-sex-till-the-wedding-night ban she had unilaterally imposed on us. Even if she finally agreed to bump the date out of June and back into July, I had the feeling that would be my last Get Out of Jail Free card.

"Thank you, young man." I felt a soft hand fall on my shoulder. The elderly woman from the row of seats across from me was getting ready to board with the help of her grandson. She looked at me expectantly.

"Oh, no problem. They really need to add more outlets around here." I wiggled the prongs of her adapter loose and handed back her Kindle, which had needed charging. "Happy to help, ma'am."

"Such a gentleman." She gave my shoulder an extra pat. "Your mother raised you well. Safe travels, dear."

"Thanks. You, too."

With a sigh, I clicked my laptop shut and glanced around. Half the passengers had boarded already and I hadn't even noticed. Amazing how one stupid e-mail could bring the weight of the world down on my shoulders. Then again, Sloane Bidwell expected the very same world to revolve around her, twenty-four/seven, so why was I surprised in the least? I released myself from my necktie's stranglehold and shoved it into the side pocket of my computer bag. If only I could loosen the grip she had on me as easily. Or her father's, for that matter. I roughly pushed a hand through my hair, upsetting the careful grooming I had gone through to make my best impression at that morning's meeting.

Trying to ungroom, Noah?
How fitting.

"Get it out of your system, Ridgewood." My boss's words echoed in my ears as I walked down the chilly gangway to the aircraft.

I've never been a game changer.

God, I really hoped Vegas was good for something.

Boarding and Departure

"Safe and sound," the flight attendant assured me as she clicked the first-class closet closed with the dress inside. "I love your hair! Are you going to wear it like that for the wedding?"

I pushed a hand through my unapologetically pin-straight tresses that wouldn't hold a wave no matter how hard I tried. *The grass is always greener on the other side of the septic tank*, Dani would remind me, with her Keri Russell curls that she considered a curse. Unlike its texture, my hair had a hard time making up its mind what color it wanted to be. A caramel-fudge combo in the winter that became streaky red-gold in the summer sun. "Nature's highlights," my mother would allow. "You can't duplicate *that* in any salon." I think it was a compliment.

"Maybe in an updo?" the other flight attendant offered. "You have enough for a French twist." Sometime over the last year, it had reached past shoulder-blade length. A last-minute decision, along with a night at home alone, a bottle of red wine, and nothing good on television, had left me with the thick fringe of bangs that I was still getting used to. I had been conservative with the cutting shears, afraid to go too short, and was now constantly blinking them out of my eyes.

"Maybe."

I hadn't even decided what dress to wear for my mom's beachside ceremony, let alone thought about my hair. All I knew was I wouldn't be in the seafoam green strapless silk chiffon Danica and the other bridesmaids were wearing. My mother made no bones about letting everyone know my best friend would look better in the hue than her flesh and blood and only child. Whatever. Apparently, my primary function for the big day was getting her dress from point A to point B, and then the pressure was off.

Not that I think she had planned on giving me such an important role in the first place. But a delay with alterations at the dress shop, along with a last-minute opportunity to combine a business trip with a prehoneymoon in Paris, had created a first-world problem for her. And the only viable solution had been to ask the problem child: me.

"Laney can't be counted on," I had overheard her telling someone on the phone at work. "I just don't know . . ." Oh, well. Desperate times called for desperate measures, apparently.

Not that I ever had a hope of measuring up in her eyes.

First class was, for lack of a better word, classy. I marveled at the size of the seats and my personal in-flight entertainment setup. Too bad I had a layover in Chicago; it would have been nice to jet all the way from New York to Hawaii in such luxury.

That grande latte had worked its way down to my bladder. "Is it okay to use the bathroom now?" I asked the attendant, who was bringing an elderly lady her first gin and tonic of the day.

"Honey!" She laughed. "Other than lounging in the cockpit, feel free to move about the cabin."

I scooted toward the nose of the plane, bypassing the next group of passengers boarding, and into the first-class lavatory, which was identical to those in the back, except for the fancy lotion. Well, that answered one of those burning life questions. Rich people had to pee in Lilliputian-sized lavs just like the cattle in coach class.

The plane was rapidly filling. By the time I made it back to my cushy seat, it was covered with ruffled *Wall Street Journal* pages, headphones, and a banana.

"Um, excuse me? That's my seat."

"But that . . . that's impossible," Tech-Boy stuttered. God, he was even better looking in close quarters. His tie was now gone. "My phone app said this seat was empty five minutes ago; that's why I switched to this row." He held up his smartphone.

"Well, clearly," I said, cocking the banana at him, "your app doesn't know its ass from its elbow." It was kind of a stupid thing to say, since a piece of software had neither an ass nor an elbow. But I think he got my point.

Grumbling, he snatched his precious paper up before my bottom landed on it, then popped up from his own spot like a jack-in-the-box. Scanning the cabin for another place to sit, no doubt. Too bad his app couldn't tell him the airline had given me the last available first-class seat.

I rolled my eyes as his finger jabbed at the attendant button. "Jack and Coke, please. Double Jack."

"That'll go good with your banana," I muttered. Which was worse, the fact that he couldn't stand to sit next to me or that he was going to need large quantities of alcohol to get through the trauma? *WWDD?* I thought. Dani would probably have the guy curled around her little finger by now, with his phone number in her back pocket to prove it.

"Anything for you?" The flight attendant touched my shoulder like a best girlfriend would.

"Just an orange juice, please." Resisting the urge to add, *What normal people drink at nine thirty in the morning.* I pulled the black and navy blue Windwest Airways sleep mask over my eyes and tried to ignore my seatmate as he powered down every gizmo he had brought on board.

Relaxation.
Starts.
Now.

"Can I have my fruit back?"

I slid the sleep mask up and stared him down. "I don't know. *Can* you?" It was unnecessary, but I couldn't resist. Yes, even comic book artists can be members of the grammar police force. Top of my class at School of Visual Arts.

"Just hand over the banana and no one gets hurt," he said in his best tough-guy voice. I reluctantly surrendered a smile and he resumed custody of his fruit.

How many hours till Chicago?

"Seat backs and tray tables in their locked, upright position, please." Our flight attendant, Anita, was preparing the aircraft for departure. She was also looking to dish and gab. "So where's the wedding?"

"Hawaii. Waipouli Beach."

"Oh, gorgeous!" she gasped, before reverting back to work mode. "Everything with an on/off switch needs to be powered down, sir."

This guy was like the Energizer Bunny, still going and going and going with that phone. I heard him mutter something about IPOs as Anita moved on.

"Are you going to go through withdrawal if that thing is off for two hours?" I asked him.

"Work to live, live to work. The market just opened."

There was a growing roar from the jet engines as they began to spool up for takeoff. He gripped the oversized armrests, just like in my cartoon version of him in my sketchpad. But no evil supervillain grin, just a grim set of his lips. His stubble gave him a rough-and-tumble, "I just woke up and rolled over here" look, but the rest of his demeanor screamed uptight and anxious.

"What do you do?" Yes, the oldest prompt in the book. But it seemed to distract him momentarily.

"Software design," he replied, jutting his chin. "Apps, specifically." I thought of my "don't know ass from elbow" comment and gave a weak grin and guilty snort. "And what, are you curing cancer?" he finished defensively.

Oh, he did not *just say that.*

The cabin lights dimmed, and the plane began to tear down the runway.

"Graphic artist," I managed through gritted teeth. It sounded better than out-of-work comic illustrator. Maybe someday I would cure the world with laughter. Or at least invent some sort of kryptonite to render pompous guys powerless and unable to say stupid, hurtful things.

Give him a break, Laney Jane. He can't read your mind.

I went for my overhead light just as he moved to punch his, our fingers grazing and almost tangling as the eight-hundred-thousand-pound silver tube suddenly became weightless, lifting us into the air.

"I'm Noah," he said quietly. "And I really hate flying."

"Laney. Think they'll serve us good snacks on this bird?"

Noah

BEHIND THE EIGHT BALL

I know it's statistically safer to fly than drive. My chances of dying on this flight are something like one in fourteen million. Still, statistics say the first three minutes and the last eight minutes in flight are the most likely times when things could go wrong. And I'm stuck next to another victim of the bridal apocalypse. Great. What are the chances of that? She took up half the first-class cargo space with her dress, and she's got the stewardesses fussing over her every move. Where's my drink? They're supposed to be *flight* attendants, not bridal attendants.

Amber, Brittany, Camille, Darinda, Emma, Fawn, and Gabi. I wondered how they would react were Sloane to tell them they weren't going to be her bridesmaids after all. Haley, Iris, and Jessie would probably be cool with it. I'm pretty sure Sloane only chose them because they fit the dresses and the alphabetical order.

There was a time when I thought we were in love and able to shut out the rest of the world. When and why did she have to open the floodgates? Ten bridesmaids! Two girls for every guy was picture perfect in Sloane's mind. I'm pretty sure she has everyone accounted for on that damn checklist of hers . . . except for me.

Wheels going up. Damn, they sound like they are falling off. What percentage of accidents are due to landing gear failure? Jeez, Noah, think of some happier statistics. Like how many freakin' lily of the valley stems your insane fiancée plans on importing from Holland to total $3,150. Nine into three thousand, carry the . . .

God, the girl in 3B smells really good. Like, warm sugar cookie good. Way better than lily of the valley ever could. I got a whiff when she pushed by me in the waiting lounge and almost took me out with her humongous bridal bag. They should charge her an extra seat for that thing . . .

Oh, great. She's reaching into her carry-on. How much do you want to bet she's going to pull out the most recent wedding porn from the newsstand? *The Knot, Brides, Martha Stewart Weddings* . . . I had a forest's worth cluttering my coffee table at home, property of Sloane. Fuel for the wedding juggernaut.

The shared armrest between us vibrated against my elbow. Was she having a seizure? I flicked a glance over. No bridal magazines to be seen; instead, she had something clasped between her hands and she was shaking, turning, and cursing it in rapid succession.

She caught me looking. "What? You've never seen a Magic 8 Ball?"

"I've never seen anyone violate one like that."

She blew a dismissive *pfft* from her bottom lip, which ruffled her choppy bangs and gave me a good look at her wide, green eyes. She rolled them in response to my comment and offered up the fortune-telling toy. "You try."

"No, thanks."

"Come on. Not one shake? You know you want to," she taunted.

What were we in, second grade? I refused to bow to her bullying tactics, turning my gaze to the window instead. I wished I could see the wing of the plane from first class. Seeing the wing always made me feel a little better about—

What the hell?

She had literally reached over, unlocked my tray table to horizontal position, and set the Magic 8 Ball in front of me. "You look like you could use a good shake," she added.

What I could really use is another double Jack and Coke. "All right, all right," I muttered, giving it a halfhearted tumble.

Will this plane land safely? I silently queried, then flipped it and watched the die inside slowly float to the top. *Without a doubt,* hovered in the display. Well, that was a good sign. I gave it another shake, thinking about my morning meeting and Bidwell's threat. Not that I would trust a ten-dollar toy to decide my fate, but . . . *Will I "get it out of my system" in Vegas?*

Get rid of my cold feet?

Get on with things?

Go with the flow?

Give in?

"The pyramid's stuck." She was leaning over my shoulder, snooping on my fortune.

"It's not a pyramid," I informed her. "It's an icosahedron. It has twenty sides."

"Well, shit." Her tone was mockingly amazed, laced with scorn. "You'd think it would give me at least one answer I want, then."

"Well," I mused, giving it another slow shake, "if you understand probability theory, you'd have to turn it about seventy times on average to see all its answers at least once." *Great, Noah. Way to put an idea in her head. She'll be shaking that thing all the way to Chicago.*

"Did you just calculate that in your head?" She sounded both impressed and slightly creeped out.

I ignored her, looking down at the ball. The raised letters displaced the liquid to show *Reply hazy, try again,* in the window. I shook it again. *Cannot predict now,* it insisted. *Of course you can't predict,* I told it. *You're a cheap, plastic plaything. I'd be crazy to trust you as an oracle of prediction on the matter of my pending marital status.*

Maybe I had asked it too many questions at once.

To marry or not to marry: that question had grown larger and more open-ended than just a simple "yes" or "no" answer could satisfy.

I wordlessly handed back the toy to my seatmate, allowing my own mind to spin over that.

In Flight

"It's a *bird*, it's a *plane*, it's . . . *Laney Jane!*"

"Allen Burnside, you give that back!"

It was hard to think of Allen and not picture him at eighteen, the lanky skater kid with the swoop of blond hair. The class clown who loved to talk with a cigarette dangling out of his mouth, squinting like a grunge version of James Dean. Who wrote poetry and played drums and totally won my heart in seventh grade when he lost the election for class president. "That's the way the cookie bounces," he'd said. "Wanna go get high after school?"

Was Allen my soul mate?

Might as well ask the Magic 8 Ball.

I squeezed my eyes shut and waited a beat to peek at the answer. *You may rely on it.*

Thanks. But really, *can* I?

We may have been voted Cutest Class Couple, but Allen and I hadn't exactly had the most reliable track record, especially after that fateful day on the beach. Over the next decade, we had taken our own sweet time, and turns, hurting each other.

Not that I was keeping track or anything.

I absently rubbed the 8 Ball like it was a genie's lamp and tried to conjure up that early spring day, verbatim, from our senior year.

"Give it, give it!" I'd hopped up from my blanket on the sand and given chase, practically climbing Allen's six-foot-one frame like a ladder to get back the letter he had swiped. He held it infuriatingly an inch from his face and out of my reach, studying it.

"Laney, this is an acceptance letter to Otis!"

"I know, butthead. It came today." I gestured toward my blanket. After pulling several fat white envelopes from the mailbox, I'd walked down to the beach to open them in solitude. The last thing I'd wanted was my mother hovering and commenting.

"That's perfect!" he crowed, pulling me into one of his signature Allen Burnside bear hugs, over the shoulders and stranglehold tight. Somewhere downwind, a radio was blasting Blink-182's "Dammit," its poppy riff ebbing and flowing out of earshot above the dull roar of the waves. "Laney and Allen, taking on L.A.! It's like they named the city after us." He rocked us until our feet faced the ocean. "Pretty soon we'll be standing, just like this, in front of the warm, blue Pacific . . . instead of the dirty, gray Atlantic. I am so proud of you, girl."

I gently butted my head against his sternum. "Thanks." The wind had picked up. He pulled the hood of my zippered hoodie up over my breeze-tangled hair and we raced back to secure the blanket, and my other letters, from blowing down Quogue Village Beach.

I remembered how we collapsed to the sand, kissing like teens are wont to kiss: with a deliberate passion, with a luxury of all the time in the world. In junior high school we had kissed for practice; by sixteen we had learned how to deliciously build up each other's libidos and how to set them free.

Looking back, I realized I was kissing him out of consolation that day. We were on the cusp of graduation, and he was heading to California with his band come fall. I had been accepted to L.A.'s Otis College of Art and Design. But my number one choice—well, my mother's—had always been the School of Visual Arts right in Manhattan, and they wanted me, too.

"I want you so bad, Laney Jane."

I remembered the conflicted feeling as I twisted his ring off my finger, Blink-182 in the background, insisting that this was growing up. I could still hear my voice, barely a whisper above the chilly ocean breeze but loud enough for it to sink in. And there was no taking it back.

"Allen, we need to talk . . ."

Will this trip be a grand adventure or would I have been better off staying home?

Better not tell you now, bubbled to the Magic 8 Ball's surface.

Why the hell not? Stupid 8 Ball. I guess it was kind of a loaded question anyway. I tucked the toy, and my thought, away for the time being.

"Ladies and gentlemen, we've reached our cruising altitude, and the captain has just informed us that it is safe to use approved portable electronics at this time . . ."

Great. Tech-Boy went to work peeling his laptop out of its case, practically knocking his Jack into my juice. I pulled a vintage issue of the Hernandez brothers' *Love and Rockets* from the side pocket of my bag and leaned on the armrest closest to the aisle, and as far away as I could get from his cologne—and his insane typing. He reminded me of one of those dipping drinking birds made of glass. His index finger would slowly come down and hover on a key before popping back, then dipping down quick and pecking out multiple characters across the lighted keyboard. Then back up and slow, like the bird with the liquid in its butt bulb. There was no rhyme or reason to his assault on the keys, no steady rhythm.

After dating a drummer for so long, I craved rhythm.

"Frittata with ham, sir." Anita reached past me to place a tray in front of my seatmate. He barely glanced at the food, which was served on ceramic rather than plastic. The egg smelled heavenly, and the sides of asparagus and fruit were plump and bright, like close-up photos from a foodie magazine.

"Hold on, hon. I've got nothing listed for you." She frowned. "Let me go check on that."

She sashayed up the aisle.

"Hmm, my app might not know an ass from an elbow, but it knows how to keep my stomach from rumbling," Noah said, tucking into his frittata. "Ordered ahead," he added, mouth full of egg. "On my app."

Anita was back. "I'm so sorry, we don't have any additional hot breakfasts, but I can give you yogurt with granola and fruit."

"Not a problem. I love fruit and granola. And yogurt! It doesn't make your pee smell funny, like asparagus does."

Noah pushed his spring veggies off to the side of his plate and continued index-fingering his way through the alphabet on his oh-so-important document. I smiled, dipped my spoon into my parfait, and went back to my *Love and Rockets* storyline. It was one with Maggie and Hopey, who were just about my favorite characters from any graphic novel ever.

"Hey, want to know why urine smells funny after eating asparagus?" The guy in the opposite row leaned conspiratorially across the aisle.

"Yes, do tell."

"Sulfurous amino acids."

"Fascinating!"

"Are you really having this conversation?" Noah inserted. I dismissed him with a wave of my spoon.

"And here's the kicker: everybody has pungent pee after digesting asparagus, but less than half the population owns up to it. Want to know why?"

"Of course," I prompted.

"Because not everyone has the *special gene* that allows them to smell it!" This guy was very pleased with himself.

"I did not know that. Thanks." I tipped my spoon politely at him and went back to scraping the sides of my dish. Noah finished his meal, including his asparagus, in silence. I wondered if he possessed the smell gene for asparagus pee or not. Something told me I'd better not ask.

"Business proposal?" I inquired instead. He had all sorts of windows with Excel worksheets open.

"Nope. Bachelor party." Noah sounded thrilled . . . not. "A weeklong extravaganza in Vegas. I've known the best man my whole life. Tim is what you'd call . . . a bit gung ho."

I glanced at the screen again, with its grids and flowcharts and color coding. It made my eyes practically cross just trying to find a spot to focus on. "Wow, looks like a wild time. Are you going to have strippers there, giving PowerPoint presentations?"

He smirked. "Ha, you're funny." He highlighted a bullet point, made a notation, and clicked save. "Really. You should do comedy."

"Comedy is exactly what my mom always hoped I would pursue." I waited a beat. "Said no child of a critical, overbearing, advice-dealing Jewish mother, ever."

Now he really laughed; it was a full-on belly laugh. The kind of laugh you'd just love to bottle up and save, to let loose on a rainy day.

"Ladies and gentlemen, we are currently looking at an on-time arrival," the captain murmured through the loudspeaker, and he ran through the time and current weather conditions in the Chicago metropolitan area.

"I've got one of those, too," Noah confided. "Minus the Jewish advice. Mine has the Catholic guilt component built in."

"Lucky you," I said.

"And, folks, we'd like to give a special shout-out today to Flight 1232's beautiful bride-to-be and her groom. They're heading all the way to Hawaii for their big day. Let's give them a big Windwest Airways round of applause!"

I gave a polite little tap to my palm as the other passengers cheered. And here my mom thought she was doing something so special, having her destination wedding in Hawaii. Sounded like all the cool kids were doing it like that these days. I craned my neck down the aisle toward coach in search of the happy couple. Looking at brides and grooms was, for me, almost like rubbernecking on a highway at a car accident. I needed to observe the situation, then thank my lucky tail feathers it wasn't me, that I had managed to escape unscathed.

Noah wasn't clapping, nor was he smiling anymore. "Do they think—"

With two crystal flutes and a bottle of champagne in her hands, Anita was making a beeline up the aisle from the back of the plane. Her dazzling grin and eyes were definitely aimed at seats 3A and 3B.

"Oh—oh, God, no." This could not be happening.

"You guys," Anita gushed, her voice choked with emotion, "are going to have a great life together. Thanks for choosing to start it with Windwest Airways!"

"Please, you don't—" I began.

"Of *course* we do!" The other flight attendant began to pass out glasses to the other handful of first-class passengers. Anita expertly filled the ridiculously phallic-looking flutes balancing on my tray table.

There was static from the loudspeaker. "Congratulations to . . ." We heard shuffling from the flight deck. "Helen . . . no, that's *Helena* and Noah!" I winced at the use of my given name from the flight manifest.

Anita rolled her eyes and giggled. "Don't worry, the flight crew is just drinking sparkling grape juice. But you're having the real thing. Cheers!" She clinked her own glass to my flute and then reached over, practically giving me a mouthful of cleavage so she could clink Noah's glass. "You lucky, lucky kids!" She looked barely older than us, but she had a knowing and nostalgic look in her eye. I noticed her hand was sporting a diamond ring big enough to need its own wheelbarrow, as well as a sparkly platinum band.

This had to be karmic payback for that little white lie I told back at the gate in LaGuardia. Now I was stuck in first-class hell, with a bunch of rowdy well-wishers, clinking their glasses with whatever cutlery was left on their tray tables. The kissing-on-demand thing always struck me as a bizarre ritual at weddings. I knew it was traditional, but always wondered what would happen if the happy couple refused to kiss at the sound of clinking glasses. Would the mob turn on them, wielding their reception forks like pitchforks and grabbing the candelabras like torches? *Kiss, kiss, kiss!*

For one insane moment, I contemplated what it would be like to kiss the perfect stranger in the seat next to me. A kiss with zero history built up behind it. He was Noah, app guy in 3A. That was all I knew. Would we go in, eyes open? Would what started as a chaste peck tease into something stronger, if my lips were to part and he happened to catch my top lip between both of his?

Kiss, kiss, kiss!

The plane hit a pothole in the sky and took a sickening drop, matching the turbulence in my stomach. Were these people blind? Yes, I had walked on board with a bridal salon dress bag. But the class ring, hanging on my finger like a hex nut, could hardly be mistaken for a Tiffany solitaire. And had they failed to notice the look on the face of my supposed betrothed? He hadn't so much as glanced at me with even a hint of affection. More like abhorrence. The short civil moment and laugh we had just shared was now long gone.

Under the red blush creeping up those impossibly high cheekbones, Noah looked green. He closed his computer screen with a hasty click, no doubt wanting to avoid puking across the keyboard. I hoped that, like the lotion in the lavatory, first class stocked a fancy supply of barf bags in the seat pockets.

Kiss, kiss, kiss!

"No, no, no, don't you know it's bad luck to do that *before* the wedding?" I tutted, fanning myself with Los Bros Hernandez. Was it getting hotter in here? I took another gulp of champagne. "We promise we'll kiss if you clink on our return flight, okay?"

My illogical statement garnered a smattering of applause.

"Aw, you guys are so dang cute!" Sometime during all the *mishegas*, Anita had disappeared and reappeared with tongs and a tray. "Hot scented towel?" An inferno of lemon-infused steam enveloped us.

"Yes, please." Noah reached rudely past me and grabbed one. He pressed it to his face like he wanted to disappear behind it, and then wiped his neck and his brow, as if he had been put through the wringer.

"Thanks, Anita. For everything." I plucked a towel from her tongs and squeezed it, determined to wipe my hands of the whole business. As if I would be caught dead kissing some uptight jerk in a matching suit and loafers. The minute we landed, this guy could move on to his gate to Vegas or to Mars, for all I cared. With his little spreadsheets and overripe banana. And I would be one step closer to toes in the sand, a margarita in hand, and a good laugh with Danica over Mr. Energy-Suck. I thought of my drawing, and the frowning photo of him I had texted her. I bet he would be the life of his friend's bachelor party. If anyone could drain the joy of sinning out of Vegas, it would be him.

"Ladies and gentlemen, from the flight deck. Looks like there's an area of weather over Chicago. We're just going to circle for a while so they can plow the runway . . ."

Delayed

"Tell me again how you managed to miss your connection?"

"Mom"—I tried to keep my voice even—"I had a forty-three-minute layover. We had to circle while they cleared the runway, and then we had to sit for twenty minutes until a delayed flight could push out of our gate and we could go in. Which gave me exactly five minutes to get halfway across O'Hare." Flip-flops were a poor choice of running shoe, and my feet stung in protest. They were wishing for those lemon-scented hot towels right about now.

"I can't believe they didn't wait for you. *I've* sat on the tarmac many times, just waiting for delayed passengers to straggle on. It's not like they didn't know you were coming!"

"Yes, Mom, I know." They knew *the dress* and I were on our way, because my mom had probably called and spoken to every supervisor she could reach on the Windwest Airways 800 number. Vera Hudson didn't mess around. "They had to leave right on time because of the weather window."

"Figures. The one time they leave on time, and they leave you behind."

"I'm on the three o'clock flight now; it's all good." I sighed, glancing out at the gray skies and swirling flakes. Bands of snow were forecasted for throughout the day. I had really hoped to leave winter behind back in New York.

"It would have been *better* had you flown out on Monday, like I asked you to in the first place."

Oh, boy, here we go with the guilt. I held the phone away from my ear, rolled my eyes at it, and placed it back before replying, "Dex was playing last night, Mom. I promised him I'd be there."

"You and your *bands.*" She clucked disapprovingly. "Isn't it time all these friends of yours stopped playing Peter Pan and got real jobs?"

"I think it's time for me to hang up now. Gotta conserve battery." *And my sanity.*

My mother gave a resigned sigh. "Ernie and I will pick you up, no matter the time."

Ernie Crystal. Or, as my mother pronounced it: Crys*tal*, like the cham*pag*ne. I had a hard enough time getting used to the idea that my mother was dating, let alone marrying, a guy named Ernie. He looked and sounded less like the millionaire real estate investor he was, and more like a guy who should be in a domestic partnership with a muppet named Bert.

"Oh, got to run, dear. Cousin Miriam just arrived with her doctor!"

"Mom, he's not her doctor. He's her husband, who happens to be a doctor."

"Yes, well." I heard my mother sniff, and I knew what was coming next. I had been there as she addressed her wedding invitations, sighing longingly over writing *Dr. and Mrs.* "You have a perfectly good doctor just waiting for a second date with you."

"Mike Weintraub really wasn't my type, despite our shared interests." The perfectly good podiatrist had been way more interested in my recently deceased rocker boyfriend than in getting to know me. "I can't believe you dated Allen Burnside!" and "So what was he like?"

were his version of breaking the ice on the first date, so I didn't feel the least bit guilty about giving him the cold shoulder.

"Your cousin Miriam had offered to bring the dress, you know. But I didn't want her to have to schlep down from Westchester with the baby to pick it up."

I knew what she was getting at. The dress would've been there by now.

And I didn't have a doctor husband.

I didn't have a baby to schlep.

I didn't have an excuse.

"And FYI, the latest batch of Veraisms should have hit your in-box. Toodles!"

I gazed at the departures screen again, trying not to be alarmed at the growing number of flights marked *Canceled* in glowing yellow letters. So far, my new flight was still on time, and I could only hope my suitcase would be on it. I had my three pairs of emergency panties in my carry-on, along with my toothbrush and other essentials my mother had hammered into me ever since I was old enough to pack my own case. In her mind, as long as you had three extra pairs of underwear, you could handle anything that came your way. Why three? I could guess her theories:

Bad things come in threes
Three strikes and you're out

My mother was superstitious. *Kina hora*, the evil eye, and all that jazz. She hated Three on a Match, the name of Allen's band, even before she heard their music just based on the lore behind the phrase.

My dad, though, he believed in luck; or rather, his lack of it. "If it weren't for bad luck, Laney, I'd have no luck at all," he'd say with a laugh. My mother used to say that luck was for suckers. But my dad and I, we didn't care. We were the dreamers in the family. My dad would always kiss my head for good luck, ever since I was a baby and even before I had a lot of hair. His preferred method was flipping me upside down with his strong arms and planting one on my forehead. "Kissing the Blarney Stone," he would say in a fake Irish brogue. Even after I had outgrown his ability to flip me, he would go out of his way to lay a kiss on me if a Big Game, a Big Client, or a Pretty Pony was on the line. "Let me kiss the Blarney Stone," he'd say and I'd giggle, because even though I had reddish hair and greenish eyes, I didn't have a lick of Irish in me, and neither did he.

I sighed; the last time I had heard from my father was eight months back, when he sent me a postcard from Ireland with a picture of the real Blarney Stone on the front. *Wish you were here!* was all it said, in his slanted, blocky script.

Ernie Crystal was behind door number three of my mother's love lottery. My dad had been behind door number two before flying the coop. And she never discussed her first marriage. The only thing she'd ever say when I'd ask about it was "Oh, that?" and wave a hand to pooh-pooh such silly talk. It was the seventies, and they were both way too young. That was all I ever got. That, along with her old engagement ring to play dress-up with. It was a gold band with an empty setting. Apparently she had taken "Oh, that?" and turned it into a lovely solitaire diamond necklace for herself. The empty prongs sticking up on the ring reminded me of those claw crane games at the mall that she would never let me play. "Like throwing money in the trash," she'd say. "No one ever wins, those games are rigged."

Why set yourself up for failure, Laney?

Says the woman on her third marriage.

Ah, but there was one of my mother's new all-time favorite sayings to balance out all the *kina hora* juju:

Third time's the charm.

A tiny fat envelope popped with a ping onto my phone screen. No doubt the Veraisms—my mother's priceless pearls of wisdom summed up in ten words or less and pimped out for $2.99. When my mom and dad split up, she had kept his last name and their greeting card company, Hudson Views. Designing graphics for her greeting card sayings was soul sucking compared to my dream job at Marvel, but at least it paid the rent. Barely.

I opened her e-mail, which contained five of her latest Veraisms. Oh, fancy that, they were all on marriage:

- *Two minds. Two hearts. One lifetime of happiness. Congratulations!*

- *Got rings?*

- *Welcome to the romantic roller-coaster ride of marriage!*

- *Knock-knock. Who's there? I. I who? I DO!*

- *Old, new, borrowed, blue—don't forget my best wishes, you two!*

My mom had pulled me off certain lines a while back, due to my "controversial interpretations" of some of her messages. Like the Get Well line, when I presented her with a sketch of a wide-eyed, wild-haired waif holding a dark mass to her mouth, bolted into a heart-shaped box, based on the Nirvana song. Feasting on tumors wasn't exactly the wish she had had in mind. "I said '*Beat* your cancer,' Laney. Not *eat* it!"

I couldn't wait for the day I got promoted to the Blank Inside line.

Hauling my sketchbook back out, I studied the drawing of Tech-Boy for a moment. Not bad. There was room on his waist for a belt, and room on the belt for a holster. A banana-holding holster. I flipped to a blank page. For wedding and engagement, I tried to stay simple and sophisticated. I began to sketch sleek, interlocked rings and the silhouette of a gown on a hanger.

"*Bichonné*? Isn't that a breed of dog?"

Speak of the devil. Noah was standing over me, eyeing the name on the garment bag I had draped over my neighboring two seats. A hard-shell, rolling carry-on sat near his feet like a sleek silver boulder. I bet it had perfect dimensions for overhead bin capacity. And I bet he had an app for measuring bin capacity, just in case.

"Um, no. That's bichon frise." I knew, because my mother had one of those, too. Bitsy was probably the only living thing less thrilled than I was about this destination wedding. The poor dog was kenneled for the next week. "You miss your connection, too?" I wondered if he'd ask me to move my bag so he could sit. That would be rich, after he had hogged half of LaGuardia's waiting area himself.

"Nah. Mechanical trouble." He rocked back on the heels of his expensive-looking leather shoes. "They're trying to scrounge up another plane for us."

I rolled my pencil between my fingers as I studied him. Its hexagonal shape was strangely comforting. "You seem pleased."

"As long as the plane gets me from point A to point B in one piece, I don't mind being late. Better than dead and early." His eyes didn't leave his phone screen. "It's looking like a two-hour wait."

I didn't comment about the departure screen displaying the same info two inches from his head. Funny how he, like me, thought in terms of point A and point B.

"Want to grab lunch?" he asked.

I hesitated to answer; I wasn't sure if he was asking me or his phone. He seemed so enamored by it. Finally, he tore his eyes away and let them settle on me.

"You sure you want to be seen with me? People might start throwing rice at us next."

He gave a short bark of a laugh and ran a hand through his hair. "Sorry about my reaction back there. It was more about the bumpy flight than . . ."

"Than having to pretend to be engaged to a complete stranger?" I finished.

"Yeah," he said slowly. "Something like that." His grin started grim but ended sheepish, and with his eyebrows raised apologetically, it was hard to hold it against him. "So. Food? My treat."

I touched my belly. It wasn't exactly full, and neither was my wallet. I hoped my mom would take five minutes out of her prewedding bliss to remember to run payroll on time. "I don't know. That yogurt really filled me up."

"Oh, bull. You totally had asparagus envy." He had me there. "Sushi in the food court?"

I could roll with that.

Noah

ROLL WITH THE PUNCHES

"So. You're a runway bride."

Laney, my dress-obsessed seatmate, smeared wasabi across her asparagus roll like it was war paint. "I'm not running away," she said simply and left it at that.

"Not *runaway*." Julia Roberts had nothing on this one. Laney had a thousand-watt smile but so far she had only flickered it in my direction twice. "No, I mean you're flying solo, on the runway. Why are you traveling alone? G.I. bride?"

I could see my own mother in my mind, smiling down at me from the wedding portrait that graced all the fireplace mantels of my childhood. A fresh-faced *signorina* about to marry a handsome man in uniform. I wondered if my dad had promised to carry her over each and every threshold—nineteen, to be exact—after meeting her during his first station at Camp Darby, in Italy. Or if she had realized she would be a single mother for months at a time while he was deployed to various other places. Unable to plan ahead, not even to schedule my sixth birthday party, never knowing when he might be on active duty. I guess that was just part of the whole "for better or for worse" vow.

"You assume too much," Laney snapped, bringing me back to the here and now.

Christ, would it kill her to make conversation? It was like she was studying me, trying to decide if I was worthy of her valuable time. I bet she had a wedding checklist a mile long, possibly even longer than Sloane's.

"Well, you've got a dress dictating your every move. You won't let it out of your sight. And you were doodling pictures of it, and sketching rings, back there." She probably had a page full of signatures of her future married name, too. Sloane had had no problem cranking out endless variations on her future acquired name: *Sloane Ridgewood, Sloane B. Ridgewood, Mrs. Sloane Ridgewood, Dr. and Mrs. Noah Ridgewood.* I was the one holding the PhD in computer science and I barely felt comfortable using the title "doctor." Yet she was ready to monogram it on stationery in order to pen thank-you letters to the two hundred guests from our engagement party.

"Yeah, right," Laney scoffed. "Although you should've seen me ready to shiv security for making me take my ring off earlier."

I frowned as I accidently lost control of my chopsticks, my California roll dropping into the little plastic cup of soy sauce. "See? Sounds like classic Bridezilla behavior to me."

She almost choked on her wasabi-laced sushi piece. "Bridezilla? I am the least likely person to turn Bridezilla you will ever meet. In fact, I am like the Mothra of the Bridezilla world."

"Mothra." I tsked. "Pedestrian. Destoroyah—no, Bridestoroyah—could totally take on Bridezilla."

"You have the chopstick skill level of a preschooler, and you dare to go around citing Japanese monster movie characters to me?" Laney seethed. "I have my reasons for choosing Mothra."

"Yeah?" I stabbed my chopsticks straight through the middle of my errant sushi piece. "Let's hear them."

"Don't, it's bad luck!" she exclaimed.

"What, to *talk* to a bride about her wedding dress before the big day?" And I thought Sloane was taking the wedding superstitions too far.

"No, to stab your chopstick through the middle of your food." She reached across the table and readjusted my sticks for me with one hand. I noticed she kept her other hand on the garment bag riding shotgun in the chair next to her. Its midnight blue sheen and fancy silver embroidery looked out of place in the middle of the airport food court.

"So, what's with guys wanting to have bachelor parties in Vegas? Are they really buying into the whole 'what happens here, stays here' thing?" she demanded.

"Dunno," I mumbled. "I'm just showing up where I'm told to." Which was the truth. Tim had made all the arrangements. Although I *had* been the one to organize the insanity the only way I knew how. The other guys ripped on me for a couple of days about creating the Excel file, but I bet they'd be happy to have it when they were drunk at four o'clock in the afternoon and couldn't remember where their dinner reservations were.

"Vegas just seems so plastic," Laney went on. "Everything's a mirage. I mean, you're in the freakin' desert. Everyone having the time of their lives, *please*." She dismissed the notion with a swat of her hand. "It seems so forced. If the groom really needs one last hurrah, take him to Amsterdam where there are real hookers and good dope, at least."

Is that where your groom is right now? I felt like asking. I wondered if she really felt that way. Either she was the coolest Bridezilla on the planet or she was trying to pick a fight. "Maybe the groom just wants to chill with his friends and have some time to *not* have to think about his wedding. A break from the china patterns and seating arrangements?" I could list five or twenty other things, but just the thought was enough to make me break out in a sweat.

"You mean a break from things that make him feel less like a man? So he can go beat his chest and act all macho? And leave the girl stuck with all the crap jobs? Where is it written that all the brides have to buy into the Martha Stewart song and dance?"

Says the diva with the death grip on the fancy dress bag. "Where's it written that Vegas has to be this Gomorrah for grooms like you're implying?" I just wanted a drink by the pool, and maybe a couple of good hands in poker. And some sorely needed laughs with my friends . . . a distraction from worrying about everyone else's happiness but mine.

"What about yours?" she demanded.

Wait, did I say that out loud? "My what?"

"Your friend. The groom. What's his story?" Laney persisted. "Is he going to stand around good-naturedly while all his single guy friends hook up? Or is there, like, pressure to make sure he gets some? What if he's a dweeb? Or if his future wife is calling him every ten minutes?"

"I don't know. Jesus." *Ever hear of don't ask, don't tell?* I really didn't want to get into it with her. Then again, I had been the one to start up with the questions. "Can't it just be about having a good time?"

"I don't know," she said. "Can it?"

We finished our sushi in silence. Not exactly comfortable silence, but I was used to not speaking while eating. Sloane and I often texted through dinner on our respective phones: finalizing work projects (me) and confirming manicure appointments (her). Phonetiquette, the phonic translation app I had created, was still in beta testing, but I threw the name of Laney's fancy dressmaker in there for the hell of it. "*Bichonné* means 'pampered.' Well, that explains first class."

"First class only happened because . . ." Laney's cheeks flared about as pink as the pickled ginger on her plate. "I got a bump up."

"Ah, so *that's* why . . ." My fingers flew over the minuscule keypad of my phone, making notes for SeatSight, my airline seating app. "There needs to be a code in the app that accounts for already ticketed passengers in the system receiving airline upgrades." I looked up at her triumphantly. "Thank you."

"No problem. If you need another test subject, you can just pay me in sushi." There it was, that thousand-watt smile. Hot damn. Whoever she was marrying, wherever he was, must feel like a million bucks when she flashed that grin his way. "Good call," she added.

"Attention, all passengers in the boarding area. This is the final boarding call for Flight 3320 with nonstop service to Las Vegas, departing out of gate 28."

"That's me." What do you say to a beautiful girl you will never see again and who's about to hurl herself willingly into a marital abyss? "Safe travels, Laney."

She gave a wave. "Later, Vegas."

Standby

"Passenger Helena Hudson to gate 14, please. Passenger Helena Hudson, gate 14."

I had no idea how long they had been calling my name. Helena Hudson had gone MIA somewhere around her second birthday and only made brief appearances at family funerals, bar mitzvahs, and any other occasion where the majority of the population was over the age of sixty and related to me.

The guy working gate 14 was none of these things, but a ticketed passenger is a ticketed passenger, and since 9/11, your name had better match every piece of photo ID you had.

"Helena, we have you on the three o'clock flight to Los Angeles with a connecting flight to Lihue. But with the weather they're predicting . . ." He leaned closer to me, as if to avoid causing mass panic in the gate area. "I wouldn't be surprised if we see most flights grounded within the hour."

Over his shoulder, the one o'clock sky beyond the airport window was darkening to shades of winter evening, and Auntie Em–type winds were blowing. The snow was flying sideways, and not many planes seemed to be moving at all. "We know you obviously have an important place to be," he drawled, flashing me a smile so large I could practically see his wisdom teeth. "So we're trying to get you on standby for a direct flight to Honolulu that leaves an hour earlier, if you are okay with that?"

"That would be great. I'll just take a puddle jumper from there to Kauai." The sooner I could get out of this weather, the better.

"Stay close to the gate area. And don't worry, we've never had a bride miss her wedding day yet, Helena."

"*Helena* Hudson!" an unmistakable familiar voice boomed from the inner circle crowded around the name tags on the check-in table at Central Bluff High School's five-year reunion. "Some heads are gonna roll when Laney Jane sees that!"

I edged around the perimeter of the gathered masses and sidled my way next to Allen. I hadn't seen or spoken to my ex-boyfriend since graduation, and the term *sight for sore eyes* was an understatement. How many times had I cried my eyes sore and swollen to sleep? And how many times had I woken from a dream only to find him gone from my life, seemingly for good? I reached for my name tag and pinned it on.

"Laney Jane's the forgiving sort," I said quietly, hoping he was, too.

Forgive and forget, and let's move on. Let's move in. Together. Laney and Allen, forever. I had dated my way through college, thoroughly miserable and mismatched.

"Oh, my God, look at you, girl!" The lanky drummer's arms I had missed so much enveloped me. "Miss College Diploma. Where's the Mohawk? No more rocking the pink?"

I had gone through a My Little Pony phase of hair, dyeing it every hue of the Manic Panic rainbow and keeping the sides shaved into a punkish little mane for years. While it had made me a standout in our tiny Long Island village, it was standard fare at SVA in Manhattan. So

I became a rare bird for going natural. Besides, it made for good camouflage in corporate America.

"I'm rocking a nine-to-five desk job on the island," I said breezily, but there was no way to make it sound remotely cool.

"Courtesy of your mom, I bet." The sneer that hooked his lip was a reminder that five years' time hadn't put enough water under the bridge for us to sail smoothly past the pain.

"I think you've got enough color for both of us now." I gently touched his tattooed wrist, letting my eyes follow the designs up his arm. Beneath the thin white cotton of his rolled-up shirtsleeve, I could see muted ink all the way up to his muscular shoulder. Cartoony moonscapes and cratered planets, rockets and sunbursts mixed with mermaids, skulls and flaming poker playing cards. I wanted to know them all.

"Yeah, well, L.A., baby. Gotta walk the walk! Everyone's inked." He pulled a Sharpie marker from his back pocket and carefully corrected my name tag, his thumb hovering tantalizingly close to my left breast. I seized the moment to study him, loving the look he had cultivated in California. Both sides of his head were shaved close, but what was left on top was unspiked and longer than I had ever seen him wear it. Leather and silver graced his throat. He sloppily crossed out and scrawled upside down over his own name tag so it read: *HELLO, my name is SATAN.*

He swung his floppy curtain of flaxen hair over to one side as he dipped his ocean blue eyes down to inspect me. "I'm surprised you don't have any tats, with all that doodling you used to do."

I laughed, I basked, I glowed under his attention. "Not anywhere you can see, anyway."

"Laney Jane Hudson, are you flirting with me?"

I sighed, inking a speech balloon around the word *"MAYBE . . ."* in my latest drawing. The lanky rogue and petite, bright-eyed waif held each other at arm's length, but the tilt of their heads and the gaze of their *manga*-style wide eyes showed they were utterly immersed, consumed by one another.

The stages of my life with Allen were like the multiple-panel sequence of a comic book. A series of starts and stops. Fresh renewals and "To be continued . . ." with every page. A girl can dream, right? Over the years I had tried to capture what I referred to as *The Short but Brilliant and Doomed Courtship of Allen and Laney Jane.* I had filled many a night, and many a sketchbook, with my attempts.

And now I filled the minutes and the hours, past the departure time for the Honolulu flight (canceled), past the boarding time for my three o'clock LAX flight (delayed, soon to be canceled). I kept working while every TV in the terminal was tuned to the weather, every caption running along the bottom of the screens the same:

. . . high winds have grounded planes in the nation's midsection . . .

. . . as much as an inch of snow an hour expected . . .

. . . 250 flights canceled . . .

My father took me to my first comic book convention when I was seven years old. I think it was the Big Apple Comic Con, certainly not the most famous of its kind. But it was a pretty big deal for the time. I remembered the crooked lines of people, and row after row of long boxes tightly packed with every comic you could ever think of. The air of the old church basement where it was held had the distinctive scent of old paper pulp, tinged with the excitement of hundreds of collectors. I hung onto my dad's pant leg and stared up at the racks stretching toward the ceiling, lined with the colorful highlights of each collection sheathed in thick plastic. My dad handed me an old Harvey kids' comic; to keep me occupied, I supposed. It was a *Little Dot*, and I was quickly caught up in her world. I wanted to live in Dotland.

By age eleven, I had read through my father's collection and was developing one of my own, devouring each issue from cover to back page filler. I accompanied him to various conventions and shyly loitered around Artists' Alley. The seemingly ordinary men sitting at their tables would transform into heroes before my very eyes as I'd glimpse their name tags and match them to the series spread out before them.

Before my parents split up, the highlight of each summer was the weekend excursions out of town, just my dad and me. With a map and a sack of peanut butter sandwiches, we'd pile in his old Cutlass and make our way to Philly, South Jersey, and Delaware in search of comic book Mecca. Some places turned out to be no more than glorified garage sales; others like the Holy Grail. One day, we drove through the Pine Barrens, which was always spooky and made me think of the Jersey Devil urban legends, to an unlikely little shop near the ocean called Gus's Last Gathering. Tina and Gus, the owners, welcomed us like family, and it became a regular stop on our itinerary.

"Laney, I've got an errand to run. Tina's going to watch you for an hour, okay?" my dad said one day.

"Can't I come with you?"

He shook his head sadly. "Adults only, kid. But I got a hot tip, it's a sure thing. One hour, tops," he assured me, kissing my forehead. Kissing that Blarney Stone. I stayed with Tina and picked through the open back issue bins, trying to imagine where my father had gone that wouldn't allow me, too. There were some comic stores with small back rooms. *Adults Only,* the signs hanging from the closed curtains would read. Or *18 and Over.* I knew there were inappropriate comics, and I knew some men read only those kinds of comics. But my dad never went behind those curtains, as far as I knew.

He came back just as he had promised, within the hour, happy and chatty. He bought me my Magic 8 Ball and five *Archie* comics for being "the best daughter in the world"; and for himself he bought the old *Justice League* comic that Gus kept in glass behind the counter.

Tina called that a "fine thank-you" and laughed when he let her keep the change from the hundred-dollar bill as a tip.

The next time we went down to Gus's Last Gathering, my dad told me he had to meet a friend in Acey. "It'll be quick, I promise." He left me with Tina again. Quick didn't feel like an hour; it felt like several. A man came into the store and stood close to me at the new issues rack. He smelled like corn chips and sweat, and I could feel him staring as I kept my eyes on the pages in front of me. After that, Tina made me come behind the counter where she worked the register. She let me play with the action figurines, but only the ones that were already out of their boxes.

Gus had a huge map of New Jersey hanging on the back wall, and I tried to find Acey on it, but couldn't. I traced along the ocean and over to Long Island, where my house was. It felt like a long way away, even though we were on the same oceanside.

When my dad finally returned, he wasn't as happy or chatty as the last time. I heard Tina say something about not having eyes in the back of her head, which made me think of some kind of alien Superman would want to punch. She sent me in the back room and set me up with some blank paper and a pencil. "Draw," she commanded. And I did. I sat surrounded by stacks of comics, breathed in that old inky air, and pretended I was in Artists' Alley. I drew as if my life and my dreams depended on it.

Finally, my dad came in the back and said it was time to go home. "Where's our car?" I asked, as I climbed into the backseat of Gus's car. He had a Cutlass, too, but it was a newer model and had fancy blue velvet on the armrests.

"It broke down in Atlantic City," was all my dad said. He stayed silent as Gus drove us to catch the train in Asbury Park back to Manhattan. Gus and I sang along to the Rolling Stones' "Ruby Tuesday" on the radio. I didn't know it would be the last time I'd see Gus, or Tina. I would've said good-bye, and thank you, if I had known.

When our train pulled into Penn, my dad finally spoke. "Never lose your dreams, Laney. You don't want to lose your mind, like me."

"Sweetie, you're still here?" Anita, the flight attendant, was click-clacking toward me with her heels, towing a minuscule Windwest Airways bag behind her. "Figured you would be halfway to Hawaii by now."

"Missed the first connection, and the new one was coming from Newark . . ."

"Lemme guess," she said with a smirk, "it's still in Newark."

"Yep. So much for 'light bands' of snow. More like full-on, death-metal moshpit blizzard."

Anita laughed. "That's the Windy City for you! More sand, salt, and ice per capita than any other place."

"The only sand, salt, and ice I'm dreaming of is a margarita on the beach," I grumbled.

"I hear you, sister. Listen," Anita advised, "you should grab a hotel room while you still can."

"Eh." I dismissed the thought with a wave of my ink-smudged hand.

"I'm serious. Get your man and go snuggle up somewhere. Hey, my cousin works at the Regency, she can totally hook you up. I'll call her, okay? You and that dress don't need to be all crumpled in an airport chair all night."

She grabbed a cocktail napkin from her bag and used one of my fine-nib pens to jot down directions for me. "I'm terrible with names, but follow the colors, okay? There'll be red shuttle signs, and it's the blue-and-white bus. Ask for Daisy at the desk. I know she's working tonight. And here's my cell number—promise me you'll text me pictures of the big day!"

"Thanks. Oh, and here." I carefully tore a sheet from my sketch-book. In between my last Starbucks and bathroom runs, I had completed a fairly detailed rendering of Anita sashaying down the aisle of first class, silver tray and tongs in hand. She had the traditional slammin' body of a superhero comic book dame, buxom and nip-waisted. I had glammed up her hair in voluptuous waves to match both her figure and the rolling plumes of lemon-scented steam emanating from her supply of towels.

"Oh, my God, you drew this? I'm so . . . Wow. I am blown away. Girl, that's amazing! This is what you do?" She couldn't stop staring at her picture and smiling.

"It's what I did."

"So professional." She pushed the paper to her ample chest. "I'm gonna frame it, I'm serious. Thank you so much. Congratulations again. He's a doll."

"Who?" As the word left my mouth, Noah occurred to me. My accidental fiancé had his head in the clouds right about now. At thirty-five thousand feet, the lucky dog.

"Stop, you're cracking me up! *Who?*" She laughed. "Have fun, good luck!"

I recalled our lunch. It hadn't been half-bad. I had figured airport sushi to be on par with mall food court sushi, but was pleasantly surprised. The company hadn't been so bad, either. But when he called me Bridezilla, sheesh. Tech-Boy had no freakin' clue . . .

My cell phone beeped to life. I was almost scared to check the text. My mother was demanding updates hourly. And Danica kept sending me pictures of her bare feet, long legs crossed on a chaise, no doubt, along with a different tropical drink strategically perched in her hand in the foreground in each. I didn't know which was more torturous.

Windwest Airways Flight Status: #3 ORD–LAX, canceled. Please call airline to reschedule.

Yeah, right. Call the airline. That was a laugh. Thousands of stranded travelers surrounded me, and with each step I took, I saw fewer and fewer uniformed employees. O'Hare was turning savage. I pulled my battered army coat from my carry-on bag, thankful I had opted to keep the liner zipped in for the trip.

Canceled. Finding hotel. Am OK, I quickly texted to my mom and Danica. **Powering down for a while.**

Meaning "no more pictures of toes and umbrella drinks, please." And no more asking about the status of the dress. The dress and I were in a holding pattern, stuck with each other for another day.

I consulted my napkin map. Red signs. Right.

My phone bleated for my attention once more; I thought it had powered down, but apparently it needed to deliver two more messages: a sad face emoticon from Danica, and an emotionless plea from my mother.

And what of the dress?

Noah

TARMAC

"Ladies and gentlemen, we're being held here for a bit longer than expected. There's quite a bottleneck of planes waiting for takeoff. Our crew members will come through the cabin shortly with snacks and water. We're keeping the cabin lights dimmed, but the in-flight entertainment service is available to you at this time. Channels for viewing can be found in the Windwest *FutureFly* magazine, located in your seat-back pocket. We hope to have you up in the air shortly."

We had pushed out of the gate forty-five minutes behind schedule due to a delayed crew, and at least a half hour had passed since. And then the plane had just rumbled around on its wheels for a good fifteen minutes, making it feel like we were turning in circles. Now we were just sitting motionless on the taxiway, waiting. Whether we were waiting our turn for takeoff or waiting for the ground crew to find the runway, it was hard to tell. The snow was still coming down in thick slanted sheets.

As much as I hated flying, I hated the anticipation of flying more. And all the waiting around was making me squirrelly. One and a half hours already shot. Couldn't we just drive there at six hundred miles per hour? We can send a man to the moon, but no one has figured out how to build one long runway across the country? Gas up the plane and just drive that sucker. So it would take a little longer. So what? At least we'd know what we were up against. Currently, we were involuntary captives.

Tarmac delays sucked.

I wondered if Laney, the dress girl, was still in the terminal. I couldn't stop thinking about that smile. And how it had lit up the dreary food court.

Turning my attention to the personal television in front of me, I flipped absently through the channels. Ah, space. The final frontier. Even though it was muted, I knew the *Star Trek* intro, and most of the episodes, by heart. "My gorgeous geek," Sloane would brag to friends, with a dramatic eyeball roll. As nerd culture became the latest social trend, Sloane pretended to understand and revel in the chic of dating geek. "I'm Penny to his Leonard," she'd say at parties. But behind closed doors, she wanted nothing to do with my movie marathons on Syfy and would stamp her high heels in horror if I so much as hinted at going to a fan convention with friends. As my internal concern that maybe we didn't have much in common grew, she'd do a Vulcan mind meld and insist, "Well, maybe I just want you all to myself," along with a wicked walk of fingernails down my bare chest and—I'll be the first to admit it—I'd cave. I might've been a dweeb, but I was your typical horny guy as well.

"After a time, you may find that having is not so pleasing a thing, after all, as wanting. It is not logical, but it is often true."

Amen, Mr. Spock.

The truth was, I had wanted Sloane Bidwell from the first moment I saw her. And because I was so used to watching everything through rose-colored glass windows, gazing at the haves with my nose pressed against the have-not side, I really thought I wanted everything she stood for.

She'd clubbed with Paris in New York; she'd shopped with the Kardashians in Paris. And she had been well on her way to becoming a binge-and-purge party girl "celebutante" when her father funneled her (along with enough money to fund a new wing) into Northwestern to reinvent herself, and our worlds collided. With my temple pressed against the cool layers of plastic and glass that made up the airtight safety window, I stared out at the frigid Midwest landscape. Chicago: the city where it all began for us.

Warren Butler prairie-dogged over the top of my cubicle. "You've got a suit and tie, don't you, Scout? Put 'em on. I scored us seats for the Bidwell gala tonight. At the Standard Club."

"You're joking, right?" The Standard Club oozed old money, and Kip Bidwell was a major money player, known throughout Chicagoland as well as the tristate New York area. The guy had his hands in transportation, real estate, sports teams, and, as of late, mobile advertising and R&D. We had been trying to land a meeting with him since finishing our alpha tests on my translation app over a year before.

"Why on earth would I ever joke about wearing a suit and tie?" Warren asked drolly. He dropped back into his cubicle and I could hear his machine-gun fingers going a million miles an hour on his computer keyboard, trying to keep up with that brain of his.

Warren had been my dad's oldest friend, and he was a perpetual funny guy, but there was always a modicum of truth in what he said. Although his mind was always on business, his body still had yet to trade in the tie-dye for a shirt and tie. While my dad had moved from base camp to base camp, Warren had caravanned from parking lot to parking lot, seeing at least two hundred Dead shows.

I got up and walked over to his side of the partition separating us. Our cubicles were just two of many designated to keep the worker drones of the IT department on task. Warren had gotten me the intern job right when I hit Chicago for graduate school, and although it sucked big boring dog balls, I was grateful for it.

I was grateful for Warren, too.

"I have the suit from my dad's funeral," I told him. "It still fits."

Warren had the keyboard resting on his lap, with his feet, clad in beat-up Birkenstocks, propped up on his desk. Pinned on the corkboard behind his monitor were pictures: Warren and my dad as kids, Warren and my dad making peace signs, my dad's hair clipped short to his head while Warren's flowed long. Warren as fearless leader of my Outward Bound experience, his arm draped around a scowling teenager (me) out in some godforsaken forest somewhere. That was around the time he'd decided to christen me Scout. And finally: a picture of Warren and my mother flanking me at my college graduation.

While I had been proudly wearing the mortarboard, my dad's convoy had hit a very different kind of mortar: 81mm rounds embedded into a roadside improvised explosive device, seven thousand miles away. Killed instantly.

"Good to hear, kid," Warren said, dropping his feet to the floor and swiveling his chair to face me. "Because tonight you're going to change our lives."

Sloane Bidwell was holding court in the center of the room, smiling and nodding with a grace I had only seen in movies. Diamonds dripped from her regal neck as she threw her head back with a devil-may-care laugh over something some ascot-wearing buffoon had said.

"Let's go talk to her. Butter her up," Warren suggested.

"What do you mean, 'butter her up'? She's not a loaf of bread," I told him. And even if she was, she was fresh-baked artisan to my day-old Wonder. There was nothing I could say to this creature without making her look down her nose at me. I could tell.

"Her daddy has more dough than God's bakery. He's got investor capital out the yin-yang. He's also got access to the highest-quality pool of testers. Our betas need Kip Bidwell. Let's go make your dad proud."

He was already making his way toward her, and I had no choice but to follow.

"You look lovely tonight, Miss Bidwell," Warren finally said, after an excruciatingly long wait by her elbow for a chance to break into the conversation. She smiled at him expectantly. "Warren Butler, of the Kennebunkport Butlers."

Her smile stayed exactly the same; I had a feeling she was trying to place him in her mind. Or her mind was trying to compartmentalize the information and decide whether he was worthy or unworthy of her time.

"And this handsome lad"—he clapped me on the shoulder—"is Noah Ridgewood."

This was his buttering-up strategy? "How 'bout those Wildcats?" I heard myself say.

She turned, but she didn't look down at me. She looked *through* me. Infinitely worse.

"Noah's at U of C," Warren supplied. A waiter passed by, balancing a champagne tray, and Sloane helped herself to a bubbling flute.

"Greek?"

"No, but he's got the Mediterranean thing going for him. Italian on his mother's side," he said as he slowly backed away to leave the two of us alone.

"I meant fraternity," she said coolly, but I saw a minuscule arch in her brow as she flicked a quick glance across the span of my chest, up to my face, and down to my groin.

"We're trying to get a meeting with your father about some apps I've developed."

She rolled her eyes as if she had heard it all one hundred times before. "Remember when an app was something you ate?" She grabbed a complicated-looking morsel from a silver tray passing by. "I'd much rather talk about that instead."

I opened my mouth to reply, and she pushed the entire thing past my lips. A perfect storm of flavors exploded on my tongue. "What," I gasped, after chewing and swallowing, "was that?"

"Sweet potato *gaufrettes* with duck *confit* and cranberry black pepper chutney," she rattled off. I liked the way the French words, whatever they meant, flowed off her tongue as fluidly as the English. "I know, because I chose every item on the menu. And none of these boring businessmen seem to care."

Warren was loitering around the buffet table, nursing a drink and scanning the crowd. He held up his phone and gave it a little shake, indicating that I should show her the apps in question. Ignoring him, I ventured, "I am sure everyone appreciates the food. They're just too busy networking to really discuss it." Kissing ass was more like it.

Sloane drained her tall flute of champagne and frowned at the strawberry wedge lodged at the bottom. "Well, what makes you any different? Tell me one thing. Make me laugh," she demanded. Using her perfectly manicured fingernail, she coaxed the fruit up the inside of her glass.

Warren took that moment to casually walk behind me and beta-test Fartrillion, an app I had jokingly made in school. Of course he chose the most obnoxious, juiciest-sounding fart noise as the prototype. Sloane's eyes widened. She glanced from left to right, then she stepped back, flaring her nostrils.

"It was the app, I swear!"

"You shouldn't eat duck, then, if it gives you gas."

I burst out laughing. "No, look." I pulled my own phone from my pocket. "One of the app*lications* my partner and I have developed. It's a silly one, I know. But I've got tons of others and I think your father might be really—"

"Let me see it."

I offered the phone to her. Biting her plumped-up lip in thought, she scanned over the choices before placing a lacquered talon on the Atomic Bomb button and letting it rip. A prominent member of the city council quickened his pace past us at the sound of it. Sloane stifled a laugh and hit another particularly ripe selection. It practically vibrated through the hallowed halls of the Standard Club, raising eyebrows and lowering voices.

"You can record your own, too," I began to say, just as she sidled up to Mayor Daley and her father in deep discussion.

"Daddy . . ." she said, her eyes taking on a maniacal twinkle and her finger hovering dangerously close to the Tearjerker button. I saw my whole career pass before my eyes, doomed before it could get started. Warren was already heading for the exit door. She leaned in close to her father and the mayor of Chicago, whispering as she manipulated the buttons on my phone.

I couldn't bear to look. Turning away, I drowned my sorrows in more duck confit. It might be the first and last time I ever got to try it. I'd probably be eating ramen noodles for the rest of my life.

I felt a weight drop into the pocket of my cheap suit. Sloane had deposited my phone back in and whispered in my ear, "You've got his last meeting of the day, next Tuesday. Thanks for making me laugh."

Later that night, I discovered her number programmed into my phone. She'd entered it as stealthily and as boldly as she had entered my life. It was a strange new world for me. Socialite girlfriend, powerhouse family. I had been dredged up from the dregs like that strawberry in her champagne glass. Her dad liked my ideas; he actually liked me. "You've got a good head on your shoulders, Ridgewood." He thought I was "a grounding force" for Sloane, who tended to chase "the wrong type," whatever that meant. "Meet the potential in-laws" turned into "manage the portfolios," and Warren and I, along with our growing family of apps, were blended into the Bidwell conglomerate with open arms. We were in the black, and in a corner office in Manhattan, quicker than you could say "hedge fund," with Warren's name hanging from the hyphen in an act of good faith. Bidwell-Butler Solutions was born.

Truthfully, deep down I never thought things with Sloane would last. Just as her father would pursue ultraspecialized bets and had the power to unsentimentally dump losing positions in his business trades, I thought for sure Sloane would wake up one morning, wonder what the hell I was doing there, and discard me like last year's fashion trend.

Turned out she must've been interested in the long-term performance of my equity offerings. In layman's terms, she said yes to my proposal.

And from then on, there seemed to be no slowing down, no—

"We're sorry, folks, but the latest news from air traffic control—" Our captain's voice was drowned out by the collective groan of the cabin.

Turning back. We were turning back.

Cold Feet

I found the blue-and-white hotel shuttle Anita had described with no problem, but my courage to brave the snowdrifts in flip-flops was elusive. *Think warm thoughts. Think toes in the hot sand.* I plunged myself into the revolving doorway to the outside world. A blast of frigid air bitch-slapped me within the vacuum and I lost my nerve, twirling back through the revolving doors a second time. On my third time around, I saw Noah standing inside and shaking his head. The garment bag and I pushed back into the airport.

"Are you done playing merry-go-round in the doorway? Because some of us would like to get on that shuttle."

"I thought you left hours ago. What happened?" I asked.

"Sitting on the runway for three hours happened." He did not look happy. "You?"

"Same shit, different plane. Although I never made it down the gangway."

"Lucky us, we get to try it all over again tomorrow. In the meantime . . ." Noah turned, making toward the revolving door. "What are you waiting for? That shuttle is filling up." He paused, looked me up and down, and rolled his eyes. "You couldn't wait till you got to Hawaii to show off the pedicure? It's still winter in most of the country, you know."

"Long story. I've got other shoes in my checked luggage." Which may or may not be on its way to Hawaii without me, I realized.

"Of course you do." He glanced once more at the door and then back down to my stupid flip-flops. Was he considering carrying me across the threshold and onto the shuttle? The preposterous thought struck me, and a giggle burst out. I covered my mouth to feign a cough, but I couldn't contain my grin. "Sit," he commanded.

I sat. Noah kneeled down beside me and thrust his hard-shell case open. He tossed me a pair of socks in a neat roll and pulled out a pair of red Converse high-tops.

"Thanks." Even with the thick white socks, his sneakers were Bozo-the-Clown big on me, but at least they protected me from the elements. Noah went to work tying them tight to my feet, like I was a kindergartner on the first day of school. I tilted my head and watched him make perfect double knots. He didn't seem like a Converse Chuck Taylor All Stars kind of guy, in his matchy-match suit and Italian loafers. So put together, and so not my type. He had added a gray wool overcoat to his getup. Very Fifty Shades of Blah. There was a tiny crepe-paper poppy fastened to the buttonhole of the coat's lapel, giving his monochrome ensemble a small pop of color the same hue as the red Chucks.

"So why are *you* traveling alone," I asked, picking up on our lunch conversation, "to a bachelor party? In a suit?"

"Meeting my friends there." He snapped the case shut. "Mostly college friends, from the Pacific Northwest. I had an early meeting. Hence, the suit. It's been a really long day." *Hence, shut up,* his look conveyed.

We boarded the bus and were met with glum looks; our fellow

passengers were clearly ready to get the show on the road and didn't take kindly to newcomers pushing on with more luggage. The driver moved to take my garment bag to hang, but I waved him away. "I'll hold it on my lap, thanks."

One seat remained in the very last row of five across. It was big enough to fit half my ass, so I perched, garment bag unable to be contained within my personal space. The mother sitting next to me shielded the eyes of the child on her lap, as if the hanger was going to reach over and poke his eye out. *It's only a dress*, I felt like saying. But it was more than a dress. It was my mother, personified. Ready to jump down my throat for poor choices, unfortunate mistakes.

Noah stood in the aisle, his stance wide as the bus lurched and lumbered up the highway ramp. With his computer bag slung from his shoulder and one hand on the bar above his head, he looked like a typical New York straphanger on his subway commute home: grumpy yet unflappable. His expression was impassive, but his stare intense as he zeroed in on a spot overhead, slightly to my left. I wondered what he was thinking about; what warranted such a strong jut of that chiseled jaw.

The snow had a way of insulating everything. Everyone was silent as the bus crawled along the highway. No horns honking; there was no frantic pace outside the windows. All traffic had agreed to play nice and inch along. The trip may have been thirty miles, or it may have been three; it was hard to tell. But my legs were pins and needles by the time we finally arrived. I tripped down the bus steps in Noah's clown shoes and into the warm, bright lobby of the Regency.

"You must be the bride!" The line of guests waiting to check in parted like the Red Sea, turning to stare at me as the woman behind the desk beckoned me forward. Her colleagues were scuttling around like crabs, fetching keys, making calls, and explaining calmly to panicky and weary travelers that there were no rooms left at the inn.

"And, whoa, Anita was right—he *is* going to look amazing in a tux!" she marveled.

I turned. Noah was at the desk next to me, tapping his credit card impatiently against the marble countertop. He was beginning to blush again, the red creeping north of his shirt collar. At least he wasn't turning green, like on the plane.

"You must be Daisy." I sighed in relief and returned her smile. At least one thing was going right.

"I've got the honeymoon suite saved for you guys," she singsonged. *What? No! Wrong, wrong, wrong!* "It's not Hawaii, but it's the last room left. Total is three hundred twenty dollars—going on your charge?"

Three hundred twenty dollars? I could rent a cabana *and* a cabana boy in Hawaii for that kind of money. But I wasn't in Hawaii. And I didn't exactly have that kind of money to burn. I had only the dress as my collateral. Noah obviously had the line of credit, and he slapped his bargaining chip down with a resigned sigh.

"Are you sure there are no other rooms?" he pressed. "We're not—"

"We're traditional," I hissed. As much as I didn't love the situation we were in, I didn't want to risk losing the last room at the inn because of Mr. Uptight Tech-Boy's hang-ups. Daisy looked at me like I was crazy. I glared warily at Noah. What if *he* was crazy?

"One key or two?" Daisy clearly didn't want to be involved.

"Two." Noah said, as she ran his card. "Thank you, Daisy."

He signed his name on the slip with a cocky flourish. Was I supposed to be impressed with the size of his credit limit and the girth of his wallet or at how fast he whipped it out of his pants?

Tech-Boy could go whiz in the snow all he wanted, the show-off. Unlike my mother, I wasn't in the market for a sugar daddy.

Noah

RAISING THE BAR

"We're sorry, folks. We have no more vacancies," the hotel manager announced to groans and protests.

"I need a drink," Laney muttered. She didn't invite me, nor did she wait for me to join her. She simply hiked her wedding bag over her shoulder and turned on her heel—in my sneakers, thank you very much—and made toward the dimly lit lounge off the hotel lobby.

I contemplated my choices. I wanted to go straight upstairs and sleep, sleep through the entire Vegas bachelor blowout and wake up on the other side of . . . what? The thought of heading back to New York sucked almost as much as being stuck halfway to my destination. A drink actually sounded good right about now.

My phone vibrated against my thigh; pretty much the most action I had received below the waist in months. It was Tim—best friend, best man, worst timing—blowing up my screen with "Dude, where are you?" texts.

When you said you'd arrive at 1300 hours, I didn't think you meant IN 1300 hours! WTF, man?

Dude, beyond my control. Delayed. Currently in Chicago, hotel bar.

Shacking up with some hot stewardess?

They're called flight attendants, you Neanderthal. And for the record, no.

I wasn't about to tell him I was sharing the last available room with some strange girl before her wedding night. Emphasis on *strange*. Knowing Tim and his dirty mind, he was already crafting porno stories to tell the rest of the guys about how I put the "lay" in "layover."

And I knew him well—we'd been friends since first grade and army brat pen pals no matter where our dads' assignments took us. We'd managed to land in the same college for undergrad, before Tim followed in his father's footsteps and enlisted upon graduation. We had been each other's wingmen for years: he had the bravado and I had the brains; he got the laughs with his personality and I got the looks with my, well . . . as he would call them, "pretty boy" features.

"Work hard, play harder" was Tim's motto and I was certain he planned to take "Bachelor Party in Vegas" to a whole new high. He wasn't exactly the kind of guy you wanted to disappoint.

You do realize how hard it was to get leave? I practically had to go AWOL to get here. You'd better show!

Yes, sir, Drill Sergeant, sir!

At ease, Private Pretty Boy. At ease.

I slipped the phone back into my pocket and ambled into the hotel's cocktail lounge. Laney was digging to China in her handbag, a stiff-looking concoction by her elbow. The bartender tapped a cardboard coaster impatiently against the bar in wait for her. No doubt counting the minutes until the end of his shift so he could attempt to make it home on the snowy roads to his family. He lifted a brow expectantly as I approached.

My credit card hadn't made it back into my wallet yet, so I forked it over. "Make it two."

"Stop. Paying. For me." Her perfect row of teeth gritted at me as the bartender turned his back and went to work. She continued to paw through her giant leather bag. I had never seen anything like it before. Its rough black hide and silver studs made me think she had ripped a biker jacket off some Hell's Angel gang member's back and proceeded to ride over it repeatedly with his Harley. Not exactly Prada material.

"I've always wanted to say that," I said defensively. "You know, like in the movies." I surveyed our stoolmates. Rumpled-suited businessmen killing the hours with their corporate card tabs, weary families making their Cokes last as they sat with their bleary-eyed children on the low couches to the left of the bar area. Some flight attendants and a captain or two were laughing over a game of darts in the corner.

"Honeymoon's over, eh?" The bartender slid my drink into my hand and winked at me. I wanted to laugh; it certainly felt like something out of a movie now.

"You don't know the half of it." I signed the credit card bill, making sure to tip well. "Over before it started."

He threw back his head and laughed. "The minute my wife said 'I do' in the church, she started saying 'I won't' everywhere else—the kitchen, the bedroom . . . If I get it on our anniversary and my birthday, I'm lucky."

I wasn't sure if it was comforting or disturbing to hear this information from a total stranger. But it really wasn't high on the list of things I wanted to hear, period. Last year for *my* birthday, Sloane got *herself* a boob job. "I did it for you," she had insisted, even though I had never expressed any particular fondness for large breasts of the silicone variety. And it seemed in direct opposition to her hands-off-till-the-wedding-night sex ban she had instituted. She threw both in my face recently—the facts, mind you; not her actual breasts—as prime examples of "nothing I do makes you happy." But in truth, they were pretty far down on a growing list of other concerns that gnawed at my happiness and had kept me awake for the last few months.

Another hotel worker, his gleaming head shaved as bald as Mr.

Clean's, sidled up to the bartender. Silver rings dangled heavily in both ears. "They just closed Lake Shore Drive, Jimmy. How much you wanna bet Phil won't make his shift?"

Jimmy swore under his breath and halfheartedly smacked his bar towel down to wipe up an imaginary spill.

"You guys serve food here?" I asked.

"Restaurant's down the corridor and to your left. There's quite a wait; you might want to go put your name down now," Jimmy advised.

Laney was halfway through her drink; her feet—in my Converse— were curled around the rungs of the bar stool. I began to drain my own for courage, and for something to do. What the hell was I going to talk about with this girl for the rest of the evening? Crown Royal burned under the tangy comfort of ginger ale. I think Jimmy had also "made it a double" when he "made it two."

"I'm going to scope out the food situation here; I'll be back in a few," I said to Laney. She nodded and shrugged in a way that could mean *good idea* or *go to hell*, for all I knew.

An e-mail pinged through on my phone as I meandered down the hotel corridor.

From: Maria Ridgewood <maria@cucinacaterstoyou.com>
Subject: INVITATION
Date: March 5, 2013 8:08 PM EST
To: Noah Ridgewood <noah.ridgewood@bidwellbutler.com>

HONEY, SLOANE SENT ME THE PROOF OF YOUR INVITATION—SO BEAUTIFUL, IT MADE ME CRY! AND WHAT A DEAR OF HER TO SHARE IT, I WAS SO SURPRISED. SHE WANTED TO KNOW IF I MINDED THE DATE CHANGE. I TOLD HER IT WAS A NICE TRIBUTE, BUT WHO AM I TO SAY? ULTIMATELY, THIS IS YOUR AND SLOANE'S DAY, NOAH. YOUR FATHER WOULD BE SO PROUD AND HAPPY FOR YOU. LIKE I AM.

WILL YOU HUMOR YOUR POOR MOTHER AND PLEASE TELL SLOANE TO SEND ME TWO WHEN THEY'RE PRINTED? I WANT TO KEEP ONE IN THE SCRAPBOOK, UNOPENED, FOR MY FUTURE GRANDCHILDREN.

ENJOY YOUR TIME WITH THE BOYS, VIVA LAS VEGAS!

CIAO, MOM

Great. Leave it to Sloane to ambush my mom about the invitations.

There would be no mistaking what they were upon arrival in the two-hundred-plus mailboxes around the globe—the hefty weight of the paper stock; the addresses all done by hand in calligraphy; the double "Love" stamps, hand-canceled. Another envelope with the engraved invitation would be nestled within. Yes, real engraving. Touch the back! Somewhere out there, custom metal plates would be created and pressed to create the announcement, the RSVPs, the works. Every enclosure card and envelope would be stacked in order of size, as etiquette dictated.

Every detail screamed Sloane.

Me, I was like the pesky piece of tissue in between. *Why is it there? What is its purpose?* The minute you pull out the all-important invitation, the tissue invariably sifts to the floor, forgotten. Crumpled underfoot.

My mother wanted two invitations: one she could open and gaze upon, to show her friends and to respond to, and one to keep sealed up like a time capsule. For the grandchildren she so desperately wanted.

I reread the e-mail as I slowly approached the restaurant. Despite all my teachings, my mother had yet to grasp the concept that writing in all caps was essentially shouting at someone. I hoped she didn't do it to her clients of Cucina Caters to You, her home-cooked meals delivery service.

My stomach growled nostalgically at the thought of her seafood lasagna, her Bolognese. And there was literally no substitute for her almond amaretto cake. Comfort food was my mother's old-world specialty, with a little dash of Catholic guilt for flavor.

The bartender hadn't been kidding about the wait list. It seemed the line of people who had been hoping for available rooms had just shifted over to the restaurant. And if the patrons looked unhappy outside of the place, the food service workers within appeared utterly miserable, dragging their feet and glumly serving up bland-looking fare. My stomach turned just thinking about spending any additional time near the place.

Jimmy had moved on to other customers back in the bar, and apparently Mr. Clean had decided to move in on Laney. Seriously? Fake fiancé or not, I was a bit pissed off. Who hits on a girl carrying a bridal dress?

You do, you horn dog. You flirted with her over that banana on the plane and teased her about envying your limp asparagus. It's a wonder she hasn't screamed sexual harassment by now.

Come on, I reasoned with myself. *She seems like the type of girl who knows a joke when she hears one.*

And who knows a joke when she sees one, too.

You.

I was so busy debating with myself over the fallacy of my phallic innuendos that I hadn't noticed Laney had climbed half on the bar and was in the process of unbuttoning her sweater. What was this, her audition tape for *Brides Gone Wild*?

"You think *those* are big?" she was saying. A cocktail waitress loading her tray behind the bar turned to survey the goods as well. Mr. Clean stood there smiling smugly with his arms crossed over his mammoth pecs, just like he did on the bottle of floor cleaner. The resemblance was uncanny. "Wait'll you see my—"

"Um, Laney. Sweetheart. What are you doing?" I asked through gritted teeth.

"He showed me his. I'm just showing mine," she said coyly, raising her bare shoulder to her chin and blinking over it seductively. So perhaps Mr. Clean wasn't the one with the dirty mind. She was flirting with him, despite my being there. "Got a problem with that? *Sweetheart?*"

Oh, she was flirting *in spite* of my being there.

"Ha, she totally has you beat, Lance. Pay up!" crowed the waitress.

"You win, angel." Mr. Clean slapped down a fiver. He turned to me and bared one muscle at a time. The wings tattooed across the span of each of his biceps appeared to take flight as he flexed. "Totally bigger than mine."

Laney grinned and shrugged her sweater back onto her shoulders, but not before I caught a glimpse of the flame-colored feathers stenciled in a blocky tribal style along her scapulae.

"She's a live one," Mr. Clean said, lifting a brow at me as he began to bus empty beer glasses from the bar. Laney did a raise-the-roof move in victory. "Don't let her fly away from you, now."

"No chance of that even if I wanted her to," I joked hoarsely. "All the planes are grounded."

"Jealous much?" Laney asked me, as he moved on.

"Of what? Tattooed beefcake bar backs?" I nursed my drink and ignored her smug look. "As if." *Good one, Noah. What are you, ten?* "Please, no dancing on the bar, or doing anything else on your 'bridal bucket list.'" I air-quoted. "Not on my watch, okay?"

"Then stop watching me," she dared, her eyes flicking flames as fiery as those I had glimpsed across her bare skin just moments before. We stared each other down in silence, with the bulky blue bridal dress bag sitting on the stool between us like some useless referee. Fine. If this was a test of wills, I could go all evening.

It was almost imperceptible, but I caught the twitch of one brow under that thick fringe of bangs, sending smoldering warmth through the pit of my belly. What would it take to break her? *Stop. Engaged. Remember?*

I wasn't sure if my thoughts were trying to send smoke signals to remind me, or her.

There was a rustling of vinyl as the garment bag slid lazily off the side of the stool, and the spell was broken as we both reached down in a Hail Mary attempt to save it from puddling onto the questionable bar carpet below.

"Brides don't need bucket lists," Laney muttered under her breath, trying to wrestle the unwieldy bag into submission. "People who throw around that term, and the 'YOLO' crap"—now it was her turn to air-quote—"and 'gotta go live my dash, dude' . . . they don't have a fucking—"

Laney's cell phone bleated for attention on the bar, interrupting her tirade. "Yay, my mother." Sarcasm dripped from her lips as she dipped to pick up the call.

"Yes, Mom. I'm alive. And I have clean underwear . . . yes, three pairs. Four, if you count my black lace thong."

I almost dropped what was left of my drink. Good God, this girl was going to be the death of me.

That probably wasn't for your benefit, you loser. She's just trying to rile her mother up.

I snuck a glance at Laney, whose eyes rolled up under her messy fringe of bangs.

"Well, put *your* Big Girl panties on and just deal with it! I'll be there tomorrow, I promise. Can you give Danny the phone? Thank you."

What was with all the panty talk? I wondered if it was wedding-day jitters, or did all girls talk to their mothers like that?

"Hey, Danny." I heard Laney sigh as she twisted on her stool for privacy. "Yeah, I'm okay."

Was it possible to feel out of place, out of line, and out of sorts, all at the same time? What was I doing in some hotel bar, fighting with some girl I barely knew over what she did with her body? The phrase *I'm a lover, not a fighter* stupidly popped into my head, reddening the tips of my ears and igniting embers that had been damped down and trampled on over time.

I righted the dress myself, pushing it firmly back in its place. I was tired of considering brides and their many lists, bucket or otherwise. Sloane certainly had a number of things she felt compelled to accomplish before life as a single woman ended. Living alone, that lasted about two weeks. Learning to cook stopped after three lessons with a Michelin-starred chef. "Good luck with that," were his last words to me before he threw down his apron. I wasn't worried about it; I could fend for both of us with what cooking skills my mother had taught me, were all of Manhattan's five-stars to suddenly close.

Many of the items on Sloane's "to do before I say I do" list began with *M* and ended with *E* and carried price tags so high, most people couldn't hope to cross them off in their entire lifetime. I didn't concern myself with the majority of them . . . but the prewedding surgeries concerned me.

"Think of it as an upgraded version of me. The Sloane 2013 reinvention! I can't wait to go shopping for my new body!" she'd crowed, poring over the bridalplasty brochures.

"But you're beautiful as you are," I had insisted.

"It's my body at the end of the day," she'd huffed after I questioned the need for the mini brow lift, cheek injections, and inner thigh liposuction. "And it's lipo*sculpturing*, not *suction*. I want to feel perfect on our wedding day."

I turned my attention to the muted television over the bar, trying not to eavesdrop as Laney chattered animatedly to Danny, whoever he was. If Danny was her fiancé, he was probably worried about her. Chewing on a whiskey-laced cube of ice, I contemplated whether it would even occur to Sloane to track my flight status, even under normal circumstances.

Our circumstances hadn't been normal in a long time.

Laney sipped her drink through the tiny stirrer like it was a straw, her cheeks sucked in exaggeratedly. Her jade eyes widened with the effort. She reminded me of a mime—a cute mime—as she listened, enraptured, to whatever this guy was saying to her on the other end. Actually enjoying listening to the person you were going to marry; that was novel.

Okay. So maybe I was a little jealous.

"Oh, my God, Dan! Shut up!" She was giggling. "Yeah, you would! I know, sweetie. Aw, I love you, too." Her lips were off the stirrer-straw and she was grinning, hanging on to her tiny flip phone with two hands now.

God, that smile! It rendered me snow-blind. I kept staring long after she clicked her phone shut, not even registering that she had hung up.

"Dude." She shot me a wary glance, lips in a reserved line. "What?"

I shook my head, but it didn't exactly bring me back to my senses. "What would *Danny* think of you stripping down for total strangers?" I blurted out.

"Didn't your mother ever teach you that eavesdropping is rude? Besides, they just wanted to see my tats. Get over it. It's not like they asked me to join them in a threesome."

"Your body, your life." I shrugged. "My mother taught me to help out strangers in need, so . . . you're welcome," I said sarcastically. She had shoes on her feet, a roof over her head, and a drink in her hand, all courtesy of me. Couldn't she at least pretend to be civil?

"Oh, am I supposed to get down on my *knees* and thank you? If you're looking for some alcohol-infused camaraderie or sleazy movie-fantasy hookup out of this, you are sadly barking up the wrong tree." She waggled her circa 2008 phone in her hand. "I've got people on the line. And they know where I am. So why don't you call someone who cares?"

Was what lurked behind that sweet glitter of her smile nothing more than a dry and tasteless experience, just like cake after goddamn wedding cake Sloane and I had endlessly sampled? Each had been just as generic as the rest when you cut past the smooth surface: just another cookie-cutter element in the generic moments making up what was touted as the happiest day of your life.

If she was just another sucker buying that, hook, line, and sinker, she had no advances to worry about coming from me.

"Christ, are you always this caustic?" I snarled.

"Caustic?" She hurled the dress bag over her arm and glared at me. "Is that a word from your thesaurus app? Better test that one. Because if it's supposed to help you pick up the ladies, it's malfunctioning."

It didn't matter that she was feisty and cute and moderately interesting. I saw her Bride-to-Be banner as a chastity belt with jaws of steel and barbed wire. Been there, done that, and currently paying nine dollars a goddamn flower for it. "Suffice it to say you are safe with me," I managed. "Not interested. Believe me."

Two Sides to Every Coin

I stormed; he trailed to the elevator. *Not interested. Believe me.* Noah's retort echoed in my ears down the empty hall. He had spit out the words with such irritation, as if they had been sawdust in his throat. *Yeah, thanks. I am that repulsive. Good to know.* The tiny pep talk Dani had just given me had almost bolstered my confidence to flirt with him. But that look he had given me—as if I were some bug in his computer code that he was determined to straighten out or something. It had immediately put me on the defensive. Could this situation get any more weird and humiliating?

"Come on," he said, attempting to reason with me. "We need to make the best of the situation—"

"Well, all I can picture is the *worst* of this situation! How do I know you're not an ax murderer?" I blurted out as the elevator door swept open. It was one thing to suffer through sushi with this egomaniac. But a hotel room?

"I went through the same security checkpoints as you," he said, holding out his hands. "Did you see me stop at the ax murderer store on my way from the airport to the hotel?"

"Wiseass."

He followed me into the elevator.

"You could drown me with your cologne as I sleep," I added.

"Who's to say you won't smother me with that dress of yours?" he quipped back, giving my mother's bridal dress bag a disgusted look.

I bit my tongue and hammered the button for our floor, while he kept his eyes on the lighted number panel. With my luck, we'd get trapped between levels and our only way out would be climbing down the shaft using the train of the dress as a makeshift rope ladder.

"Look, what do you need to hear to make you feel better about this?" he asked, trailing me down the corridor. "You know my name. How about my birth date? How about my Social?"

"How about you shut up and let me open the damn door?" I hissed, but he ignored me.

Every time I stabbed the key card into the slot in an attempt to open the door, he gave me a new fact.

"I'm an only child."

Stab.

"I've lived in three different countries and nine different states. My favorite ice cream is rum raisin."

Stab-stab. The little light winked its red eye at me again. Denied.

"I'm allergic to feather boas."

"Well, then," I said through clenched teeth. *Stab!* "You'd make a horrible drag queen."

"*May* I?" He plucked the card from my hand and, with one smooth swipe, got the green light.

So he had a steady hand. And was a quick study on grammar. *So what?*

"I enjoy rock climbing and stand-up paddleboarding," he supplied.

"Are you saving some of this for your online dating profile?"

Once we were in the room, he tossed his carry-on onto the luggage rack. I had clearly tested his attempt at pleasant-guy patience.

"You can check my bag," he offered flatly, throwing it open. I peeked in. It was neat as a pin, everything rolled and folded, including three pairs of boxer briefs.

I wondered if his mother had taught him the Golden Three emergency rule, too.

"So. Any questions?" he demanded. "Comments?"

You're behind a closed and locked door with him now, Laney. And you've seen his underwear. I could just hear my mother now. Giving the eulogy at my funeral and explaining to all my mourners that I had failed to listen to her time and again on the hazards of stranger danger. *You've made your bed, poor Laney.*

I could think of nothing more to say on the matter.

Other than "That's disgusting."

Noah raised a brow at me. "What is?"

"Rum raisin ice cream."

I carefully laid the garment bag on the bed and turned to find him standing behind me, a mound of extra bedding from the closet in his arms. If he was going to smother me, he sure wasn't wasting any time.

He pushed past me. "You take the bed. I'll take the tub."

I watched as he spread a large down comforter in the oversized heart-shaped Jacuzzi that sat regally (well, as regally as a gaudy heart-shaped tub could) upon a tiled platform near the windows. He added the decorative pillows from the bed for cushioning before laying a blanket over the top. It looked like a large fluffy nest by the time he was through.

"You look like you've done this before."

"Done what, slept in a bathtub?" Noah gave a grim smile. "My roommate in college snored. I guess this will be good practice for Vegas when I see him."

While he knelt by the Jacuzzi, preening and poking at his nest, I took in the rest of our accommodations. Besides the gargantuan king-sized platform bed, there really was no other sleeping alternative. Two wingback chairs flanked the decorative fireplace, but they would be more uncomfortable to sleep on than the seats at the airport.

Sleep.

As in, actual resting. Was I really expected to get any sleep with this—this *stranger*—this "I know I'm handsome so I'm allowed to be incredibly obnoxious" stranger—three feet away from me? I didn't even have my requisite can of Mace in my pocketbook. Stupid TSA, with their prohibited items lists and three-ounce rules.

There was one thing I had in my bag that could possibly prevent any sticky situations. I sprinted over to the bed and pulled it out of my bag in an "I've got the conch!" *Lord of the Flies* move.

Duck Tape. I gave the end of the roll a fierce tug, and it emitted a loud *pffffffft* as I stretched a length of it.

Noah sat up rod-straight. "What was that?"

"Duck Tape." I thrust my hands up in the air to show him.

"You mean *duct* tape. For sealing ducts. Not *duck*. Ducks quack. They don't go *pffffffft*."

What a smart-ass. I held up the label, which clearly said my brand of duct tape was Duck Tape. It was also fuchsia-and-black zebra print, and fabulous.

"All right. So the names are interchangeable," he allowed. "Still. What are you planning to do with it?"

Gee, I don't know. Gag you?

I bent and, beginning at the wall next to the bedside table, stretched it all the way to the opposite wall, pushing it down to the Berber carpet as I went. I tried not to think that he might be checking out my butt as I waddled along.

"Come nighttime," I dictated, "we don't cross this line to each other's side." I had seen it on an old episode of *The Brady Bunch.*

"You may want to rethink your boundaries. My side has the bathroom."

Huh. It hadn't ended so well for the Brady boys, either, come to think of it.

Noah tossed his suit jacket onto one of the wingbacks, kicked off his shoes, and hopped into test the nest. He looked so cozy and insulated.

"Well, that's hardly fair. I say we flip for it."

He cracked an eye. "I gave you the bed, and you're giving me a hard time?" I crossed my arms. Noah sighed and dug into his trouser pockets for a coin. "Heads or tails?"

"Heads," I called as he flipped the coin from his reclining position. It bounced off my Bozo shoe, rolled over near the bed, and landed in his favor. "Phooey." I picked up the coin with a frown.

"What's your problem?"

"I . . . I really wanted to try the nest," I admitted.

Noah slowly pushed himself up and out. "It's all yours," he said slowly. "Go nuts."

I was sure he thought *I* was nuts, but I didn't care. Smiling, I untied his Chuck Taylors, pulled them off, and plopped myself in. "Nice." I looked up at him. "Well built."

"Eight hours of nice?"

"Maybe." I curled on my side. "Maybe not."

"I'll take it, Miss *Bichonné*," he mocked. "You can have the big white fluffy bed. I'll bet it matches your dress."

I stuck my tongue out at him as he began to set up his base station at the desk, firing up his laptop and unwinding his power cord. I knew he couldn't see me but it felt good to do it. For spite, I stayed in the nest. Had I been alone, I could have stripped and soaked all the snow and cold away with a bubbly Jacuzzi and a minibar drink. And maybe called down to room service and ordered up a tattooed Lance from the bar. Having a fake fiancé was really cramping my style.

nest and rummaged through my bag for my cosmetics and requisite quart-sized Ziploc for carrying liquids on the plane. I stowed them on the bathroom counter, opposite Noah's leather shaving bag. It was understated and elegant, of course, just like him. Padding back to my carry-on in the middle of the room, I pulled out a picture of my cat in a tiny heart-shaped frame and Allen's vintage Batman alarm clock and set them on the bedside table. The clock wasn't exactly travel sized, but it was from the seventies and virtually indestructible.

"What the hell is that?"

Jeez, put a bell on the guy. Even with his fancy loafers back on his feet, he was catlike—quiet and stealthy.

"I inherited it from a friend. Still keeps great time. Oh, and that is Sister Frances."

Noah contemplated the frame in his hands before gently setting it back down. "I like her milk mustache."

"Yeah, her full name is Sister Frances Tappan Zee Got Milk. After my favorite nursery school teacher. I found her near the bridge, hence her middle name."

Noah ran a finger over the top of the molded plastic of Batman's cape as if he were wiping a layer of dust off. His fingers were long and elegant, I noticed, and squared off at the tips. Probably from all that blunt-force typing. "Your friend was a fan of the Distinguished Competition, huh?"

I whipped my head to face him. He raised his thick brow, allowing a slight smile to escape his lips. Only a true fan of Marvel Comics would know the nickname it gave its main competitor, DC.

"Yeah, he was," I said quietly. "Two years gone."

We sat in silence until the minute hand wrenched forward and Noah cleared his throat. "My pop used to buy me comics when I was little. I lost him when I was in college."

"Cancer?" I couldn't help it. My mind just invariably went there.

I reached an arm length away to my carry-on bag and pulled my *Love and Rockets* book once again. At least I had good reading escape into.

"You might want to put down your comic book and start looking for another flight," Noah advised.

"It's a graphic *novel*," I informed him. "About Hispanic gang warfare, 1980s California, punk rock, women wrestlers, and the subtle battle to stay true to oneself."

He swiveled in the desk chair to face me, staring down that regal Roman nose of his. "The airline's website is a total clusterfuck, but I've DMed them on Twitter and I'm searching across multiple travel platforms right now. If you give me your criteria, I'll prepopulate in another browser window and set alerts."

A ball of panic began to rise in my chest. I imagined it like a storm cloud scribble across a blank page, animating as it grew. Loneliness overwhelmed me. I missed home. How could I get to Hawaii if I couldn't even breach the chasm from the Jacuzzi to the desk chair? This guy and I were speaking very different languages.

"I thought the airlines would just rebook us," I squeaked.

"*Force majeure*, baby." Noah leaned back and huffed air over his bottom lip with such force, his hair ruffled. "Act of God."

"You mean that bitch Mother Nature?"

"Yeah, her, too. The airlines are scrambling just like us." He rolled up the sleeves of his crisp white button-down and got to work.

I mumbled my itinerary, holding my book closer to my face so he wouldn't see my lower lip tremble. I wished Mother Nature would stop acting like a spoiled brat, the kind of kid who packs up her toys and leaves in a huff if the play date isn't going her way.

Noah was clearly in his element, clack-clacking away and zooming his mouse around. Well, if he was going to make himself at home, surrounded by power adapters and blinking routers, I was going to surround myself with my favorite things as well. I rolled out of the

"IED." He paused for a moment, then added, "Roadside bomb in Afghanistan."

I didn't know what to say to that. "Holy crap" was the only thing that came to mind.

"Hey, still got that quarter?"

I flipped it up to him, and he caught it between his palms. Sitting down on the edge of the bed next to me, he deftly rolled the coin down his knuckles from index finger to pinky, then back again. He let it fall into one palm, then the other. And back again, as if he were working up to something. Finally, he closed his fist around the coin and held it out to me. "Blow on it." I hesitated. "Go on. My dad taught me this one."

I pursed my lips and blew lightly on his hand. His fingers opened to reveal an empty palm. "Now, logically," he said softly, "it stands to reason that the only place the coin could possibly be . . . is here." He reached his hand up to my ear and, sure enough, he had the coin again.

"Hey!" I broke into a broad grin. "How'd you do that?"

"Stick with me, kid." There was that tough-guy impression again, like with the banana showdown on the airplane. "We'll go places. What do you say we raid the vending machine? The hotel restaurant's kitchen is closing at nine."

"Vending machine, huh?" I laughed. "I guess the honeymoon really is over."

"Yeah, no more wining and dining you with champagne and caviar. But I'll share my bag of pork rinds."

With only granola for breakfast and sushi for lunch, I was ready to devour dinner, even if it came rolling out of the coils of a vending machine. I was starving.

For food, Laney Jane? Or attention?

I decided I was far too hungry to dwell on the fact that I didn't exactly mind sharing another meal with the perfect stranger in the matchy-match suit and loafers.

Ghosts and Whiskey

"So," I asked, after swallowing a bite of a Pop-Tart, dessert to my peanut butter crackers and Doritos dinner. Our dining music was my iPod docked into the bedside clock, accompanied by the cool mood lighting of Noah's open MacBook screen. "What's doing in Vegas right now?"

Noah consulted his computer, a Slim Jim between his teeth. He plucked it out like a cigar and pointed it at the screen. "According to the spreadsheet, the guys are having drinks at Casa Fuente in Caesar's Palace."

He had been receiving text messages intermittently from the bachelor party throughout the evening, letting him know about all the fun he was missing out on. "Tomorrow morning they're renting Harleys and driving out to the desert," he announced, swiveling in the desk chair to face me.

"After smoking cigars and drinking cognac all night?" I snorted. "Doubtful."

Noah laughed from behind a mouthful of Slim Jim with a Coca-Cola chaser. "Is Hawaii surviving without you?"

"Apparently so."

My mother had texted an hour before with my new flight information; leave it to Mom to take charge from four thousand miles away. I hadn't heard a peep from her since, but Danica had been drunk-texting and sent me at least six pictures of the beach at sunset. "Looks like my best friend is getting bombed in honor of Pearl Harbor." I showed him her latest toes-and-tropical-drinks picture. "This was supposed to be our girls' week together." I pouted. "She moved out of state last year for a job and I haven't seen her since."

"That sucks. You'll be there soon, though."

"Yeah, Mom to the rescue." I smirked. "She booked a 10:05 A.M. flight for the dress, and I am allowed to fly free as its companion."

"Come on, it's not that bad."

"Yeah, it is," I said softly. My entire teenage existence revolved around gaining and losing that woman's trust. No amount of years or therapy had changed our mother-daughter dynamic. "She always has to run the show."

"Well, if it makes you feel any better, I never even wanted to go to Vegas for this stupid party, anyway." He turned his attention back his laptop.

"Gee," I said mockingly, "I didn't know there were sour grapes in that vending machine."

Cruising the Strip, blackjack and comp drinks, partying till dawn, and then motorcycling through the desert? I would've gladly traded places with him. I'd even stuff the stripper's G-string with dollar bills. He could go to Hawaii. My mother would probably be too preoccupied to notice if I sent a surrogate as the dress bearer.

Noah didn't comment right away. The glow from the screen high-lighted his face in profile: lips pursed, brow slightly furrowed.

"At least it's a good excuse for getting all us guys together. One teaches high school"—he ticked items off on his fingers—"one works at a college, another is in the military, there's a doctor . . . it's hard to find time for a Skype call, let alone a week together."

"And the groom?"

"General consensus among his friends is that he's a lucky bastard." He gave a short laugh. "On the fast track at work, engaged to the boss's daughter, blah blah blah. Sounds good on paper, I suppose." He didn't look up from his computer.

"You don't think so," I observed.

Using his foot, he pushed himself away from the desk in the rolling chair. "I don't know what I think anymore, Laney," he admitted, running both hands through his thick, dark locks. "I've been up for, like, nineteen hours at this point."

I brushed Pop-Tart crumbs off my leggings and hopped off the bed. "The hell with cigar bars and beach cocktails for now. Let's have our own party right here." The minibar had been singing its siren song to me all evening. "Come on, it's time to leave the office," I singsonged.

Noah had already booked himself a new flight that left an hour after mine. Keeping tabs on the weather and the Vegas itinerary was futile; nothing was going to change no matter how many times he refreshed that browser. We had two fresh cans of Coke and ginger ale in the hotel ice bucket and a minibar filled with overpriced but limitless opportunity.

Back in the day, everyone relied on Life of the Party Laney to get the festivities started. Granted, I was rinsing out empty cat food cans more than beer bottles after a blowout Saturday night these days, but my alter ego still remembered how to get my drink on. "Happy hour's waiting," I tempted, wiggling tiny bottles of Jack Daniel's and Crown Royal between my fingers. "Turn off your computer, Tech-Boy."

"Tech-Boy, huh?" He swiped the bottles from me and mixed us our first drinks in the glasses provided. "Cheers, Bridezilla."

With just twelve hours until my flight, half of which I hoped I'd spend passed out sleeping, I reasoned there was no harm in failing to correct him when he called me that. Let the pretty-boy, all-put-together techie think I *was* someone's bride from hell. Self-absorbed to the max, without a care in the world except making sure that the world revolved around starting our new life together? That sounded a whole helluva lot better than the pathetic, lonely truth.

But I had to admit, I kinda liked when he called me Laney.

I took a healthy gulp, relishing the burn. "Oh, my God, look!" I choked, gesturing. We had the television on with the volume down.

"*Giant Monsters All-Out Attack*!"

"No way! That's my favorite Godzilla movie of all time." Noah hopped onto the bed and perched cross-legged like a little kid. "Let me guess. You're too old-school to like this one?"

"What can I say? I'm a purist. Although"—I balanced my drink on the flat wood of the footboard before sprawling belly down—"any movie with Mothra in it is okay in my book." Propping myself up on my elbows, I watched the citizens of Japan flee in silent terror.

"But Mothra dies in this one, remember? Godzilla kills her with his atomic breath."

"He must've been eating Slim Jims," I teased, sneaking a look back at him.

Noah gave my leg a mock kick. And he gave me that adorable, sheepish smile.

Maybe it was the Alice-in-Wonderland-tiny bottles of alcohol or maybe it was the bonding over awful monster movies, but I felt very content. Even Noah's cologne, a heady vanilla and lime woodsy combination, was growing on me.

Suddenly I became very aware of sharing such a small, intimate space with him. The king-sized bed may have been movie-monster large, but it felt no bigger than our first-class row on the plane. Especially with his leg still resting so close to mine. And there was no Anita or other flight attendant to save us with hot towels.

"I lived in Tokyo for a year," Noah supplied.

"That's right, three countries, nine states." Saved by small talk. "Where else?"

"Well, born in Philadelphia, moved to Bel Air—"

"Like the Fresh Prince?"

"No." He laughed. "Bel Air, Maryland. G.I. brat. I've also lived in Virginia, North Carolina, Texas, Ohio—"

Anywhere
I don't care
I'd follow you
but you wreck me
wreck me
through and through

"Oh, jeez. Sorry, let me, um . . . crap—"

My iPod had shuffled onto a rowdy surfer-punk anthem by Allen's band, rousing me out of my reverie. I reached over Noah and practically pawed the iPod off the dock in the process.

"Sorry. That song was just so . . ." *Heartbreakingly perfect, painfully nostalgic, blaringly truthful?* "Loud." I gulped.

Realizing I had practically foisted myself into the poor guy's lap in my haste to change the song, I scooted off the bed and fiddled with the shuffle.

"It sounded cool to me," Noah said. "Who was that?"

"Three on a Match," I answered, trying to keep my voice light. "I went to high school with them." *Et cetera, et cetera.*

"Never heard of them."

"Seriously? You don't know Three on a Match?"

"Oh, wait. That dude what's-his-face, Rob Thomas, who was on *The Voice* last year. His band?"

"No, that's Matchbox Twenty. Not even close," I said.

"I know now—they had that hit song 'Kryptonite,' didn't they?"

I stared stonily at him. "You're joking, right? Three *on a Match,* not 3 Doors Down."

Noah scratched his sexy scruff in thought, then tapped his chin. "Do they sing that one song, what's it . . . 'Cumbersome'?"

I nixed him with an obnoxious beep. "Wrong again. That's Seven Mary Three."

"Okay, then I'll take 'Wrong Lyrics by Bands with Numbered Names' for five hundred, Alex," he joked, the corners of his mouth pushing into that adorable sheepish smile.

I guess there were a lot of bands with a variation of that magic number in their name: Third Eye Blind, Three Days Grace . . . I couldn't recite the U.S. presidents to save my life, but I could match bands and songs all evening.

"Before you go asking if they wrote about a bullfrog named Jeremiah," I teased, "that was Three Dog Night."

Noah tsked, as if I could be so silly as to suggest he didn't know *that*.

I put the iPod onto a more benign playlist. "Three on a Match is a psychobilly band out of California."

"Psycho-what?" he asked, looking like a deer caught in headlights.

"Psychobilly. Like rockabilly with a punk slant. Koffin Kats? Bang Bang Bazooka? Not even Reverend Horton Heat?" Noah was still shaking his head. "No? How about Southern Culture on the Skids?" I asked, incredulous. "Wow, you could use some schooling."

He had to be around my age. Music had been such a big part of my friends' and my lives growing up, that it was hard to believe all my peers didn't share the same soundtrack. "I was in the glee club at school," he offered.

"Ah, no wonder." Actually, it was oddly refreshing to know that this guy had no clue who Three on a Match was, or Allen Burnside, for that matter. "Just kidding. I guess they're kind of . . . obscure, then. If you aren't into that scene."

Obscure, that was, until they had recorded a scathing rock rendition of Bananarama's "Cruel Summer" the first year they were out in

L.A., which made it into a big, blow-'em-up, bullet-filled beach movie starring Hilary Swank.

We sat on opposite sides of the bed and watched in silence as a missile ripped Godzilla from the inside out. Down he went, disintegrating to dust. The citizens of Japan rejoiced.

The poor bastards had no clue that the monster's heart was still beating far below on the ocean floor.

"Refill?" Noah asked.

"Why the hell not."

His thumb grazed against mine as he reached to take my glass. *Holy pulse rate, Batman!* Mine was alive and kicking, keeping time with Godzilla's heart at the bottom of Tokyo Bay.

I blamed the Crown Royal; my libido always had liked the liquor. Noah mixed two more drinks. "Hey, what're these?"

My sketchpad, along with an oversized deck of cards, had found its way out of my bag and onto the floor. Probably around the time I was playing the role of DJ Jazzy Denial to Noah's Fresh Prince.

"Nothing. Work stuff."

I hastily scooped up the sketchpad, almost clocking heads with him, as he had reached down to help. It had fallen open to the picture from the boarding area.

"Is that . . ." Noah leaned closer and took it from my hands. "That looks like me."

"You were hogging every electrical outlet in the entire boarding area." I giggled, looking at the exaggerated depiction now.

Currently Noah looked nothing like his alter ego. Back in the airport terminal, he had been hardwired to all those gadgets like they were his armor. Suit jacket and crisp button-down shirt were now long gone, and I couldn't help noticing, even in my fuzzy state, that he filled out his plain white tee quite nicely. And no evil supervillain ever had such nice hair as Noah's. Whatever grooming gel had been taming his slightly long locks had been worn away throughout the evening by him running his hand through his hair. It was a gesture I noticed he repeated when he was nervous, but also when he was laughing that great laugh of his. I had a crazy urge to run my fingers through those thick, full curls, just to make sure they were as soft as they looked. The smoky, vanilla lime scent that had repelled me at the airport was now drawing me in with a pull that had nothing to do with gravity. His shoes had been kicked off over by the door, but even had they been on . . .

I could kinda see myself kissing the guy in the loafers.

"The detail, it's just . . . incredible."

"Mmm-hmm," I agreed absently, fixated on just how perfect his eyelashes were as he gazed down at my rendering. So dark and lush, perfect for butterfly kisses against the cheek . . .

"Like, pro incredible." He blinked up at me and snapped me out of my trance.

"I was, once." I cleared my throat and added, "I worked for Marvel."

His eyes widened. "Get out of town."

"Dude!" I laughed. "I've been *trying* to."

He swatted me with the sketchbook. "No, seriously. That sounds like the best job ever. Why did you leave?"

"There aren't enough bottles in the minibar to get into that *mishagas*." I gave a wave of my hand to dismiss the topic, but Noah didn't seem to want to let go of it; or the sketchpad, for that matter.

"Can I look through it?"

"No."

"Why?"

"Because it sucks."

"*No*," Noah said vehemently. He grabbed the hotel pen and small pad of paper sitting near the telephone and started scribbling away. "*This* sucks."

He held up his drawing of a stick figure, clutching what looked like a drawing of a stick figure and puking a rainbow out of his mouth at the horror. "What you drew was the opposite of suck."

I heard a sloppy, drunken laugh and realized it was my own. "No, what I meant was, most of the subject matter sucks." I took back the sketchbook, holding it tightly to my chest. "Wrongs I cannot right."

I had tried; believe you me. My Pink Pearl and kneaded erasers could do little to minimize or soften the low points in my life.

Noah was studying me, but it wasn't in a bug-under-a-microscope kind of way that got under my skin. "Fair enough," he said slowly, and he reached for the box of cards that had fallen to the floor as well. "'Naughty Sleepover Q and A.' Work stuff, huh?"

"Well, those were for girls' night, for when I got to Hawaii." Danica was spiking the drinks, my cousin Miri was bringing good chocolate, I was providing the entertainment, and we were going to have someone from the spa come and do facials. Kind of like a bachelorette party, except we weren't going to invite the bachelorette, because she'd ruin all the fun. "Just something goofy to pass the time."

"Well, since *we've* got nothing but time . . ." Noah raised a wicked brow.

I almost choked on my Crown and ginger. Oh, he should not do that, or say those words, in the presence of a lady . . . especially while she had a strong drink in her hand putting dirty thoughts in her head.

"Seriously? Mr. Rigid Tech-Boy, who could barely deem the Magic 8 Ball worthy of a shake?"

"Hit me." His eyes were chocolate truffle dark with a sea salt sparkle to them. Did this guy know how tempting he was?

I took possession of the deck of cards and slowly shuffled them. Noah grabbed his drink and lowered himself into the Jacuzzi nest.

"Okay, then, first question: What's the most important item in your makeup bag?" I giggled.

He took a haul off his drink. "Pass."

"You have to keep drinking till you answer, you know." I settled on the edge of the Jacuzzi with my bare feet dangling in. "How about . . . what's your favorite"—*oh, Laney, don't go there*—"body part of your partner?" *My mouth just keeps on talking and drinking.* "Assuming there is a partner." *Argh, shut up! God, I hope he's as buzzed as I am.*

"Body parts," Noah began, raising his glass as if he were going to toast a limb or a digit. "Body parts are overrated. What about the mind? The mind can be a sexy tool."

He's talking sexy tools. And he's sprawled in a hot tub. Mind you, it was dry and swathed in three-hundred-count cotton sheets, but could I help it if my mind was in a far wetter and hotter place right then?

A hand circled my shin. Was he going to pull me in?

"Ankles. I'll go with ankles."

"Final answer?" I asked with a gulp. *Wait, did he confirm or deny partner?*

"Yep, just a simple, surgically unenhanced ankle." Yeah, he was buzzed if he was talking about cosmetic surgery for cankles. "Your turn."

Noah relieved me of the deck and very deliberately extracted a card from the middle of the pile. "Name one thing in your purse that you can't live without." He snorted. "Let's see, is it going to be the Magic 8 Ball, Batman, Duck Tape . . ."

"Very funny." I gave him a nudge with my toe. This was a no-brainer. "My sketchpad and pen."

"That's two things, but you're cute. I'll let it slide." He winked and laid the deck back in my palm again.

"Here's a benign one. Name one thing you wish you had done differently today."

I discreetly studied his features and waited as patiently as a girl with a couple drinks in her could. His lips twitched, and I wondered if he was thinking about the kiss request close call we had had on board the airplane. I knew I was.

His eyes widened, and I swore I saw a spark of something: realization, regret? He looked pointedly at me, and I felt my face flush.

"That quip I made on the plane. About curing cancer. That was low. Sorry. About your friend."

Oh. That.

"Whatever," I said softly. "How could you have known?" I gave him a tiny smile to let him know his apology was accepted. I was, after all, the Queen of the Daily Do-Over Wishers. Fanning the deck out like a magician, I let him extract his next card.

"Favorite guilty-pleasure music," he announced. "The kind that you jump around and dance to when no one else is looking?"

"That would have to be . . ." I cringed a little before continuing. "Billy Joel."

"Seriously?" He laughed. "The piano man?"

"Come on, he was raised a Long Island boy; it's a local pride thing." That and my mom used to wear the grooves out on his albums *52nd Street* and *The Stranger* when I was little. Dani, born and raised in Jersey until she moved to my town as a teenager, would always have an undying love for Springsteen and Bon Jovi, no matter how much I tried to brainwash them out of her system.

"I *guess* it's rock and roll . . . to some," Noah teased.

"Pick your passion," I said, swallowing hard as I read the next card aloud. "Dirty talk, or role play?" *Talk about a loaded deck . . .*

There was that blush, creeping up his neck again. "How come I'm getting all the naughty ones and you're getting all the snoozers?" he demanded.

"Because the deck of cards is trying to corrupt you? I don't know! But you were the one who wanted to play this," I reminded him, fanning myself with the card and blinking my eyes expectantly.

"I believe it depends on the person you are with," he finally admitted. "I think . . . playing off each other's passion is a turn-on in itself."

"Yes. I tend to agree. But the card specifically asks *your* passion. What turns you on?"

Did that just come out of my mouth?

"Wait, wasn't I supposed to save some of this for my online dating profile?" he said mockingly, taking the card from me and tucking it under the pile. "I like a healthy dose of both, okay? As long as she is into it, too."

Adventurous *and* accommodating. And looks good hanging out in a dry Jacuzzi.

"Best"—his eyes scanned back and forth, and he bit his lip—"pass."

"Hey! It's my turn. You can't pass for me. Drink!"

Noah took a big swig, shaking his head. "Best sex of your life, who-where-when." It all came out in a rush, and he wouldn't make eye contact with me. Ha, I bet he was wishing for a snoozer card now.

"Allen Burnside, Lake Shore Hotel, five-year high school reunion," I answered without hesitation.

While it was one of the few Allen encounters that had not morphed into a graphic novelization on my part, the milestone had been played out in my mind more than once in the last eight years. Perfectly perfect. We had ditched our classmates before dessert was served and hightailed it back to his hotel room, stripping each other of those silly paper name tags and every stitch of clothing. There was nothing awkward or fumbling as we fell into each other's arms at last, crashing and moving together perfectly. Fresh, but not foreign. Allen's hands had gone to work laying claim to every inch of my skin that had missed his touch since high school. And my lips rememorized every cut of his muscular frame, my tongue slicking its newly colored landscape as his sighs punctured holes through every lonely night without him.

He was back. Allen. Mine. Those strong drummer's fingers tangling through my hair as we kissed like mirror images; knowing exactly how the other would respond, anticipating and absorbing it, then throwing it back like a thousand points of light on a disco ball.

"That good, huh?"

Noah was watching me over the rim of his cup. I don't think he had stopped drinking since I had ordered him to imbibe. Good thing the card didn't ask how or why.

I flipped my next card over with a raised brow. "Who's the one that got away?"

"Jemma Fine."

"Jemma Fine? Sounds like a porn star to me."

"Yeah, well . . . she's not," he sniffed. "She's a veterinarian. And she had it going on back in the day. We'd have these long talks for hours, lying on our backs watching the clouds. She always knew what to say when things were bleak for me. And she could make the most amazing grilled cheese sandwiches."

Jemma was sounding less like a porn star and more like a keeper by the minute.

I covertly watched him, lost in his memories, as I drained the dregs of my glass. Going from head in the clouds with Jemma Fine to lying in a dry Jacuzzi fully clothed with Laney Hudson must've felt like a crappy hand dealt to him.

"So what happened?"

"She raised her rates and my mom found another babysitter." He shrugged, a slow smile teasing into a full-on grin. "My heart was broken and my grilled cheeses were burned from then on."

"Cheat!"

"Ah, fifty-two-card pickup, my favorite game," he said, as I showered him with the deck. Hard to believe this joker was the same uptight guy from Flight 1232. "How is that cheating? I answered my turn and now . . ." He shifted his hip up and unearthed a card that had slipped to the bottom of the tub. "Now I believe it is your turn. The million-dollar question."

With a flourish, he whipped the card up to his face, those dark brows knitting in mock concentration.

"Worst night you've ever spent with someone."

"It doesn't say that."

"Who-where-when," he insisted, holding the card close to his chest. I sighed. "You can always take a pass. And drink," he reminded me.

"I'm past drink," I said with a groan. "I am drunk." Time to change my nickname to Lightweight of the Party Laney. Only drunks would stretch the word *drunk* out to two syllables. I drank anyway. And I still answered.

"Five-year high school reunion."

Noah tapped the card to his lips, waiting for me to go on.

"Lake Shore Hotel."

"Allen Burnside?" he finished for me.

"Yep." My warm-fuzzy buzz had gone from flirty to fizzled.

"Wanna talk about it?"

"Not particularly."

It was never something I spoke about. But I saw it in vivid four-color panels like a comic strip, even though there was nothing funny about it.

I had used my ever-handy artist pens to sketch one of his favorite heroes, Mighty Mouse, on his biceps, in flight, with drumsticks in hand. "Ace," Allen had said. "Can't want to get this inked when I hit the road. Speaking of which . . ."

He gave my forehead a kiss. A kiss of consolation if I had ever felt one.

"You're leaving?"

"Bus lobby call is at six A.M. We're midtour. This was just an off day, kid."

Off day? *Kid?* I thought we were basking in the afterglow, getting ready for round two. "I thought—"

Things in the memory got hazy then. What I thought wasn't exactly what I said, and it all ended with Allen blowing up like I had never experienced before.

"Were you expecting a tidy arc for us, like your characters in comicbookland? For me to be part of your benefits package, like your 401(k) and your health insurance? Nothing's guaranteed in this world, Laney! You gotta live and learn that shit."

I was being dumped, ditched after the first course. Just deserts, I supposed.

"But I love you!" My wail was pitiful, even to my ears.

"Don't use that word with me." His voice was quiet venom. "Not if you're trying to harpoon me with it. Love isn't a weapon, Laney! Love is wanting the best for someone, even if it makes you feel fucking awful.

"Working on the island, at a job you hate? Living with your mom, too, I suppose? What the hell happened to your art? You blew off California, and you're not even in Manhattan? It's like . . . like living next to fucking Everest and never attempting to climb it," he had informed me, lifting his hips off the bed and snaking his boxers up.

"The view's nice," I remembered saying softly.

"Yeah, well." He tossed my blouse and skirt from the mingled pile of our clothes at the foot of the hotel bed. "You can't conquer a view."

I didn't know what hurt worse: the fact that he had turned on me or the fact that he was right. Allen had spent the last five years conquering his dreams and earning the view. What the hell had I been doing?

"*You changed the goddamn plan, Laney. You went with your mother's master plan instead of ours.*"

Noah's gaze was lost to the inside of his glass as he swished the liquid around. "*La verità è nel vino.* Ever hear that?"

I shook my head, unable to really speak. "Latin?" I managed.

"Italian. It means 'In wine there is truth.'"

"Yeah, well." I drained the rest of my glass with a hard swallow. *In whiskey there are ghosts.* "You don't want to hear my sob stories."

He looked up from beneath those impossible eyelashes. "Try me." The stare he fixed on me dug under my psyche for secrets I had forgotten I'd even placed there.

No way. Not all of us had apps and spreadsheets to navigate us neatly through the "multiple travel platforms" of our lives.

"Just forget it," I muttered, and vaulted myself toward the sanctuary of the bathroom.

How many minutes of my life have been spent in bated breath behind a closed door?

I looked around the pristine, impersonal hotel bathroom, as if it held the answer somewhere in its polished faucets or cool tiled floor. Nope, just the last seven years of my guilt, bouncing off the gilded hotel mirror and back into my memories. It made me want to smash the glass with my fist, but the last thing I needed was seven years of bad luck to add to my lot.

"Danica! What a lovely surprise, dear. Laney's home but she's not feeling well."

"I know, but I brought her some magazines and candy to cheer her up. I love your sweater! That color looks great on you, Mrs. Hudson."

"Well, aren't you sweet?"

I listened to the murmured pleasantries from behind my closed bedroom door and slowly counted seconds. Dani was always good at handling my mother. Her patience and knack for dealing with the crazy must've come from her father, a professor of psychology at Hofstra, and her mother, a noted animal behaviorist. I knew from experience that she was usually able to extricate herself from my mother's interrogations in less than a minute.

"Hey." I heard Dani's breathy greeting and a quick knock as I got to thirty-three.

I cracked the door and she slipped in. "Did you get one?"

"Yeah." She shoved the drugstore bag into my hand. "Two, actually. Your mother really shouldn't wear florals."

"I know, she looks like the bastard child of Lilly Pulitzer and Vera

Bradley down there." I hopped on one foot, and then the other. "I must've drunk a gallon of water while I was waiting for you. Were you coming from the Walgreens on Mars?"

"Go, go." She had shooed me into the adjoining bathroom and kept up a running commentary from the other side of the closed door. "I got caught up reading all the headlines in the checkout lane. Hey, remember when we were in ninth grade, and I was out sick with mono? You brought me *Sassy* magazines and Bubble Yum to make me feel better. I'll never forget that."

I peeked into the bag and smiled. Dani had brought me the latest issue of *People*, a big bag of peanut butter M&M's, and two pregnancy test kits.

"Um, why are they already opened?"

"I forgot my book on the train, so I read the instruction pamphlets. Besides . . . I figured you'd want to have an educated second opinion."

I made quick business before joining her on the edge of the bed with the magazine and offered her an M&M. "Two minutes on the one with the pink plus or minus sign. Three minutes on the one with the purple lines."

"I hope you washed your hands," she joked, jostling my shoulder as she popped a fat blue candy into her mouth.

After two surreally slow minutes, I abandoned the magazine and went to peek.

"Second opinion, please?" I managed to get out.

Dani trotted into the bathroom. Her long ringlets brushed my cheek as she tilted her head to examine the first stick.

"It's still a minus, right?"

Dani made a face. "A minus sign with arms? That's a plus, honey."

We each held our breath and focused on the backup stick, sitting shotgun on the side of the tub.

"Two lines doesn't mean twins, does it?" My brain had gone numb and I had already forgotten what the directions said to look for.

Dani hadn't. "It doesn't predict quantity. But it confirms you have the grade-A, quality pee of a pregnant woman."

The years dropped out from beneath me, causing the floor to tilt. Allen and I had had a pregnancy scare back when we were fifteen. We both got As in biology that semester, fervently studying reproduction and fertility while we played the waiting game, too broke and scared to buy a test kit back then. It had turned out to be "almost an oops," much to our relief, and we had been fastidious about protection after that.

Until that night at the Lake Shore Hotel.

I gripped the cold, hard edge of the tub and brought my brain back to the present.

"I need more M&M's."

We went back into my bedroom. I paced, inhaling my favorite candy without even tasting it, and Dani sat and stared at the magazine for a while.

"Are you going to tell him?"

"You mean interrupt the Australian tour and ruin his life? Um, no."

I had done the walk of shame out of Allen's hotel room five and a half weeks prior and had punished myself by stalking Three on a Match's tour page ever since. I had imagined he'd had sex with girls in Denver, Salt Lake, Portland, and Seattle before winging his wang across the Pacific to do assorted girls Down Under. Maybe he had a girl in every port, and I was just his safe harbor on Long Island.

But I hoped not. If the road had to be his bride, I wanted to be his sole mistress.

"He'll probably think I did it on purpose, that I'm trying to trap him. Which you know I would never do."

Dani kept quiet, her nose in the magazine.

"Talk about changing the plan!" Pregnant at twenty-three had definitely not been on the agenda. "We wanted to see the world and party and make records and comics and maybe get a cat, to test-drive domesticity," I moaned. "Kids were for when we slowed down."

A flash of Allen with a baby cradled in his tattooed arms gave me
a fluttery feeling in the pit of my stomach. How silly. I knew it was too
early to feel anything, but just thinking about something so fresh and
new that Allen and I had made together . . . maybe . . .

"Do you think he would—" I stopped midsentence.

My best friend was slowly and discreetly ripping a page from the
new magazine.

"Dani . . ." My voice wavered in a warning tone. "What—?"

M&M's rained down and the bedsprings of my old canopy bed
creaked under our combined weight as I wrestled for the torn glossy
photo page she held in a death grip between her shirt and her bra.

*A Match Made in Heaven? Victoria's Secret Angels model Geska
Nielsen spotted in Bondi Beach frolic with rock drummer Allen Burnside of the scorching alternative band Three on a Match: exclusive
pics!*

I splashed cool water on my whiskey-warmed cheeks and blinked the
moisture away. The hotel's towels were plush and decadent against my
face as I stalled for time and an excuse. Noah had to think I was a
nutball by now, drinks or no drinks. I took a sobering breath and went
back to face the perfect stranger I'd left behind in the not-so-hot tub.

"Sorry. Had to break the seal."

*Seal? Sure, Laney. More like whack the eight-hundred-pound
elephant hanging out with us in the room.* I cringed weakly. *Lame.*
"Guess the game's over?"

"It was fun while it lasted." Noah had drained his drink dry. "Anyway, forget about it. You're obviously in a better place now."

He propelled himself up and out of the Jacuzzi, leaving a litter of
Naughty Sleepover party cards in his wake.

"What's that supposed to mean?"

"Someplace named Hawaii? A little thing called your wedding?"

He cracked the minibar like it was a bank safe and stood back to admire the bounty within.

I toed the cards into a messy pile with my stocking feet. "Still assuming too much."

"Meaning?" He turned to glance at me.

La verità . . . whateverthehell.

Tired of pretending, I winced and went for broke.

"Meaning it's not mine. Not the dress, not the wedding. None of it."

Noah

LAST CALL AT THE MINIBAR

"You've heard of a ring bearer, right? Well, I'm just the dress bearer. For my mother."

My brows shot up. I didn't know what I was expecting when Laney emerged from the bathroom. Weepy, prenuptial nostalgia over some old flame, perhaps. But certainly not . . . she wasn't even . . .

"You're not even in the wedding?"

"Nope." She gave a wry smile. "I escaped the Creature from the Seafoam Blue Lagoon dress. My best friend wasn't so lucky. Fortunately, Dani's so cute, she would make pond scum look good."

"Dani's a girl?"

"Do those look like a guy's toes?"

Laney held up the latest beach picture on her phone. Realization washed over me like a tidal wave; or maybe all those Jack and Cokes were finally hitting. I reached a hand behind me to make sure the bed was really there before I sat.

"I'm sorry I called you a Bridezilla."

"Told you I was more like Mothra," she replied quietly.

The pieces began to click into place for me. "You're helping your mother."

"Even though she is the enemy, yes."

I shook my head. "So, that ring—"

She bared her fist, tough-guy style. "Class ring. Sentimental."

I gave an understanding chin bob. The ring's stone winked under the hotel lighting. She held her hand out for me to inspect it. Music notes were etched into one side of the ring, and the other side displayed the tiny tools of an artist's trade: brushes, pens, and paper.

"But what was with all the drawings?" I asked. "Of rings and cakes and stuff?"

"Oh, you mean like these?" She opened her sketchbook to the page I had seen her working on in O'Hare. "Ever hear of Hudson Views?"

"'Hudson Views has got a card for you'?"

"Yes." Laney gave a dramatic eye roll. "When you barely care enough to send the next best greeting card. That's my family's company. I do the graphics."

"Ah, that makes sense. Laney Hudson, Hudson Views."

I guess that also explained the witty one-liners and sharp barbs she'd been lobbing my way since landing in my first-class row.

"Well, the office is on the West Side Highway, so it also overlooks the river."

"Clever." I thought back to that killer caricature she had sketched of me back at LaGuardia. "Wait—my picture isn't going on a greeting card, is it?"

Watching her toss that glossy hair back in ribbons of red and gold and making her laugh a full-on belly laugh felt like winning the lottery.

"No, No-ah." She teased my name from her lips. "That's for the private collection." She sobered a bit. "More superhero than sappy sentiment. I draw for fun, too. See?"

She flipped the page to show me a busty crime-fighting babe: catsuit, cape, mask, and all. She was poised in midair between various city skyscrapers, and instead of fighting a villain, she was punching out a disembodied wedding dress. And instead of the usual "sound effects" like "POW!" and "KA-BLAM!" inside spiky speech bubbles, Laney had added funny wedding-related ones, like "VOW!" and "RRRRRING!"

That was right; she said she had worked for one of the Big Two. As a kid, I would've given my left nut to see the inner workings of the Marvel Bullpen or the headquarters of its rival, DC Comics, whose offices I imagined were like the inner sanctuary of the *Daily Planet*, the fictional newspaper where Clark Kent worked.

How and why had Laney gone from comics to greeting cards?

"I love it. What's the *WF* stand for?" I asked, gesturing to the logo gracing the superwoman's sexy bod.

"Oh, that's my alter ego." Her tone was a sarcastic and nonchalant mix. "Laney the Wonder Fuckup."

A knock drew both of our gazes to the hotel door, then back to each other.

Paranoid, silly, and completely illogical thoughts swarmed in my head. Had Daisy the desk girl noticed our strange behavior at check-in? Suspicions aroused, had she alerted the police to come evict us? What if it was Lance the bar back, coming back to claim his five dollars or, worse yet, to claim Laney?

What if it was Sloane or her father, ready to drag me home by the ear?

That's your guilt talking, Noah.

Just when Laney had dropped her bombshell, just when I felt my own defenses begin to fall. What if, as they said in every comic book, cartoon, and superhero movie, the jig was up?

"We'll go together," Laney whispered.

The peephole yielded a fish-eye view of a young hotel employee with something in his hand.

"Sorry to interrupt your night," the kid, probably a bellhop, said upon greeting.

His reddened yet sly expression told me what his dirty adolescent mind was assuming he had "interrupted."

He held up a bottle of champagne like a peace offering. "For the happy couple, compliments of the hotel manager."

Laney's relief was palpable. "Isn't that sweet, honey?" Her melodic giggle was music to my ears.

"Absolutely," I said, dropping my arm casually across her shoulders and giving her a gentle squeeze. She didn't pull away. I smiled.

"We know you didn't plan on staying at the Regency before your wedding," he continued on his bad script, "but we do hope you'll come back and visit us after the big day."

Laney grabbed the bottle by the neck like a sailor and rapidly rolled her other fingers in a cute, "take the hint and get lost" little wave.

"Thanks, man." I palmed the guy a ten and closed the door on his wink.

"Good job, Tech-Boy," she said teasingly. In her best Johnny Depp doing his best Keith Richards as Jack Sparrow, she strutted back into the room with bottle in hand. "You didn't turn red this time. Or green."

"Deception gets easier with time, I guess."

I thought of Laney, blushing over her sushi when she mentioned getting bumped into first class. She had had plenty of opportunities to set the record straight, to say she wasn't a bride and that wasn't her dress she was lugging around. I wondered why she hadn't.

Then again, I was one to talk. I still hadn't said a word about my own situation.

It occurred to me that I hadn't so much as given a thought to the wedding, or the bachelor party, or even Sloane, until that knock on the door. I had been having such a good time joking with Laney about Godzilla's cheesy special effects and flirting with her during that silly

Q&A game. Trying to figure out what made her tick was a bit of a turn-on, and now that I knew she wasn't the Bridezilla I thought she was, I felt even more—

"Ha, there it is! Delayed blush reaction!"

Guilty as charged.

As usual, my id tried to reason with my superego. Was a little bit of old-fashioned fantasizing and flirting with Laney any different from what I'd be doing in Vegas? Looking with my eyes but not with my hands, not ordering from the menu, and all that jazz?

Of course it's different, you idiot. Laney isn't a plastic mirage, like Vegas. She's a living, breathing, very cool girl. A girl who some asshole named Allen must've hurt pretty bad in her past life.

"I'm gonna go get some *gratis* ice for our *gratis* alcohol," Laney said, but not before flipping to an early page in her sketchbook and tossing it to me. "You might as well start here," she said with a resigned sigh, as if she had read the earlier thoughts in my mind. I stared after her as she sashayed toward the door; Laney seemed to possess superpowers of her own. I dragged my eyes back down to the page and studied the first panel.

A young girl was sprawled, belly down, in front of a roaring fireplace, propped up by her elbows. Paper and crayons littered the floor in front of her, and she was dreamingly clutching a pencil. Her knees were bent, her stocking feet pointing up to the sky. The speech balloon was a puffy, cloudlike thought balloon, with the classic bubble tail pointing toward her head. *"When I grow up, I want to be a cartoonist . . ."* Off in the top right corner, another balloon was roughly inked, reminding me of the monster comics I'd devoured in my youth. Someone off panel was reminding her *"You'll never be GOOD enough, so stop DREAMING!"*

The next panel showed a teenaged girl, her hair spiked into a Mohawk. Eyes squinted, teeth gleaming in happiness. *"I've got my pick of art schools! California, here I come!"* is inked above her head. Each hand was clutching school admission letters triumphantly.

Another rough balloon burst the hopeful art student's bubble: *"I'm not about to sit back and watch you squander your future, running off with some high school flunky! You'll stay at school here in New York, where I can keep an eye on you."*

My eyes zoomed to the last panel of the page. It was heart shaped, with a big jagged break splitting it down the middle into two. With a sunset on the beach as the backdrop, two hands reached for each other in the foreground or, perhaps, were pulling away. The hand on the left side of the broken heart was smaller and more feminine. With a speech balloon dashed to indicate a whisper, it read: *"We need to talk . . ."* The right side of the broken heart showed a larger, more masculine hand and a balloon containing the universal curse word symbols: *"@#$%&!"*

My eyes lingered a moment on the bottom panel before flipping to the next page. A new set of panels greeted me. The girl was newly graduated in her cap and gown, her hair now tame, shiny, and hanging straight. *"Marvel Comics wants me!"*

I could practically hear the shouting inside the jagged speech bubble: *"After I spent $80,000 in tuition? Not on my watch!"*

"That's called a burst balloon." Laney was at my shoulder, her finger grazing the words of rage on the page. "Fitting, huh?"

I tried not to inhale too deeply, but her sweet scent was too good not to. I directed my sigh toward the open page.

"Have you ever had someone shutting you down at every turn?" she asked quietly.

I shook my head. "No. With a high-ranking general for a dad, I grew up in a 'be all that you can be' type of household. It was a different kind of pressure."

"I can still hear the scorn in my mother's voice." Laney scraped her own voice up an octave and imitated: "'You'll never earn enough drawing to support yourself, Laney!' and 'No one will ever take your job choice seriously.'" She ground the bottle down into the ice bucket angrily. "As if the artists in the Marvel Bullpen were a bunch of kids playing Dungeons and Dragons and goofing off in their parents' basement rec room!"

I thought about my own parents' basement, where I had built my first computer at age twelve. There had been no put-downs in the Ridgewood household. But there had been plenty of pick-up-and-go, which was enough tumult to keep me reaching desperately for the brass ring as my father kept moving us in his quest for top brass.

Looking back down at the penciled and inked panels, I shook my head. "I take it your mom wasn't impressed with the best of the best coming to court you?"

"There was what my mom thought was the best—whether it was schools or boyfriends or places to live and work—and then there was *all the rest*." Laney snorted. "'Let me know when it's the *New Yorker*, Laney; then we'll talk!'"

I loved how she threw the obnoxious, stereotypical Long Island inflection into her bit, drawling out *Yawka* and *tawk*.

"My mom never trusted me to figure it out on my own. She pulled some strings and got me a cushy cubicle job doing graphic design for an elite women's magazine." Laney mimicked sticking a finger down her throat. "Monday through Friday, nine to five—"

"Bang-your-head-on-the-desk boredom?" I finished for her.

"Stick-your-head-in-the-oven torture."

"I've spent a few nine-to-fives there myself." I gave a knowing smile and flipped the page.

"YOU'LL BE THE DEATH OF ME, LANEY."

There was no graphic to go along with that caption. Just purple and red lava drips and plumey yellow vapors indicating some form of purgatory for all involved.

Laney knelt on the edge of the bed next to me. "The night at the Lake Shore Hotel was a wake-up call. It took five years, but I finally realized it was my life, *my* choice. No one was going to save me but myself."

She sounded so resolute, yet so vulnerable at the same time. I wanted to gather her to my chest and hug those years away, but I had no right. I had no power myself, as I sat questioning my own choices.

"So I quit the magazine, applied at Marvel"—the hint of her smile told me that went well—"and moved into the city. I got my dream job, dream apartment . . ." Her fingernail traced the hellish vapors around the word *death*. I remembered that her two question cards, best sex and worst night, had shared the same answer. *Lake Shore Hotel. Five-year high school reunion. Allen Burnside.*

I had to ask.

"What about the dream guy?"

Laney shook her head, as if to clear the past, and her messy bangs, from her line of vision. Then she smiled and reached for the champagne. The walk down memory lane was over, at least for now.

"Compliments of the hotel, for the *bride*"—her chortle was derisive and dead sexy—"and the *groom*."

I flicked a glance at the label. "Classy."

Not that I was an expert, but after courting Sloane for so long, I knew better than to try to pass any brand off on her that spelled its name with a lowercase *c*. "One must never capitalize unless it's from the actual *region*"—I could practically hear her haughty tone.

"Hey, don't question free booze," Laney countered. "This says 'Michigan's Finest.'"

"The Midwest isn't exactly known for its sparkling wines."

"Snob," she teased, slowly tilting the bottle back and forth. "I say we open it."

"In the bathroom," I instructed.

"Bathroom? Classy," she echoed mockingly, with a wink and another shake.

"Careful," I warned, following her. "A champagne cork can pop out of a bottle at a speed of over twenty-five miles per hour. You could put an eye out."

"Please," Laney scoffed, picking at the foil. "I was on tour with a rock band for six months. I *know* how to pop the bubbly."

"And rock bands are known for trashing hotels," I pointed out, reaching for the bottle. Although I was curious to hear more of *that* story. "Allow me."

Uncorking a bottle of champagne followed a ritual, almost like a ceremony, yet Laney was treating it like a cage match. "I've got it. It's just"—she struggled—"this wire thingy won't—"

"It's a *muselet*," I informed her. "Turn it six times."

"Like I was *saying*," Laney said defiantly, "the wire thingy won't budge—and I turned it 'six times.' How do you know so much about champagne, anyway?"

"Champagne school," I admitted. "At Flûte Gramercy."

"Champagne *school*? Is that like obedience school for rich guys?"

"Yes," I deadpanned. Sloane had enrolled me as an engagement present. I had learned the fine art of tastings, food pairings . . . and how to roll over and play dead. "I can pair prestige cuvée champagnes from the top of the producer's range with caviars from Petrossian Paris. And I can certainly open this bottle if you'd let me help."

I felt a victorious jolt as she relinquished a tiny bit of control, allowing me to sidestep next to her and give it a try. How was it possible I could find such a stubborn person so seductive?

She tilted the bottle under my instruction as I opened the *muselet*, keeping my thumb on the cork. "Turn the bottle now, like this," I said. Probably overkill, but I placed my hand over hers to guide her. *Jeez, Noah.* The cork wasn't the only thing ready to pop.

I felt her other thumb rub against mine on the cork. Just a bit of pressure was all that was needed for it to escape with a little sigh. "Here we go," I said under my breath. "Listen for the *soupir érotique*."

Laney lifted her eyes to meet mine in questioning camaraderie. "What's that?" she asked.

"If we do it just right . . ." I trailed off. *Find neutral ground, take the high road, don't go there.* "It makes this sound, like . . ."

The playing field had been so even before, back when I thought she was a Bridezilla and I had been dragging my cold, miserable feet across the country. Now my feet were against hers, in matching pairs of socks, bolstering us as we braced for the release.

Laney pulled the bottle a little closer to her chest for leverage, taking my clutch with her. My chin grazed her bare shoulder, setting the strap of her tank top askew. Shit. If I moved back, I'd let go, and we'd run the risk of getting soaked in a shower of champagne.

"Like what?" Laney turned her head, her lips just inches from mine. If I didn't move away, we were in danger all the same.

The cork hit the shower wall and she shrieked, jerking back into my arms. Her thumb slipped over the bottle opening and it was all over; the movement of her landing against me shook the effervescent contents just enough.

Champagne geysered from the small space between her thumb and the lip of the bottle. It rained down the shower curtain, dripped from the ceiling, and cascaded over us. Laney's unbridled laughter bounced off the walls of the small space, shoulders hunched as she shook what was left and aimed the neck at me.

"Don't you dare, Hudson!"

"And if I do?" she challenged, with a gleam in her eye.

Laney squealed as I took charge of the bottle and turned it on her, but not before I got blasted square in the jaw. Her bangs were sopping and her top was bordering on wet T-shirt contest–worthy by the time the bottle was spent, but we were both laughing so hard, it didn't matter.

"Oh, my God, that was fun," she gasped. I took a haul off what was left in the bottle and then offered the rest to her. She guzzled the dregs of Michigan's Finest and deposited the empty bottle into the bathroom wastebasket with a thud and a giggle. "Serves them right for not bringing us champagne flutes, right?"

"Damn straight," I agreed, wringing out the bottom of my T-shirt.

Laney wiped her mouth with the back of her hand and grinned. "So what were we listening for before that thing exploded?"

"The *soupir érotique*." I grabbed a hand towel from the rack behind her. "Sometimes uncorking makes a sound"—I ran the towel gently down her dripping hair and across her collarbone before I even realized what I was doing—"like an erotic sigh."

"*If* it's done right," Laney added, her tone soft and serious, her smile now gone.

She reached up tentatively to my cheeks, her fingers on my stubble, sticky to the touch. My left hand, still holding the towel, moved down her back. When my right hand reached for the other end of the soft cloth, encircling her waist and pulling her closer to me, she let a breath escape that was by far the most erotic I had ever heard.

"I think we did okay," I said, trying to remember how to breathe in her presence.

"I know I ranted about alcohol-infused camaraderie and sleazy movie-fantasy hookups earlier—" Her thumbs moved across my lips to silence me as I started to protest. "And I know you said 'not interested,' but that was back before you knew it wasn't my dress, right?"

"Ah, Laney . . ."

The look in her eyes was absolutely slaying me.

"I wish you could skip the bachelor party," she blurted out, "and I could skip the wedding and we could just stay here, like this."

I closed my eyes, turning into her caress.

In wine there is truth. *You stupid idiot.*

You have to tell her.

"I wish we could, too," I said, my own sigh catching in my throat. "But I kinda think the guest of honor is expected to be there."

She laughed in my arms, and I hated myself.

"I told you, silly. I'm *not* getting married."

"I know. But I am."

Burst Bubbles

"It's my bachelor party, Laney. In Vegas," Noah added, as if I was stupid and I needed it spelled out.

Seriously? He couldn't have worked that in earlier? No *by the way* while we were having sushi at the airport? No *I've been meaning to tell you* over drinks in the hotel bar? Or even *wow, what a funny coincidence, you're not really a bride but—surprise! I'm really a groom* when I confessed? Name, birth date, and social security number . . . but this little detail slips his mind?

Erotic sigh? What the hell was that, if not a moment to seize?

He was still holding me.

And my hands still wanted to touch his cheeks, even though they should have wanted to slap him right about then. Traitors.

My brain called a truce and commanded them to move away. I reached behind me and extricated myself from his embrace.

WWDD?

Laney, just walk away.

Dani had given me that sage advice after seeing the picture of Allen

frolicking with the lingerie model in Australia. We'd dubbed the billboard bitch "King Kong in a bra" and joked about the possibility of her
airbrushed ta-tas hanging out with P. Diddy and Mr. Peanut on a billboard twenty-three stories high in Times Square. Let her have him.

Just walk away.

Dani was never one to beg a boyfriend during a breakup; she never
got teary or upset in front of one of them, no matter how hurt she was.
"Okay," she'd say, and simply walk away. I can't tell you how many guys
ended up crawling back and making total asses of themselves, but
Dani? She always kept her dignity intact.

"Well," I managed, "that's the way the cookie bounces, I guess."

Walk away. And leave him to clean up the bathroom.

"Cookies don't bounce." He followed me out of the bathroom,
looking genuinely perplexed. "Do they?"

I smiled, remembering having the exact same exchange with Allen
after he lost the seventh-grade class election. "More often than balls
crumble."

"I'm sorry, Laney."

"For what?" I barked out a bitter laugh. "For getting engaged? For
getting drunk with me? For flirting?" *For getting my hopes up?*

"Yes. No, I mean . . . oh, damn it, Laney."

This guy was smooth. And all I could picture was him effortlessly
sailing through the blowout bachelor party, once he was rid of me.
Then gliding through his nuptials with a gorgeous, adoring bride.
Everything would be perfect, down to the satiny sheen of fondant
draping their wedding cake.

Noah didn't need someone like me anywhere near that happiness.
I was like a finger dug into the frosting, personified. Messy and undig-
nified.

I grabbed my sketchbook and pencil. "I think I need some air."

"Air?" Noah sputtered. "It's twenty-one degrees out. And we're on
the twelfth floor where the windows don't even open anyway."

I laced on his Chucks once more. "Okay. There's a dartboard calling my name downstairs, then." I reached for the doorknob. "See ya."

The bar was slightly transformed late at night, its small dance floor lined with flexi LED rope lighting. A motley-looking assortment of patrons were swaying their hips and sipping their drinks to some benign flavor-of-the-day dance song. I recognized the two dart-playing flight attendants from earlier. They were now in jeans and shimmery tops, shaking their rumps with a couple of *Saturday Night Fever* types. Obviously the women were used to flight delays and probably packed their bags for any possibility. Converse sneakers, leggings, and a champagne-splattered tank top was hardly club attire, but it wasn't like I was up against a velvet rope and a VIP bouncer.

Lance and Jimmy were no longer behind the bar. I ordered a ginger ale from their replacement, a flirty Filipino who was aptly name-tagged Phil, and took to the corner stool. Who needed company when they had a sketchbook? I flipped through mine until I caught a glimpse of the rough sketch I had done of the Manhattan skyline on my way out to the airport.

When you lived in Manhattan, it was easy to forget to look up at the wonder around you. Sometimes it took crossing a river to remember.

Noah wasn't a boyfriend; he wasn't much more than a stranger. A handsome, funny, and seemingly nice enough stranger. Who, it turned out, was taken. Off the market before I even knew him. There would be no crying or begging on my part. But still, it was nice to follow Dani's advice, walk away, and get some perspective.

The bellhop who had brought the bubbly to our door skittered through the lobby with a big rolling cart. I thought back to those few minutes after I had told Noah the truth. There's that stupid saying about the truth setting you free, and for a moment, I had freed myself up to the possibility of getting to know this guy. It had felt like we were on the same page. On equal footing.

I looked down at his sneakers on my feet. Of course he was taken. All the good ones were, some way or another.

That's the way the cookie bounces.

Turning my attention to my work, I ran my pencil up the top of the Empire State Building, sharpening the spike. It didn't matter where I was in life—in the dusty back room of a comic book store at twelve, in the inner sanctum of one of the world's largest comic conventions at twenty-five, in the corner of a hotel bar in real time—when I started to draw, I was transported into the page.

"Holy shitballs, it's crowded in here," griped Pixie, shifting in her metal folding chair. The two of us, pencilist and colorist for the fledgling *Dreamer Deceiver* line, were relegated to the end of a table so far down the row, it felt like another zip code from the rest of the Marvel creators, but I was in my element. This was the heart and soul of the New York Comic Con; everyone and anyone in comics was in this very place: Artists' Alley. Over two hundred tables were crammed into the narrow upstairs area of the Javits Center and the room was abuzz with industry, press, and fans.

We were rolling into the last day of the convention, and the novelty was wearing off for Pixie. She had been thrilled to learn of our table's proximity to some of the hottest names in the business, but quickly realized their fan lines were forced to form a tight seal that eclipsed any space or business we'd hoped to have in front of our table.

"I'm really tired of staring at ass," she complained. "I'm gonna go find a Monster or a Red Bull. You want anything?"

"I'm all good, thanks."

The nonstop barrage of people bustling by with their totes crammed full of free swag was a bit overwhelming, but I found it easy to shut out simply by doing what I loved to do. The atmosphere buzzed with potential and creativity, and I had spent the weekend drawing, inking, and chatting with fellow artists. I loved the intimate feel of the Alley and had barely strayed onto the main floor except to say hi to friends at the big Marvel booth.

Each day of the convention had had a slightly different feel to it. Friday had the jumpiness of first-date jitters, opening early to industry and press. Saturday carried an exhausting, sold-out rock star exhilaration; and now I was settling into a full-blown affair with Sunday, luxurious as lounging and lingering with a new lover in bed. A few eager fans of the line we were working on had come and gone earlier in the day. I had happily signed and sold a few sketches and had given my card to a handful of people interested in commissioning. Pixie had spent most of the day texting her boyfriend, coloring a few pieces I put in front of her, and making rude commentary on the backsides in our direct line of vision.

I crossed my legs under the skirted table and leaned over to lavish attention on my newest creation.

"Hey. Big fan."

Hands dropped a comic in its bag and board on the table in front of me. It was the first *Dreamer Deceiver* comic I had ever worked on, its cover as familiar to me as my own face.

And the hands were familiar as well, down to the blisters-turned-calluses on the lowest pads of each index finger.

Drummer's hands.

I glanced up from the sketch I was working on and saw the line of asses had parted like the Red Sea. Allen was standing at my table.

He looked rock-god amazing, legs splayed in expensive dark wash jeans, with a full head of blond locks touch-me tousled. Beneath his perfectly broken-in leather jacket, the pearly white buttons of his black western-style shirt glistened. Shades covered eyes that I knew were a piercing blue.

How the hell he had found me, out of the fifty thousand people milling through the place, I'll never know. He didn't wear an attendee badge or a press badge or anything to indicate he hadn't just magically descended from the sky.

Allen pushed his shades up on top of his head. "Sign, please?"

I stared up at him for a long minute, before letting my shaking hands move on autopilot, slipping the comic from its polypropylene.

"You're a hard woman to track down, you know?"

Yeah, right. Look who's talking. "I'm not the one who changes cell phone numbers every couple of months," I countered.

His guilty smirk turned into a sexy grin.

Pixie was back, sliding in behind me. "Freakin' madhouse out there. I did catch a glimpse of Chewbacca, Peter what's-his-name. Hey." She nodded at our "fan" before plopping herself down.

"Mayhew," Allen and I said in unison.

"That's it, thanks. Yeah, he's, like, at every convention and will be until the end of time. I really want to see—" She suddenly did a double take. "Holy fuckballs," she whispered.

Pixie and I had worked together long enough for her to know that the guy standing in front of us was the same guy from the cover of the *Rolling Stone* magazine that I had tacked to the wall of my cubicle, behind my monitor and next to the autographed photo of Stan Lee. It was just about as famous as the naked cover of the Red Hot Chili Peppers, with the trio from Three on a Match all holding fire in their hands. Even though Pixie didn't know half our history, she knew me well enough to judge when I needed privacy.

"I'm gonna—uhhh, go find a Monster or a Red Bull," she said, delving into a weird déjà vu, smile pasted to her face. "You guys want anything?"

"No, thanks," we said in unison.

I signed Allen's comic with trembling hands, feeling his eyes on me the entire time.

"So what are you in town for?" I asked, my attempt at casual coming across as woodenly formal.

"Recording our new album. Over on Fifty-seventh Street." He extended a hand to me, like it was a Couples Only skate at our local roller rink. "Now, come on out from behind that table and let me get a look at you, girl."

I hooked my fingers into his and practically twirled out in front of him.

"Check you out, Wonder Woman. At your Comic Con debut. And those boots, va-va-voom!"

"Bought them with my first Marvel paycheck," I said proudly, feeling like a badass superhero myself. I'm sure Allen's first record label advance afforded him a Porsche out in La-La Land, but I was perfectly happy strutting around town in my va-va-voom boots.

"You must be the talk of the island back home in those," he said, baiting me. I knew he was fishing for info, confirmation that I had taken the catalyst completely around the circle.

"This island is home now. Forty-seventh and Ninth Avenue."

"Making Hell's Kitchen even hotter," he said with a smile. Obviously he approved.

"Find anything good?" I asked, gesturing to the large brown paper bag under his arm.

With a smile, he unsheathed his bounty. "Vintage talking Batman alarm clock. In the box. Wanna come over to my hotel to make sure it works?" he asked slyly.

"What about Gwyneth? Or Giselle? Or whatever the hell her name is?"

"It's Geska. She's Danish."

Of course she was. "I bet she's sweet."

"Yeah. I guess she is."

I wished he had used the past tense to let me know she was stale and that he had kicked her to the curb like a day-old doughnut. Instead, he shrugged. "She's around. We're not really *together* together. You know how it is. As long as there are rock stars in the world, there are always going to be models and actresses who want to be seen with us. We could be hideous monsters with six eyes and it wouldn't matter."

"Funny you should say that, since that's how I've been drawing you lately." I held up the *Dreamer Deceiver* sketch I had been working on, which happened to feature just such a creature, busting through a steel door. Allen gave me that adoring, "you're such a smartass" look that I so missed, I so craved, all these years.

"Can you write *1603* there?"

He pointed down to the page, where my monster had crumpled the door of Dreamer's secret hideout like it was a piece of aluminum foil. I reached for a fine-tip and added a number plate to what was left of the door, customizing it to his specifications.

"That's the number of my hotel room over at the Meridien," he supplied. "In case you change your mind about coming over to test-drive my *clock*."

"You wouldn't dare take it out of the box, now, would you?" *Shameless, Laney. Shameless. And juvenile. Look where flirting got you last time.*

Allen was like my drug, and I needed that shot.

He winked. "I'd be very careful taking it in and out. Mint condition and all."

Somehow we always managed to slip into the double entendres and dirty talk, as smoothly as we used to pass love notes to each other in high school. The memories time-lapsed through my brain before pausing on our last night together, in the Lake Shore Hotel.

"Is there somewhere private we can go here?" he asked. "To talk?"

I could tell Allen had fast-forwarded to the exact same memory moment. It hung there over us, the image burning into the plasma. Pushing play would take us down two divergent paths that I didn't really want to think, or talk, about.

We were on my turf now, in this *moment*. Why did we need to rewind back to the regret and the pain of the past?

"I'm not really supposed to leave the table unattended . . . and besides, you shouldn't be out there," I warned, gesturing into the sea of spectators.

The Venn diagram of rabid comic fans and music fans was known to overlap a bit too fervently at times. I once saw a throne, as in an "all hail the king" type of throne, being carried into a convention for Rob Zombie, where he was scheduled to do a signing. A musician of Allen's caliber would be jumped on as quickly as a hot girl wearing skintight cosplay around here.

Allen chuckled. "That's what these are for." He tapped the shades resting on his head. As if a mere pair of darkened glasses could mask the entire rock star essence that was oozing from his every pore.

We ducked behind the booth, on the other side of the black pipe and drape. Allen gently pulled on the artist's badge lanyard hanging from my neck, luring me into his arms and meeting my lips in a kiss so tender that it almost felt like dreaming. My hands ran up the smooth leather covering his chest and over his chiseled shoulders, squeezing as if to make sure he was indeed real. His hand clenched my ass as if to confirm that yes, he was very real.

"I'm so proud of you, Laney Jane," he murmured. "And I'm so sorry for being such a dick to you after the reunion."

"You have nothing to be sorry for," I sputtered. "I needed to be pushed out of that nest."

Allen had given me more than just two purple lines on a pee stick that night at the Lake Shore Hotel two years before. He had given me back my courage and my drive. Yes, the anger, hurt, and betrayal had brought me pretty much to rock bottom. But woven with his words, they had fueled my strength to stand up to Vera Hudson.

"You'll be the death of me, Laney!" my mother had raged, shaking the drugstore receipt in her hand. She had gone into my room "on a hunch" while I was out. "Pregnant? By that . . . that deviant? For heaven's sake, you're not a fifteen-year-old dum-dum. A baby?"

When I was fifteen, she had broken the binding on my diary and my teenage trust based on one of her "hunches." After the Lake Shore Hotel incident, she tried breaking my spirit and my heart by railing against my lack of foresight, my unrealistic expectations, and the two people who had ever truly believed in me: my dad and Allen.

That day she came up with her two worst Veraisms ever: "Absent fathers make for promiscuous daughters!" and "Are you happy, Laney? You've tethered yourself to that loser for life!"

Finally, after she had sighed and said, "We'll just have to take care of it," I had the tiniest glimmer of hope that, for once in my life, my mother had my back, supporting me, accepting my choices. Until she picked up the phone to call the clinic and I realized what she really meant. It was the same day I told her to go to hell. I was quitting the job, moving into the city . . . and I was keeping the baby.

"I shouldn't have pushed you so hard, that was mean. But I was in a bad place," Allen said, stroking back my hair.

I tried not to think of the photo of him, playfully pulling the bikini string of a supermodel whose hands rested intimately on his bare body in an Australian paradise. It looked like a far better place than the "bad place" he had been in with me.

"If you hadn't pushed me, I would still be on Long Island, juggling that meaningless job and living in my mother's basement."

Mother-daughter apartments were a common feature in our suburban neighborhood, and if my mother the martyr had had her way, I'd still be in hers. I tried to picture being there, a single mother myself. Three generations trapped under a single roof. Forever in debt to my mother and her priceless advice.

"Laney Hudson!"

Allen and I both froze.

My mother had grilled me over the phone the previous night about my exact coordinates within the Javits Center, down to the row and aisle number, but I thought she was just being her usual nosy self.

"Hello! Where are you?" my mother trilled, crashing back through the pipe and drape separating us from the crowd.

I was equally horrified and touched that she had bothered to come see my "little show," as she referred to it. And a bit mortified, as she had brought a cookie bouquet and a big Mylar balloon that said *Way to Go!* on it.

"Mrs. Hudson," Allen said formally.

He was still holding my lanyard, but at least he wasn't holding my ass any longer.

Her eyes reduced to slits. "Allen Burnside, you are dead to me." And turning on me, she wailed, "Laney, how could you? After what he did to this family! I'd rather sterilize you like a deer with a salt lick than go through that heartbreak again!"

Her heartbreak?

I was the one who had lost the baby, four months in. *Incompetent cervix*, my doctor told me. Giving my mother a new adjective to throw in my face, along with *irresponsible*.

It had been Dani who had nursed me back from the devastation, shielding me from my mother's big, fat "I told you so" and "Must be God's way of telling you something." And Dani who had hacked us through the snare of our high school friends, using a machete of words to cut down their tangled grapevine of gossip about Allen and his newfound, A-list love life.

"Laney?" I heard a waver of that fifteen-year-old kid in his voice, but the haunted look on his face aged him more than his twenty-five years. "You told me it was a safe time . . . What—"

"Please," I pleaded, "not here."

I didn't want to discuss my ovulation cycle, my state of mind, or my miscarriage in the middle of the Javits Center. Not in the middle of Artists' Alley. This was supposed to be my turf. My safe haven.

"You didn't even *tell* him? Laney, that is *rich*!" My mother slammed the cookie bouquet down so hard that the cookies came off their stems.

The balloon tethered to the box bobbed violently overhead. When I brought my eyes back down to focus, Allen was gone.

New score: Laney, 2. Allen, 1.

Way to go!

Later that evening, I brought myself to knock on door number 1603 of the Meridien Hotel, with Allen's forgotten Batman clock tucked under my own arm like a peace offering.

He took it from me silently over the threshold and didn't invite me in.

"It's not what you think," I stammered.

Because it really wasn't.

"Who's at the door, baby?"

Allen. Baby. Someone else.

It was my worst nightmare.

Geska was more horrifyingly beautiful in real life than in her photos.

Allen had said she was "around," but I was thinking he meant in the vague, "somewhere" sense. Not in the way she wrapped her hairless, poreless, perfectly toned arms around his waist and peered over his shoulder at me. Her long legs, bare from beneath the hem of Allen's black western button-down shirt, didn't need boots to be va-va-voom.

I tore my eyes from her and met Allen's steely gaze.

"She's nobody," he said pointedly.

Allen had evened the score.

He slammed the door, leaving me to consider exactly just who was the real monster lurking around room 1603.

Match point.

"Do you know what the spire on the Empire State Building was originally built for?"

"I hope that's not your newest pickup line," I joked lamely, as Noah slid onto the stool next to me with a fresh drink.

He had changed into a dry tee and thrown his dress shirt back on, but it was unbuttoned and the sleeves were rolled up. I wondered how long he had been in the bar, watching me. I probably hadn't looked all that approachable, hunched over my sketchbook with a death grip on my pencil.

"It was designed to serve as a mooring mast for dirigibles. You know, zeppelins?"

"Frightening. And fantastical."

"Can I buy you a drink?" Noah asked, as if we were meeting for the first time. And in a way, we kind of were.

"Sure. My usual." I laughed. Funny how you could know that about a person in just one day. Alcohol was the greatest bonding tool since the peace pipe. "Hi, I'm Laney. And I don't take rejection well."

"Noah." He shook my hand and grinned. "And I'm really good at sticking my foot in my mouth."

I clicked my glass to his and put one final detail on my drawing: a tiny *Way to Go!* balloon wafting toward the heavens.

"Okay, I get the *kaiju* in the dress," Noah said, contemplating my picture. "But why is King Kong wearing a bra?"

I looked down at my Manhattan skyline. Bridezilla, in Badgley Mischka and kitten heels, was thirty stories tall and storming up the West Side Highway. The Javits Center was crushed, accordion style, like a tin can underfoot. She had a cookie clenched in one of her tiny theropod fists. In the background, hanging from the Empire State Building, was Geska the billboard bra bitch.

"Just a few of my foes." I had depicted Allen's Danish ex as the damn dirty ape, but instead of the usual airplane or damsel in her fist, she held a tiny replica of Allen's Batman clock. "You know that old saying, 'if you can't beat 'em, join 'em'? Well, if I can't beat them, I draw them."

I gave him the rundown on Geska, whose billboard still taunted me every time I walked through Times Square. "I mean, seriously, what's the shelf life on a girl like that? Skinny as a rail, with lips like a hemorrhoid doughnut and a chest like Silicon Valley?"

Actually, I knew exactly what her shelf life was, as far as Allen was concerned. It was around the time that Dani let it slip to Gloria Boyner, biggest mouth of the North Shore, that I had miscarried. That was the one time the high school grapevine came in handy for me.

"You're gonna get him back," Dani had promised. "And he's gonna marry you. Just like Dorothea Hurley and Jon Bon Jovi. They were high school sweethearts."

What I did get, about a week later in the mail at Marvel, was a CD. *All You Had to Do* was written on it with a Sharpie in Allen's handwriting, nothing else. No return address, nothing. It contained one song, written and sung by him, accompanied by Bryan on guitar. It was the most beautiful thing I had ever heard.

Allen Burnside was the forgiving sort.

Noah held up the drawing to the light.

"I hope you defeated Queen Kong by dipping her in hot wax. Her cleavage could use a good depilatory."

"That's a big word. For a guy," I teased.

But seriously, Noah was like no guy I had ever met. He knew things, and said things, that surprised me every time he opened his mouth.

"Sixteen points on the Scrabble board. Unless you landed on a triple-triple and got the fifty-point bonus for using all your tiles, in that case it would be something like one hundred and ninety-four."

"'Something like,' huh? You've got a photographic memory, haven't you?"

"For some things." Noah stabbed at the ice in his Jack and Coke with the stirrer. "My fiancée certainly doesn't. Or she just doesn't care."

"About what?" I set down my pencil and studied him.

"How's this for a start? She changed our wedding date on a whim,

without consulting me." He threw back half his Jack and Coke before
continuing. "To the anniversary of my father's death."

"Are you serious?"

Noah nodded grimly. "And when I asked her, 'You know that's the
day my dad died, right?' she never answered yes or no, she just began
to list her reasons why the fifty-one other Saturdays in the year just
weren't for her. Especially if they put her flowers out of season. And
didn't jibe with her favorite photographer's schedule. And then she
told me to take the lemon"—he plucked the garnish from his drink
and tossed it over the bar, making a perfect rim shot into the garbage
pail—"and make *lemonade*."

"What a . . ." I trailed off. *Would it be socially acceptable to call
your fake fiancé's actual bride-to-be a colossal cooze?*

"She's been doing these . . . these enhancements, too, that I'm not
really on board with. Maybe that makes me sound shallow or controlling, but I like the natural look," Noah confessed.

Ha, yes! Take that, *billboard bra bitches of the world!*

"Not shallow at all," I murmured.

"Most brides would be happy if their grooms got a fresh haircut
and a hot shave before their wedding. Mine suggested a chin implant
to balance out my somewhat 'ethnic' nose." He smirked and rubbed
his already strong, square jaw.

God, was she delusional? Noah was the easiest guy on the eyes
that I had ever had the pleasure of meeting.

"It's all about Remy Georges and his 'fine-art photojournalism' for
the big day," he continued.

The name sounded familiar. "Isn't he that street photographer, the
one being called the Banksy of the camera world?"

"Yeah. He does those Manhattan truisms. Gum on the sidewalk
and all that." Noah laughed. "We went to see a retrospective of his
work on our first date. So she thought it would be meaningful to have
him shoot the wedding."

"Huh. Romantic enough, I suppose."

I tried not to imagine Noah and this beautiful creature in their wedding attire, smiling for the camera. They'd be the couple whose photo comes inside the frame when you buy it. Making you feel lame for throwing it away to replace it with your own watered-down substitute.

"So, is she aspiring to be a model?" For all the joking I made about Allen's day-old frosted Danish, I really didn't know how much was genetics, how much was Photoshop, and how much was surgery. But I had to assume that some cosmetic upkeep was a necessary evil in that profession. "Why else would anyone in their right mind want to willingly go under the knife repeatedly?"

Noah made a face. "She's not aspiring to be much of anything beyond a totally pampered wife, like her mother. Well, she does carry a business card around. It says she's a Tastemaker."

"Tastemaker . . . is that a club, like Toastmasters?"

Noah laughed. "No. It's a person who decides or influences what is or will become fashionable in a given sphere of interests." He gave me that sheepish smile I was beginning to quickly become addicted to. "Except her interests are somewhat limited."

"Sounds like pretty much to a party of one." I snorted.

Noah gave a sad smile. "You probably think I'm nuts for putting a ring on her finger in the first place, don't you?"

Actually, I was thinking he should go find some hobbits to throw that ring into the fiery pit of Mordor. It sounded like pure evil.

"There's just a lot riding on this," he finished softly.

It sounded like something my father would say, back when he'd hole himself up in the bedroom to watch the Big Game or the Pretty Pony, or to call his bookie. "There's a lot on the line here," he'd say, covering the mouthpiece of the phone to address me if I were to interrupt him.

"Besides your future happiness?" I mumbled.

I didn't add *for the rest of your life* because I supposed marriage was a gamble, after all. Experts would say a fifty-fifty shot. Was it the intermittent reward system that kept Noah coming back for more, like the psychology behind playing the slot machines?

Aside from the Naughty Sleepover Q&A, which had been mainly for flirty fun, Noah had been a closed book to me. I remembered the first image I had of him, all buttoned up in his suit and uptight. Perfectly groomed and put together. Sitting next to me now was an entirely different guy. Beneath all the PowerPoints and calm control there was a passion and vulnerability that I craved to know more about.

"Sloane makes her"—he tapped my gowned Godzilla—"look like a gecko. She was a Bridezilla before we even got engaged."

Noah

STUCK IN THE MIDDLE WITH YOU

Sloane's name hung stubbornly in the air of the bar, like cigarette smoke used to before all the smoking bans took effect. Laney tapped her pencil against her sketchbook thoughtfully.

I couldn't believe I was discussing this with her. What on earth did I have to gain by opening up to Laney? I wasn't going for sympathy, and I wasn't trying to get laid. I just wanted . . . the connection.

If I complained to my friends, they'd rip on me for being whipped and joke about the first-world problems of falling in love with a rich bitch. To confide in my mother would heap heartbreak on top of what she already had. She had put up a brave front for so long, first as a military wife, then as a widow. The simple reward of a doting daughter-in-law and abundant grandchildren was all she wanted.

But if I told Laney, she would understand. Something told me that she would. Still, I felt a tiny tug of guilt . . . a betrayal, perhaps.

The Bidwells, Sloane included, were WASPy, close-to-the-vest types when it came to airing the family's laundry. Although I had grown up with a hot-blooded Italian mother who talked with her hands and loved with her fierce hugs, I had acclimated myself to the closed-door policy that came with marrying into old money.

For the second time that night, the exchange went something like this:

"Wanna talk about it?"

"Not particularly."

I really didn't. Sloane had had a way of making sure she occupied my thoughts 99 percent of the time, front and center, for the past three years. Tonight was about allowing that 1 percent to sit back, relax, and enjoy the break. Like a death row inmate ordering up his last meal, I was going to savor every morsel.

"I Will Survive" appropriately came onto the jukebox, predictably followed by "Shout," always a favorite at bars and football games. Laney and I hung by the bar, leaning into each other and making up life stories about the people on the dance floor. "See that guy?" I pointed to a heavyset businessman who was boogying on the sidelines near the flight attendants, hoping to be waved in. "Lives at home with Mom. Collects My Little Pony memorabilia."

Laney was emphatic. "No way that guy is a Brony!"

I practically did a spit-take with my Jack and Coke. "There's a name for that?" I turned to her, incredulous.

She laughed and nodded. "Oh, you have so much to learn, dear boy."

"How about the flight attendants? Think they're bi?"

"You wish." She rolled her eyes at me and gave me a little bump with her elbow. "No, that one is curious, though. See her body language? The other one is having an affair with the pilot playing darts over there."

"I thought you wanted to play. Shall we challenge them to a game?" I asked her.

"Nah. Making up stories is more fun. What do you think people would say about us?"

"Well," I drawled, leaning in to be heard over the thump-thump

of Foster the People, "now that you aren't carrying around that ridiculous dress bag—"

"Yeah?" she prompted. "And now that you're not hardwired to that
freakin' computer . . ."

Our own body language was changing. Whether made bolder by
the alcohol or feeling safer under cover of the dusky bar lighting, we
orbited into each other's personal space. The typical nightclub cacoph-
ony of music, laughter, and glasses clinking was the perfect excuse to
lean in closer to be heard. Bumping shoulders as we joked, nudging
each other with our knuckles, our hands hanging on to our drinks all
the while to keep them occupied and away from what was off-limits.
It was a heady and torturous game.

"You could be heiress to the breakfast cereal kingdom, and I could
be your bodyguard." My upper lip hit her earlobe very time I enunciated a *B*, and I literally felt her body sigh closer.

"General Mills, or Kellogg's?" she asked.

"Both," I made sure to say.

"Or maybe"—she turned toward me and I could feel the whisper
of her breath on my collarbone—"we're Amish kids and we're off to
explore the real world. On *Fahrvergnügen*, or whatever they call it."

"I think you mean *Rumschpringe*."

Her laugh rang out. "You're the one in the suit." She set down her
drink and fastened the very top button of my open shirt. "You would
know."

The gesture was somehow both innocent and intimate. And indicated the joking was over. She went for the next one in the row, nim-
bly buttoning that one, too. The glass in my shaking hand met the
smooth finish of the bar top and I slid it away from me.

Laney's fingers were still playing with my buttons. "Sometimes,"
she started, keeping her eyes level with them. "Sometimes I have to
ask myself 'What Would Dani Do?' 'cuz she's not only my best friend,
she's also the smartest, and wildest, girl I know."

A new song came on, a party anthem whose volume seemed double that of its earlier competitors. The flight attendants were already swaying their hands in the air as the music began to build. Laney rolled the next button in the row between her thumb and forefinger and stole a glance at me. Desire boiled low in my core and threatened to volcano up. I had never met Dani, this devilish voice of reason that perched on Laney's delectable shoulders. Would I be thanking her, or resenting her?

"She would," Laney said, slowly breaking away from me, "totally get up and dance to Steve Aoki and Laidback Luke right about now."

Her smile was much too wicked for the girly giggle that accompanied it, as she shimmied in my sneakers onto the dance floor.

Good God. The guys could brag and moan about the blatant debauchery of Vegas as the ultimate in seduction until they were blue in the face, and in the balls. But I'd bet they had never experienced the sheer, erotic torture of being stripteased in reverse by a beautiful woman. Talk about your agony and your ecstasy.

"Turbulence!" the flight attendants yelled in greeting to her. "Are you ready? Are you strapped in?"

Laney whooped, pumping her hands as the bass-thrashing, electro-frenzied beat picked up. From my spot near the bar, I just grinned and shook my head, watching her. She was crazy. The flight attendants sang along, obviously versed in the song, all about initiating emergency procedures at thirty thousand feet.

With one hand, I worked the tight top button of my shirt open once again. I watched the trio on the dance floor and strained to eavesdrop on the girl who was blowing out Laney's eardrum.

"Why isn't your guy up here with us?" she shouted over the music.

"He hates flying!" I could read Laney's lovely lips.

Your guy.

Five hours before, Laney would've denied even knowing me. Now she was using a crooked, come-hither finger and a sexy squint to beckon me. I just crossed my arms, aiming for cool, but couldn't control the smile spreading across my face.

The women shook their heads, threw them back in laughter, and raised their arms higher and higher as the song began to build. Laney hopped and headbanged. Her dancing wasn't overly provocative to the casual observer, but it threw my mind into overdrive as she flung that curtain of hair over one shoulder, eyes closed, lost in the music. I noticed her tattooed wings were on full display as she swung her body uninhibitedly to the beat. There had to be a story behind them, and I intended to find out, whether it was drawn in her sketchbook or not.

"Come on, Noah!" She had bopped over to me and was grabbing at my hand. "Let's go make a clown bitch out of your aviophobia."

"Big word," I said, echoing her earlier tease, as I let her drag me out to the dance floor. "For a girl."

"Loosen up," she coaxed.

My legs were moving, but my arms stayed stiff and unnatural at my sides. I must've looked like the typical, self-conscious white boy.

"Not exactly my comfort zone," I said apologetically. Or my kind of music. The beat was frenetic yet seemed to be reaching toward a crescendo.

"Come on, like a roller coaster!"

She laced her fingers through mine and lifted our arms up, up, up as the bass thundered around us. My nervous chuckle gave way to genuine laughter, freeing up the space in my lungs and throat as we bopped to the pounding club mix. Laney's smile flashed at me brighter than the lights on the dance floor, skyrocketing my pulse rate until it was in synch with the crazy strobe light overhead. The flight attendants were clapping and stripper-shimmying around us.

AC/DC's "Highway to Hell" hit the speakers next, a classic yet respectable song to rock out to on the dance floor. Certainly worth the dollar I had spent on it, along with two other tunes on the TouchTunes jukebox, before seeking out Laney at the bar. I became Angus Young, duckwalking in circles with an air guitar as Laney mouthed every lyric. The rousing song got everyone in the bar up on the dance floor, shouting the chorus. It was liberating, especially after being trapped on a plane, at the airport, and then in a hotel for the last eighteen hours.

"I love this song!" Laney exclaimed next, over the rattling drums of the Talking Heads' "Once in a Lifetime," and danced around me. We sang along to the preposterous proclamations and asked ourselves those burning questions in unison. I slicked back my hair with my hands and played the perfect part of frontman David Byrne in my half suit, doing the funny big-stepped dance and herky-jerky marionette moves from the old eighties video. I knew all the old rock classics; I think my parents used to put me in front of the television and let MTV babysit me.

"So much fun," Laney gasped, fanning her hands in front of her face as the song dwindled down. We wound our way off the floor, back to our watery drinks and to Laney's sketchbook waiting on the bar. We gulped gratefully and settled back into contemplative silence.

"So . . . here we are," I said, for lack of anything better, just as Laney started with "Where were we?" and the jukebox began to play that old seventies folk rock tune, "Stuck in the Middle with You."

"You picked this song, didn't you?" Laney accused.

"And if I did?" I asked, shaking my ice innocently.

"It's pretty damn perfect." She grinned.

"Thanks."

She cocked her head at me. "For what?"

"For saying that. For noticing. I don't get 'perfect' right very often these days."

I didn't have to say Sloane's name again, but it still lingered, stale and irritating, over our heads.

Laney made a face like she smelled something rotten. "She sounds like a perfect bitch." Clapping her hand over her mouth, she added, "That was rude of me. I'm sorry."

I shrugged. "I'm thinking we could make a new drinking game out of 'I'm sorry.' We'd both be plastered in no time."

"Oooh, me first, me first!" Laney said. And with each confession, starting at our first encounter on the plane, we began to clear the air.

"Last but not least, I'm sorry for spraying you with champagne and hitting on you." She laughed and took a final swig of her Crown and ginger.

"Let's not get carried away here," I said with a smile. "But seriously, if I put you in an uncomfortable position by not fessing up sooner . . ." I tapped her glass with mine and took a drink. "Well, then, *I'm* sorry."

"Yeah, you should've been holding up a sign in the airport like one of those valets. One that read, 'I'm Engaged,'" she teased.

It was true. I was engaged.

To Sloane.

But I was also allured, bewitched, captivated, enchanted, and utterly fascinated.

By Laney.

And I didn't need a thesaurus app to come up with those.

The Dress Dictatorship

Talk about your roller coasters. The entire day had been more of a thrill ride than I had experienced in the past two years.

Each conversation with Noah was like hitching slowly up that steep hill; each flirtation throwing me into that heart-hammering, belly-dropping descent and making me want to yell, "Again! Again!"

The moments I spent thinking about the past, lost in my sketches, were the contemplative darkened tunnels needed for regaining equilibrium. Fleeting moments of memory chased away by the bright, dizzying light and pace of the present. Noah was gripping the guard bar in front of us, right along next to me for the ride, yet on his own personal journey.

But, like all good things, we kept coming to a screeching halt.

Reality.

Jerking us forward and back in a cruel game of inertia.

He's getting married. Soon.

And your mother's waiting, Laney Jane. For you to show up.

To grow up. Get your act together. You're late. As usual.

"Ready to head up? Or do you need more air down here?" Noah asked.

Up or down. The ride had to go one way or the other. But at the very top, time suspended and the air was still. I savored that teetering moment with closed eyes, but only for a second.

"Race you!"

We hightailed it back to the elevator, pushing each other out of the way to press the button. Noah whistled the "Once in a Lifetime" chorus and I leaned nonchalantly against the wall as we glided slowly up, up, up. But the moment the doors slid open, we were racing back down the hallway, laughing. He won, but only because I overshot the room, forgetting which number was ours.

Noah threw his key card down on the bed next to my blinking phone. "Looks like your people on the line are messaging you," he observed.

I checked my texts. "Oh, you've got to be kidding me."

"What is it?"

"My mother took it upon herself to schedule a wake-up call for me through the front desk. 'Just in case, Laney.'" I tossed my phone down and reached for the hotel's corded one, punching the call button angrily. "Can you please cancel the wake-up call for tomorrow morning? Yes, I'm sure . . . I've got at least four clocks with alarms in the room, I have no doubt one of them will succeed in waking me up. Thank you." I plopped myself down on the bed and reached for the drink I had left on the nightstand. "Just in case, my ass."

"Your mom doesn't trust you?"

"Never has, never will. I'm sure she gave me this task just to *prove* I'll mess it up. I bet there isn't even a dress in that bag. It's probably wadded-up newspaper. Or live snakes or something."

Noah's laugh washed over me like the alcohol did, making me feel fuzzy inside. "So no wedding waiting in Hawaii, then?" he said, teasing me. "Just a bunch of judges holding scorecards?"

"I wish! No, it's going to be the wedding from hell, I'm sure. Let me tell you, if I ever get married, I'm doing it quick in Vegas, with no one in attendance. No, better yet, with a roomful of Elvis impersonators . . . no one *I* know who can tell me I'm doing it all wrong."

"Come on, what have you done that's so wrong in life?"

He sat himself right down next to me and waited expectantly. What could I say? In my mother's eyes, I had quit a sensible job, I had gotten myself pregnant—and dumped—by a deviant loser, and yet I kept going back for more. And where had it gotten me?

In her opinion, I was completely incompetent, right down to my cervix.

"Don't be so hard on yourself, Laney." Noah flipped up an invisible collar, raised a lip, and actually made a passable Elvis impression. "A-don't be cruel . . ."

Now it was my turn to laugh. Which just encouraged him to keep up the act.

"Now, when I was your age, little lady—"

"You had tons of hit songs and millions of bucks?" I quipped.

Noah Elvis—*Noavis?*—ignored me. "I had invented an app that made me a good hunka money to burn, yes indeed. I bought the fancy house, the nice car. Took the big promotion in the Manhattan highrise. And I thought the next logical step was finding a pretty young thing and settling down . . ."

"So you're marrying Priscilla?"

Sloane. I couldn't bring myself to say it. I swallowed her name and practically gagged on the bitter aftertaste. My overactive imagination put her on a pedestal and pelted her with rotten fruit. Gorgeous, entitled, and covered in pulpy goo. *How do you like them lemons now, Sloane?*

The lip curled higher. "Fools rush in, darlin'. I thought she was the peanut butter for my hot banana sandwich."

He shook his head, and a rogue curl fell to the middle of his forehead. "So just goes to show . . . even when you think you're doing the right thing, you might still end up singing the blues."

"Sucks to be us, here at the Heartbreak Hotel, huh?" I said softly.

He bumped my shoulder with his and didn't miss a beat. "That's all right, mama."

I reached up and twisted his lone curl. "You make a good Elvis."

For God's sake, Laney. Get your hands out of the man's hair. And get off the bed!

I knew it was all kinds of wrong, yet all I could picture was climbing into Noah's lap and kissing him. Talk about a hot peanut butter and banana sandwich. I wanted to press up against him and—

"And you . . ." he said huskily, no trace of Elvis to be found, "make a good mixed drink."

Great. You want to make out with him. He wants you to make him a drink. Way to read those cues again.

Or maybe he's just being a gentleman, Laney Jane.

Engaged, remember?

"A toast, then." I mixed one last batch of drinks.

"What are we drinking to?" Noah bit his lower lip and fixed his gaze on me. I felt a buzz that had less to do with the whiskey than I dared to admit.

"To . . ." *Get yourself back on neutral territory, Laney.* "To Tokyo?"

"Tokyo." He clinked my class. "And to asparagus."

I giggled. "Definitely asparagus. And hot towels."

"And don't forget bichons frises."

"Oh, shit, the dress!" I had moved the garment bag to the edge of the bed earlier so I wouldn't get Dorito crumbs on it. Sometime between Godzilla and the champagne shower, it must have slipped between the bed and the wall, where it lay in a crumpled heap. "I'd better hang it up."

Noah watched, amused, as I attempted to shove the monstrosity into the closet. The space was wider than the one on the plane, but the bar was too low. Half the dress would be wrinkled from pooling on the floor all night. Hmm, maybe the back of the bathroom door would be better.

Hurling the bottom half of the garment bag over my shoulder like a fireman's carry, I lugged it across the room.

"I thought for sure you were some dress-obsessed diva," he called after me. "Why didn't you just check the darn thing?"

"You don't know my mother." I gave the hook a test tug and set the hanger down firmly before continuing. "This is the woman who used to control the marshmallow ratio in my breakfast cereal."

"You're putting it on."

"I'm totally not putting you on. She would literally count out my Lucky Charms every morning."

"No, I mean, the dress. Put it on." His voice was closer now, serious and sexy as hell, from the other side of the door. "You need to face your fears, Laney. Walk a mile in that dress's shoes."

"Dresses don't have shoes," I said lamely. Just like apps don't have elbows.

"Come on, just do it. What are you afraid of?"

"When it comes to my mother? Everything. And she's like a tiger. She'll smell my fear clinging to the dress. She'll know."

"She'll never know. Your secret will be safe with me."

He clicked the door closed and left me alone with just the garment bag, its reflection mocking me from every angle in the mirror.

Aren't you a little too old to be playing dress-up in your mom's closet, Laney Jane? It felt a little naughty. But this wasn't the 1980s and there were no racks of blazers with linebacker shoulder pads to hide behind. *Face your fears,* Noah had said.

You're a little too old to have to ask permission or seek approval from your mother about everything, I told myself. Or maybe that was the Crown Royal talking. I scowled at the drunken girl in the mirror. Was she trying to pick a fight with me?

With shaking fingers, I unzipped the bag slowly. After lugging the thing eight hundred miles, the least I could do was take a peek at it. Sure, my mother had shared some of its physical detail with me. But each utterance—*Eggshell white! Silk! Taffeta! Beaded and sequined!*—had felt like pepper spray to the eyes—a stinging insult.

You've got a dress dictating your every move. That's what Noah had said back in the airport food court. And he was right, even before knowing that it wasn't mine. It was as if the dress, even flat in its bag, embodied my mother. And everything she had ever criticized me for, disapproved of, and forbidden me to do was stitched into the very fabric and held fast.

Resentment and terror sobered me somewhat. But I still had enough alcohol fueling me to propel me forward. I roughly pushed open the garment bag and it fell away from the hanger, like a creature shedding its cocoon.

Wow.

I couldn't fault my mother's taste, when it came down to it. With all her controlling and planning and single-mindedness, it was no surprise she had chosen this specimen. It didn't scream virgin, it didn't hint at skank ho. A smattering of pearl beads and Swarovski crystals allowed the eyes to dance and linger on the dress's curves.

Wait. Those were my curves. I turned one way in the mirror, then the other way. Its bodice was modest, with a sweetheart neckline, but had a gauzy lace coverlet attached that draped down the shoulders in a sleevelike attempt. I flapped my elbows out: bat wings.

I turned and peeked over my shoulder. The lace dipped to a V at the waist, allowing much of my phoenix tattoo to show, but not all. The skirt was long but not too busy, with tiers of scalloped fabric. At least it had one thing going for it: it made my waist look minuscule.

When I was twelve years old, my favorite comic was the giant-sized annual, #21, of *The Amazing Spider-Man*. It was the special wedding edition and featured Mary Jane Watson and Peter Parker standing as bride and groom in front of a crowd of well-wishers, with a big heart-shaped Spidey face in the background. To my preteen sensibilities, M.J.'s dress was the epitome of gorgeous at the time. I had read somewhere that a real-life fashion designer had created the wedding gown especially for the comic book bride. It had a mermaid-style skirt that clung all the way past her thighs before fanning out, down to the floor, and a Playboy Bunny–style top softened by an overlay of sheer fabric up to her neck. M.J. looked as if she had been poured into the thing, and she hung on Peter's arm and smiled a carefree, million-bucks-lottery smile. *That* was happily ever after to me.

Until, of course, alternate-universe issues of *Spider-Man* were released, along with the "One More Day" plot that erased the marriage from both their memories.

In comicbookland, anything was possible, and improbable.

"Checkout is at eleven A.M. . . ." Noah's teasing reminder brought me out of my reverie.

"Give me another minute." I leaned on the bathroom counter and stared down the girl in the mirror.

In an alternate universe, this could be my dress. My wedding. In an alternate universe, my dad would've stuck around long enough to walk me down the aisle. But life, as Allen had reminded me, wasn't comicbookland.

The girl in the mirror stuck her tongue out at me.

"Now, now," I said to her. "Be polite."

She smiled demurely. Then she reached up and pinned one side of her hair back with the rhinestone clip I had stashed in my cosmetics bag for Hawaii. She popped a breath mint and glossed her lips. And with a wink, she reached for the doorknob.

"Hey, now, look at you!"

"Speak for yourself," I mumbled, suddenly feeling self-conscious. Noah was in his blazer.

"I thought you might feel more comfortable if I got back in the monkey suit."

"You could be wearing a gorilla suit. That wouldn't make me feel any less foreign in this thing." I wriggled a bit. "Itchy."

"So not exactly the dress of your dreams, huh?"

"What do you think?" I asked, hands on hips. I could feel the corset bones under my fingers getting tighter by the minute. I had to pee, too. But that was another story.

Noah cocked his head. "This part is nice." He waved his hand in the vague direction of what my mother would refer to as my décolletage, but I wasn't about to utter that word. "Maybe get rid some of that stuff"—he gestured to the lace overlay—"or make it a shawl or something." Secretly, it was kind of fun watching him struggle to find the words.

"Admit it. It's a nightmare."

"Yeah," he hastily agreed. "It's pretty bad. But that's good."

It was my turn to cock my head at him and his logic.

"Your mom chose this dress. This is her dream, for herself. Not for you. You have your own dreams that you would choose. Hers don't fit you." He paused by my shoulder. "Nice tat, by the way."

I turned this way and that in the length of the mirrored closet doors. My wings were clipped. I frowned at the thought. How drolly appropriate, my mother finding a way to hold me back once again.

"You're quite philosophical at a quarter past midnight, aren't you?" I commented to both the girl in the mirror and the guy standing next to her. Neither responded, except to provide a twisted smile.

"So what's the story behind the phoenix?" he asked.

"Sacrifice and renewal," I said simply and left it at that.

I had gotten the tattoo shortly after the Javits Center debacle with Allen. A reminder that if I ever felt the urge to look back, I should, well . . . look back at it. I'd offered my memories of Allen up to the rebound gods and vowed to reinvent myself as a sharper, more focused Laney.

But, like the tattoo itself, those lines had blurred a bit over the years and faded. The pain was a vague memory, buzzing permanently below the surface.

"Oh, wait. Something borrowed." Noah fetched his red Converse high-tops from where I had ditched them near the door and held them out to me.

"Perfect!"

They looked even more Bozo-hilarious peeking out from under the flouncy gown. I gathered a bit of the skirt at the waist so I wouldn't trip and did a little soft-shoe shuffle in them.

With a bow and a flourish, Noah held out a hand. As soon as I accepted, he maneuvered us in fluid circles through the hotel suite.

"Shall we expand the dance floor?" he suggested, swinging the door open. I twirled right under his arm and out into the hallway.

"That's one long 'aisle,'" Noah commented, with a nod of his chin toward the end of the hallway. "Let's boogie."

"Where'd you learn such smooth moves?" I laughed as he waltzed us past the elevator doors. He may not have been the master of freestyle on the dance floor, but he cut a respectable rug.

"Junior cotillion." He grinned, leading. "El Paso, Texas."

"And that was city number . . . ?"

"Four and six. While my dad was at Fort Bliss."

"Bliss, that sounds . . . blissful." I laughed, then squealed as he dipped me dangerously low to the hallway carpet.

The doorway of 1209 across the hall flew open, and out popped a head full of hot rollers. We had apparently disturbed our neighbors. The woman's sourpuss expression softened upon sight of me in the dress and Noah in his suit. Behind her came a gruff male voice, demanding to know what all the ruckus was.

"Oh, pipe down, Hal," she said with a sigh. "They're just newly-weds. You remember what that was like, right?"

With a smile and a shake of her hot rollers, she clicked the door closed.

Noah and I stifled our giggles and fled back to the safety of our room before bursting out laughing.

"Oh, wait. We forgot something old."

Noah unwound the green wire stem of his boutonniere and pulled it from his coat's lapel. I recognized the small red flower now: it was one of those crepe-paper poppies the war vets handed out in exchange for a donation in front of the post office every Memorial Day. I had always equated them with Santas ringing bells outside department stores during the holidays and regarded them as the same: an annoyance. But now, after hearing how Noah had lost his father, I began to grasp the significance. It was telling that he had managed to keep the delicate flower intact from May till March.

He reached for one of our empty minibar bottles and popped the bloom into it. "There," he announced. "A bouquet for the blushing bride. It matches your shoes."

"Thanks." I clasped the bottle between both hands and smiled up to the sky angelically.

"Gorgeous."

"Oh, please," I scoffed. "I'm just the lowly dress bearer."

"Hold that pose." I heard a click, and then another.

"Hey, who said you could take blackmail photos?"

"These will be just between you and me, promise."

Thank goodness he was staring at the phone and not witnessing the goofy smile spreading across my face.

"What's your number?" he asked.

I recited it and watched as he entered the info into his phone.

"There," he said, hitting a final button. "Saved. And when's the wedding?"

"Saturday, at three o'clock."

"Okay, setting a task reminder . . . Nevada will be two hours ahead of Hawaii, so . . . there we go. I'm going to send these to you while your mom is walking down the aisle so you can have a good laugh, okay? Come on—selfie!" Noah squeezed in next to me and held up the phone to capture both of us. "And to remind you," he murmured, his cheek practically pressed against mine, "that you are an incredible person, with or without her approval."

I inhaled his amazing scent, and breathily exhaled my thanks. "Wait, I think my eyes were closed. Take another?"

"You got it."

Shameless excuse, but it kept him closer for another few seconds.

Noah

CROSSING THE LINE

She was just the dress bearer?

That changed everything.

Actually, Laney passing out changed everything. Part of me was disappointed, because I wanted to stay up all night talking with her. I can't remember the last time I had so much to say or felt so in tune while listening to someone else. But the more practical part of me knew it was better to get some sleep. It was oh-dark-thirty, as Pop used to say. Beyond late. Time to let gravity take over. And reality.

She looked divine in that dress. Something about the color made her skin shimmer. I thought about the way the back of the gown scooped below the bones of her shoulders, allowing all but the tips of her fabulous wings to show through. I know they say that every bride looks magical in her wedding gown, but forcing Laney to put on a dress that wasn't even hers turned the table on every tradition and old wives' tale I had ever heard.

I had no idea what Sloane's dress looked like; its classified intelligence was tighter than national security. All I knew was its "say yes or else" price tag was roughly the same as a compact car's. And many shouting matches between her, the bridal consultant, and poor seamstresses had ensued over the months it took to choose, purchase, fit, and alter the dress. I remembered the look on my mother's face when I had to break the news that Sloane didn't even want her to come dress shopping with the bridal party. Having no daughters of her own to marry off, I knew Mom had hoped to be more included in the planning festivities. But looking back, I was relieved she hadn't been subjected to that couture cage fight.

Laney sighed in her sleep as I carefully arranged the coverlet around her. She had passed out in the damn dress, and I debated whether to try to rouse her to get her out of it. One arm was up in a "Walk Like an Egyptian" move, and her knees were tucked to the left and hidden under the poufy layers of wedding fabric. Her hair was like caramel sauce pooling down a scoop of creamy vanilla ice cream as she turned her head on the pillow and settled deeper into slumber.

She mumbled something that sounded like *"kissloafer"* to me.

I rolled gently off the bed and did a parameter check. Door locked, lights off. Then I crossed to my side of the zebra Duck Tape. The only thing in my carry-on that passed as sleepwear was a pair of Tommy Bahama swim trunks. I wasn't sure what I had been thinking when I packed them. Perhaps that I would just laze around by the hotel pool in Vegas, waiting for my luggage, in the event it was misplaced? Ironic. They came in handy as I climbed into the padded Jacuzzi to go to sleep.

I stole one more glance at Laney. In just the quiet light of the gas fireplace, she looked like an angel, caught under a light, gauzy layer of snow. A true snow angel.

My dad used to bring home snow globes whenever he traveled. In fact, that was usually how he would break the news to me that we were moving once again. He'd place a different trinket on my palm each time, its liquid world churning, and announce, "You're going to love this place, son."

Some of them were frighteningly ornate: heavy glass domes on delicate bases of porcelain. Glycerin in the liquid would slow the descent of the glitter inside. Others were just cheap plastic, filled with water and glitter that clumped stubbornly in one spot. I had always hoped that one of our new homes would feel like the magical world suspended inside, but in the end, all the places felt the same. And we were never really there long enough to find out.

But tonight, sealed in a room full of warmth and light while the snow swirled beyond the windows in the dark sky, with a stranger like Laney, I could think of no better place to be.

Reality could wait a few more hours.

Noah

WAKE UP AND SMELL REALITY

I woke to my cell phone alarm chirping and Laney's insane Batman-from-Hell talking clock yammering. Before I had a chance to ponder what was worse to wake up with, a raging headache or a raging hard-on, she was up in a flash and pacing around the Jacuzzi nest like an angry white swan.

"I could've drooled on it or puked on it. Or worse!" she railed. Cradling her face in her hands, she moaned. "My head feels like a coconut that someone was bashing a straw into all night. Like they sucked it dry and tossed it on the beach."

"That's quite an image."

She was quite an image, but I didn't dare tell her that. *Mind over matter*, I instructed my nether regions. *Think kittens. And grandmothers. Kittens in baskets. Grandmas holding kittens in baskets.* "I believe there were bottles of coconut water in the vending machine, if you want to replenish."

"I blame that stupid vending machine and its lame-ass excuse for a dinner! I'm not usually such a lightweight."

Her left arm flailed over her head and her right stretched behind her, elbows flapping like a demented chicken. She hopped. "I can't unzip this thing, help!"

"Stand still, I'm kind of seeing double."

I pulled myself up out of the Jacuzzi bed and surveyed the zipper situation. Holy hell. It started above the small of her back and went down to no-man's-land. With shaking fingers, I carefully eased the zipper down an inch, then froze.

"I'll take it from here, thanks."

She was sliding away and slamming the bathroom door before I knew it.

Great, Noah. Way to go catatonic at the sight of her leopard-print panties. I ran my hands through my hair and surveyed the room. How much had we drunk? I counted a dozen minibar bottles. At some point during the evening, Laney had duct-taped them together into a glassy bouquet. They perched in the ice bucket, its ice long melted. I fingered the remembrance poppy poking from the neck of the middle one before plucking it out and winding it back into the buttonhole of my overcoat.

I should call my mother, I thought. It wasn't like me to go completely off the grid.

The shower hissed on.

It wasn't like me to have a naked girl in my hotel shower, either.

I envisioned Laney, turning into the spray to rinse soap off those flaming wings tattooed across her naked back . . .

No amount of cute, cuddly kittens in baskets was going to keep me from getting turned on at *that* thought.

Flight times. Go check the flight times. I pulled up my browser window and navigated my mouse to the refresh button. But the search bar to its right was just so tantalizingly blank. What harm could a quick search do? I typed in *Alan Burnside* and quickly got schooled on misspelling his name. *Allen Burnside,* the search engine's display read beneath a small montage of photographs, *was an American drummer who played in the band Three on a Match.*

Was.

I clicked the first link.

1982–2011.

I'll take "Dead Boyfriends in Bands with Numbered Names" for five hundred, Alex.

Poor Laney.

Her schoolgirl dreams crushed. Her schoolgirl crush, just a dream now.

Thinking back to her drawings and the things she had said, it was easy to piece some of the details together now. Allen was the guy on the beach, the "flunky" her mother didn't want her to follow out to California. He was the guy who gave her the best and worst night of her life at the Lake Shore Hotel. He was the rocker who dated supermodels.

And now he was dead.

I remembered how she had closed the book and held it close, claiming there were wrongs in there she could not right.

Her sketchbook sat by the Batman clock on the nightstand. Probably a few flips through the pages would provide me with a breathtaking rendering of this girl's past. Moments she had captured in time to ponder, to work through. To lose herself in.

Private property, Noah. Not cool.

Besides, what good would it do? In a few hours we'd each take to the sky and leave behind the few surreal, slightly drunken hours we'd spent in each other's company. We would both become each other's doozy of a flight delay story, to be told over drinks in another hotel bar. I didn't need to know her life story.

But I craved to know her.

I heard the shower turn off. Minimizing the browser, I turned my mind to other things, like dismantling the Jacuzzi nest.

All those Elvis tunes I had joked about the night before looped through my head. Around and around they went, like my parents when they used to waltz through the living room to Elvis's "It's Now or Never." My mother had always had a soft spot for the King, and that song especially, as it was sung to the tune of her favorite Italian folk song, "O Sole Mio."

I debated whether to pull up Laney's zebra-striped no-fly zone, but ended up leaving it. I was sure housekeeping had seen far kinkier stuff left behind. It's not like we had fashioned duct-tape handcuffs on the bedposts.

The Naughty Sleepover cards were still scattered on the floor.

Name one thing you wish you had done differently, I heard in my hungover state, her voice just a hazy recollection. As I bent to retrieve the cards one by one, my mind automatically gave answers different from the one I had voiced the previous night.

I wish I hadn't groveled like a dog to Bidwell in that morning meeting.

I wish I had just packed up my desk and left right then and there.

I wish I could rip Sloane's hold on me off like a Band-Aid, smooth and quick, and tell her how I really feel.

I wish I didn't care so much about what other people thought.

I wish I had kissed that girl on the plane.

Laney. The dress bearer.

The thought of her lugging that dress around like a sack of couture potatoes made me smile.

God, we were both such a mess.

"It's all you."

"Huh?"

I turned to find Laney standing in the bathroom doorway, back in her traveling clothes, with a towel turbaned atop her head. She had the dress back in the bag and draped over her arms.

"Your turn."

"Oh. Thanks."

We brushed wordlessly by each other. That sweet smell of hers reminded me of pulling pink tufts of cotton candy from a paper cone as a little kid at the fair. It made my head spin and my mouth water.

What was wrong with me? Normally I ran my life like I coded an app, moving carefully and methodically along, allowing no distractions. Suddenly I was daydreaming and cyberstalking. What was it about this girl? I closed the bathroom door and leaned against it for a moment to get my bearings.

Her makeup bag was on its side, its contents spilling across the counter. It was unbelievably small to have contained that much stuff: like the clown car of cosmetic bags. Sloane never traveled with less than her case, a professional one that had a split-hinge top and a lock. Her lipstick selections alone would bust the seams of Laney's bag.

There was no sighting of the source of the warm sugar cookie smell, no perfume or lotion bottles to prove to me that she didn't naturally produce that heady scent that made me salivate like one of Pavlov's dogs.

I noticed an almost full, uncapped tube of toothpaste, dented in various spots from where she must have gleefully squeezed and released it without giving it a second thought. Mine, in contrast, was flattened and rolled neatly from the bottom up. Its cap was on, straight and tight. All my life I had been the kind of guy who carefully pushed from the bottom and worked his way up, slowly, methodically. Taking my time to make sure I was on the right path before moving forward.

Congratulations, Ridgewood. You've just summed up your entire life using a tube of toothpaste.

"You decent?" she called.

"Um. Yeah." I poked my head out the door. "What's up?"

"Forgot to grab a few things."

I pulled the door wider and she squeezed by.

"Whose idea was it to rebook us at ass o'clock in the morning?" she grumbled, tossing one item after another willy-nilly into her cosmetics bag.

"Um, your mother's?"

She gave my reflection in the mirror a dark look.

"It's an hour later than in New York, at least," I added.

With one swipe, she knocked the rest of her products back into her bag and hustled out.

I had no more witty one-liners for her that morning.

Ladies and gentlemen, Elvis has left the building.

Dashboard Confessional

Hangover city. And I was in a hotel room with exactly zero coffee, zero Tylenol, and precisely one hot guy, whistling in the shower. My head throbbed. No matter how hard I had brushed my teeth and how much toothpaste I had used, they still felt like they had mittens on them. My mouth was dry and cottony. Blech.

I flopped down onto the bed, next to where I had laid the garment bag out. After being forced into wearing it the past night, I regarded it slightly different in the morning light. Sort of like the morning after you had a nightmare; the dark shadows in the room didn't look so spooky come sunrise. I touched the crumpled thick plastic of the zippered bag. Maybe the dress, having been worn, was slightly more yielding.

Maybe this was the beginning of a truce. A democracy, forged between the layers of eggshell white silk and taffeta, the beads and sequins, and myself.

Maybe.

I smiled; Noah was whistling that Talking Heads song again. The previous night was a haze, but what I remembered hadn't been all that bad. More fun, in fact, than I had thought being delayed and snow-bound could ever be.

Speaking of which, it was probably a good idea to check my flight status. I sat up too fast and felt a head rush, not unlike when Noah had twirled and dipped me in our hallway waltz. I knew he wouldn't let me fall, but it had still given me a scary thrill.

Noah's laptop glowed warm and invitingly on the hotel desk. I marveled at its neatness, everything he needed stored in a straight line of folders down the right-hand side of the screen. I thought of my own office space at home, with both my physical and my virtual desk-top in perpetual disarray.

Navigating the mouse to the dashboard, I went to click the browser but landed on the widget next to it. Oops. I swerved back like a race car driver and hit the correct icon, but not before iPhoto popped open.

I might have had a hard time saying the name Sloane, but pictur-ing her wasn't going to be a problem. Not when a million thumbnail photos of her clawed their way into my brain:

Sloane at a regatta in sailor whites, toasting the camera with her champagne glass. Sloane in a bikini on a schooner, her sunglasses and her smile movie-star large.

Sloane before the boob job, Sloane after the boob job.

Sloane cutting the ribbon at a new nightclub, Sloane making the duck face, Sloane eating calamari, Sloane, Sloane, and more Sloane.

Photo after photo displayed her obvious beauty and wealth; demon-ized her. And pretty much desensitized me. Just another pretty face.

That was, until I saw the one lone photo of Sloane and Noah, toward the bottom of the screen.

The rock that hung from her finger was huge, as her hand splayed coyly across her lips. *I've got it all,* her smile mocked. *I win.* She was propped up on her elbow, leaning in toward Noah, who was in profile. Kissing her cheek. His eyes were closed. But hers were open, as if she were taunting the camera. *Go ahead,* her eyes seemed to say. *I dare you.*

I felt a little sick to my stomach. Maybe it was guilt for spying. Or maybe because I wanted to take that challenge. She didn't deserve to have it all. And she certainly didn't seem to deserve Noah. I hit the little red X at the top of the window and closed it, turning my attention to the Internet for my flight. But something familiar caught my eye.

Noah came into the room, dressed and rubbing his head with one of the hotel's fluffy white towels.

"You *Googled* Allen?"

He froze, towel in hand, at my accusation.

"With your vast knowledge of computers, you consulted the divine oracle of *Wikipedia* about my love life? How dare you!"

"What were you doing on my computer in the first place?" Noah demanded, striding over and taking possession of it.

"I wanted to check my flight time."

"Yeah? Then why is my iPhoto open?"

I had exited out of the picture gallery, but I hadn't closed the program, apparently.

My temper flared; how dare he get angry with me! Sneaking a look at his rich, gorgeous girlfriend was hardly on par with him cyberstalking my dead boyfriend. I wanted to grab the wet towel draped across his neck and smack him with it. Hard.

"I guess I hit the wrong button by mistake," I said, glaring defiantly at him.

"Well, how would you feel if I said I turned a page in your sketchbook by mistake?" His words sent my heart pounding. "I didn't, by the way, touch your sacred book. All I looked at was one lousy website."

My eyes blurred down the timeline of text. "Well, Allen was more than just . . . just this jumble of discography and death. He was . . ." I struggled for words and breath, "he was my home. My heart. My best friend."

"So you got back together? After all?"

"After everything." I nodded.

Ever after.

"Ten years too late," I whispered, "but better late than never."

Never after.

I marched over to the bedside table and deposited Allen's Batman clock and the picture of my cat back into my bag. "He didn't have the big rock star, better-to-burn-out moment, okay?" I grabbed my sketchbook. "There was nothing sudden or romantic or mysterious about it." I flipped page by page as I continued my rant. "He didn't die in a bathtub like Jim Morrison; he didn't walk into a river and never return like Jeff Buckley."

I dropped the open book across the keyboard of his computer and gestured for him to take a look. The panel I had drawn had a *MEANWHILE* . . . caption box up at the top. A hospital bed, a machine marking vitals could be seen. And a tiny, wavy balloon holding only breath marks. In art school, we called them "cat's whiskers" or "fireflies." At work, they were known as "crow's feet." They usually came before and after a cough or sputter to help the reader visualize the actual sound.

When you use a set of breath marks with no word in between, it looks like a tiny burst bubble. Usually indicating unconsciousness of a character.

Or death.

No visualization needed.

"Cancer just goes on until it's done. And then *you* go on," I said softly.

Noah gingerly picked up the book, cradling it open-faced in his large palm and gazing at it. With his other hand, he clicked his laptop shut. Then he set the book on top and closed it.

"Laney," he began and reached for me.

"Don't," I said. "Don't do that because you feel sorry for me."

"I'm not," he said quietly. I closed my eyes as his thumb ghosted along the top of my brow, brushing my bangs off my forehead. Warmth radiated at my temple as his fingertips lingered. I felt his lips touch my forehead, not a kiss of consolation, not one for good luck. Whatever it was, it was exactly what I needed, right there and right then.

We stood just like that, for a while, and I don't think either of us wanted to be the one to break the seal.

"Come on," he finally murmured against my skin. "We've got places to be, flights to catch, and people to see, right?"

Noah

GOTOHAIL

"Oh, thank you, little baby Jesus."

Laney had spotted a Keurig in the lobby the minute we stepped out of the elevator. She made a beeline to the machine while I dropped the key cards at the front desk.

I turned to find her holding the hanger of the garment bag in one hand, an unopened packet of sugar in the other, and staring blankly at the steaming cup of joe on the counter in front of her. Jeez, she really couldn't function without caffeine.

"One lump or two?" I asked.

She growled at me. I didn't take it personally. She had warned me she was a bear without her caffeine. Whatever anger or hurt that may have lingered over the Google and iPhoto incident had dissipated. It was as if we'd locked up all that we had revealed to each other during the drunken evening and hungover morning and sealed it with that innocent forehead kiss, leaving it behind with a Do Not Disturb sign on the door. And all that was left was a comfortable calm.

Obviously she didn't want me messing with her coffee, so I wordlessly relieved her of the garment bag instead. She went to work, smacking the sugar packet on her palm like a junky prepping his arm for a vein.

"I'm going to survey the transportation situation. Meet me outside. After you've had your fix."

Arriving in the previous day's late afternoon blizzard, I had been unable to see three feet in front of me. Now the sun glinting off the snow was blindingly bright, and I could see the Regency was just one of several hotels on the road, close to the slow-moving snarl that was I-294.

The hotel staff was out scattering salt on the walkways, and the white-gloved doormen were huffing cold clouds of breath in their labor as they pushed winter to the curbs with their shovels. It was the heavy, wet kind of snow that made your bones cold just looking at it. Across the way, several cabbies were hunched over, digging impacted snow from their wheel wells where the street plows had repeatedly pushed it. The road was still a mess of slush and drifting snow, and the wind whipped a reminder that its wrath wasn't quite through yet, despite the cold, hard glare of the sun.

"You've got to be freakin' kidding me."

Laney was next to me now, coffee in hand, looking slightly more chipper. Staring at the huge queue waiting for cabs and the measly number of cars rolling up to the taxi stand, she groaned. "This is going to take forever!"

I smiled. "Actually, more like three minutes." I held out my phone for her. "See the star on the map? That's our location. And the pulsing red dot? That's Ruel. He's driving a 2011 Signature L Lincoln Town Car and he's coming to pick us up."

Laney's eyes were more hazel than green in the bright morning light, and they widened. "Let me guess: one of your fancy apps?"

"Yep. I just plug in my location, and it works off a pool of partici-pating car services in the area. The driver closest pings you back to tell you arrival time and estimated fare based on your input destination. Everything is included—tolls, tips—and payment is done through the app so no money even exchanges hands."

"That's fan-freakin'-tastic," Laney exclaimed, as the pulsing red dot—and the car itself—turned onto our street.

I thought so, too . . . aside from the unsettling fact that Sloane's father owned half the fleets in the Midwest and a few in the tristate area as well. His backing of this app venture was apparently his equivalent of a dowry that, he'd warned me in no uncertain terms, I could kiss good-bye if the wedding didn't happen.

Like the doormen pushing snow off the walk, I shoveled the thought to the back of my mind; it was too heavy to deal with at the moment.

"Ruel's got a five-star rating. That means he speaks great English, knows the local roads, keeps his car clean, and is a good conversationalist," I explained. "Riders can rate their experience afterward, and the drivers, in turn, can rate the user."

"That is wild," Laney marveled.

Ruel pulled smoothly up to the least slushy part of the curb and hopped out. "Good morning, Mr. and Mrs. Ridgewood. Let me help you with your bags."

I winced, anticipating Laney's reaction, but she merely giggled. "Hey, it got us free champagne," she reasoned, "twice. And the last available hotel room in Chicago." Ruel held the door for her, and she dipped into the luxury sedan as regally as a queen. "Own it, Noah."

"Hi, Ruel." I grinned. "Careful, we've got a wedding dress on board."

I handed off the bulky bag, and he carefully draped it over our luggage before securing the trunk with a wink.

"I trust you had a good night, sir?"

"One of the better ones, of late." I ducked in after Laney, who was already playing with all the buttons on the car's interior like a little kid.

"Look! Heated seats back here!"

She popped her coffee into the cup holder and waved to the

grumpy-looking crowd still waiting for any sign of a cab on the horizon. "Later, suckers."

"Too bad they didn't GoToHail."

Laney lifted a brow in my direction. "GoToHail? Who comes up with these app names, anyway?"

I chuckled. "Geeky computer software guys, after one too many drinks at their hotel bar. I was out at a convention in San Francisco when the idea came to me."

"You travel a lot, then? For work?"

"Yeah. But I've always been used to moving around. We picked up stakes so many times when I was a kid."

"I guess it makes sense, then, that you try to make traveling as hassle free as possible. Airplane seat assignments, translation devices, car service apps. Is this the one that made you the gazillion dollars?" she queried.

"I never said a gazillion," I mumbled, shifting in the seat, which was growing warmer by the minute. "A solid six figures, maybe. But no, it was a different app."

Laney squirmed and fiddled with the buttons. "Wow, there's a fine line between warming your butt and feeling like you wet your pants."

I laughed; her quirky, honest opinions were such a turn-on.

"So . . ." She sidled closer and leaned on my shoulder. "Which app was it?"

"It's not that important." I made to slide my phone into my jacket pocket, but her fingers were lightning fast.

"Come on, show me."

She tapped my display but couldn't find a way off the main screen.

I pried the phone from her hands. "I don't let the ladies touch my app on the first date," I joked.

"Oh, God, you're calling *that* our first date? If so, I want a do-over." She reached across my lap and swatted at the phone while I held it at arm's length. "I'm just going to touch them all," she threatened.

God, would it be so wrong to kiss her? Hell, it would be so easy right now. Her body was twisted toward me, her arm flailing across me in pursuit of the phone. All I had to do was reach behind her back with my free hand and pull her close. I could imagine the softness of her hair as I wove my hand through it, to the back of her neck, and—

"Fartrillion? Is that what I think it is?"

Talk about a mood killer. I surrendered my phone to her with a sigh. "Yes, and yes. That's the one."

"You designed a fart app?" she sputtered.

"I'm not proud of it."

"Oh, come on. Why not?" She was all up in my apps now, zooming around. "Where's the volume control?"

"It's so silly. It makes zero sense why that thing is a best seller and all my other ideas . . ." Laney giggled as a particularly rude noise burst from my phone. "It's like pissing in the wind," I finished.

"Oh, come on. Lighten up." To drive her point home, she hit the Squealer, the highest-pitched sample on the screen.

"Now you know why I never went to any of *my* class reunions. Can you imagine; I'd spend the entire evening fending off 'dude, pull my finger' jokes from all the jocks," I muttered.

"Matter-Eater Lad. Codpiece. Arm-Fall-Off-Boy. Granted, those were all DC. But Marvel has had some doozies, too. Asbestos Lady. Whizzer. Squirrel Girl."

"Your point?"

"Every successful enterprise has a few prototypes they aren't proud of. And there is no accounting for taste when it comes to the buyers' market. That's all," she said simply. She set my phone down on my thigh and wasn't quick in taking her hand away. "Just keep doing what you love."

I reached as though I wanted to take possession of the phone, but got her hand in the process. "Thanks." I gave it a gentle squeeze as I threaded my fingers through hers. She had artist's hands, for sure. Her nails were bare and close clipped, unlike Sloane's impeccably lac-

quered talons. And I could feel a bump on her index finger from where
she had gripped her pencil all those years.

"You're welcome," she said sweetly. "Why are you laughing?"

"So I guess coffee is your kryptonite, then?"

"What do you mean?" she asked.

"It turns you human again."

Laney grimaced. "Kryptonite never made Superman *human*. It
merely made him lose his powers. He became weak."

"Oh." I hesitated. "True."

"Unless you equate being human with powerlessness?"

Sloane came to mind, as did the meeting I had had the previous
morning with her father. "We all have our weak moments, that's for
sure." It was a nonanswer at best; the topic hit me in a sore spot
between my head and my heart.

She studied me for a moment. I felt heat blossom in my belly and
radiate upward. Instead of pressing me for further explanation, thankfully she changed the subject.

"I still can't believe you got me into that dress." She shook her head,
chuckling in disbelief.

"Yeah, usually guys try to get girls *out* of their dresses. I'm so not
normal."

"Eh." Laney bit her lip to fight back a smile and cocked her head.
"Normal's overrated."

"Totally."

For the first time in my life, I wished for Chicago traffic to stand
still. I'm talking bumper-to-bumper gridlock traffic, clogging every
major artery of the city. Anything that would keep her hand in mine,
on my knee, indefinitely.

No such luck.

"Uh-oh." Laney dipped into her bag and came up with her phone.
"I'm getting a text message, and it's way too early for Hawaii to be up."
Her text alert sounded like an elephant trumpeting. Or maybe it was

Godzilla roaring. "Shit. I don't believe this!" She tilted the phone to me. "My flight is delayed indefinitely. The airline is claiming 'system-wide computer problems.' Yet their text alert system is working just fine. Great. I'm screwed. Why me?"

"If it's systemwide, it's got to be affecting the entire country," I mused.

I knew a bit about the industry from developing the seat assignment app, and I knew that an airline's computer system was its intricate brains. Not only was it responsible for bookings and reservations, but it also managed online check-ins, ticketing, boarding pass printing, and bag tracking. Whatever was wrong with it, it didn't sound like a quick fix.

"How about you?" she asked.

Laney's mom had rebooked her onto a different airline. I thumbed through my e-mails to locate my new Windwest confirmation and clicked through to the flight's status. "Still on time."

"Well, whatever. I'll just camp out at the gate. This hotel lobby coffee is burning a hole through my gut. I'll eat something there and wait it out, I guess. Get some work sketches done."

The thought of getting on a plane to sunny Vegas and leaving Laney to eat a greasy airport breakfast, with just her sketchpad and that damned garment bag to keep her company, depressed me to no end.

She had moved away from me, her elbow propped on the door's armrest and her chin in her palm, gazing out at the icy gray Chicago landscape as it whizzed by. In another few minutes, the vast flat expanse of O'Hare Airport would come into view.

The tune to "O Sole Mio" echoed in my head. *Now or never, dude . . .*

I lowered the privacy partition.

"Hey, Ruel. Hang a left up here and jump on the Skyway."

"You got it, boss."

"But the sign for the airport is pointing that way," Laney exclaimed.

"I know. But we've got time to catch the best breakfast in Chi-Town."

Noah

CANDY GIRL

"Noah!" Laney protested. "The last thing I want is for you to miss your flight after the hassle you had yesterday. And think of your Vegas spreadsheet!"

"We left extra-early to catch your flight, and my flight was still a good hour later than yours," I reminded her. "There's room for food on the agenda."

"Oh, and I am sure you have just the app to locate it, right?" she teased.

"Actually, I don't need an app. Chicago was city number eight of nine that I lived in for a time. Ruel, we're taking the next exit. Then make the first right, okay?"

It had been at least a year since I had been to Jughead's Diner, but it had been an institution in my old River North neighborhood, so I assumed it was still there. And I knew it was the absolutely perfect place to bring a girl like Laney. Sure enough, my heart leaped when the twenty-four-hour blinking sign, shaped like a crown beanie, came into sight, and I heard Laney gasp in recognition.

"Oh, my God! Like Jughead Jones, from the old *Archie* comic?"

"Yep."

"How perfect; he was always obsessed with food." Laney was totally geeking out, and she was so cute. "I'll keel over if Pop Tate is working behind the counter."

"Doubt it. The place has been owned and operated by some sort of lesbian cooperative since the eighties. I've never seen a guy working there, come to think of it."

Laney was out the door before Ruel had managed to put the car in park, and she stood with her hands on her hips, staring up at the place.

"Sure you don't want to just grab an Italian Beef down the street at Portillo's instead?" I teased.

"No way."

The diner's small, boxy building was unassuming from the outside, but I knew she would flip out over the interior, as well as the food. Jughead's breakfast menu was the stuff of legend, as evidenced by the crowds.

"Can we keep you on the clock, Ruel? I think it might be a bit of a wait."

"I've got no problem with that. As long as you bring me back one of their famous chocolate bacon milk shakes, man."

"Deal."

Laney hesitated when I held the diner's heavy door for her. "Should we bring our stuff in?"

I realized that, other than our dance fever stint at the hotel bar, this was probably the farthest she had been from her mother's dress since she'd embarked on her trip. I didn't think it would hurt to distance herself from it for a little while, physically and emotionally.

"This place is hole-in-the-wall tiny. We're better off leaving it in the car. It'll keep."

Laney saw what I meant the minute we stepped inside. "Wow. Just . . . *wow*."

The tiny foyer was a roving landscape of Pez dispensers, hundreds and hundreds of them; every kind of character you could think of lined the wall-to-wall shelves. Above our heads was an AstroTurf field of tiny green plastic army men, glued upside down to the ceiling. Several couples and young families hovered in the vestibule, waiting for available tables.

"There're so many kids here. I bet schools are closed because of the storm," Laney observed.

"I've got room at the counter now, but a booth could be about a fifteen-minute wait," the hostess said.

"We'll wait for a booth," I said, reaching for my phone.

The Windwest page was still up on my screen, my flight, ironically, still on time. *For once in your life,* a voice inside me screamed, *grab life by the balls. Squeeze from the middle of the tube!*

Fuck it. I clicked on "change flight" and chose the nonstop leaving at 4:45 P.M., before glancing up guiltily. I needn't have worried; Laney was no longer next to me. I spied her kneeling in the corner where several brightly colored pillows and stacks of books and magazines kept children and adults alike cozy and occupied. She and a little girl, probably around six or seven years old, were busy coloring and gabbing away, while the girl's parents pored over a menu nearby.

"Would you look at that," I said, shaking my head upon approach. "Now my flight is delayed."

"Ugh, really? Chicago is, like, purgatory or something!" Laney lifted her gaze toward me, and I saw brightness in it, reminiscent of my first encounter with her.

She had been camped out on the floor that time, too, at the gate back in LaGuardia. And she had been sketching then, as well. I'd stolen several glances at her while she worked, until she caught me. I knew all about "being in the zone" when you were doing something you loved, but Laney brought it to a whole other level. Laney brought it to life.

"At least there are colored pencils in purgatory," I observed, giving my trouser legs a tug at the knees before squatting down next to Laney and her new friend. The purse I had likened earlier to a leather motor-cycle jacket turned out to be a magical bag full of cool writing tools, as Laney pulled out one after the other.

I turned to the little girl. "Whatcha got there?"

"It's a bunny," she said, holding up her drawing and making it hop across the low coffee table before her. Laney had done a quick pen-and-ink sketch of a cute and fluffy bunny for her, and the girl had colored its fur a trippy rainbow of colors. "He's hopping through the snow to find his friends."

"This is Samantha," Laney supplied. "Are you done with that one, honey?"

"Yes. His name is Bruce. He's my friend, and he's alllllllll done."

"Cool, don't forget to sign your name. All good artists sign their names at the bottom of their creations," Laney said. "This is my friend Noah. And he's—"

Something had caught her eye behind me. I turned and saw a magazine rack lining the wall. Oh, for the love of Pete.

"He's one of 'Thirty under Thirty'?" Laney finished, hopping up and reaching for the dated *TechnoByte* magazine. She grinned, dancing the tattered cover back and forth between her fingertips in front of me.

"Hmm, they really need to update their magazine collection around here."

"Stop with the modesty! You didn't tell me you were the poster boy for"—she tilted the magazine so she could read the title—"*TechnoByte* magazine. But it makes total sense, Tech-Boy."

She brazenly tucked it into her bag.

"You're stealing it?"

"I need something to read on the plane."

"Laney, will you sign my picture, too?" the girl asked shyly.

"Of course I will, Sam-I-Am."

"Hey," the little girl exclaimed in wide wonder, "my uncle calls me that! Did they have Dr. Seuss when *you* were little?"

"Sure did," Laney replied, sending a wink my way. "*Green Eggs and Ham* was my very favorite, too. Think it's on the menu here?"

"If it's not, it should be," I murmured.

Samantha scrawled her name in the top right corner. She took extra care with her *M*, but Laney waited patiently. When it was her turn, she rotated the paper to the left and signed it parallel to the rabbit's upturned foot.

"Noah, party of two!"

"That's us." Laney shifted from her cross-legged position up to her knees. "'Bye, Sam-I-Am, have a great breakfast. I hope Bruce finds his friends." She handed the girl a new sketch to color. It showed three happy bunny faces, hiding in the crook of a fallen log. Although it was a monochromatic sketch, Laney had looped what appeared to be large overhangs of snow along the log. But where the bunnies sat, it looked warm and safe and cozy.

"Thank you, Laney! Mommy, Mommy, do you have my crayons?"

I held out a hand to Laney and pulled her to standing. Smiling, she crammed her drawing materials back into her magic bag and we followed the hostess to our booth built for two.

The counter would have been fine to sit at, but I knew each of the booths held a theme, displayed in old comics pressed flat under the glass tabletop. I could recall every one of my meals here during graduate school simply by which table I had landed in: *Peanuts*, *Richie Rich*, *Millie the Model*—they were mostly older nostalgia comics, but there were more modern superhero comics as well.

Laney spread her fingers wide and flat in wonder. "Cheryl Blossom!" she breathed, as if she were greeting an old friend. "I haven't thought of her in years."

I pushed my menu aside and glanced down at the strips containing a buxom, smiling redhead. Sheesh, she looked like a caricature of the very girl sitting before me! It had been a long time since I'd gotten turned on just by looking at a drawing. I comforted myself with the fact that it was the likeness sending my mind into overdrive. And the fact that Laney's feet, still clad in my sneakers, were bumping against my ankles under the small table.

"Good morning, you two." Our waitress, a petite brunette with a rose tattoo snaking around her neck, gave us a knowing smile, as if she were in on some secret with us. "Coffee?"

"Please," I said gratefully.

"Actually, I'll have a root beer float," Laney said. "Two straws." She turned to me after the waitress left. "Seriously. Best hangover cure ever. You'll see."

We proceeded to order; my mouth had been watering for their crème brûlée French toast since we had pulled up in front of the place. Laney opted for the "Eighteen-Wheeler" breakfast, complete with three eggs scrambled, two pancakes, bacon, hash browns, toast, and a side of grits.

"Carb overload." She grinned. "Perfect for a cross-country flight. Maybe I'll sleep through the whole thing."

"Hey, I thought you were saving that for the flight," I protested, as she pulled out the magazine with my cover story and smoothed the pages out.

"Can't read it on board if I'm sleeping, now, can I?"

She was merciless.

"'Profiles on thirty of the most successful young innovators in the industry today,'" she read aloud. "Noah, this is seriously cool."

I glanced her way to see if she was joking, but she was totally absorbed in my half-page feature. "It's not exactly accurate anymore. I'm no longer under thirty."

"Is this accurate?" she asked, pointing at the box that showed my net worth in bold, blocky numbers.

"Um, yeah."

She let out a whistle. "That explains first class, then."

I had to laugh; I had said the same thing to her over our sushi lunch, back at the airport, when I learned the name on her bridal dress bag meant "pampered."

"You should be proud; this is a big accomplishment."

"Oh, I am." I had worked hard to get where I was by age twenty-nine. The number was not lost on me, thinking back to Allen Burnside's Wiki page. "I can't take full credit for landing the cover story, though. That was Sloane's doing. I think she knew the publicist or someone."

"That was nice of her," Laney commented.

"Yeah. She can be nice sometimes." It was supposed to be a joke, but it fell somewhat flat. "Sloane's not a monster, Laney. Sorry if I made it seem that way last night."

Airing my grievances to Laney about Sloane kind of felt like playing hooky from school. It had been thrilling and exhilarating while we were holed up together in the hotel. But now that we were out in public, in broad daylight, I felt a little paranoid and weird.

"She must be proud of you, too," Laney said, tucking my smiling glossy face back into her bag and retrieving her sketchbook.

"She probably would've been more excited had it been *GQ* or *Details*. Kind of like your mom with *The New Yorker*. But yeah, she thought it was bragworthy, for sure."

Leaning back with her sketchbook propped against the edge of the table, Laney smiled and dropped her gaze. I couldn't tell what she was drawing; all I could see was her hand moving, making broad strokes here, or tight, fluid movements there.

We chatted as she worked, about snow days we remembered having as kids and that feeling of utter reprieve when the TV announced that all schools in the area were closed. I didn't admit it to her, but I think I would've felt that same elation had both our flights been canceled at that very moment.

Is it really Laney making you feel that way, or is it just an excuse to delay reality? I told my mind to shut up and enjoy the distraction. I really didn't want to consider the source right now.

She let me have a sip of her root beer float, which did seem to have hangover healing properties. Or maybe it was just the brain freeze combined with carbonation bubbles in your nose that took your mind off your hungover state.

"Look at us." She giggled as we simultaneously came up for air from straws on either side of the old-fashioned soda fountain glass. "We could be two teenagers at Pop Tate's Chocklit Shoppe after the sock hop. Like Cheryl Blossom and Archie Andrews! Gee willikers, and all that jazz."

"Who is she, anyway? I only remember Archie with Betty and Veronica." I sat back and sipped my coffee. The diner got it from Intelligentsia, a local artisan roaster, and it made me long for an all-nighter just so I could drink cup after cup of it.

"Cheryl Blossom was Archie's *third* love interest."

"Third time's the charm, right?"

Laney snorted. "According to some." She fiddled with her straw. "Poor Cheryl didn't last long during their teenage years. Apparently she was deemed 'too sexual' for a children's comic." She used air quotes to show her disdain for this theory.

"She does have it going on," I said, pointing to a strip of Cheryl on the beach in a teeny-weeny bikini. "That's a lot of junk in the trunk for a two-dollar comic."

Laney laughed. "I used to hate Cheryl for trying to steal Archie away from the other girls. She's the not-so-nice-but-still-sweet kind of rich girl. You know, the kind you love to hate, but you sorta love anyway? Mostly she's devious and conceited and will stop at nothing to get what she wants."

"Oh." My stomach clenched, partially from hunger but mostly from the fact that I was engaged to a girl who sounded just like Cheryl Blossom. I was thankful when the waitress reappeared with several plates that took up the entire table and covered the vixen smilingly wickedly up at me.

Laney was much easier on the eyes, anyway. And warm and three-dimensional. A girl who could sit coloring with a little kid one minute, and scarf down a meal fit for a trucker the next.

"Check it out," she said shyly, and held out her sketchbook over the eggs and bacon and French toast for me to take.

Oh, wow.

In light pencil, she had captured a cartoonlike me in a sequence of three panels across the page. Mostly from the chest up, sitting at the table. She kept my trench coat on and had raised the collar. My hair curled out in darkened points and chunks, falling characteristically away from my face and across my forehead like it did in real life. She had paid special attention to my cheekbones and eyes, I noticed. No speech bubbles or narration, just moments caught in time, capturing me unawares: adding sugar to the coffee cup in front of me, stirring said coffee and looking off into space, lips pursed in a jaunty whistle. I smiled and snuck a glance at her: watching her watching me looking at her work with a proud smile on her face. I wished someone had a camera to capture both of us.

The last box was my favorite. A close-up angle with elbows on the table, resting my chin in the palm of one hand and raising the cup to my lips with the other. Dark eyes flashing over the rim, one brow arched slightly higher than the other. The hint of a smirk peeked out from one side of the cup. "Is this how I look to you?"

"How?"

"I don't know. Remotely cool?"

"In a cartoony, *GQ*-ish kind of way?" She laughed. "Yeah, I guess."

Cartoon Noah looked impish yet aloof. I liked him.

"You're really talented, Laney. Why did you leave your job at Marvel?"

She shook her head as deliberately as she had shaken that Magic 8 Ball on the flight to Chicago. And her answer was just as vague. "Ah, you know . . ." *Reply hazy, try again later.*

"How do you do it?" I pressed. "Capturing that on the first go-round . . . with no eraser?"

She held out her hand for the book. "I've learned to tread lightly," she said, a softness in her voice. "I try not to use an eraser for mistakes, just as another artist tool."

With that, she molded a soft, white bit of eraser between her fingers and gently pushed it down on the last panel, making a soft highlight to the graphite darkening my raised brow. It was a subtle but perfect change. She gave me a shy and apologetic shrug before tucking her supplies away.

We silently dug into our meals, until her phone jangled to life next to her root beer float. "Oh, it's Danica. Sorry, I'd better grab it."

I nodded, taking the opportunity to check my e-mails. Nothing from Sloane, not even a forwarded e-mail through my secretary, Kiwi. And nothing from any of the wedding vendors. Perhaps my trip to Vegas would be good after all, giving Sloane time alone to consider my simple request.

There was a new text from Tim: **What time do you land, slacker?**

Change of plans, I thumbed back. **TTYL.**

Tim's response was almost immediate—and most definitely obnoxious.

Enjoy your lay . . . over, you lucky bastard!

"Yes, still alive . . ." Laney relayed into her flip phone. "I don't know, there's some systemwide bullshit going on now . . . Yeah, he's with me . . . Oh, get this—he thought you and I were getting married . . . I know! Okay. Hang on." She leaned across the table, gesturing at me with her phone. "She wants to talk to you."

"All right," I said slowly. This was a little weird. And kind of reminded me of high school, when girls you liked would put their friends on the line so they could size you up. "Hey, this is Noah," I said, because I didn't know how else to begin.

"Oh, good," came a smoky, radio personality voice. "So you're not a figment of her imagination. It's Dani."

"No, I'm quite real. Hi."

Laney was smiling at me and sipping the dregs of her float.

"I'm not on speaker, am I?"

"No. Do you want to be?"

"Uh-uh. I just wanted to thank you for keeping an eye on my BFF. We've all been kind of worried."

"Understandable."

"And one more thing. Just answer yes or no. Do you know about Allen Burnside?"

How the hell was I supposed to answer that? I didn't know how much there was to know. "A bit," I confessed.

"All right, then. I'll take that as a yes. Whatever she told you, though, is probably not the truth, the whole truth, and nothing but the truth. Remember that song 'Jack and Diane'? Yeah? Well, that little ditty was nothing compared to the classic that was Allen and Laney. Her breaking up with him right before prom was huge. So he left her in the dust for California; it was the cruelest summer ever. And then he proposed to her in front of a thousand people, at a concert of all places, ten years later, before earning his goddamned dash. It was like being left at the altar, only worse, because when she goes back home to our tiny town, she has to face tons of those people and see the pity in their eyes. And her mother? She gave Laney a big, fat 'I told you so' and Laney hasn't been able to move forward since. Classic case of self-fulfilling prophecy, you know? Her mother blames Allen, and Laney blames her mother; it's a total mess. So please know that I will hunt you down and kill you if you cause her any further pain. 'Mmkay? 'Byeee."

I found myself saying, "Nice speaking with you," even though she had already hung up.

"So when did you live in Chicago?" Laney asked, buttering her toast nonchalantly.

She either didn't want to know what Dani had said or didn't have to know.

Proposed to . . . like being left at the altar . . . pity . . . mess . . . pain . . . I compartmentalized her friend's confession, throwing it into the small rubber box section of my brain that allowed "WTF?" items to bounce around for a while until I could analyze and make sense of them at a later time.

"I came here for grad school at UC . . . the University of Chicago. I ended up staying to work and pursue my doctorate in computer science. I liked it here. But Sloane wanted to move back to New York."

She had been at Northwestern when we met, majoring in sociology with a minor in wife-ology. Definitely one of those rich girls with no true academic aspirations.

"Let me guess, Priscilla's from the Upper East Side?" Laney asked, stabbing a forkful of hash browns. "Summers in the Hamptons, winters in Aruba and Saint-Tropez? Matching salt-and-pepper Beemers for quick jaunts to the Cape?"

"Hey, don't make fun," I said, reddening. Mine was imperial blue, actually. And Sloane's was champagne quartz metallic. "But that is eerily accurate. How did you—"

"I'm a townie for life. I know all about people who summer." She stole a bite of French toast from my plate. "But I know you're not a native New Yorker. Home for you was . . ."

"Before Chicago? Seattle. City seven of nine. I did undergrad there, and that's where my mom still lives."

"Wow." Laney chewed on her bacon thoughtfully. Which reminded me I had to order Ruel's milk shake. I flagged down our waitress.

"Can we also grab a chocolate bacon milk shake?"

"With or without alcohol?"

"Seriously?" Chocolate and bacon sounded lethal enough. Since it was for our driver, I added, "Without, please. In a to-go cup, thanks."

Turning to Laney, I asked, "Wow, what?"

"I'm trying to imagine living on the opposite side of the country from my mother."

"You're an adult now. You said you were on tour with a rock band for half a year; you must've seen some cool places. What's stopping you from picking up and moving where you want?"

Wrong question. She prickled, and a steel door rolled down over her expression. Shuttering her off from whatever pain and guilt her past seemed to hold. I wished I could take it back, take her hurt and box it up and ship it off to parts unknown.

I thought back to the sketches she had shared the night before. And in the morning. What had really happened between breaking up before prom and Allen earning, as Dani had called it, his dash, at the age of twenty-nine? And why was she still not out from under her mother's thumb?

She swirled a bite of pancake around and around her syrup-heavy plate, doing figure eights and loopty loops.

"Long Island and Manhattan are all I've really ever known," she finally said. "I like islands. You sort of always know where you stand, you know?" She gave a short laugh. "You're either at the middle of it or at the edge of it. There isn't this, this . . ." She waved her arm in her search for words. "This whole gray expanse. I guess I'm more small-town-in-a-big-city kind of girl."

She looked lonely, and a little lost. *I will hunt you down and kill you if you cause her any further pain*, her friend's voice echoed through my ears.

"Let me show you a bit of Chicago," I pressed. "It's not New York. But it's a great city."

Laney finally popped the soggy pancake piece into her mouth and eyed me skeptically. Then she picked up her phone. "What time's your flight rescheduled for?"

"Four forty-five. But that could change again."

I wanted to keep spending time with her, in the middle of the country. I didn't want to think about the East Coast, where decisions weighed heavily. Or Vegas, where I had left my best boys hanging. Truthfully, they were probably having more fun on their own without me.

"Looks like I'm back on the grid," Laney said, thumbing through her messages. "New flight at four forty."

"Perfect, it's only eleven thirty. What do you say, Mothra?"

Our waitress arrived with our bill, Ruel's milk shake, and, instead of after-dinner mints, a small roll of Pez candies. Laney gave a little yip of excitement and dove into her magic bag, coming up with an Incredible Hulk Pez dispenser. She deftly loaded his green cylinder up and snapped it closed. With a smile, she set him facing me on the table.

"You just happened to have that in your purse, then?"

"Good-luck charm."

"Tell old Jade Jaws he needs to get cracking in the flight department," I said, sputtering a laugh.

Laney's fingers tipped Hulky's head and a pink Pez candy protruded in my direction, like he was sticking out his tongue at me. I pinched it out and popped it in my mouth.

"Do you believe in luck?" She cocked her head, contemplating me, perhaps anticipating my answer.

"I'm a numbers guy. I believe in statistics." Laney made a face. I spun the Pez dispenser toward her. "I believe in strategy and product placement."

"That's just fancy talk for being in the right place at the right time." She took two Pez for the road and gave me a grin. "Lead the way, Tech-Boy."

Noah

MAGNIFICENT MILE

Ruel was happy to sip his milk shake and cruise the town as I played host to Laney. In the city, the main streets were clearer and traffic wasn't its normal heavy assault for a Wednesday. Laney had fiddled with the heated seats until they were just the right temperature and sidled up next to me in the middle of the backseat so she could easily see through both windows as I pointed things out.

"Okay, Magnificent Mile might feel a bit like Fifth Avenue," I explained. "Lots of tourists and rich shoppers." Sloane could probably name every block from the Chicago River to the Near North Side by each of their landmark stores: Cartier, Escada, Bulgari, Van Cleef & Arpels, Harry Winston, Prada, Gucci, Tiffany & Co., just to name a few. "But it also has five of the world's tallest buildings."

Laney leaned over me, craning her neck and staring in wide wonder, as if she expected to see Batman leaping from one building to the next. I saw her hand reach for her sketchbook, but I gently pulled it out of her hands. "Look now. Sketch later," I advised.

She gave me a long look, then acquiesced. I gave a salute to the water tower staidly standing sentinel as Laney pressed her nose to the glass and tried to see how high the hotel next to it rose, its top half enshrouded in morning winter fog.

"Good thing you weren't here in December. You'd probably want to sketch the Santa Speedo Run down Michigan Avenue for charity," I ribbed her.

Laney shivered. "Brrr, sounds cold. And that would depend."

"On what?"

"On whether you were running it," she said slyly.

I laughed and flipped back to the diner picture of me. Cool *GQ* Noah might do something off-the-cuff like that.

He'd definitely squeeze the toothpaste from the middle of the tube once in a while.

"May I?" I asked, my thumb poised to flip back a page.

"You may."

The sketch before mine showed a gentleman also holding a cup of steaming coffee. But, unlike me, he was clasping his cup in both hands, grateful. A frayed cap sat atop what looked like a balding head, but his beard was full and bushy, and Laney had shaded it in various patches for a salt-and-pepper appearance. Wrinkles fanned out from the corners of his eyes, and while his lips were pursed to enjoy that first warm sip, you got the feeling his eyes were smiling.

"Kitchen of Hope," Laney said, glancing down, and then back out the window again. We were sitting in a bit of traffic, so people-watching was the only touristy thing to do. "I volunteer there sometimes."

"I think I've seen their sign before," I said, flipping to the picture before it: a young girl, cornrows in her hair, with a fork poised over a steaming plate. She looked unsure of where to dig in first, but the grin on her face spoke volumes. "Above Union Square?"

"That's the one," Laney said.

"How did you get involved there?" I asked.

"It actually started as my bat mitzvah project when I was thirteen.

My dad wanted me to understand that there was more to the day than just throwing a huge, lavish party and collecting lots of loot."

I fell quiet, thinking about passing the soup kitchen on my way to meet Sloane and her parents at the Altman Building just a few blocks away, the historic carriage house where our decadent reception was supposed to take place. It was staggering to think about spending two hundred dollars a plate on one meal, when that same amount of money could probably feed many more of Manhattan's hungry and deserving.

"Your dad sounds like a wise man," I said.

Laney made a production of tucking her sketchbook back into her bag. "Yep, Charlie Hudson's a wise man," she said, her voice breezy with false cheer. "And, as my mother would say, a born con man. Who else could convince a thirteen-year-old sucker to sign over all her bat mitzvah checks to him?" She ignored my stare. "Yep, that sucker would be me. My mom still hasn't recovered from that one. Irresponsible, head in the clouds, gullible Laney. Earned those nicknames all by age thirteen."

I swore under my breath. "You were just a kid. If you can't trust your parents at that age, who can you trust?"

"Yeah, he basically said the same thing. He promised to pay back every penny; he was just . . . in a bad way. I don't think he was lying," she said softly. "Desperate times call for desperate measures. The money must've paid off some of his debts, but not all. He used some of it to leave the country, and he hasn't been back since. Eighteen years ago this April."

No wonder her friend Dani was so protective. Laney had loss coming at her from every angle. "I'm sorry you had to go through that."

"Thanks." She fiddled with the seat warmer again. "When I was little, he used to kiss my forehead, kind of like you did today. For luck. So when things got bad, with the gambling and the divorce and stuff, I thought it was my fault. That somehow, the luck in me had run out. And I was no longer good enough. It's silly." She shook her head to rid herself of the thought and gave a little chuckle. "I know he loved me.

I was the apple of his pie, he used to say. You know, instead of eye? He was always silly like that. And he encouraged me to draw. He really believed in me. My mother, not so much."

We fell into silence as the car glided through green light after green light. I wondered if Laney surrounded herself with all the trinkets and tokens as an attempt to harness back some of that childhood luck she thought she lacked. I had the strongest urge to shield her, to leap out of the pages of her comic sketches as a superhero and protect her from further hurt. But my own reality pinned me to the ground. Its gravity, in every sense of the word, was pressing down and closing in.

"What do you say we do a little of Michigan Avenue by foot?"

"Sounds like a plan, Stan."

"Ruel, whatever it takes to keep you on the clock?" I began.

"No problem, my good man. Just page me when you're ready. I'll stay in the Michigan–Randolph area, okay?"

"Perfect." We didn't have too much time left, and I wanted to show Laney the Bean, Chicago's most famous tourist attraction. I had a feeling she would love it not only for its artistic value but for its magical properties as well.

Laney had talked about being a small-town girl, but she definitely had the big-city smarts built in. She walked the cold, congested streets with purpose, keeping her pace even with my long-legged strides. I imagined her conquering New York the same way and wondered whether we had ever crossed paths there. When you think about it, Manhattan becomes a bit of a small world once you've lived there a while. It's only a few miles wide and—what, twelve miles long? The thought of traipsing the same grid as Laney brought a smile to my face.

"What?"

Of course she had noticed.

"Nothing. I think we need reinforcements if we're going to stay outside," I told her, as we passed a street vendor selling hats, gloves, and scarves to the unprepared tourist and the random Chicago kid who *had* to have the latest street fashion fad. Laney gravitated right toward a zoo's worth of knitted animal hats on display.

"Aw," she cooed, plopping one on my head. "Sad panda!" Then she grabbed brown fleece earmuffs and dropped them over her own head. "Hey, do I look like Princess Leia? 'Help me, Obi Noah, you're my only hope.'"

I laughed, and we ducked down to see our reflections in the display mirror. The panda hat had a built-in scarf thing, with little flaps on the ends, decorated like paws, for your hands.

"As much as I appreciate the three-in-one combo, I think he's more your speed." I pulled off the hat. "Trade?"

"Deal. But only if you let me buy."

The earmuffs were seven dollars; I could swallow my chivalry for a cheap and useful gift.

Laney got herself the panda hat and a pair of woolen mittens that hid half gloves underneath a flap that could be pulled back and buttoned.

"Perfect for an artist, when winter inspiration strikes," she explained. "So where to?"

"First stop on the Noah Ridgewood ten-dollar tour . . ." I pointed down to the skaters whizzing around the ice rink in Millennium Park. "You game?"

Laney stopped in her tracks. "I'm game, but . . . I'm not good," she warned.

"Me, neither," I said, "but it's worth a shot."

We rented skates and stowed Laney's big biker purse in a locker. "Wait a sec!" She flung the locker back open and checked something in her purse. Relief swept across her face. "Oh, never mind."

"What?"

"I thought I had left my Hulk Pez behind. You know when they say your life passes before your eyes? I saw, like, the King Kullen checkout lane where he began his shelf life."

"You remember the supermarket where you bought him?"

"Yeah," she said softly. "Where Allen's mother had a job as a cashier. I was back on the island one day and she was working the register . . . I wanted to talk to her so I grabbed the first impulse item I saw and got on line: Hulk with lemon-flavored Pez candy. That's when I learned about Allen's cancer, his first diagnosis. We were still broken up then."

She looked down and took a long time lacing her skates.

"To this day, I cannot eat that flavor. Lemon Pez tastes like cancer. Cherry is fine."

I bent and double-tied her laces.

"Oh, I don't know about this," she warned, her ankles wobbling dangerously as she tried to stand. "I could be a hazard to myself and others out there!"

"It gets easier once you're on the actual ice."

I clamped a hand under her elbow and helped her hobble toward the rink. "So much cooler than Rockefeller Plaza, no?" I gave her a gentle push and she glided for about a yard.

"I don't know," Laney confessed. "I've never skated there. Way too—" Her arms flapped up to maintain her shaky balance. "Way too intimidating."

"You don't have to worry about that here," I assured her, skating in little circles around her as she practiced moving her feet back and forth in one spot without making any headway. "All different levels here. And isn't it amazing, amid all the buildings?"

"It's really pretty."

She gazed toward Michigan Avenue in wonder, but almost lost her balance in the process. I swooped in and caught her around her waist, righted her, and led us out toward the center of the ice in gentle, sweeping strokes.

"Noah Ridgewood, you lie like a rug," she laughed.

"I've had a few lessons." I smiled and shifted my weight, pulling her with me so she could get the rhythm. "I've lived in a few cold-weather cities over the years."

"Well, I grew up on a beach," she informed me. "The water got cold but it never froze. I'm feeling a little out of my element."

"You're doing great."

I raised her hand in mine and guided her by the small of her back so she could do a little spin underneath our raised arms. "See, almost like dancing."

"Almost," she admitted, as her left leg gave way like a baby giraffe's on its first day and she went down on her ass, laughing.

"My dad taught me how to skate by pushing two stacked milk crates along the ice in front of me," I told her, hauling her back up. "How about I'll be your milk crate?"

"I've called you worse things." She giggled, grabbing the sides of my overcoat from behind.

I gave a gentle shove off and she followed suit.

"Hey, not bad," she said, as we continued to glide along. I stayed as still as possible, but helped by leaning slightly forward and cheating every so often with a quick flick of my skate to help propel us. She was laughing so hard, eventually I was doing all the work and she was just hanging on and taking a joy ride.

"Wow, you are getting so good at this," I taunted as I began to take longer strides. We whizzed past the other skaters, Laney's shrieks lost to the wind. I grabbed her hands and turned quickly, and now skated backward, facing her and still pulling her along.

"Show-off! What do you think this is, the Ice Capades?"

"And you thought I was just in the glee club." I swirled her around.

"You're a lot more fun when you're not strapped down to that computer, you know."

"As are you, when you're not saddled down with that dress."

"Oh, you ain't seen nothing yet, mister!"

In a flash, she pushed off on bolder legs with the panda paws of her hat flapping behind her. I had no choice but to pursue. After all, she was a danger to herself and others out there.

She was doing surprisingly well, but I quickly gained on her. I got a hold of one of her panda paws and she squealed, her hair striking my cheek like a velvet whip as she tried to pull away and stumbled instead. She overcompensated to try to center herself and toppled right into me. We both went down together, bellies aching with laughter as people continued to zoom around us at dizzying speeds.

"You know what this ice needs?" she gasped. "Seat butt warmers, like in the car."

"I dunno, that might defeat the purpose," I managed between wheezes and snorts.

All the time and energy spent on jumping through hoops to make Sloane happy came to mind. It was exhausting and not very gratifying. Despite everything Laney had been through, despite her somewhat tough exterior, she had an inner joy that was infectious. Talking to her—hell, just being with her—was effortless. Easy—even as I pulled her sorry ass off the ice.

"Let's get out of here." I held out my hand, and she placed her mittened one in mine. She became my milk crate, and I pushed her, locked-legged, off the ice.

"Ah, now here's the best part of skating." I offered up a steaming cup of hot chocolate from Park Café to Laney once my Chucks were back on her feet and she had shaken all the snowflakes off her panda hat.

"I actually don't like hot cocoa. I know: how weird am I? But I'll hold it for a moment and warm up my hands." She took the cup and walked over to the park map as I went to grab her bag from the locker.

"Hey. Grant Park!" she exclaimed.

"What about it?" I asked, relieving her of the hot chocolate and taking a tentative sip.

"Can we go there, too? I want to see the fountain."

"It's closed for the season," I said hastily. "Nothing to see."

Laney put her hands on her hips. "Let me guess. A little app told you that?"

"No," I said lamely. "It's just common knowledge that they shut the water off in the winter." I gulped the cocoa a little too fast, scalding my throat as my ego took a slow burn as well.

I loved my second-to-last adopted hometown, but for me, visiting Buckingham Fountain would be like a criminal returning to the scene of the crime. I had proposed to Sloane there, and at this stage in our strange nuptial holding pattern, it was really the last place I cared to contemplate. But Laney was whistling the looping chorus of that stupid Frank Sinatra song and giving me the big sad panda eyes, in that silly panda hat. How could I deny that?

"We'll see," I allowed. "If time permits."

Laney grinned.

"So where's this mercury-flavored jelly bean? I must lick it."

"Cloud Gate?" I laughed. "I wouldn't advise it in this weather."

Despite the chilly conditions, people were out in droves, braving the weather to see Millennium Park's biggest treasure up close and personal. I remembered my first time gazing at what Chicagoans fondly call the Bean, coming at it from every angle and snapping a million pictures. It was a must-stop, and I was glad Laney was getting to see a little of the fun Chicago, instead of just the inside of the airport and the hotel.

As we made our way toward it, she grabbed my hand and yanked me back. "Oh, my God!"

"What?" There was no traffic endangering us, but I didn't exactly mind her grip on me.

"Watch."

She pulled me back another few steps and then jutted her chin in the direction of the Bean. As we crossed over again, the city skyline seemingly disappeared from the reflection, due to its concave shape. Something I had never taken the time to notice before.

"The whole city just falls away behind us," Laney marveled. "I feel like we've just stepped onto the edge of the earth. Or off of it."

With her hand in mine, I wholeheartedly agreed.

Head in the Clouds

We had nothing like Cloud Gate in New York. Well, maybe the Cube at Astor Place came close. But it was a dirty little block compared to the majestic Bean.

The sun had baked off most of the snow from the shiny silver sculpture, but a little still remained in certain sections, like make-believe continents on some fantastical globe. People were reaching up to trace their names in the residual dusting. I approached it slowly and reverently before deciding on a shiny spot to claim as my own.

"Could you?" I asked shyly, holding out my phone so Noah could take my picture. After a lifetime of nonchalance in New York, it was fun being a tourist in another city.

"Turn around and face it," Noah recommended. "Now you have a photo of you, and you."

My mirror image and I laughed at the notion before ducking under the center of the Bean's arch. It was like playing ring-around-the-rosy with a fun-house mirror.

"Laney, over here," Noah called. He grabbed my hand and pulled me right down underneath the thing. People looked at us like we were crazy; it was probably something few tourists were brave enough to do in the dead of winter, the day after a storm.

The ground was cold, but at least it was dry under the arch. And totally worth it. We looked up and, as if counting stars, we pointed out the number of Laneys and Noahs above us.

"Can I tell you a secret?" I said, my breath forming a frosty cloud above us.

"Of course." His own breath mixed with mine.

I lifted the earmuff off his left side and whispered, "You're the best layover I've ever had."

He smiled. "Likewise."

Stiff legged and chilled, we relinquished our spot so others could walk under. But not before I stole a quick lick.

"How'd it taste?" Noah asked, laughing.

"Shiny."

His phone pinged in the pocket of his overcoat, and he reached to consult it. The expression *his smile slid from his face* was an understatement.

"What is it? Is it our flights?"

"No . . . no goddamn way. She did it. She fucking did it. I can't believe her!"

The string of expletives that followed suit was impressive. Honestly, I wouldn't have thought Noah had it in him.

"I'm so goddamn—argh!" Noah raised his fist in frustration, but apparently thought better of it. He'd either break his hand or get arrested if he punched the Chicago landmark. "Sorry," he grumbled, shoving his phone into his pocket. "So not cool."

"Dude, let it fly. I lived on a tour bus with seven guys. There's nothing I haven't heard before. Trust me."

"She signed off on the freaking proof." He ran both hands through his hair and clenched it at the crown of his head before letting out a ragged breath. "For the invitations."

I instantly knew what he meant by that. And what that meant to him. That day had a solemn sacredness for Noah, and Sloane had trampled on it.

No, worse, she was going to parade down a petal-strewn aisle and throw rice on it.

Noah stomped down the stairs and across the snowy courtyard. I had to step lively in his Converse to keep up.

"I asked her to wait until I got home, so we could discuss it, but she didn't. What's worse?" He whipped to face me. "The fact that she took the liberty, or the fact that I had to hear it secondhand?"

He held up the phone so I could see the e-mail from the printer. Sloane hadn't even bothered to reach out to him directly. A defeated laugh broke from deep within him.

"It doesn't end there," he assured me, shaking his head. "The programs, the menus, the cocktail napkins will all have that damn date on them. She wants everything dated and monogrammed."

"Everything?"

"Everything! Down to the eco-friendly, heart-shaped, biodegradable seed-paper wedding favors." He shook his fists to the winter sky, each word freezing and hanging in perpetuity.

"Eco-friendly, heart-shaped . . . is she high?" I shook my head and sputtered, "Does she really think Aunt Marge is going to go home and plant a tree with that packet of spruce seeds after tying one on at your wedding?"

Noah's rant was reduced to a snort of sardonic laughter at the preposterous statement. I didn't want to laugh, given the situation, but one look at him trying to bite back the hilarity made me lose it. Our giggles fed off of each other's until we were doubled over with uncontrollable laughter.

"Nothing says I love you like a fucking evergreen!" he howled into the wind.

"Stop," I gasped, waving my mittens in surrender. "I'm crying, and my tears are going to freeze!"

Struggling to recover his own composure, Noah stepped closer. "We can't have that," he murmured, still laughing and out of breath himself. "That just won't do."

The cool press of his thumb was a sobering reality check as he whisked the moisture away. It seemed to shock him, too. He traced one hot trail down my cheek, his own expression just as serious. His brow wrinkled with worry and doubt.

"It's like, everything she says or does is leading up to this one big day in our lives and I feel so not a part of it. It makes me wonder what it's going to be like *after* the big event. One big letdown?"

"I wouldn't know," I admitted. "Allen and I never got that far." I pulled my panda hat down lower over my ears. I hadn't opened up this much to anyone about Allen, save for Dani, who had been right there in the trenches with me.

He looked mortified. "Oh, my God. I have no right to— Jeez, Laney. I'm—"

"Don't say it," I warned. "Use your thesaurus app to find another word for *sorry*, okay?"

"No, I'm an idiot. I wasn't thinking about what I was saying."

"You're allowed to have feelings, Noah. You're allowed to get angry or upset. Or feel unsure. Don't censor yourself because of what I went through. Don't censor yourself, period."

I lifted my heels; the white rubber rounded toes of Noah's All Stars practically cracked in the freezing temperature as I tipped forward and laid a kiss upon his forehead.

My turn.

I wished I had the power to erase memories like my favorite comic book heroine, Zatanna Zatara, who was the bomb even though she was DC. I wanted to make him forget he ever knew Sloane.

Or, at the very least, forget how much she had hurt him.

I heard his whisper. "I'm afraid to hurt anyone. I'm afraid of what people will think."

Dropping down to my regular height, I locked my eyes on his. "Who told me to face my fears? To walk that mile?" Maybe it was silly to compare our situations, but I didn't care.

He gave me that stony stare I hadn't seen since LaGuardia. "I think we're done walking. I'm going to page Ruel and have him bring the car around."

"No, not yet." I wasn't ready to give up and go back to the airport and leave him like this.

"I've been in your shoes. I *am* in your shoes." I laughed, but this time he didn't join me. "Come on, no fear."

I pulled on his hand, but he didn't budge.

"I can't."

"Can't what?"

"I can't just walk away from it all, Laney! I'm not like you. Quitting doesn't come easy for me."

"What's that supposed to mean?" I demanded.

"I don't know. You tell me!"

I knew a dig when I heard one. I had let my flaws slip out in increments: I had quit the California dream; I had walked away from Allen all those years ago and spent that decade in limbo, letting my mother think for me, get the best of me; and even when it appeared I finally had everything I wanted . . . I had quit Marvel.

Never lose your dreams, Laney. My dad's voice was as clear as the stereo speakers in Gus's fancy Cutlass Supreme, that night he drove us with the Stones on the radio.

I had lost my dad, I had lost Allen, and I had lost our baby. But I hadn't quit dreaming.

My tears had the icy burn of liquid nitrogen; this time they weren't from laughing, and this time I wiped them away myself.

"Where do you think you're going?"

"I want to see the fountain."

"It's not really worth the walk," he said, his voice flat. "It'll be a letdown. I'm paging Ruel."

"You said if time permits. We have time." Why was he being so stubborn?

"I changed my mind."

"Changing your mind is just a fancy way of quitting, isn't it?" I called over my shoulder and kept walking.

He caught up with me. "Five minutes, tops. I'll have Ruel meet us over there. Then back to the airport. Deal?"

"Deal."

Noah

COINS IN THE FOUNTAIN

Even though it was always a bit cooler near the lake, the wind had died down. We walked in silence for a while; our deal like an unspoken truce. I pointed out the Art Institute, along with some smaller places of interest along the way, and she soaked it all up. It was nice to see the city through someone's fresh experience. The midday sun kept poking through the clouds every so often, giving us a rare glimpse of the diamond brilliance dusting the virgin snow on either side of the shoveled path.

Grant Park was an untouched Sahara of white, save for the flocks of pigeons turning in circles like confused old men. The sun shone on their dark iridescent feathers like a shimmering mirage.

"It was pigeons that made me do it," Laney said matter-of-factly, staring out at the dotted expanse.

"Do what?"

"Quit Marvel."

She rubbed a mitten across the bridge of her nose, and I held my breath, waiting to hear more.

"I was taking my lunch break around the corner from the office, in Bryant Park. You know, right behind the New York Public Library? It was a few months into Allen's treatment. And there was this old woman, alone on a bench. She was feeding the pigeons bread from her sandwich. You could tell people were annoyed with her; the birds were swooping everywhere. But she was smiling, happy. I wondered what it would be like to be that old, and that alone."

Laney squinted into the sun's glare off the snow.

"But then a little old man came shuffling up and joined her on her bench. They were married, you could just tell. There was that unspoken comfort as they sat together. He had a book under his arm that he offered her. And she gave him the rest of her sandwich. And then he started eating and tossing crumbs as she read aloud to him. And I realized, I knew then: I was going to lose Allen. We weren't going to get to grow old together, like that couple. But what little time we did have together, I didn't want to waste another second of it. I didn't even go back into the building after lunch. Left the project I had been working on, and that was that."

She smiled at me. "It was the best eight months," she finished quietly.

I was blown away. I knew it took a lot for her to tell me.

I needed a moment to find the perfect words. But when I told her I thought she did the right thing, she smiled, and I knew I had.

"Hey, whoops." She stopped in her tracks to pick something up. "Your poppy!"

I must not have wired it on tight enough back in the hotel room. Laney dusted it off with her mitten, then pulled her fingers free from it so she could rewind the remembrance flower through my buttonhole. "Don't want to lose that," she murmured as she tightly worked the wire around and around. The panda hat pushed her long bangs even lower, but I could still make out her golden lashes below them, as they fanned across her rosy-red cheeks.

"Thanks, Laney."

"No problem." She grinned up at me, and then she was off again.

"I'm telling you, you're going to be in for a big bowl of disappointment," I warned, as she skipped ahead of me. "It's definitely shut down for the season."

"I don't care," she called over her shoulder. "You don't travel all the way to Chicago and not see the Love and Marriage fountain!"

Her breath huffed little clouds of locomotive steam behind her. With my hands crammed into my pockets, I halfheartedly jogged to catch up with her. "It's called the Buckingham Fountain," I corrected, just as the structure came into view.

She halted in her tracks.

"Definitely more impressive when it's on," I added, apologetic.

Laney shook her head and smiled. "I don't know," she said, taking in the sight of the dry basins. "I'm sure all the lights and water are nice, but"—she placed her mittened hands on one of the loops on the waist-high iron and copper fence—"they're probably a little distracting."

I laughed. "Distracting? A fountain is designed to pump a stream of water into the air and then the water falls down. What could that possibly distract you from?"

But when I followed her gaze, I saw what she saw. The unique patterns in the granite, the intricate details of the Georgia pink marble. And the majestic seahorse sculptures, sitting patiently amid the bronze bulrushes and waiting for the next low tide. Their blue-green patina lent itself well to their mythical aquatic qualities.

"Aren't they gorgeous?" Laney breathed.

She had her sketchpad out and the tops of her mittens turned over so the tips of her fingers were bare and better able to hold her pencil.

"You're going to freeze," I said, because I knew I already was. We had clomped through enough snow to numb my ankles, and I knew those Converse high-tops she wore were not exactly water-resistant.

"Look, there's Ruel, waiting." I pointed to the black car idling along South Columbus.

"Just another minute," she pleaded, as she stood rod-straight, her pencil moving like lightning.

I stood back and snapped a picture of her at work. I made sure to capture the Chicago skyline in the distance, with only the red neon of the Congress Hotel breaking up the gray expanse of the background.

"There are probably millions of pictures out there," she called to me, "of people posing in front of the fountain when it's running."

I couldn't argue there. I had even hired a professional photographer to capture my big moment with Sloane.

"But how many pictures while it's sleeping, like this?"

She smiled, glancing to her left and her right. "We are practically the only ones here. In this moment. Right now."

I walked back to join her, but she was already stowing her drawing supplies. "Can I see?"

"It's rough. Needs some more work. I'll do it from memory, later."

Later, I mused. When this moment is *only* memory. And no more.

The thought of that struck me sharp and sad. I crammed my numb hands into the pockets of my overcoat, and they touched upon something hard and cold. *A penny for those thoughts,* I mused. Pulling it out, I flipped it into the basin, where it sunk into the snow, out of sight. *I wish . . .*

"Is Mr. Numbers Guy wishing on a coin?" she teased, her eyes wide.

"Laney," I started, but an enormous gust of wind shushed me like an icy finger to the lips. It teased her hair across her ruddy cheeks and threatened to play keep-away with her panda hat. We both gave chase.

"No fear!" I thought I heard her yell, but perhaps it was the wind in my ears as I ran, playing tricks on me.

Laney dashed toward of the sea of pigeons and they scattered, taking flight southeast. There had to be hundreds of them. Suddenly they seemed to change their collective mind and swooped west. She lifted her head in wonder to watch them go, and two things struck me:

Next to my father, Laney was the bravest person I knew.

And I wasn't going to have a chance to grow old with Sloane.

I was going to grow old, and she would keep operating to stop the clock, locking herself in some time period she considered her prime. Without considering me.

She never once considered me.

"I know Chicago is called the Windy City"—Laney laughed, catching up with me—"but because the politicians are full of hot air, not because of the weather!"

"Where'd you hear that?" I offered her the wayward hat, and she crammed it back on her head.

"Read it. On a Snapple cap."

She grinned up at me, that smile brighter than any light display, and I felt my hopes shoot higher than the water in the fountain ever could.

"Politicians, huh?"

My brain made a beeline back to watching TV with my dad at ten years old. I couldn't understand why my dad was so upset, watching the president's speech. After all, he had voted for the guy. "It's because he wasn't honest, son. He lied to the people. And then he lied to himself, to make him feel better."

His words had concerned me; at ten, I had already told my share of fibs. But I was a kid. Weren't adults supposed to know right from wrong? "How do you know the truth from a lie?" I asked him.

"You'll know the truth by the way it feels, Noah."

My father's words rang clear then, and I heard them now, despite the winter wind whistling in my ears. And standing in this very spot, while looking down at Laney that very moment, brought them full circle.

Things with Sloane had never felt right. No matter how hard I had tried—had lied—to convince myself. And things with her weren't going to get better. No amount of turning back the clock or slowing down our engagement could deny that fact.

And yet here I stood with Laney, freezing my ass off in the last possible place I wanted to be, listening to her talk about Snapple caps and why the fountain was better off dry.

And yet I felt happier than I had been in a long time.

That was the God's honest truth.

I had treated my love life like a spreadsheet, trying to solve problem after problem with reason and logic. Cramming my emotions into equation after equation that just didn't add up. I had experimented with every variable I could think of to find the formula for happiness between Sloane and myself, and none were valid. We were like a #NULL! error: the message that occurs when two or more cell references are not separated correctly in a formula.

"You were saying?" Laney was back on her tiptoes now, leaning against the wind, close to me.

There was so much I wanted to say to Laney.

But first I had to put things to rights. No more walking on eggshells, trying a wait-and-see approach. No more "don't ask, don't tell" non-discussions. I had to call Sloane. And her father.

It was time to quit. For good.

I reached for my phone.

And that was when Laney kissed me.

Her lips, utterly refreshing, brushed up against mine in a cold whisper. I felt the warm shock of her tongue and I tasted cherry Pez for a brief moment, all too brief, before she reeled back.

Embarrassment and hurt passed over her face, faster than a bullet from a gun. She turned and ran, kicking up snow as she went. I stood shocked, silent and still, no better than a weathered statue in an empty basin. My reaction had been a nonreaction, my head lost in the lies I had fallen for in my past.

The truth, and my future, was receding in the blowing drifts of snow.

"Laney!" I roared.

Cut and Run

"Laney, wait!"

By the time I reached Ruel's car waiting by the curb, my lungs were on fire. Every breath in was like a thousand tiny ice needles. I slammed the door of the Lincoln Town Car, shutting out Noah and his pleas. He could go to hell. And GoToHail and find himself a new cab.

"Airport," I choked out, "now!"

"But, miss—"

"I don't care! I'll pay you double. Go!"

I pushed the button on the privacy partition, sealing myself up in my misery. Pulling off my panda hat, I shoved the dumb thing in my bag and closed my eyes as we lurched away from the curb and into traffic.

God, was I stupid! The day with Noah had been no more reality than my silly comic book sketches. What the hell was I thinking? I should've never left the airport, I should have slept there and taken the first available plane out, not even caring where it was going. Ten layovers to Hawaii would've been preferable over this.

I no longer wished to have Zatanna Zatara's power. Sentry's would be far more preferable. The most powerful character in the Marvel universe, Sentry could erase the memory of himself from the entire world.

My ego had taken a direct hit, and I was flooded with nonstop feelings of shame and worthlessness. Punishment, I fumed, for allowing myself to be distracted from my goal. How would I ever prove to my mother—hell, to myself—that I was capable of doing something right for a change, if I kept making the wrong choices? Reading the wrong signals. I would've had more reaction had I kissed one of those stupid seahorses.

Despite all his issues with Sloane, Noah clearly still had, as he had sworn in the bar the day before, zero interest in me. So we bonded over a few drinks. And he showed me around his town. I had let my imagination and my impulsive nature get the best of me.

My phone was roaring for my attention in my shoulder bag, but I ignored it. Noah had my number now, I thought dully. In more ways than one. I must seem like some pathetic female to him. Desperate for attention, starved for affection. Ughhhh.

Could it get any worse?

A horn blared behind us, and I turned to see a yellow cab. It toot-tooted again, as if to get our attention. I cringed. If Noah was pursuing us, it was only because I had made off with his bag and his precious computer. I remembered his big flowchart of bachelor party fun. He would be back on track and in Vegas before nightfall, where he would delete any memory of the ditzy broad he had passed time with during his day from hell.

And I would be heading to Hawaii. No lessons learned. One wrinkled wedding dress in my possession and a mouthful of mumbled excuses to those I had, once again, disappointed. Same old Laney, waiting on standby for her real life to start.

The green-and-white airport signs were coming into view now, as well as the sprawling buildings of O'Hare snaking across the flat Illinois landscape. The same yellow cab was still riding our bumper as we merged and headed toward the lane for departing flights. I blotted my cheeks with my palms and composed myself. It had been childish to run from Noah, but now that I had had a few moments of alone time, I felt better equipped now. We could divide our stuff up and part ways. Different airlines, different gates. Totally separate destinations. I would hand him his Bozo shoes at the security checkpoint, and he wouldn't have to deal with me again.

Noah

WAKE-UP CALL

"I'm on my way to an appointment, Noah. I don't really have time to deal with you right now."

I heard a horn honk impatiently back in Manhattan, matching my fiancée's tone.

"I'll make it brief, then." Gripping my phone with one hand and the taxi's headrest in front of me, I didn't take my eyes off the taillights of the car carrying Laney.

If anyone had told me one day earlier that I'd be ending my engagement, by phone, in a hired car driving way past the speed limit toward the Tollway in pursuit of another woman, I would have said they were out of their fucking mind.

Funny, I finally felt like I had come to my senses.

"This ends now. You had no right to change the date without consulting me first."

"Enough with the dramatics. I get it. You don't want to marry me in June. We'll move it. Point made," she snapped at me.

"No, you don't get it! I don't want to marry you. Not in June. Not in July. Not two years from now. Not anytime."

I felt like I was reading from the Dr. Seuss book Laney had quoted to the little girl at Jughead's Diner. *Not in June, not on the moon, not in socks, not in a box. Never, never!*

"I'm done, Sloane."

There was a pause. Who was being dramatic now?

"You can't do this to me!"

"Me, me, me!" I seethed. "Just because *marriage* starts with an *m* and ends with an *e*, it's not all about you!"

"Well, the word *mistake* does, too, but you can't blame *me* for the one you're making, mister. Just wait until my father—"

My cab careened past Ruel's and the other cars idling along the curb for departures and swung into the first free space. I had caught up with Laney. I breathed a sigh of relief.

"Have a nice life, Sloane."

In Reverse

The car had barely had a chance to grace the curb before I was popping the locks and yanking on the door handle. A gust of wind practically took me, and the car door, with it as I struggled to exit.

"Damn it, Laney!"

Noah's yellow cab had bypassed us and parked up ahead. My feet felt rooted to the frozen concrete as I watched him, his long arms waving like an air traffic controller's over the crowd of people's heads. With his open overcoat flapping behind him like a superhero's cape, he raced toward the Town Car, dodging the maze of luggage at curbside check-in and shooing an eager skycap out of his way.

"Why the hell did you just cut and run?" he demanded, pushing the car door shut so nothing was in between us. Except, of course, the last twenty-four hours.

"I guess that's just what I do! I don't go down with the ship!" I hollered.

"You didn't even give me a chance!" He slammed his palm down hard on the roof of the Town Car. "Because if you had, you would have heard me on the phone, telling Sloane it's over."

"Seriously?" I squeaked. *Is he saying what I think he's saying?*

"Do you think you've cornered the market on epiphanies?"

He stood in front of me, chest heaving, eyes ablaze. There was that vulnerability and that passion that had stopped me in my tracks soon after meeting him. And now it was directed at me. It was because of me.

"I had that whole cab ride to stew over"—he panted—"not kissing you when I had the chance. But I had to end it with her first."

He stepped into my airspace, and winter melted away as his hands found my cheeks.

"All my life, I've been hardwired to do the next logical thing," he said softly, pushing my windblown hair off my face and weaving his fingers through it. "You were *so* not part of the equation."

He dropped his forehead gently against mine and closed his eyes. A speck of a snowflake dotted his perfect lashes where they fanned out above his cheekbone, and dissolved in an instant. I threaded my arms between his open wool coat and his suit jacket, pulling myself into his solid warmth.

"Do—I—compute?" I asked in my best robot voice. Not exactly a come-hither, sex kitten move, but it made his chest rumble with laughter against mine.

"Yes, you factor in perfectly."

I lifted my forehead from his, and we were practically nose to nose. "Well, hurry up and kiss me, because the meter's running."

He caught my top lip between both of his, and a ragged sigh escaped me as his fingers lingered on my jawbone, gently coaxing me closer. It was a sweet gesture, made even sweeter by the cocoa on his breath. I closed my eyes and felt the busy airport terminal drop away behind us, just like the world had seemed to disappear from the reflection in the Bean.

Our lips fully met in perfect unison, creating heat and awareness. The kiss had boldness in its buildup, and an intensity that we never would've been able to muster during that first missed opportunity on the airplane. His tongue hit the tip of mine and I felt warmth roll down to my toes, hitting all my pleasure points along the way.

"Get a room!" some guy muttered as he brushed past us. I could feel Noah's mouth, still pressed hard against mine, as it broadened into a grin.

"We had a perfectly good room, didn't we?" I murmured, giving Noah's lower lip a gentle tug with mine. His groan buzzed against my mouth, making me hot despite the single-digit Chicago windchill.

"You said you pay me double now, miss?"

Ruel brought us back to reality . . . except Ruel was not Ruel. He was some Jamaican guy with dreads pulled back in a thick ponytail. He looked like a younger Bobby McFerrin. And he was standing expectantly next to the car I had vacated.

"What the—where's Ruel?" Noah demanded. "Pop the trunk."

"Easy, man. I don't know any Ruel. And there certainly ain't no Ruel in my damn trunk, you hear? I get a fare, I get them *there*. Get it?"

He gave the trunk a pop with his fist, like something the Fonz would do.

Oh, this is not happening. No, no, no. Show me something, anything.

Even a body back there would have been preferable to an empty trunk.

"You were parked on South Columbus, where it meets Congress, right? That's exactly where I texted Ruel to meet us."

The cogs in Noah's brain were turning, trying to bring reason into play. Me, I had no cogs. No paddle, either, and I was up shit creek. I just kept staring into the empty trunk, hoping it was another one of Noah's magic tricks.

Shit, shit, shit. I wanted to rewind back to the morning, even if it meant sacrificing that first incredible kiss. I just wanted—no, I *needed*—the dress back safe in my hands.

"Ruel a dog?" the guy asked. "Your kid? Be more specific, man."

"GoToHail!"

Noah's response wasn't exactly understood or welcomed. The guy made a face like he smelled something foul.

"No, *you* go to hell! What's this kind of crazy shit? Your girl jump in *my* car. I drive her with *my* gas. She even say she pay me double, and you tell me—"

"Hail, hail, not hell. GoToHail; it's a car service app."

I thought back to my rushed getaway. I hadn't noticed any other black Lincoln Town Cars. And I hadn't let the driver get a word in edgewise before throwing up that partition panel.

My mother's words chanted in my head. *Whatever you do, do not let them check it, Laney. Do* not *hand it off.*

The airport should've been the least of her worries. Letting me loose in a strange city, well . . .

Laney the Wonder Fuckup strikes again.

"Here, here, I'm sorry." I offered up the bills, just about the last I had on me, from my purse. This seemed to make the driver happy. At least I could do one thing right.

Noah had his phone jammed to one ear and a finger in the other to shut out the noise. I watched his face for any sign of relief or hope.

"I tried Ruel at the number he texted me from originally when he accepted the GoToHail request," he said. "No answer. I am going to track the car down a different way."

"No more flashing red dot?" I asked, ever hopeful. Ever delusional, more like it.

He held up the phone display for me to see. "He's off the grid."

"But he had five stars!" I wailed, butting my head against Noah's shoulder.

He leaned over and kissed the crown of my head. "I know. We'll find him. Don't worry."

His screen display said 2:47. Our flights didn't leave for another two hours, but the window quickly shrank when you factored in security checkpoints and boarding time.

"We're going to miss our flights and it's all my fault," I whispered.

"First things first." His fingers flew over the tiny touch screen. Funny how his typing speed varied from device to device. Placing it back up to his ear, I heard him say as he turned away, "Hey, Kiwi. It's Noah."

A traffic cop was monitoring the drop-off line, waving cars on if they stood too long. Dreadlock Guy got in his car to leave, but not before rolling down his passenger-side window and beckoning me over. "What you leave behind?" he wanted to know, his Jamaican accent lilting.

"Wedding dress." It came out barely above a whisper. "And his computer. And luggage."

He shook his head with a smile, his dreaded ponytail smacking each shoulder, back and forth. "Clothing is easily replaced. Computers, you can back up the data. Insurance covers what you lose."

I looked at him expectantly, figuring that at any moment, he'd utter "Don't worry, be happy." *Say it and I'll pull you out your car window by your dreads and put the hurt on you.*

"But a kiss like *that*, miss—" He clucked his tongue. "Irreplaceable. Don't let that go the other way."

It took me a moment to process his last words, as they came out *"gowdee otterway."* But as he put the car in reverse and backed up in order to swing around the shuttle parked in front of him, it sank in.

"Laney, quick. Grab a pen."

Noah was beckoning me over. Digging through my bag, I triumphantly produced one and handed it over. As I tried to find an empty page in my sketchpad for him to write on, he didn't wait for me; instead, he began inking numbers and letters right onto his palm.

"Great, I owe you big-time when I get back," he said to whoever was on the other end of the phone. With a name like Kiwi, I tried not to think of how cute and juicy she might be.

At least she wasn't a day-old Danish.

Hey, no jealousy, Laney Jane. This guy just broke up with his fiancée so he could kiss you.

After hanging up, he turned to me. "My company back in New York was able to get the VIN and license plate number. They traced the car to the Central Auto Pound."

"Well, Bobby just left, so we'll have to get cab," I said.

"Bobby?"

"Long story," I supplied. "Can we skip GoToHail and just grab an old-fashioned, take-your-life-in-your-hands yellow taxi?" I had had my fill of black Lincoln Town Cars for the day.

"Where to, bub?" asked the pug-faced driver, as we hopped into a recently vacated cab.

"City pound on East Wacker," Noah replied.

The driver gave a bark of a laugh. "Oh, I know the place. You want under Lower Wacker, actually. I'll getcha there, bub. Not to worry."

"How many layers does this city have?" I whispered to Noah as we careened down the ramp toward the highway. "That sounds like it's in the bowels of Middle-earth."

"It probably is," Noah said grimly.

"I swear this wasn't a ruse to spend more time with you," I joked lamely. "If that were the case, I would've picked a much more romantic place than the city pound."

"Yeah, you really know how to show a guy a good time."

Squeezing my knee, he admitted, "I really do want to spend more time with you. Any way I can get it. I, um . . . I canceled my own flight reservation earlier and rebooked, so I could have those extra hours with you."

"Seriously? That is, like, the most messed-up, but sweetest thing anyone has ever done for me." I giggled. "Thanks, Vegas."

"My pleasure, Hawaii."

Two Hearts Pound as One

"So there's your East Wacker Drive," our cabbie announced, gesturing toward a street we weren't even on, "and down there's your Lower Wacker Drive. And we're going under that."

He seemed far too pleased with himself, and soon I understood why, as he took the car through twists and turns with the calm, collected coolness of a Jedi master. There was no way we would've found the place ourselves, even with Noah's GPS superpowers.

The pound was exactly what my mind had pictured: dimly lit and dank, with rows of darkened cars sitting dejectedly, waiting for their owners to spring them.

"This was definitely not a stop on the Noah Ridgewood ten-dollar tour itinerary," he murmured, holding the door of the double-wide trailer for me. "Here we go."

"For the dress," I said, taking a deep breath.

Noah approached a woman who appeared to be sleeping at her desk. Like, literally sitting upright in her chair with her eyes closed and fooling nobody.

"We're looking for a black Lincoln Town Car that probably came in within the last hour."

She had either been awake after all or was sleepwalking, because she got up and grabbed paperwork for us to fill out. Noah slapped down his license and credit card, and I read his palm to fill in the necessary information on the papers.

"You aren't Ruel Da Silva," she said to him, before turning to me. "And you don't look like a Ruel Da Silva. We can only release the car to the registered driver."

"Actually, we don't want the car," I explained. "We just want what's in the trunk."

She was totally wide awake now and giving me the stink-eye once-over like I was some drug mule. "Bring Ruel Da Silva of KTL Limo down here and then we'll talk."

"Can I speak with your supervisor?" Noah asked, sweet as pie. I think I even heard a hint of Noavis in his voice.

She lumbered away. Noah and I exchanged a look. "I'm going to get KTL Limo on the phone," he said. "Perhaps they can be of help."

Sleeping Beauty had fetched another woman, who seemed even more annoyed that we had interrupted her alone time than the first one.

"We can only release the car to the registered driver," she droned, as Noah opened his mouth to speak.

"I've got the limo company on the phone right now. The driver was admitted to the emergency room," Noah said, handing the phone to the supervisor.

"Ruel's in the hospital?"

That was the last thing I would've expected to hear. It gave me pause, especially after our other driver's divine words of wisdom. And here I was, worrying about a couple of yards of fabric. "What happened?"

"His dispatcher didn't know," Noah admitted.

Supey handed him back his phone. She also pushed his license and credit card back across the desk toward him, as if she were ruler of a land that didn't accept such items as proof or currency. The phone call hadn't made a lick of difference, apparently.

I noticed she had a thick band of yellow gold around her pudgy ring finger, as well as a tiny chip of an engagement ring. It reminded me of April, the June bride, back at the check-in desk at LaGuardia.

Time to be an oversharer.

"Maybe this just wasn't how it was meant to be," I said to Noah, and I bit the inside of my cheek until tears came. Tugging on his jacket, I added, "Maybe eloping was a crazy idea."

Noah developed that deer-in-headlights look again. Could I blame him? A half hour earlier, he had still been engaged to Bridezilla. Now he was fake-eloping with me, Mothra.

"But I know . . . I know you had your heart set on it?" he floundered.

Definitely glee club, not drama club material.

"My dress." I turned to the women, my throat thick with emotion. "My wedding dress is in the trunk of that car."

Supey looked me up and down, from Bozo shoes to panda hat. At least Noah, in his suit, looked a little more the part.

"Getting married, huh?" she asked, leaning in on her elbows. "So how'd he propose?"

I couldn't tell if she was genuinely interested or just trying to call our bluff.

"It was so romantic," I started, stalling for time by rubbing Allen's class ring like it was Aladdin's lamp.

"I went to Cartier," Noah cut in, "and ordered a setting exactly like the one her grandmother had."

He zipped through his phone's photo gallery and flashed them a close-up shot of the ring I had previously seen when I spied on the picture of him and Sloane in his iPhotos. It looked museumworthy, the stone large enough to rival the Hope Diamond. Supey and her buddy Sleeping Beauty flicked a glance at my army jacket. My demeanor screamed Carhartt much more than Cartier, but I went with it.

"It wasn't ready in time for the big day when he wanted to propose," I added quickly. "So he ended up using his class ring. I loved it so much, I told him to cancel the Cartier order and use the money to start a college fund for our baby." I rubbed my stomach and thought longingly about my Eighteen-Wheeler breakfast from Jughead's. Those were some good eggs.

Noah was getting into the part now. "So I dragged her to Buckingham Fountain," he began, "even though it was Valentine's Day and she had probably hoped for a carriage ride, or dinner at the Signature Room at the 95th—"

"He's crazy. I could eat Slim Jims and Pop-Tarts for dinner and be perfectly content," I told the women. "As long as I'm in his company, who cares about fancy dinners?"

They were both leaning on the desk now, in rapt attention.

"I thought I had planned for everything, down to the time of the sunset. But the one thing I forgot to check was—"

"The fountain itself. And wouldn't you know, it was closed for the season!" I finished triumphantly.

Supey slapped her thigh and hooted. "Everyone knows that they turn the water off for the season!" Her underling just shook her head and tsk-tsked.

"So there I was, in an utter panic," Noah said. I couldn't help noticing his brows were knitted in what looked like a genuinely painful reminiscence. "I thought for sure she was going to be angry. And disappointed."

Wait—could this have really happened? Back when he thought Sloane was the Priscilla to his Elvis? The peanut butter for his hot banana sandwich?

"I had wanted everything to be just perfect."

"And it was," I said softly. "You couldn't have planned it better. It's supposed to be 'for better and for worse,' anyway, right? In sickness and in health . . ." Now the tears were really rolling, as I was thinking about Allen. And my parents. "Marriage isn't just about sticking around for the pretty light show and water features. You've got to be there for the dry season, too."

I had reduced Supey to tears as well. "Greg! *Greg!*" she shouted.

A uniformed guard appeared in the doorway. "Give me the keys to the Lincoln."

She came around the desk to give his beefy arm a squeeze. "My husband of twenty-five years. Good times and bad."

Greg had sad eyes and jowls like Droopy the Dog. "Just as pretty as the day I married her," he said in a molasses monotone.

"You're not springing the car," Supey said, as our entire motley-looking party straggled out to the impound lot, "but if there's a wedding dress in the trunk, I'll just charge you a hundred-dollar convenience fee and turn my back."

"Thank you. Thank you very much." Noavis was back.

"There's a blue garment bag that says *Bichonné Bridal Couture*," I started.

"Oh!" Sleeping Beauty clapped her hands together. "My dog's a bichon!"

"There's also a computer bag." Noah choked out the words from behind relieved laughter. "Monogrammed with my initials, N.L.R., and two small carry-on bags. His and hers."

He squeezed my hand, and I silently reminded myself to ask him what his middle name was.

Supey popped the trunk and I couldn't bear to watch. What if . . .

"Well, I'll be double-dog-damned," Droopy the Dog said slowly, and he turned to stare at us as if we were prophets of the parking lot.

I peeked out from behind Noah, who had been bracing himself as well. His whole body relaxed under my touch.

"Can you give them a ride out, Greg?" Supey asked.

"Send a picture of the big day!" Sleeping Beauty called after us.

"How's about I drop you at the L?" Droopy said, as we stuffed ourselves, and our bags, in the front seat of the tow truck next to him. He practically used my knee as a gearshift and we bumped up out of the bowels of Lower Wacker and onto surface street level once again.

"Sure, where are we?" Noah asked.

"Randolph/Wabash."

A few moments later, we found ourselves standing under the rumbling elevated train tracks, no closer to our destinations but happy and relieved to have our stuff back.

"By the way, I owe you fifty. My share of the 'convenience fee.'"

"Oh, please," Noah scoffed. "Save it for the baby's college fund."

We broke out in hysterics. "That was a bit over the top, wasn't it?" I managed, wiping my eye with a panda scarf-arm.

"Just a tad." He checked his watch.

"So it's four o'clock," he said, sobering up a bit. "Do you want to go to the airport and try to get on standby somehow? There's no way we'll make the other flights."

"I think there's something we should do first."

Noah

HOME, HEART, HEAT

"Ruel Da Silva is in room 7305. Take the last bank of elevators to your left."

We followed the hospital receptionist's directions and crowded into the elevator with all our bags. People must've thought we were moving in.

Seeing the small mixed bouquet of colorful flowers from the lobby gift shop in one of Laney's hands, and the bridal dress bag in her other, I couldn't escape the irony as we linked arms and walked down the long, quiet corridor together toward Ruel's room.

"Hey, you guys!" Ruel was sitting up straight in the hospital bed, genuinely happy to see us. "Can you believe this?" He gestured to his predicament.

"What happened to you?" Laney asked, rushing to his bedside.

He accepted the flowers, tucking them in the crook of his arm like a beauty contestant.

"One minute I was sitting in the car, sipping my chocolate milk shake . . . the next, I'm out of the car, puking my guts out. Violently."

"Was it the bacon?" I asked, making a face. "I thought that was a strange combination."

"No, not the bacon, boss. It was a spiked milk shake. And I'm intolerant to alcohol," Ruel said, shaking his head sadly. "It actually induced a seizure."

"Oh, my God, Ruel. We're so sorry," Laney gushed. "Noah told the waitress no alcohol when he ordered it—I heard him. She must've messed up."

"No worries! I got a CAT scan, and no damage done. Ruel is A-OK. They're keeping me overnight for observation. I got my own remote and I don't have to fight my kids to watch TV." He grinned. "I felt bad leaving you in the lurch, though. You probably missed your honeymoon plane, huh?"

Laney and I exchanged a smile. "I got the best damn tour of Chicago instead," she replied. "It was worth missing the flight."

"And we got our stuff back. Thanks to the best performance the Central Auto Pound has ever seen," I bragged.

Ruel slapped his leg under the thin hospital blanket. "Now, that I would've liked to see!" He hooted with laughter. "Those ladies down there don't want to give up nothing."

Gesturing for us to sit, he asked, "So where were you two headed to, anyway?"

"Hawaii," I automatically replied, at the exact moment that Laney stated emphatically, "Las Vegas."

"Well, um . . ." We both started and stopped, then laughed.

Ruel gave us a sly look and a wave of his hand, as if to say *I know you'll figure it out, you crazy kids.*

"You two should totally stick around. My wife, she's bringing up paella . . ." he said temptingly.

Before we could even begin to politely protest, the smell of saffron and garlic wafted into the room, followed by what must've been a dozen of Ruel's relatives. I guess being held for observation didn't include holding off on eating a home-cooked meal.

Ruel's wife ladled the first bowl lovingly for him, then climbed onto the hospital bed right next to him with her own spoon in hand. Now, *that* was for better or for worse.

Laney stepped up to serve paella for the rest of the Da Silva clan as they eagerly crowded around the bed to chat with him. I helped pass the steaming plastic bowls around, catching her eye and smiling over the heads from across the crowded, and very small, hospital room.

After everyone was served, she filled two more bowls, scooping from the bottom where the flavor was best. Waving a silent good-bye to Ruel, we snuck away to the lobby.

"I'd hate to be the one to tell *that* family that visiting hours are over." Laney dug in. "Oh, my God, best paella ever!"

"Seriously," I agreed, around a mouthful. "Nice that they all came. Being an only child, I've never experienced that sort of family chaos."

"I'm an only, too," she confided. "So your mother . . . she never remarried?"

I shook my head. "I wish she wasn't alone. But she says she's okay so I don't push it." We tossed our empty bowls and pushed our way back out onto the chilly Chicago street.

"Speaking of mothers . . ." Laney groaned. "I'd better call mine."

When Laney's mother shouted, there was no need for speakerphone.

"Helena Hudson!"

I could hear her loud and clear, even with the phone pressed to Laney's ear.

"Your luggage has arrived. Your flight has arrived. Where in green hell are you?"

She barely let Laney get a word in edgewise. We must've covered three city blocks with Laney mumbling only "uh-huh" and "for sure" before they finally hung up.

"Ugh, my mother still has the ability to make me feel nine years old."

I reached for her free hand and gave it a squeeze. "I think I felt like an old man by nine years old."

"How so?" She threaded her fingers through mine as we strolled, and suddenly it didn't feel so cold outside at all.

"Well, whenever my dad would get deployed somewhere—and it was often—he would take me by the shoulders and tell me, 'Son, you're the man of the house now.' It didn't matter how small I was. He'd get on his knees, or he'd stoop down. So long as he could look me square in the eye. 'Take care of your mother, Noah. Until I get back.'"

"That's a lot to put on a little guy."

"It's a lot to put on anyone," I said grimly.

I remembered the final time my father had made the request. It was my junior year of college. We'd joked about the routine, the formality. But there was something sacred about it as well, passing between father and son in the household. He had to actually reach up and lift his head to meet my eyes.

"When I was about eight or nine, we had already moved I don't know how many times. I had started at a new school, which I liked. But the first week, I drew an utter blank while on the school bus home. Nothing out the window looked familiar. I couldn't remember the name of the street. Poplar? Pine? It might have involved a tree; it might not have. Stop after stop, but I stayed glued to my seat, terrified to get off the bus, lest I was wrong. Finally, I was the only kid left on the bus. The driver was kind. But when he asked me my address, I couldn't tell him. When he asked my phone number, I didn't know it. I became so upset that I didn't even want to say my name. He took me back to the school, and the principal called my mother, who was of course frantic by then. When she arrived, I shouted, 'I don't want to be the man of the house! I'm not a man! I don't even know the color of my house!' My mother held me for a long, long time. Her English still wasn't great . . . well, it was better than she thought but she was self-conscious in front of my principal and all the office staff. *'La casa è nel cuore,'* she assured me. Home is in the heart."

"I kinda love that saying," Laney said softly, pulling me to a stop. *"La casa . . . ?"*

"La casa è nel cuore," I repeated slowly, and I watched her lips try to imitate mine. *How many hours ago did I kiss her at the airport?* Too many. I twirled the hanger out of her hand and swung the garment bag behind my shoulder. "Home"—Laney reached up and fiddled with the crepe-paper poppy in my lapel; my cheek grazed gently against hers as she leaned up toward me—"is in the heart," I whispered.

Kissing Laney was like stepping into a hot shower on a cold day; that luxurious tingling sensation that starts at the back of your brain and rushes pleasure through your nerves. Once you were in, you craved more heat.

City to Ourselves

I was in danger of losing myself completely to the guy with the matchy-match suit, in the doorway of a Methodist church, on a freezing cold street corner in an unfamiliar city. A grand adventure? I didn't exactly need the Magic 8 Ball to tell me, *Hell yeah*.

I was also in danger of frostbite.

As much as I envied the heat of Hawaii and Vegas, I really wasn't in a hurry for either of us to leave Chicago. But we couldn't stay out in the elements forever. Noah rubbed my arms as I reluctantly pulled back.

"Cold?" he asked. "Let's get out of here."

"Do you believe that's true?" I nudged him slightly as we walked.

"What's that?"

I pointed to the illuminated sign on the lawn of the church: THE HEAVIEST THING TO CARRY IS A GRUDGE.

"I don't know . . . this dress is pretty damn heavy," he joked.

I rolled my eyes at him. "Ha, very funny. I mean, seriously, think about it," I said, stopping in my tracks. He turned to me, hunching his shoulders against the cold.

"I think you were right about having to walk a proverbial mile last night. Putting on the dress made me realize that. It's stupid to still be angry with my mother after all these years. Like you said, nothing's stopping me from going where I want to go."

Noah picked up my hand and kissed the back of it gently, before flicking his gaze up to meet mine. "And where is it you want to go, Laney?"

"We've missed every available flight out tonight, haven't we?"

"Pretty sure we have."

I suddenly felt shy, after the overwhelming events of the day. We had killed time, raced for time, chased the dress, and each other, all over town. And now it was just Noah and I, alone on a quiet, freezing-cold street corner.

"Do you think there's room back at the inn?"

"I know there's room at the Drake. I called."

Hey, WWDD about getting wrinkles out of a wedding dress?

UH-OH, WHAT DID YOU DO?! & WHERE R U?

Hey, don't go yelling at me in all shoutie caps, Dani. Still in Chicago.

I know that—it was rhetorical! Your mom just let the entire island know. Still with Tech-Boy?

Yes. And don't tell my mother (about the dress)!!!

"Finally, a good reason to hang the Do Not Disturb sign," Noah rasped as we came up for air.

We had barely dropped our bags in the room and closed the door before we were bumping up against it, pawing at each other.

"Before we get too busy to be disturbed . . . please tell me you have something in your carry-on, because I don't want to open the door and let you out," I breathed, practically climbing him like a ladder. He responded with a tortured groan. "Not very prepared for the big Vegas bachelor party, were you?"

"I was going to Vegas for the steaks and motorcycles; I wasn't exactly planning—oh, yeah, that's the spot!" I bit his earlobe, and he pinned me up against the door, pushing open my jacket and kissing my neck. "Besides, I wasn't the DCP for this trip."

"The what?"

"Designated Condom Provider. That was my buddy Tim's job. Knowing G.I. Joe, he bought a surplus supply."

"Fat lot of good that'll do us now," I murmured.

He felt so good, I didn't want to let him go. But if we wanted to feel even better . . .

"Gift shop!" we both said in unison.

Noah was out the door in a flash. "Leave a light on for me . . . but not much else."

I closed the door behind him and leaned against it. Closing my eyes, I hugged myself and smiled, relishing the recent memory of his hands and lips all over me.

My phone went off in my jacket pocket. It was a new text message from Dani, with an answer to my earlier question.

STEAM! It read, in capital letters.

You got that right.

I rushed into the bathroom, unzipping the garment bag as I went. Turning the polished bronze shower taps on full blast, I hopped in and took the quickest scrub ever. Might as well kill two birds with one stone, I figured. The dress would be wrinkle free and I would be squeaky clean. And ready to get dirty with Noah.

I skipped getting my hair wet, jumping out and drying off while the steam began to build. *What to wear, what to wear?* I contemplated the his-and-hers terry-cloth robes. Going commando under the robe seemed a little too "playground flasher" for me. As badly as I wanted Noah, I wanted him to "want" a little more.

Padding out to the bedroom in just a towel, I pulled the luxurious curtains closed on the magnificent view of Lake Michigan and began to paw through my carry-on bag. Noah had said to leave a light on . . . but the overhead lighting was really harsh. I tested the wall sconce next to the bed, on and off. It made for a good lone spotlight.

Inspiration struck.

I quickly pushed one of the overstuffed chairs toward the bed, grabbed my carry-on, and raced back into the bathroom.

The lingerie I had packed for under my formalwear was neatly folded at the bottom of the bag. Perfect, perfect, perfect. The black lace bra was a push-up, with a black rose design. It was a wickedly sexy little thing, with scalloped lace trim to soften it. I pulled on the matching black lace boyshorts and, once again, reached for the rhinestone clips to pin up my hair.

I couldn't wait to see Noah's face when he saw me. We had come a long way since that hostile first encounter on the airplane. Thinking of it made me remember his tie. *Now, where would he have stashed that?*

My Spidey sense led me over to his computer bag. Sure enough, it was stuffed in the front pocket. I smoothed the blue-gray silk, with its intricate square-and-dot pattern, between my hands. So conservative, so luxe. Luckily, it still had the knot on it from where he had loosened it and pulled it off. Lucky for me, since I had never tied a tie from scratch in my life. I looped it over my head and turned to the mirror as I pushed up the knot toward my bare throat.

In my reflection, I caught sight of Allen's ring. I contemplated it. Had I kept wearing it because I couldn't bear to part with it, or was it to keep me safe: to keep new love away? Its peridot winking, warding guys off like an evil eye? *Don't come too close!*

Whatever the reason, I was ready now.

With a pause, and a slow smile in the mirror, I removed the ring and dropped it into my cosmetics bag on the marble counter. The finishing touch was donning the hotel robe, its thick waffle weave luxuriously rough against my freshly washed skin.

Another beep of the phone from Dani, texting again.

BUT NOT TOO MUCH STEAM! it warned.

The thought of Noah, those blazing brown eyes and long, strong fingers, weakened my knees. *Too much steam?*

Impossible.

Noah

WHERE LOYALTY LIES

The gift shop in the hotel was closed, but I struck gold at the drugstore down on East Chestnut. As I reached into my pocket for money to pay, my hand hit my Bluetooth and, as if on cue, my phone began to blare.

Tim and his great timing. Although I had promised in my last text I'd talk to him later. Later had to be short, and it had to be now. Popping the hands-free piece in so I could pay and hurry back to Laney, I answered it.

"Dude. You are missing wall-to-wall pussy here!" he said in greeting. I could hear pounding club music and the clinking of glasses in the background. "Not to be believed! You're such a lame-ass. Why aren't you here by now? No excuses!"

"It's kind of a long story, best shared over a beer." I turned my collar up and pushed against the wind whipping up from the lake.

"What? I can't hear you, I'm drowning in pussy!" Tim bellowed. "I just wanted to tell you, you have the coolest freaking boss ever! He totally hooked us up at the Palomino! Limo ride, VIP line passes, premium bottles, and the best seats in the house! Free floor dances, too."

"Which boss: Butler or Bidwell?" I pushed through the revolving doors of the Drake and stepped back into the hushed warmth of the lobby.

It had to be Butler, I reasoned. Bidwell would be sending nothing short of a noose for me, after my phone call with Sloane.

"The one who doesn't have a daughter you're boinking," he quipped.

"Oh. That's Butler." I paused, but didn't correct him. *Like I said. Long story.*

"Did you show him the itinerary? How'd he know we were going to hit the Palomino?"

"Yeah, I gave him a copy. He said he wanted to live vicariously through us for the week." Warren was my only groomsman who, iron-ically, couldn't get off work to go.

I pushed the up button on the elevator and smiled politely at an elderly couple, dressed in their theater best, who stepped off when the doors opened. Tim continued to drone on about the abundance of nameless women shaking their nakedness in his face in celebration of the almighty dollar.

"Did you know there's a law here in Vegas that they can't serve alcohol in the all-nude places? Only the topless places can, except for the Palomino. Best of both worlds! It's nudie, with a full bar! God bless the grandfather laws in the U. S. of A.!"

Leave it to Tim to wax patriotic about pussy.

"Listen . . . and tell the guys. No posts on the social networks or anything. If Sloane—or her father—gets word I'm somewhere else . . ." I was on our floor and literally counting the doors that would lead me back to Laney.

"Dude." Tim was all of a sudden as serious as the war veteran he was. "I will always have your back. No questions asked. You know that. But you should call your boss and thank him."

"I will eventually," I said, giving the hotel key card one smooth pass through the lock and swinging open the door of the darkened room. "I'm a little preoccupied right now."

"Oh, yeah?" Tim laughed. "What's her name?"

"That's classified, Sarge."

Looking up from the door, I spied Laney standing in the bathroom doorway. The lone light from the bathroom silhouetted her form exquisitely. She had her hip cocked and one arm languidly over her head, leaning on the doorjamb. Even in the dim lighting, I could see her long, bare legs peeking out from beneath the short robe she was wearing.

Tim had no idea what VIP treatment was.

"A one-woman private show, huh? You lucky bastard!"

I ended the call and tossed the phone down on the nightstand, along with my all-important purchase.

"Doing a little feng shui in here?" I asked, noticing a chair in the path.

"Hit that light behind you," she said huskily, "and have a seat."

I did what I was told, the sconce casting a warm light over her path as she sashayed toward me.

"Straight from Sin City," she announced, "live on our stage for one night only . . . Miss Laney Hudson!"

Smiling and shaking my head, I raised my brows and leaned back to appreciate the view as she swiftly bared the robe off her shoulders and dropped it to the ground.

Good God. She was perfect.

And she was wearing my tie. Along with little else.

Strutting those last couple of feet toward the chair, she straddled my lap and draped her arms over my shoulders. "Long day at the office," she said breathily. She pulled the clips slowly from her updo and swung her hair to its full length. "I can't wait to unwind . . . all over you."

"Hard work, huh?" I gulped.

"So hard."

"Must be all those PowerPoint presentations," I quipped, remembering her comment about strippers on board the airplane.

With my thumb and index finger, I lightly flicked my tie hanging in the hollow between her breasts and trailed my pinky down along the inside curve of her barely-there bra.

She smiled and leaned toward me, opening her legs even wider across mine as she murmured, "You know it. Can you help a girl out with her spreadsheets?"

Oh, man, I was in danger of blowing a wad over computer geek dirty talk. She was good. "You are driving me absolutely wild. You know that, right?" I told her.

"Really? And I haven't even mentioned my flowcharts yet," she said with a wink.

I shook my head and groaned and ran my fingertips along the interiors of her thighs until she quivered.

"Who's the wild one now?" she asked in a husky whisper.

It was a straight shot from the chair to the bathroom, and the huge vanity mirror in there was angled perfectly over her bare shoulder to give me a view of what I was missing from the back. Her lacy black boyshorts dipped in a slight V where her tailbone curved, and the fabric hugged each rounded cheek. Even that black lace thong she had unknowingly taunted me with back when I eavesdropped on her phone call in the hotel bar could not have made her sexier than she was right now. Those fiery wings tattooed across her shoulder blades fluttered as she arched and trembled under my touch.

As she reached behind her to unhook her bra, I turned my attention away from the mirror and focused on her. God, she was so beautiful. Creamy skin, with that reddish gold hair spilling over her breasts like a velvet curtain. She still had that warm sugar cookie scent, but it was suddenly more complicated, mixed with the heady scent of her desire.

She had just one more tattoo, and there was no way I could've spotted it before that night. Wisps of black ink plumed from her left hip, starting somewhere below her waistband, and followed the curve of her rib cage. It was the plume of a different kind of feather, a beautiful lone peacock feather, stunningly realistic in its color and detail, that proudly sat on the side swell of her left breast.

It literally took my breath away.

She glanced down as I reacted, and whispered, "Oh, that. For luck."

Wow. So much better than a Pez dispenser.

"Talk about product placement," I breathed, my fingers memorizing its lines.

Her face close to mine, she parted her lips in a sexy pout. With just my tongue, I touched the top one, right below the spot where it pinched up in a bow.

She gasped, flicking her own out to meet mine, and we lightly teased each other with French kisses, lips never touching lips. It was the hottest thing I had ever experienced, closing my eyes and not knowing when or where I was going to feel that gorgeous tongue of hers next.

I reached to remove the Bluetooth from my ear.

"No, leave it in," she insisted, whispering in my free ear. "I like a challenge. Good boy."

"I can't guarantee . . ." I started.

She began to nibble her way down my neck, and I lost all track of what I was saying.

"Is that a banana on your tray table," she cooed, "or are you just happy to see me?"

"Oh, I am so, so happy to see you . . . so ready."

My cell phone began to angrily buzz for attention on the nightstand. She leaned over my shoulder. "Warren Butler?"

"Oh, fuck." Warren had even worse timing than Tim. "It's one of my bosses. I'm sorry."

"Well, it is technically a workday. Night." Laney giggled, her breasts tantalizingly close as she leaned to hit the talk button on my phone.

"Warren," I said, with more bravado than I had intended.

I placed a finger to my lips. Laney smiled wickedly and began to unbutton my shirt. "How are you, sir?"

"I was about to ask you the same thing, Scout. Did you get my gift?"

"Yes, thank you for hooking us up! What a pleasant"—I sucked a breath of air as Laney began nibbling her way from my earlobe down to the hollow of my throat—"pleasant surprise. You really didn't have to."

I heard the bleating of traffic in the background. It was nine o'clock in the evening back in New York, and Warren Butler was no doubt just leaving the office. "Well, I thought it might go a long way toward 'getting it out of your system,'" he replied, his voice grim.

"So I take it Bidwell told you about our morning meeting yesterday?"

I wondered if he had heard the latest. Thinking about my dire straits at work, along with the two powerhouses there playing me like a pawn, would normally work wonders against my libido.

But with Laney in my lap, using her superpowers of seduction, nothing was getting me down. Literally. She was freeing me of my oxford dress shirt and peeling my undershirt over my head.

Taking true advantage of my hands-free device, I gripped her luscious bottom and lifted her toward me, tonguing her ripe nipples and kissing my way, openmouthed, down her smooth belly. She trembled against me, her fingers running through my hair as she threw her own head back with a ragged sigh. Two could play at this game.

"Yeah, kid. He told me. So this is my way of saying sorry." He probably took my silence as disapproval, because he hastily added, "I wish I had never introduced you to her, Noah. I feel like I threw both of us under the bus, son."

Both of us? I figured my head was on the chopping block, but Warren's?

"Wait, what do you mean?" I asked, leaning back.

Laney judged this as my assent and took over, running her hands up my pecs and across to my bare shoulders. As she moved to kiss her way down my abs, I felt her hands busily work my belt buckle.

It took all my concentration to stay in the conversation, because all I could picture was throwing Laney down on the bed and making her scream with pleasure. But in the back of my mind, I knew what he was going to say and braced myself for it.

"I brought in the wunderkind. You. So Bidwell basically let me know, in no uncertain terms, that our little partnership will be kaput if this wedding doesn't happen."

I was speechless, but not because I had a mouthful of Laney this time.

"But Noah . . . Scout. Listen to me. I will understand your decision, either way. I know you want to do what's right. But you need to do what's best for you."

"Yeah, okay," I managed, leaning back and squeezing my eyes shut as Laney's nimble hands freed me. I noticed he didn't add his customary "your dad would be proud of you no matter what" pep talk, and I was grateful.

"Enough of the doom-and-gloom crap. Now tell me, are the seats as good as I was told they'd be?"

I sat up and watched Laney, beautifully clad in just my necktie and her panties, as she began to shimmy her way down between my legs.

"The view is spectacular," came my strangled reply as she took me in her mouth and began to roll slow circles with her tongue.

"That's what I wanted to hear. It's the least I could do. We'll talk when you get back next Monday, okay?"

I threw off the earpiece after we'd ended the call, and let out a long, low growl. Laney had me so deep, so gone. I ran my hands through her hair as she moved, taking me dangerously close to the edge with each inch.

Fuck. I was going to blow this deal. Bidwell was going to pull out if I stood my ground, and it was going to screw one of the most important people in my life in the process. The thought was enough to paralyze me.

But I didn't let it. I didn't care. Tonight, the only thing that mattered was Laney. I was going to shut everything else out and make her scream my name all night.

All systems go.

Three Little Words

I felt every muscle in Noah's body clench. His side of the conversation with his boss was less talking, more just listening. If he really was, in fact, listening at all. I loved trying to break his cool, professional exterior, but the truth was, he was revving me up just as high as well. Just the way he looked at me so intensely, those dark eyes a night storm of desire, was enough to make me want to moan. I absolutely ached for him. His fingers tangled in my hair, rubbing slow circles behind my ears, and his breathing was becoming more irregular.

"I want you, Laney. So bad. Come here, baby."

His strong arms were coaxing me up, back into his lap, and in one deft move he flipped me over the side of the chair and neatly onto the crisp sheets of the bed.

Leaning over me, he began to pepper my face slowly with kisses: my temples, my forehead, down my eyelids, and over my cheeks before finding my mouth with his. Softly and seductively, his tongue made me forget about time and space.

I could hear him shedding the rest of his clothing, his lips never breaking contact with my skin. My body yearned for his touch; I felt like a goddess as I arched to meet him.

"Oh, Noah," I gasped, as he lightly bit my neck, giving my nipples just the right amount of pressure between his thumbs and forefingers.

I pushed his curls back off his face so I could watch as he slowly made his way down to each one, nuzzling them with kisses as his thumb found my navel and his fingers began to lightly play on my panties.

"Please," I whimpered, but I had no idea what I wanted.

I was crazy with wanting all of him, all over me, everywhere. Those nimble fingers grazed the lacy hem of my panties, skimming them off my hips and down my legs.

I felt his tongue flick at my waist and slide up my side, tracing the long path of my lucky tail feather tattoo. He kissed the blue-black eyespot on the side of my breast before coming back to my center.

"Mine," he said throatily, giving a gentle tug on his tie, still around my neck, and claimed my lips with his once more.

"Do you want it back?" I whispered against his mouth.

Noah sat up and didn't say anything for a moment. Taking the end of the tie, he lightly brushed it along my cheek. Then his fingers deftly loosened the knot out, and he began slowly sliding the length of it down my naked body, moving along with it. I felt a delicious, silky sensation as he passed it over my delicate parts, giving me wild fantasies.

"I want you. Just you," he answered, tossing the tie to the floor. "It's what I've wanted since you sat down next to me on that plane."

I thought back to the first glimpse I had had of him, of how I had stolen glances so I could sketch him. I wished he would let me draw him now, rising above me in all his naked glory. He was gorgeous, an Adonis, all for me.

"Tell me again what my favorite body part on a woman is," he dared huskily, as he hiked my leg over his smooth, chiseled shoulder.

"Ankle?"

The word caught in my throat as I felt his scruff, rough against my foot, and he started kissing his way up my leg.

"That's a start," he murmured, his breath hot against my skin.

I fell back against the pillows as he took his time, inch by inch, up to his desired destination. The glance he flicked up at me, just as he hooked his tongue on the very tip of me, set me on fire. His curls were so soft against my thighs, and his strong hands found mine. Lacing our fingers together, he rendered me useless.

For the third time that day, I felt as if I had dropped off the face of the earth. Falling and shattering into a million pieces as he brought me to a screaming finish on the edge of his talented tongue.

Noah Ridgewood.

Drake Hotel.

Right now.

Best. Sex. Of my life.

"Condom," I begged, pulling him up to the top of the bed.

"I'm on it."

I heard the crisp tear of the packaging and then I was on him, mewing, kissing, and pressing up against him. His hands were on my ass, guiding me. "Laney," he panted, as he thrust up to meet me. I could tell he was barely hanging on, teetering on that cliff he had had me gripping just moments before.

"Come with me," he moaned.

I bit my lip, my eyelids fluttering as I rode him high and hard.

"No, you come with me."

"You mean to Hawaii?" He heaved against me, and I took him to the hilt.

"You were talking about Vegas, right?" I asked, slowing my pace, but keeping him deep.

"Oh, God," he groaned. "Laney!" He gripped my hips. "With me, here, now."

"I don't think I—"

I felt his fingers between us, spreading me, and he tilted his body so I had complete control, bucking and quaking as another impossibly hard wave crashed over me.

"Oh, Noah!"

He gave in to his own release, crying out with me, kissing me in wide-eyed wonder as his body wracked with hard, shuddering spasms beneath my quivering clench.

"That was fucking incredible," he managed, as I settled myself into the crook of his arm. His fingers toyed with my hair, and we were quiet, spent.

"Best layover ever," I agreed, waiting for my heart to resume its normal rhythm.

"Totally." He laughed. "I might never fly direct again."

"You know, I could come to Vegas," I said, running my fingers lightly through the goody trail of hair near his navel. "I could be your all-you-can-eat buffet, your lucky roll . . ."

He kissed my shoulder, sobering up for a moment. "Ah, Laney, I wish . . ." As great as that sounded, I think he and I both knew what the answer was.

"Yeah, I guess there isn't room on the Excel itinerary for me," I joked, trying to keep my voice light.

Jeez, Laney. Are you going to pop out of his cake, wearing pasties and your boyshorts? Get a grip. Don't overstay your welcome.

"The hell with that. I'd clear the whole damn schedule for you. It's just—"

"I know. It's boys' week."

"And they're pigs. But no, you haven't come this far just to be short of your goal. Those judges are waiting, with perfect scorecards for you."

I smiled. "You could come to Hawaii. I mean, it's a wedding and you do have a monkey suit . . ."

"Speaking of which, what are you wearing? All I've seen of your ensemble is black lace lingerie and flip-flops."

I giggled, trying to even remember what I had thrown into my checked luggage that could pass for wedding attire. "I guess I'm a bit of a disorganized packer."

"You're cute." He nuzzled his nose against mine. "So I guess I'll forgive you."

Propping myself up on my elbow, I turned to face him. "So what do you say? You could teach me to paddleboard, we could make love in a hammock on the beach under a palm tree . . . My mother would think it the scandal of the century if I brought you to crash the wedding."

Like the day's clouds passing overhead, made swift by the wind, I detected a stormy shadow flicker across Noah's face. "I wish this delay would never end," he said quietly. I detected more words under the surface, but he just gathered me into his arms like precious cargo. I rubbed my cheek against his scruff, and he turned to lightly lay kisses on my eyelids, the bridge of my nose, and the pulse point on my neck. In the dim light of the room, I could see the bridal dress bag looming on its hook on the open bathroom door.

There's a honeymoon phase with a new lover, halfway between awake and dreaming, and Noah and I were drifting through it. We lay past midnight, squeezing and dozing, chatting sweet nothings into our dream cycles, and rousing each other with lazy kisses.

"Hey, what's your middle name?" I whispered, tracing his strong jawline with my finger. He tilted his head on the pillow toward me. "The mystery letter *L* on your monogrammed bag."

"Would you believe me if I told you 'Lucky'?"

I laughed. "No."

"Luciano. My mother's maiden name."

"Noah Luciano." I kissed the tender spot under his ear and felt his jaw relax. "Very melodic."

"What's yours?"

"Just plain old Jane," I mumbled. "I don't use it much." *Anymore.*

I felt his lips brush my bangs away from my eyes. "There is nothing plain about you, Laney Hudson."

Noah's phone began to do a little song and dance across the nightstand. He reached up to silence it, but got an armful of me. "Forget it," he croaked, rolling closer.

Spooned with my back up against him, I could see, and reach, the phone. "It's Tim."

He groaned. "Just swipe the screen across to unlock, then swipe up to reject it."

I reached with my index finger and did as I was told. Up popped three choices to send an automatic text to the rejected caller:

1. *I'm driving.*
2. *I'm in a meeting.*
3. *Why are you calling? Send a text like a normal person.*

Chuckling, I chose number two. Then I rolled over in his arms.

"I said you were in a meeting," I murmured against his chest.

"I am. It's a meeting of lips," he said, drowsily kissing mine. "And a meeting of hips." Noah's thumb found my hip bone as his fingers came to rest on my backside. His eyes closed once more, and a small smile played on his lips.

I gently wound a finger through the curl hanging over his forehead. Morning was going to come too soon, taking him with it. We'd both be going our separate directions. I knew it was inevitable, as was sleep. As my eyes began to close, Noah's phone beeped and buzzed once more.

"You're getting a text now." I sighed. "Should I reject it with a 'go to hell'?"

He mumbled something indistinguishable, but didn't move. From the corner of my eye, I could see his screen display lit up as bright as a Christmas tree.

I picked up the phone for him. It was still in unlocked mode, and there was no avoiding the text splayed in caps across the screen.

CAN'T BELIEVE U R MISSING YOUR OWN BACHELOR PARTY FOR SOME PIECE OF SNATCH IN CHICAGO.

I dropped it so fast you'd have thought the buzzing phone was a rattlesnake. It went off again.

GET YOUR ASS TO VEGAS, MAN!
WHAT HAPPENS HERE, STAYS HERE.

Whether Noah felt the same way his buddy Tim did or not, the words hit me sharp, and stung. Bravado bolstered by booze made guys talk a good game, but I had no idea whether Noah had told his best bud and best man that the wedding was off.

Come to think of it, how do I really know he has told Sloane, for that matter?

Maybe I really was just some piece of ass, some bullet point on his agenda. Just some cheap thrill to nail before he tied the knot? Easy prey?

Absent fathers make for promiscuous daughters, I could hear my mother say. Maybe Noah had stockpiled all my insecurities and flaws I had shared and used them to bait me with all the hooks, lines, and sinkers needed to get lucky.

Would you believe me if I told you my middle name was "Lucky"?

No.

Check his call history, Laney.

No.

I needed to believe in myself for once, and believe Noah wouldn't hurt me like that. Thinking back to sneaking a peek at his iPhotos, I filled with guilt. Trust was a two-way street.

He's not as perfect as you first thought . . . but he's still pretty much a perfect stranger.

I turned to Noah's sleeping form. Gorgeous in dreamland as well as in the real world. No, I refused to give in to the demeaning demons of my self-esteem that were trying to deceive me. Noah was one of the good guys. It was wrong of me to look at his conversation with Tim to prove it, but I couldn't help myself. It was like I was under a spell.

Change of plans

Those three little words Noah had written to Tim hit me harder than *piece of snatch.*

You changed the goddamn plan, Laney.

I couldn't let Noah do this. Not for the wrong reasons. Not for me.

The regret of my own decision back on that Long Island beach so many years before made me sure as hell I didn't want to be responsible for anyone else messing up their lives.

You lucky bastard, Tim had replied. Suddenly I could hear Noah, back in our first hotel room. Unbeknownst to me at the time, he had been describing himself. *A lucky bastard . . . on the fast track at work . . . engaged to the boss's daughter.*

He wasn't just breaking off his engagement. He was committing professional suicide.

I swiped my bra from the floor, my panties from the foot of the bed. *Go, leave, now.* My brain was barking one-word commands with each step I took. I needed to get my things, all my things. The dress. My clothes. My bag. My jacket. My shoes? Where were my shoes?

I left Noah's sneakers in a neat row by the door, and I left the sketch I had drawn of him on the hotel desk. Adding a handwritten good-bye message that I hoped he would understand, forgive, and act upon, I fled, my flip-flops sounding like gunshots as they slapped against the marble floor.

Dramatic exit by elevator was kind of impossible. The door coolly slid open the moment I pushed the down button. As if it had expected me all along. *Here comes Laney Jane, going down in flames once again.*

Once the elevator hit ground level, I was off and running. Past the tables overflowing with gargantuan floral bouquets, away from all the glitzy glaring chandeliers, through the lobby, and down the blue-and-gold-carpeted stairs. I paused only to catch my breath when I reached the other side of revolving door. The frigid night air pierced my lungs, but mentally I was already so numb I didn't care.

"Miss?" The concerned face of the bell captain peered down at me. He had followed me from inside and was now clutching his arms in the cold as his valet staff looked on. "Are you all right? Can I call someone for you?"

The only soul I knew in Chicago had written her phone number on a flight cocktail napkin.

The Scary Truth

Even as the cab glided up in darkness, I could tell Anita's neighborhood was desirable and trendy. The streets of Andersonville were dotted with interesting-looking restaurants, boutiques, and bakeries, although most were shuttered and sleeping at that hour.

I paid my fare and hauled my bags to her doorway. Had it really only been a day and a half before that I'd glided through LaGuardia Airport with ease? My shoulders screamed and my legs felt leaden.

Anita pulled open her door. The long legs that I remembered sashaying up the airplane aisle were lost under a pair of men's flannel pajamas, and her blond hair was piled in a messy bun on top of her head. A wailing child who looked less than a year old bounced on her hip.

"I am so sorry," I blurted out. "I just had nowhere else to go and I didn't know anyone else in Chicago but you and I'm almost down to my last pair of emergency panties."

Anita beckoned me in like an old friend, not even batting an eye as I stood in her doorway with snow on my flip-flops and rambled about my underwear while the baby smacked her in the chest with a flailing fist.

"Did I wake her up?"

"No, no. This is our nightly ritual around this time." She attempted to appease the baby with a pacifier that had what looked like a small, boneless plush giraffe hanging from its handle, but the baby refused it. "Don't worry. My husband's warming her bottle," she hollered over the baby's relentless squawks. "And he's got the kettle on for tea. Come, come. Sit."

I followed her into a beautiful living room. Wide-plank hardwood floors were softened by worn but obviously real Persian rugs. A chocolate-brown leather couch beckoned from between two huge bookcases. CDs, framed photos, and small art objects were tucked sweetly between the colorful spines of the books. I draped the dress bag over the arm of the couch and collapsed next to it. "Oh!" The wall facing me was literally filled floor to ceiling with jewel cases. I had to pop back up and inspect it closer. I couldn't remember the last time I had seen such a vast collection of music.

Anita swayed with the baby. "My husband," she said by way of explanation. "I keep telling him he'd better start babyproofing his precious goods. This one is ready to hit the ground running any day now."

"Do you have any others?" I asked, running my fingers through the Ds. Yes, with an Alexandria Library's worth of albums like this, you needed alphabetizing. "Kids, I mean?"

"We've got a thirteen-year-old, too. Holly will sleep through anything, though. Teens." Anita tsked, kissing the baby's blond wisps at her temple. I bet she smelled sweet, but I wasn't about to break my eardrums getting close enough to inhale her.

"All right, all right, all right!" A guy bustled in from the other room, clutching a bottle like it held the elixir of life. A mess of black curls exploded from every direction in the worst case of bed head I had ever seen, but his features were ruggedly handsome. Muttonchop sideburns angled toward his strong jawline. "C'mere, you little demon."

Anita handed off their daughter. The baby homed in on the bottle like a guided missile and eagerly began to suck. Father and daughter settled in on the leather couch. "Daddy to the rescue." Anita sighed. "This is Laney. Laney, Scott. But everyone calls him—"

"Scary!" I knew he looked familiar. "You're the drummer of the Scary Marionettes, aren't you?" Allen had worshipped this guy's playing, and their bands had appeared on festival bills together back in the day.

He grinned, propping bare feet up on the coffee table in front of him. The tattoos began at his ankles and snaked their way up, disappearing beneath the hem of his fleecy leopard robe. The baby reached up and twisted one of his curls around her tiny fingers contentedly.

"Scary Scott Thomas, I can't believe it." I turned to Anita in awe. "I never would've guessed the stewardess on my flight was married to, like, the primo stoner rock drummer of all time!"

"And I never would've guessed a passenger on board *my* flight would be one of the three fans who would recognize him," she quipped, laughing. "What are the odds of that?"

"Oh, please, Nita," Scott scoffed. "You never got to see me fight off the thongs of—oh, I mean, *throngs* of women, back in my heyday." He winced as the baby gave his hair a hearty tug.

"I saw you totally blow the roof off Nassau Coliseum back in 1999." I remembered it was the show that set Allen's mind on the path to California. He was convinced the fickle New York music scene would never embrace his sound, and had felt an instant affinity with the Orange County rockers. "I remember it like it was yesterday," I said softly, more to myself than anything.

"What's the difference between a drummer and a large pizza?" Anita teased. Scary rolled his eyes, but he took it good-naturedly. "The pizza can feed a family of four."

"Yeah, I'm just the kept man now. She brings home the bacon, ain't that right, Amelia?" he cooed.

"We met when I was doing long hauls," Anita explained. "The band was on my flight for their first European tour. It was the first, right?" He confirmed with a nod. "I didn't work for a long time after Holly was born. But lemme tell you, being stuck in Cali with a kid all by yourself while your husband is on a month-long tour is enough to make anyone crazy. And I missed my job. I love flying. So . . ."

"So she dragged me back to the Midwest and now we take turns."

"And I've got my whole family here to help out." She sidled up to Scary and Amelia on the couch. "We didn't plan on this little surprise, but it's all worked out."

"No, we didn't plan on this sweet little cupcake baked by the devil, did we?" Scary dropped kisses on the crowns of each of their heads in turn. "Shit, the tea!"

"I got it, sweetie." Anita ran to silence the kettle. I slipped into the overstuffed chair near the CDs. The *T*s were at eye level, and I spied the familiar inserts of Three on a Match's albums, five releases over the span of Allen's lifetime. But there were two more as well, unfamiliar to me. They had been recorded with a new drummer. The realization hit me: the band had moved on.

I spanned them with my hand and felt the bottom of my stomach drop out at the sight of my bare ring finger.

I had tried to move on. I thought of the girl smiling in the mirror back at the Drake Hotel. I wanted to punch her. A sucker punch, for being such a sucker. Falling for a guy who was taken. Knowing he was goddamn engaged.

Why set yourself up for failure? I needed to mail myself a card with that Veraism on it as a reminder the next time I fell for a guy. Save me some trouble.

"So." Scary flicked his eyes toward the bridal bag, then back to me. "What's your story?" He set down the empty bottle and brought his daughter to his shoulder, rubbing and patting her back in a soothing rhythm.

After dating a drummer, you crave rhythm.

Suddenly, it was all too much. Barging in on this beautiful family, thinking about drummers and bands and Allen and marriage and love. It mixed in my head with visions of Noah at Buckingham Fountain and the press of his body against mine at the hotel door. *Change of plans.* The evening with Noah had cut deep down to the scar tissue of my past, ripping jagged holes in the places I had thought were smoothed over, and leaving me feeling raw and exposed. The floodgates opened.

"Scary! What'd you do to her? Jesus. I leave you for two minutes!" Anita scolded, pushing a mug of what smelled like peppermint tea into my hands.

"No, it was all me! I changed the goddamn plan." I choked, bringing the warm mug close to my face. Its steam mixed with the hot flow of my tears. "I was engaged to Allen Burnside."

"Hot damn, really? I remember him. Nice kid. Helluva drummer. We used to call him Burns. Played so fast, he left scorch marks on the skins." He shook his head and smiled at the memory. "He had that energy and enthusiasm that made the old guys like me jealous. Shame what happened." I saw him mouth the word "cancer" to Anita. Baby Amelia turned her head and gave a sleepy burp.

"Oh, honey." Anita's brow crinkled with concern. "I'm so sorry."

"It's been two years now. I thought I was doing okay and moving on, but—" I gulped my words and tea. It was too hard to say it out loud. "I just keep making all the wrong choices," I managed to say.

Scary carefully hoisted himself up. "Crib time," he whispered. He was probably glad he had a sleepy baby in his arms as an excuse to vacate out of there. Crazy stranger crying in your living room at one A.M. will do that to you.

Anita plopped herself right down on the floor next to my chair, like we were two friends having a slumber party, getting ready to listen to CDs. "Girl to girl," she said, blowing across the top of her mug and not meeting my eyes. "Are you leaving Noah at the altar?"

"I didn't even know Noah two days ago," I confessed. "It was all a misunderstanding gone haywire. I let it go too far. The storm came and—"

"Hold on, hold on, back up. Take a deep breath."

I inhaled, the smell of peppermint calming my nerves and thoughts. Somehow I was able to touch upon my time line without lugging out my sketchbook or doing the ugly cry again.

"It's my mother's dress," I explained. "I was in charge of bringing it to Hawaii for the wedding. I'm sorry I led you on. But getting bumped to first class felt like the consolation prize I deserved."

"And Noah?"

"He just happened to be sitting next to me, on his way to Vegas."

"No, I mean . . . do you see him as the consolation prize, too?"

I sighed. "Noah turned out to be amazing. He made me see things about myself I don't think I wanted to see. I was playing the martyr, having to carry my mother's dress around. But it's really anger I've been carrying. Toward my mother, for being so controlling all my life. And toward Allen. For leaving me." I felt a new wave of tears threatening to brim, but I blinked them back. "We were supposed to have this great life together." It came out as a pathetic wail. "He proposed to me when he was in remission. I knew what I was signing up for. But when the cancer came back . . ." Fuck it. The tears forged rivulets toward my chin and I just let Mother Nature take its course. "He broke it off. He said I would make a horrible widow." I laughed through the hot mess of my tears. "And when he . . . his last word to me was 'free.'"

Anita's eyes were wide and glistening.

"But Noah's the prize I can't have," I said bitterly. "He's off to Vegas for his own bachelor party." It hurt, but I had to be honest with myself. "I was just the pregame warm-up."

"I don't know, Laney." Anita rubbed her own mug in thought. "I've seen my share of Mile-High Club hookups and sleazy business trip behavior, but I truly don't believe that was Noah's m.o."

"Maybe not. But he said I wasn't part of the equation."

"Well, perhaps he was struggling with his own choices."

True. But those late-night texts, spelled out in black-and-white and all caps, canceled out any hope of me factoring into his life.

We sat in contemplative silence for a while.

"I don't tell many people this, but Scary wasn't the first guy from the band that I, well . . . you know. Hooked up with." She picked at the worn tweedy fabric of the chair. "And I beat myself up for a long time about it afterward. Call it being in the wrong place at the wrong time; call it lack of foresight, I don't know. But it ultimately led me to the guy I really wanted to be with. So can I really call it a wrong choice?"

I mulled that over. My mother had made so many decisions for me while I was growing up, I guess I had just assumed it was because I couldn't be trusted to make the right ones. But perhaps there were no right or wrong choices . . . only choices themselves. It was easy to wallow in regret rather than to move on and take a new chance, a different choice.

Anita set her mug down and laid both hands on my knees. "I'm sorry you lost Allen. But I'd feel even sorrier for you if you let the next chance slip away because you can't let go."

She hugged me, and it was more comforting than a tray full of steaming hot, lemon-scented towels any day. "Come on, let's pull out this sofa and get you some rest. Scary will take us both to the airport tomorrow, after the school bus comes for Holly. I'm on three days, then off two this week." She carefully hung the dress from the cornice of the bookcase. "Don't worry, I won't let you forget it for the final leg of your trip."

I smiled and sighed. I was already in a better place in my mind, but knew I still had a ways to go.

Scary emerged once the coast was clear and the terrifying girl talk was over. "She's finally asleep."

If babies dreamed vividly, I imagined Amelia and that boneless pacifier giraffe happily galloping through a moist and milky rain forest right about now.

He plopped the baby monitor into his wife's hand, and she stood on her tiptoes to kiss him on his fuzzy cheek. "You go up. I'll help with the sofa."

"The bedding's in that cedar chest. I'm just going to rinse the baby's bottles so they aren't stinky and then I'll go up. Bathroom's right down the hall if you want to freshen up. 'Night, Laney."

"Thanks again. Good night."

Scary scooped the neat stack of bedding from the cedar chest by the bookcase.

"What the heck is this?" I asked, pulling out a strange plump thing that appeared to be a question mark–shaped pillow.

Scary laughed. "That," he announced, "is a Snoogle. And apparently you have to be at least eight months pregnant to think it's a comfortable thing to sleep with. I'd leave it in the chest, if I were you."

"Enough said." I dropped it back in, and something familiar on the bookshelf caught my eye. "Aw, she really did frame my drawing!"

"Totally. Thanks for that, by the way. It totally made Nita's day . . . and mine." He winked and maneuvered the pullout with one strong arm.

We worked in silence, tucking corners and wrestling pillows into their cases.

"Being a musician is harder than it looks, as you know," Scary said, smoothing the last blanket in place.

I nodded, wondering where he was going with that.

"But being married to one is even harder. I know there are definitely days when she must think, 'This isn't what I signed up for.'" He reached to dim the sconces on the wall flanking the couch. Thank goodness he did—I was weepy at the drop of a hat . . . and the flick of a light switch.

God, what was wrong with me?

"I think you need to knock Allen off that pedestal." Scary looked pointedly at me. "Or better yet, off that drum riser."

I laughed through the hot mess of my tears. "Easier said than done. He made me promise to always love him, no matter how big of a famous asshole he became."

"Yeah, that's just like a drummer." Scary chuckled, shaking his head. "We're such attention whores."

He waited until I was under the covers to turn out the other lights. "Anyway, I'm sure you'll find a way. Good night, Laney Jane."

And Scary Scott Thomas left me staring, long into the dark, and wondering how he knew Allen's nickname for me.

"Who's the drill bit, Laney Jane?" Allen placed a hand on the concrete block above my head and leaned in, essentially pinning me to the backstage corridor wall.

"His name's Gordon, and he's not a drill bit." Maybe it had been bad form to bring a date to my ex-boyfriend's sold out New York City show. But then again . . . "He's a publicist, actually. For your record label." Ironically, my date was the one who'd gotten us on the guest list, with VIP passes.

"Laney, you *know* I would've totally hooked you up with tickets." Allen planted his other hand on the wall next to my waist, and now I was most definitely pinned. Over his shoulder and down the hall, I spied Gordon across the crowded, smoky greenroom of Roseland Ballroom, taking a hit off a joint and passing it to Paul, Three on a Match's bassist. We had only gone out a few times, but Gordon's constant name-dropping and hipster habits were already wearing a bit thin. "All you had to do was ask."

I thought all I had to do was tell you. The song he had sent me three years before was on a constant loop in my mind, and I wondered if we'd hear it live that night. But they hadn't so much as hinted at it in the first half of the show.

"Goddamn, I wish I could get you somewhere alone, Laney Jane."

Set break for the band had turned into Old Home Days; it was our tenth reunion weekend, and at least half of Central Bluff's graduating class of 2000 had turned out for the show. And now everyone was backstage, clamoring for a chance to talk to the hometown boys done good. There was no chance of being left alone. Funny, though, cornered there by him in the narrow hallway, I felt like we were.

He snaked his arm around my waist and murmured close, "I really don't want that tool looking at you like I'm looking at you right now."

"Now you know how I feel." I pouted. "At least there's only one of him. There're at least five hundred hot girls out there in the audience, lusting after Three on a Match."

"Oh, please." Allen dropped his hands and plunged them modestly into the front pockets of his long black board shorts. Even January in Manhattan didn't affect his skater-turned-surfer look. "No one looks at the drummer way back there."

He looked boyish and adorable, shrugging his ropy bare shoulders. Allen could pull off a Hanes wife beater like nobody's business. It had been a shock to see his signature golden locks sheared to stubble length, but with his new goatee that eked a path along his chiseled jawline, he was the epitome of cute Cali rocker.

"You feeling good?" I floundered, not knowing how to ask about his cancer. "Your mom told me, but—"

"It's okay. I'm okay. Remission, one full year." He gave me the thumbs-up. "You look amazing tonight, L.J."

God, when was the last time he called me that? Probably not since we were sixteen. *El Jay.* It always rolled off his tongue so exotically.

He pushed my thick curtain of hair off my cheek so he could look me in the eye. "Perfectious."

"That's not even a word," I scoffed. Allen loved to mangle the English language in an attempt to get laid.

"It is to me." His crystal blue eyes roamed hungrily over my bare shoulders as he stationed his hands against the wall above them once more. "It's you."

I had dressed carefully and mindfully, on the off chance that maybe he would catch sight of me at the show, and here we were. The Robin's jeans that Dani had convinced me to spend way too much money on, with their signature silver-stitched wings perched above my ass, were dynamite. My silky, midnight blue handkerchief top clung in all the right places and dipped enticingly at my cleavage. I felt confident and strong, especially as I slipped under his arm and made to walk away from him.

"Nice tat. How long have you had that?"

"Since the last time you acted like an asshole to me."

Allen laughed and cartwheeled his lanky arms, trapping me between them on the opposite wall. "You're right. I've been a total asshole since our fifth-year reunion."

I was silent, reaching to trace the Mighty Mouse tattoo he really did get inked after I had drawn it that night. His brow puckered and his eyes turned down.

"I've hated myself since slamming the door on you that night at the Meridien Hotel," he quietly confessed. "And for what I did to you at the Lake Shore Hotel. Hell, you and I need to stay away from hotels."

"Get a room, you two! No one wants to be a voyeur to your exhibitionism!"

Bryan, the band's lead singer, was breezing by. He had a beer in one hand, along with the unmistakable long half sheet of paper covered with Sharpie marker chicken scratch. It was the night's set list.

"Can I look at what you guys are playing tonight?"

Bryan retracted his arms to *T. rex* small and waved the set list back and forth. Caged under Allen's arms, I was just too far away to be able to read it. And when I tried to reach for it, I got a grade school playground "Look with your eyes and not with your hands!"

Allen plucked the set list from Bryan's grasp and resumed his lean with me against the wall. The paper stayed infuriatingly out of reach above my head, just like my college acceptance letter had that day on the beach.

"You butthead. You're not going to let me see?"

"He wants it to be a surprise to you, Laney Jane. It's *always* about you. He made me change it tonight, because you're here. When are you going to let us record 'All You Had to Do' anyway, Laney?"

I threw a questioning look at my ex. Allen crumpled the copy of the set list in a death grip. "Bry, go find a groupie to bang or something, why don't you?"

"Yeah, right. I'd need more than the five minutes we have left in the break to bang her properly." Bryan's laugh echoed as he receded down the corridor.

Five minutes wasn't nearly enough time to make things right with Allen.

But ten years had been much too long.

"He's right, Laney Jane. It is always about you. And I make sure everyone knows that, everywhere I go. Every band we tour with, every interview we take, every girl backstage wanting a piece—they all know my heart belongs forever to Laney Jane."

"So whose turn is it now?" I gulped.

"For what?"

"To hurt the other one. Because currently it's match point."

Allen gave a start, then a slow smile. "It's no longer match point." He gave me a sensual, probing kiss that sent every nerve simmering. Once they were open, his eyes met mine. "It's the flash point."

When I wanted characters to tell the truth in my comics, out came the dripping syringe of sodium pentothal. No, no! They'd struggle, before succumbing to the shot. What I wouldn't give for a little truth serum right now.

What I got was even better.

Allen reached for the hem of his undershirt and slowly pulled the thin cotton up and off his frame. I had spent years poring over anatomy books, learning to draw the wide pectoralis major muscles characteristic of any great and powerful superhero, with Allen never far from my mind as I worked. And now his smooth, chiseled bare chest was just inches away from my touch again, like a blank canvas. Except it wasn't blank. A new tattoo graced his heart center.

The letters *L* and *J* were etched on a banner across the middle of a big, fat, old-school "Sailor Jerry"–style red heart. I loved that the scroll bearing my initials was slightly antiqued like a treasure map, with little nicks and cuts in it, the beating it had taken over time.

Instead of a traditional arrow through the heart, a syringe was plunged through it on the diagonal. Crystal-clear liquid filled the chamber, and the superfine needle poking through the top had tiny heart-shaped drops coming off it, rather than teardrop shapes.

"No more tears," he whispered, touching my cheek.

"What's with the needle?"

You have always been my drug.

He smiled, pulling his shirt back on. "It'll make more sense after the show."

I needed that shot.

"Tell me what's on the set list."

"How about Lose the Drill Bit > Your Place > 47th and 9th > Sex Type Thing > Reprise > Encore?" he said cockily.

"No 'All You Had to Do' tonight?"

"That's always implied," he said softly.

"What did Bryan mean, when will *I* let you guys record that song?"

Allen smiled. "Didn't you ever notice the copyright on that demo I sent you?"

Backstage guests and VIPs were pouring from the greenroom, eager to get back to their spots before the lights went down. Any moment, Gordon would come looking for me.

"The music, the lyrics . . . it all belongs to Laney Jane Hudson."

He touched his chest as the tour manager came like a cyclone through the hall, hustling everyone out so the band could take the stage once more.

"Just like my heart."

Maybe it was my imagination, but the band's second set was pure fire. I could spy on Allen perfectly from my spot up front, stage left. And I was pretty sure he could see me, too; every time Gordon leaned in to scream something in my ear or to touch me, the drum tempo seemed to speed up.

"We've got a new song for you tonight, courtesy of Mr. Allen Burn-siiiiiiiiiiiide!" Bryan crooned melodically into the microphone. At the sound of his name, Allen began a *gunka-thunka* heavy beat. It sounded like he was hitting the snares and the double-bass drums all in time with the pounding of my heart. "He needs an intervention, New York! He's got it bad for—the—Love Juice Injection!"

The trio dove into what would become their biggest hit ever, and even to my virgin ears, I knew it was a keeper, with its funky rhythm and punchy lyrics. All of Roseland was singing along with the chorus by the second time around.

> *I'm in need of that Love Juice injection,*
> *Can't you feel my resurrection, baby?*
> *Your love juice is infectious,*
> *Pure, uncut, and perfectious*

Love Juice injection,
Love should never be a weapon,
Bay-hey-bay-aye-be-e

I knew the song was about me. Shared initials and all. The girls were clamoring for a piece of Bryan, yanking at his pant legs as he strutted across the stage, but he was merely the vehicle. The Cyrano de Bergerac behind the kit was running the show.

Three on a Match became many people's new religion that night. But me, I felt positively born-again. Stretching my wings as I raised my hands in time with the beat, basking in the glow of the spot-lights and the five-thousand-watt warmth of the music was pure catharsis.

Gordon started begging off before the band did their encore. "Come on, Laney. I want to be able to grab a cab before the rush. Plus we've got to deal with coat check. Who cares if we miss one song?"

I did.

We were toward the back, near the bar, when the band began their signature good-bye. Ever since their inaugural show in Paul's parents' backyard, the band would stage dive into the crowd. Bryan, ever the front man, always kicked it off, yelling, "Good night, fuck you!" into the mic and hurling himself into the abyss of arms. If you weren't really paying attention, it almost sounded like "good night, thank you," but it wasn't. Especially if you got a steel-toed boot to the head like Davey Robbins did at the beach party blowout junior year. Paul dove next, and he loved to sail out into the crowd Jesus-style—arms wide, eyes closed—and let the wave carry him.

"Laney Jane! Where's Laney Jane?"

Gordon had been pulling me by the hand as he threaded through the crowd. I froze, turning to peer over the heads. Allen was out from behind the drum kit and had the mic, still clipped to its stand, clutched in both hands.

"If you're still out there, Laney Jane . . . *will you marry me?*"

The audience roared as Allen took a running leap off the stage, flipped into the air, and was swallowed up by the crowd.

"That's me!" I pushed through the back row, trying to worm my way closer. "I'm still here!"

Gloria Boyner, known for her big mouth and famous for getting suspended three times freshman year for smoking in the girls' room, spotted me. "She's right here! Allen! She's right here!" she screamed in her hoarse, pack-a-day rasp, hopping up and down.

Chris Machetti, the star quarterback from our class, was also in the crowd with a group of friends. He handed off his full beer to the girl next to him and said, "I gotcha, Laney." He hurled me up and over his head. Someone grabbed my legs to keep them from flailing, and I relaxed into the hands that began to pass me forward.

I could hear Gordon hollering my name, but then I couldn't. The houselights hadn't gone up yet, but I could see Allen's hands reaching for me across our strange, undulating surface.

"Laney Jane, promise me you will always love me, no matter how big of a famous asshole I become?" That got a laugh out of the handful of people below us.

Ten years of missing him melted away as he opened his fist and revealed his class ring. It still had the string tied around the back. He had flung it down into the sand that long-gone day as I had fled. I had searched frantically for it the next morning, but it was gone; lost to the million grains of sand that rubbed my wounded heart.

The kind souls beneath us brought us close enough to wrap our arms around each other. It was an all-body experience, being groped by unseen hands everywhere, but as his lips locked and lingered on mine, an out-of-body experience as well.

We holed up, honeymoon-style, in my apartment for three days—encore, encore, encore. Skipping the tenth-year class reunion altogether, as we knew we would be the talk of the grapevine there anyway. His band had to practically drag him back onto the tour bus. "No, not without Laney Jane," he told them. So the guys made room on the bus for me and I finished out the tour with them.

Finally. This was it. Our life together. Once the tour finished, I walked on cloud nine, packing my things, arranging for a transfer at work, and preparing to move.

But his cancer beat me to it.

Metastasis.

It's in my bones, Laney Jane. It's not going away this time.

Scary maneuvered his small Prius to the curb of O'Hare and hit the flashers. I let myself out and walked back to pop the trunk, giving Anita and Scary some privacy as they leaned over their daughter's bobbing head, kissed, and said their soft good-byes. My eyes welled up again. So many good-byes in this world. Even the happiest ones were bittersweet.

Maybe it was perverse wishful thinking, but peering into the trunk, I almost expected the dress not to be there once more. I wished for that gift of object impermanence, wasted on the youth Amelia's age. I wanted out of sight, out of mind where the dress was concerned. And definitely where Noah was concerned.

Anita joined me, giving my shoulder a squeeze before grabbing her own carry-on. She looked so put together, her blond hair swept back in a ponytail, her makeup perfectly applied. How was she not falling apart, walking away from her amazing family? Scary rolled down the backseat window. "'Bye, Mom!" he called, taking Amelia's tiny hand in his and gently bending down her thumb, middle, and ring fingers against her pudgy palm to make the universal "rock horns" sign. "You rock!"

Anita laughed, shaking her head, and blew them both kisses.

"Knock 'em dead off their feet, Laney!" he called after me. It was a sweet sentiment, as well as a title of a Three on a Match song. I threw him the horns as well, letting him know I got the reference.

"I'll see you on the other side," Anita called over her shoulder, as she wound through the cordoned-off entry area for actively working airline personnel. I joined the ranks in gen pop, which was, thankfully, a fast-moving line. Every guy carrying a computer bag, every gray suit that caught my eye, set my pulse pounding. Chicago O'Hare International Airport was huge . . . but the fact that Noah was flying on the same day pressed down on me, making the terminal feel claustrophobic. I itched for boarding time. My heart just wouldn't be safe until it was armed and cross-checked behind the plane's plug door, and in its full, upright, and locked position. Until then, it was in danger of being hijacked by a guy in a matchy-match suit and loafers.

"How are you doing?" Anita asked, linking her arm through mine as we walked. We must've looked like quite the pair: me in my flip-flops, with my mother's garment bag slapping against my thigh as I tried to keep pace with Anita, in her clickity-clackity heels, with her sexy hard-shell case rolling behind her.

Walking through the airport with Anita had a privileged thrill to it, like walking backstage with a musician. She moved like she owned every inch of that tiled floor. People nonchalantly turned their heads and snuck glances. Catching sight of that little bronze badge on her ample chest, they couldn't help but stare and smile. Every coordinated detail, from her neck scarf to her blazer and down to her form-fitting pencil skirt, created an air of intrigue that made you want to swoon. I felt assured with her; I felt *chosen*. But most of all, I felt grateful that I didn't have to do the walk of shame to my gate alone. Granted, she was going to have to board her aircraft an hour before departure to begin her workday. But right now, I had a friend next to me.

"Where do you lay over?" she asked.

"Um, this time . . ." I fumbled with my boarding pass. "I change planes in San Diego, then I have a two-hour layover in LAX and should be in Kauai by six o'clock. How about you? Your next flight isn't to Las Vegas, is it?"

"Nope, back to LaGuardia." She flicked a glance in the direction of the Windwest Airways frequent flyer lounge but didn't slow her pace. Perhaps he was behind the darkened windows, throwing back more Jack and updating his Excel file. Excelling at moving forward with his bachelor party and impending marriage. Or maybe he was brooding again in one of the lounge's chairs, surrounded by his force field of aftershave and power adapters. Rewiring the hard drive of his heart to forget all about Laney Hudson.

"What's on your mind, Laney?" she asked, although I knew she was already reading it.

"Allen. Noah. Ghosts of one-night stands past." I knew I had to exorcise them, and there was no time like the present. "But I am off on a grand adventure. Hawaii awaits."

"Good mind-set." We had arrived at her gate. "This is where we part ways. I still want you to send me pictures of the big day, you know. To let me know you arrived safe, and to see how pretty you look."

I hugged her in thanks and promised I would. She gave a little wave before joining her fellow attendants at the boarding podium, and then she was gone. I grabbed a coffee and a muffin and trudged on to my own gate. It was fairly empty, and I had my pick of seating. I chose a bank of seats facing the window, deciding it was better to look at where I was going, rather than where I had been.

Noah

HELPLESSLY HOPING

Every cab carried Laney. I expected to see her face appear from every door that opened at the curb of the airport terminal. I expected to see that bridal dress bag when the trunk popped at O'Hare one final time. But it was just my own pathetic baggage waiting for me.

I slowly walked toward my gate, searching the faces. Looking for some sad panda hat, somewhere. And when I could no longer stand meeting people in the eye, I began to look at their feet. Looking for cheap flip-flops and toes painted like blue glass made smooth from the sea.

"We will begin boarding for Windwest Airways Flight 907 nonstop to Las Vegas in about five minutes. At that time, we ask anyone needing extra assistance . . ."

I saw myself as I was, settling into my first-class seat back on the tarmac of LaGuardia. Face after face passing by, bumping their bags against their knees as they made their way back to cattle class. And then, over the tops of the seats, I saw her coming toward me.

I'd had no idea what was walking into my life forty-eight hours before. And now, I couldn't believe I had let her walk away. It had all happened so quick, way too quick to get attached. So how come I felt like my heart was being ripped out from the roots?

All you've ever wanted were roots, Noah.

That's why you rushed balls out into proposing to Sloane. That's why you've stuck around a company you no longer believe in.

Trying to find roots. Trying to find home.

Casa è nel cuore.

I had found Laney.

And having her was just as pleasing, if not more, as wanting her. Blowing Mr. Spock's theory out of the water.

I had had her.

And I had lost her.

Boarding was an automatic afterthought. I found myself sitting in my seat, but didn't really remember the journey there. Leaning my head against the window, I stared out at the other planes on the runway. Was she still here?

All my texts and calls had gone unanswered.

She was gone. I felt it.

Another businessman took the seat next to me. We gave each other a curt nod of acknowledgment; monkey suit code. Was he heading to or from a meeting, some novelty that took him out of his office existence for a brief time? Or had he just met and had his heart broken by someone incredible? I couldn't ask. I could barely even exchange pleasantries.

We buckled, we cross-checked, we prepared for departure, and we were up in the sky before I even had time to worry about engine failure. It didn't matter. I had already crashed and burned.

I opened my tray table to accept the coffee I had requested and moved to stow my powered-down phone in my bag. Paper grazed my fingertips, and I pulled.

Laney's first sketch of me. She had captured everything I thought

I had admired about myself with a few sweeps of her pencil. Sitting rigid, unwilling to bend, when in reality, I was spineless. My fingers gripping the armrests, my eyes wide. Power-mad and single-minded. But she had caught the exact curve of my cheekbones, the slight jut of my jaw when I was deep in thought. The slant of my brow when I was trying to make sense out of the nonsensical. She had seen those details the moment she laid eyes on me.

I had shoved it into my bag along with everything else that morning, my eyes unseeing, my head dull, and my heart in disbelief. I hadn't noticed there was writing along the top of the page where there hadn't been anything before.

You have more power than you think, Noah.

There Goes Tokyo

I didn't trust myself to check my phone until I was truly out of Chicago airspace and on Pacific Coast Time. I waited for the command.

"Local time on the ground is 10:25 A.M. and weather is clear with a light breeze, at sixty-seven degrees. You are allowed to use phones at this time, if they are safely in reach. Please keep your seat belt fastened until we come to a complete stop and the Fasten Seat Belt sign is turned off. Thank you."

I could no longer restrain myself. I had to respond to Noah. He had flooded my phone with texts: long ones, short ones . . . never shoutie caps. He just wanted to know why.

And he had used an emoticon. Knowing Noah—and it was safe to admit I knew enough—he was not the kind of Tech-Boy who typically used emoticons. Certainly not the colon-open-paren combo to show they were sad.

Maybe he had run out of words. Run out of patience with me.

The second I hit "compose," my heart began to thud, dull and frantic. It didn't feel like it was still in my chest; it was that lower-in-the-pit nervous beating. Like Godzilla's unstoppable heart on the sea floor. With shaking fingers, I wrote:

I'm sorry I made you feel : (

His reply was almost instantaneous, meaning he was on the ground somewhere, too.

No, you made me FEEL. Not weak, not powerless. Incredible. You're my anti-kryptonite.

I typed and erased a dozen times before getting what I wanted to say right.

The good guys do win sometimes. I'm rooting for you from afar, but you don't need me there to complicate things.

The truth was, I didn't trust myself. I was three days late in delivering my mother's dress, and after one mind-blowing night with Noah, I had been ready to run off to Vegas with him.

I've never been a game changer, Laney. But then again, I've never had someone like you on my team. You are incredible. I've never met anyone like you and I want to get to know you better. I want you in my system, and in my life.

I couldn't bear to disappoint one more person. I needed to be responsible and get the dress delivered, but I didn't want to be the one responsible for Noah losing his job and the investors for his app company.

Like Godzilla, I felt like I was being ripped from the inside out.

You need to get me out of your system and move on.

Down I went, disintegrating to dust.

"No . . . noooo. Daddy. No . . ." The pitiful plea repeated on loop and finally tore my eyes from my phone to seek out the source. The little girl in the San Diego gate area had bright copper curls springing high above her pale forehead. "No plane, Daddy. No . . ." The parents, not much older than me, sat in matching denim and Disneyland T-shirts, desperately attempting to reason with the unreasonable preschooler.

The dad tried coaxing her to calm down with his phone, but the little girl refused to be appeased, those copper springs swinging wildly as she shook her head.

"Look, Daddy has the fart app," the mom said, in one last-ditch effort to quiet her daughter.

The little girl reluctantly took the phone and blasted a button, still visibly upset. But the tears and carrying on had at least ceased momentarily. I noticed she had a Sesame Street character on her shirt, an unfamiliar one. The puppets of my youth were primary colors—yellow, blue, red—this one was an orangey tan of unknown ethnicity, with a tutu and some pearly bling around her neck. I flipped to a blank sheet in my book and quickly sketched a plane, adding the little character's face in a window, waving a furry hand.

"What's her name?" I whispered to the dad.

"Tallulah."

"Come take a trip with me, Tallulah!" I read the words aloud as I wrote them, and I enclosed the words in a big cheery bubble above the window. Then I added a smiling pilot in the cockpit window, lest the girl think the plane was flying unmanned.

"What do you think of this?" I asked Tallulah.

The little girl's eyes widened, and she dropped her dad's phone into his hand in favor of grabbing the picture with both of her small, pudgy ones. "It's Zoe! Daddy, she made Zoe!" The mom mouthed a "thank you" and gave me a weak smile, still embarrassed that her daughter had made such a scene. "Here, Tally, come eat your carrot sticks, like Cookie Monster. He loves his vegetables."

I looked at the dad in alarm, and he just rolled his eyes in agreement. "I know. They had to get all politically correct and ruin Cookie Monster's rep. Crazy, right?" He leaned forward, his smartphone balancing between the meaty digits of his hands.

"Hey, that wouldn't happen to be the Fartrillion app, would it?" I asked, leaning a bit closer to take a look.

"Totally! Best dollar ninety-nine I ever spent," the guy said, gesturing to the multitude of choices. "It entertains my kids, annoys the women in my office, cracks up my fishing buddies—other fart apps crap out, freeze up. If you want a quality joke app, this is the one." He laughed, realizing he was giving me the hard sales pitch based on flatulence. "I know, sounds silly, right? But life's too short to not loosen up and have some fun."

I thought about the looks on the faces of Anita, the little girl Samantha in the diner, and now Tallulah when they saw the sketches I had made for them. And of Noah's expression when he had realized I had drawn him. I wondered if he had found the sketch I left that morning.

My drawings made people happy. Just as Noah's app clearly made people happy.

Would we ever allow ourselves the same courtesy? The thought saddened me. I hoped someday we both learned to please ourselves, instead of always worrying about what others thought. I hoped, wherever he was, he was finding a way to be happy.

"Are you sitting down?"

"Dani, I've been sitting down, on and off, for the last five and a half hours." I tucked the phone between my chin and shoulder and shifted the garment bag so I could grab the latest issue of *People* magazine from the airport newsstand. "And now I have an hour and forty-six minutes to kill in Los Angeles. Spit it out."

"Your mom is making a photo collage to display at the reception. You know, one of those poster boards that show them before they met, while they were dating, et cetera?"

"Yeah, yeah," I said, scouting out a snack on my way to the register. Something smothered in chocolate, preferably. "They're both in their late fifties and they've only known each other a year. I can't imagine it's going to be that exciting of a collage."

Out of the corner of my eye, I spotted a floor spinner rack with the familiar river and sun logo of Hudson Views displayed on top. Leave it to my mom to convince the airports of the world that greeting card Veraisms were impulse items just as necessary as Airborne, neck pillows, and personalized shot glasses. I swear she could sell sunscreen to the sinners in hell if she had to.

"Um, imagine again. Because I helped her sort the pictures, and remember that one we used to sneak out of the hope chest in your attic?"

"From the marriage to her first husband?"

It was a great picture, all seventies golden tones, with my mom and her ironed hair looking like a young Grace Slick. Dani and I had decided that the handsome hunk on her arm looked like Jordan Catalano with a porn 'stache, and we had giggled at the powder blue ruffles of his wedding attire.

"Why would she include Porno Catalano in her wedding collage?" I wondered if she would include pictures of my dad as well. "And what will Ernie think?"

"Laney. Don't you get it? Ernie *is* Porno Catalano."

"What? There's no way Ernie is . . . is . . . what my mother always refers to as 'Oh, that.' No way."

"Apparently, he is 'Oh, that,' all that, *and* a bag of chips. You should see all the pictures he's kept of her! Laney, he was her first . . . and now her third."

I felt the need to grab something solid, but the only thing near me was the damn card spinner rack. Full of Veraisms for every happy occasion, from *Happy birthday* to *New baby* to *Congratulations on your new house/job/pet/kidney.*

I had been waiting years for an *I'm sorry I kept you from the love of your life* Veraism from my mother. Or even just a simple *I trust and believe in you.* But apparently, she reserved all her positive sentiments for her $2.99 cards, and I just wasn't worth it.

She couldn't even be bothered to tell me anything.

"Laney, are you still there? I probably should've waited to—"

"No," I said hoarsely. "It's okay. I'm gonna go."

"You sure you're okay?" I could hear Dani's concern, genuine and gentle, drip through the phone.

"Yeah. I gotta go."

Magazine forgotten, chocolate mission aborted, I fled the small store in a daze. But not before a swing of the garment bag, lethal as the sweep of Godzilla's tail, took out the spinner rack like it was a Tokyo skyscraper just waiting to be leveled.

New texts from Dani popped up immediately.

Wait. Go WHERE?

Laney. Don't do anything drastic.

Laney?

EXIT ONLY, NO REENTRY BEYOND THIS POINT

TICKETED PASSENGERS EXITING NOW WILL BE
REQUIRED TO PASS THROUGH ADDITIONAL
SECURITY SCREENING CHECKPOINT
TO GAIN REENTRY

I stood on the cusp, contemplating the warning signs. On this side of the sliding glass door, a plane would eventually pull up at a gate to take me on the last leg to my final destination. I would land and, with dress in hand, my journey would be over.

Success.

On the other side of the sliding glass door . . . was the trip I had never trusted myself to take.

The journey would never be over if the questions stayed unanswered. But I was going to need more than a two-hour layover.

"Welcome to the Los Angeles International Airport," a seductive voice oozed from the loudspeakers. "Please do not leave bags unattended. They will be confiscated and may be destroyed. If you notice an unattended item or suspicious activity, immediately report it to airport personnel."

I pictured myself leaving the dress bag behind, abandoning it on the hook of a bathroom stall. Flags would be raised, alarms would be sounded; personnel would come running past me as I calmly exited the airport. The bomb-sniffing dogs would scramble by me, toenails clacking eagerly across the tiles, off to check it out.

Whatever you do, do not, Laney. Do NOT. My mother's words rattled vague warnings as well, but for once, my internal voice was louder than hers.

Do not tell me what to do.

I stepped onto the escalator, hauling the garment bag clear of the moving stairs. In my mind's eye, I saw Noah standing at the bottom. Holding a sign like a valet—grinning that sheepish grin at our private joke—I'M ENGAGED.

And then I saw Allen. Standing next to him, looking rock-god amazing. And holding a sign that said: WELCOME TO L.A., LANEY JANE. IT'S ABOUT TIME YOU GOT HERE.

Noah

WITS AND GUTS

Tim waved his arm back and forth, palm out, to get the bartender's attention, then raised his arm straight up and used the "rally" command to bring him over. "Two Hendertuckies, please."

"Nice to know arm-and-hand signals work in a crowded bar," I quipped.

"Shall I start a tab for you gentlemen?"

"Please do." I slid my AmEx toward the bartender. It was the "company" card Bidwell had given me to handle any wedding incidentals that fell into my lap, and I never saw the bill. It probably landed in some pile on a desk in Accounts Payable a month later and was paid with no questions even asked.

Incidentally, I was going to use it to get good and drunk.

"Where are the ground forces?" I asked Tim. I had arrived an hour before from the airport, only stopping to drop my bags in my room, and had come straight to the lobby bar to meet him.

"Jules is playing craps; Mike and Nate went to see some bullshit over at the Bellagio."

"The fountain?"

"Yeah, with all the lights and junk. It's just you and me, Private."

Thinking about fountains made me think of Laney. Actually, I hadn't stopped thinking about Laney for a moment. Not even on the casino floor, with all the sensory overload of bells clanging and glaring lights. And especially not while sitting at the Vesper Bar, with its million mirrors forcing me to look myself in the eye.

The bartender set down two frothy red drinks in front of us, each spiked with a sprig of mint. "I've been drinking these things since I got here; they are off the chain," Tim said, clinking my glass with his.

"So you're telling me you actually called things off with Sloane? In a phone call?" He shook his head and let out a slow whistle. "Aborting a mission of that magnitude takes balls, Noah."

I took a haul off my drink. "My balls were taken a long time ago, I'm sorry to say. What the hell is in this?"

"No clue. Good, right? You could've told me, you know."

I took a long look up at the mammoth chandelier above our heads, as if the answers could possibly be hovering up there.

"I didn't want to admit I fucked up," I finally said.

"Noah," Tim sputtered. "I was the definition of fuckup my entire childhood, you know that. It took enlisting to finally straighten me out, and there are still days I don't know what direction I'm headed. You've always had that calm, cool, and collected thing going on, always landing on your feet and keeping your wits about you."

I gave a sardonic chuckle. *He should've seen me upon waking and discovering Laney was gone.*

He continued. "It's a survival skill I've admired . . . fuck, I've been jealous of you my whole life."

"See, and I've always envied how you go balls out and take no prisoners," I countered. "You speak your mind and you don't worry about how anyone's going to take it. That's guts."

"To wits and guts!" Tim toasted, and we touched glasses. "Yeah, you do tend to overthink things."

We worked our way through our drinks. I tasted rhubarb. And smelled a hint of wet dog. "I need to know what's in this thing."

"See? There you go. You need to pick things apart and reassemble them so they make sense to you," Tim pointed out.

"No, I just want to know what the fuck I am drinking."

"Rumskey," the bartender supplied. "Equal parts rum and whiskey. A little Aperol and Hum liqueur, a couple of drops of rhubarb bitters and lime juice, blueberry preserves . . . just a bar spoon. And a splash of egg white."

Aha, there was the wet dog. "Great, now I know what I'm going to throw up tonight." I said, and raised my glass in thanks.

"Tell me about her."

"Laney?"

"Of course Laney. There's nothing you can tell me about the rich hottie I don't already know."

"I bet you didn't know the rich hottie has declared herself a born-again virgin, awaiting her wedding night."

Tim's mouth gaped like a flounder's. "Um, hold that thought. Back to Laney."

"She . . . she's like . . ." The glittering chandelier caught my eye once more, and I saw straight up through it, crystal clear.

"Laney's like home," I finished, looking Tim in the eye. "When I was with her, it just felt right. Easy and comfortable, but in a super-charged way. It's not settling, by any means." If anything, I had been settling when I succumbed to Sloane. "My dad once told me I would know the truth by the way it feels."

"And?"

I unfolded Laney's sketch from my pocket and smoothed it flat on the white marble bar in front of us. We both studied it for a moment. "The truth feels powerful," I admitted.

"Then you've got to blow this Popsicle stand and go after her, man. To hell with the two hundred guests, the invitations, the registry, the so-called virginity, and the future in-laws breathing down your neck. Hell, to hell with this stag week . . . as fun as it's been, even without you, bro." He bumped shoulders with me. "She's your one-in-a-million girl."

I thought about the way she'd pulled me onto the dance floor the other night.

"No," I corrected. "Laney was once in a lifetime."

I didn't need the fancy house, the nice car, or the too-beautiful wife like Sloane. Laney was all the fancy, nice, and beauty I needed. I could live in a shotgun shack with her, and I'd be happy. "But she left. There's no way—"

"There's always a way," Tim insisted.

He ran his hand over the soft stubble of his crew cut, starting at the wicked Eddie Munster–widow's peak in front, and down to the occipital bone in back that had been fractured during Taliban gunfire. I only knew the fancy name for it because of the *JAMA* and *New England Journal of Medicine* articles written about his case.

My best friend was a walking, talking miracle, and I felt humbled just being in his presence, sitting with him and sharing a drink like two everyday normal dudes. I often wondered if it was how Warren had felt, every time he saw my dad on leave. If he sometimes felt undeserving, like I did.

As if he had somehow hacked my thoughts, Tim gave me a one-armed bro hug. "Kauai's a pretty small island. We'll do some reconnaissance. With your wits—and your Platinum AmEx"—he tapped my card in the leather check holder with a grin—"combined with my guts and special ops training, we're sure to find her. And I'd be proud to lead your platoon."

"I love you, man."

Tim straightened himself up to all six feet of him, his eyes darting like a hawk over my left shoulder.

I saw his hand subtly rise and flick, and then he brought both hands toward his neck, mimicking taking aim of a tiny invisible rifle. I had to think back to the days of playing soldier in the backyard with my dad in order to interpret. They were "take cover, enemy approaching" kinds of moves.

I slowly followed his gaze through the decadent lobby of the Cosmopolitan and felt icy dread buckshot through my center, leaving my heart leaden.

Sloane and her parents were advancing straight for us. And gathered in my formerly betrothed's arms was the enormous, unmistakable bulk of a bridal dress in a garment bag.

I Sat by the Ocean

Perhaps I am being overly optimistic, but I made you an appointment at the salon for Saturday morning along with the wedding party. Unless you've shaven it all off on a whim again? Is no news good news, because I haven't heard from you all day. We'll be at the airport 6 p.m. sharp.

I ignored my mother's latest text, just as I had ignored all of Noah's, and set my mind on reaching the ocean.

"Here we are, Santa Monica Pier. Told you I'd get you here in less than thirty," my cabbie bragged.

It wasn't Los Angeles proper, but it was close enough.

"Can I keep you on the clock? I won't be long."

I couldn't be long, as my money and my time were running low. We had passed a pawnshop after exiting the freeway, and I was half tempted to go hock the dress that had been dictating my every move since Tuesday. That would show my mother.

The one who thought she could dictate my every move, and criticize my every choice, in perpetuity.

The vast vista of beiges and blues of the Pacific greeted me with open arms.

I would've preferred a bear hug.

Laney and Allen, taking on L.A.! It's like they named the city after us.

Spreading the garment bag across the sand like a beach towel, I popped on my earbuds and brought up Three on a Match's playlist.

It was perfectious.

"Are you sure you're ready for this?"

"Please. We used to shave each other's heads all the time back in high school, remember?" My voice was up an octave and sounded foreign to my ears. *Keep it brave, Laney. Don't let it waver.* "Hand them over."

Allen relinquished the clippers with a grateful smile. "I'd rather nip it in the bud now. No pun intended. Because it gets everywhere once it starts to fall out."

That was right. He had been through this once before. Without me. He knew the deal.

"You might want to lay some newspaper down, or that damn cat will be doing the hairball conga all night."

"Oh, you're right." I grabbed a week-old *New York Times* and spread it across the hardwood floor of our loft while our disinterested (for now) tabby licked a paw. "We can't have that, now can we, Sister Frances?" I cooed at her.

"You love that cat more than you love me, don't you?"

It was a fond, familiar exchange, one that we had had ever since I had spotted the cardboard box of kittens while sitting in standstill traffic on the Tappan Zee a year before. "Only you could convince the driver to open the tour bus door in twenty-degree weather on the middle of a three-mile-long bridge. Only you, Laney Jane!"

I got "only you, Laney Jane!" a lot from Allen during that tour. Like the time he sent me to the store to buy gaffer tape for an emergency drum repair, and I came back with the fabulous fuchsia-and-black zebra print Duck Tape instead. "Only you, Laney Jane!"

Between the band and the road crew, we had managed to find homes for the entire litter of kittens before the tour was over. But we had kept the littlest one for ourselves. "To test-drive," Allen had reminded me with a smile.

Was that really only a year back?

The clippers buzzed to life in my hand, and I focused on my task.

"Are you using the number two?"

"Um, no. This one is the number four." I touched down to the crown of his blond locks, trying to keep my hand from shaking. It had been a while.

"The half-inch? I'm gonna look like a hedgehog."

"A cute hedgehog," I assured him, leaning to kiss the freshly mowed strip.

I tightened my grip on the clippers and began to move them steadily, finding my groove. Golden tufts sifted past his shoulders as we talked about music, about books, and just about everything but the reason why we were sitting in our loft while the sun streamed in, while the leaves fell down, while the band was midtour. While life was moving on around us and we were holding our breath and waiting.

Those long, strong drummer's fingers ran across the top of his head. "Too long, L.J. I told you number two."

"You sure?"

"You're gonna thank me when I'm not shedding all over the house and stopping up the drains."

Fine snips of hair mingled with the longer pieces on the floor. The new clippings were straighter and darker than the sun-kissed curls that he had let grow all summer. They scattered across the open news pages of the Travel section, covering photos of beaches and sunsets Allen and I would probably never see together. They fell across the faces of the musicians pictured in the reviews in the Arts section, who strutted across stages Allen might never again play on.

"That's probably my mother," I said, as my phone buzzed for attention on the coffee table. "I'll call her later."

Allen picked it up anyway. "Hello, Mrs. Hudson," he drawled, insisting on speakerphone even though he followed up with, "Laney can't come to the phone right now. She's shaving my head. You know. Because the chemo to keep me alive is making it fall out."

Silence followed, then sputtering like static through the speaker. "Tell her to save the hair for my garden. It will keep the rabbits out."

I plucked the phone from his hand, but there was no use in hanging it up; she had already disconnected the line.

"I must be growing on her," he said sarcastically. "She's allowing me past the hedgerow."

Closing his eyes, he began to whistle Led Zeppelin's "Stairway to Heaven" as I guided the clippers over his cowlick.

"Shorter. Let's go down to number one."

I didn't question him. I simply swapped out the removable length guard with the shortest one and made another pass. The clippers were growing hot, numbing my fingers with their incessant vibration.

My hands belonged to a woman thirty years older than me: red, dry, and raw from all the constant scrubbing and sanitizing. Protecting Allen's compromised immune system was paramount. Even if I hadn't quit Marvel, I wouldn't have been able to draw. My knuckles cracked and bled every time I tried to grip a pencil.

I rested my free hand on the side of Allen's newly shorn scalp as I took care around his ears and down the back of his neck. Places I had kissed in the past. Places I would make sure I languished kisses upon that night. But first, it was my turn.

"I'm gonna leave you a landing strip," Allen joked, as the first pass of the clippers hungrily chewed through my shoulder-length shag haircut and spit long russet lengths of it to the floor. "You know I love you with a landing strip."

"And I love you," I echoed. Tears pooled as I watched my hair mingle with his, smothering the black-and-white photos of happy newlywed couples in the Styles section.

I sat on the Santa Monica Beach and rolled Allen's ring between my fingers, rubbing the stone and all its raised etchings. I hadn't been without it since that night he'd given it back to me, ten years after I thought it had been lost to the million grains of sand on Quogue Village Beach. It would somehow be fitting to lose it here.

Noah

LET IT DIE

"Thought we'd find you here, Noah!" Bidwell said with his customary forced joviality, as he threaded his way through the crowded bar, family in tow. He was clutching what looked like our Vegas itinerary in his hand.

"They must've water-boarded Warren," Tim hissed in my ear.

"Son, we know you've been a little off lately, and I'll be the first to admit, all the pressure of the big day has taken its toll on all of us," Bidwell boomed loud enough for the entire bar to hear. I swear the chandelier actually trembled above us.

"So we've put a pin in it," he said, pinching his thumb and index finger together and sweeping the air. "And we're here to take a relaxing vacation, to give you kids some time to talk, and if, by the end, you are ready to go ahead with the big wedding, great. If not"—he swept his hand as if he had all of Vegas at his disposal—"you can just have a quiet ceremony here. No fanfare."

No fanfare. No witnesses. Not even my mother. I was a POW. Prisoner of Wedding.

"Hi, Timothy," Sloane said in her usual flirty tone that she reserved for any male over the age of twelve. She completely ignored me.

"Sloane. Looking lovely as usual," Tim allowed. He was the only one of my college friends she had met before, and she went swooping in for the Euro double-cheek air kisses.

"A word, Ridgewood." Bidwell's voice was still forced, but no longer jovial. He beckoned me out of the bar and over to a tufted purple velvet couch tucked against the lobby wall. It looked like it belonged in Liberace's living room, with an old-fashioned, corded black phone on a wooden table nestled between the couch cushions.

"Here's how it works in the Bidwell household, son. If Sloane isn't happy, my wife isn't happy. If my wife isn't happy, I hear about it twenty-five hours a day. Now, we've got a big year coming up, son. Big profits. With lots of points riding on it for you . . ."

He fixed a stare on me that previously would have sent me cowering back to my corner office. But fuck the corner office. Fuck the profits and the points. I stonily stared back.

"And *your* point is . . . ?"

"Two choices." He picked up the receiver of the old-timey phone for dramatic effect. "You call Butler and tell him to pack his shit up, because security is coming to escort him out of the building. You both lose your shares in the company and any claim on the prototypes in current development. Kiss the Series C equity financing good-bye."

He egged me on to take the handle of the phone but I kept my fists in my lap, mainly to keep myself from punching him.

"Or," he said simply, dropping the receiver back on its cradle, "you marry her, call me Dad, and give Anne and your lovely mother some grandchildren, and we can forget this conversation ever happened. It's a no-brainer, Noah."

"Is this a threat?"

"No. It's a promise I made to myself, after Remy Georges almost destroyed her."

I was taken aback, not so much by the venom in his voice, but by the familiarity of the name.

"Remy Georges? The photographer?"

"That dirty Frog playboy broke my princess's heart, and I'm not about to let a two-bit Wop hack off the street do the same."

I let the ethnic slur slide in favor of breaking the news to him like a steel pipe to the knees. "But . . . Sloane's hired him, sir. As our wedding photographer."

Bidwell's mouth gaped as wide as the mounted barracuda back on his office wall; when I was first hired, he'd bragged about hiring the best taxidermist in the business to create a fiberglass replica of his big catch, so he could release the poor sucker back into the wild.

"But . . . but why would she—"

For once, Bidwell and I were on the same page. The hell if I knew. Was Sloane looking for revenge? If so, an elaborate wedding to rub her ex's nose in it was pretty extreme. Then again, this was Sloane we were talking about.

"Oh, that little girl of mine holds a grudge a mile long." He shook his head. "Always has. But I won't stand for it. You call that money-grubbing piece of trash and tell him his services are no longer needed. Got it?"

He touched the Liberace phone between us again, as if to remind me of his earlier threat. Now the barracuda look was in his toothy grin. So much for the catch-and-release program; he wasn't going to let me off the hook anytime soon.

"And book a chapel here. Let's get this over with."

He stood, giving his suit jacket a tug. "You have until Saturday. Might want to have that suit pressed, while you're at it," he added, and strode back to the bar.

I followed him stiffly, my mind still reeling over this bomb that had been dropped. This *bombe nucléaire*. I thought about all the French phrases Sloane slipped into just about every conversation. She must've been obsessed with the guy. And now she was using her money and influence—and me—to get back at him. Before he left for Paris.

No wonder she had been so insistent on the date change.

She wanted him there, to torture him with what he could've had.

And what was I? Just some weapon in her stash. Riding along in Bidwell's deep back pocket. She didn't love me. She probably never had.

I felt like a tool.

It was as if the phone call to Sloane had never registered, never stuck. She and her mom were yapping about—what else? The wedding. They had been incapable of discussing anything else for the last year. Tim's eyes must've glazed over at the first mention of pomander balls and *bombonieres*. "We'll leave you two," Bidwell said, and with that, he adjourned the board meeting by clapping a hand on Tim's shoulder. "Alone."

Tim was determined to leave no man behind. Least of all, his best friend. "Noah and I were actually just discussing my best man duties, and—"

"It's okay, Tim. We'll reconvene later," I told him.

"You sure?"

I picked up my drink with my left hand. "As you were, Sergeant," I said, pointedly toasting him with my first two fingers crossed. "I need some alone time with my bride-to-be."

He gave me the thumbs-up, drained his drink, and pushed off the bar stool. "Nice to see you all."

"Carry it flat, Mother. I want it to be perfect."

Sloane unloaded what appeared to be twenty pounds of wedding dress across her petite mother's outstretched arms. "The steamer says she can't be here until Friday."

Anne Bidwell remained impassive, either used to her daughter's demands or unable to express emotion due to all the Botox injections in her once-beautiful face.

I flicked my eyes in Tim's direction once more. With one palm flat, the other hand making a small circle above it, Tim turned on his heel and walked toward the casino. I saw him swing one arm around. *Map check and move out.* He was going to assemble the troops in one place.

Knowing Tim, he was planning a military maneuver to blow this Popsicle stand.

"Daddy booked us a luxury suite at the Paris," Sloane was saying. "I want to try the new Gordon Ramsay there, and of course, Le Provencal." Suddenly her French didn't sound all that exotic or impressive to me. But apparently it did to her, since she kept rattling on as if she just liked hearing the sound of her own voice. "And Mother arranged a private backstage tour of *Jubilee* for the four of us at Bally's, tomorrow at two. It is supposed to be gaudy and fabulous, with all those crazy outfits. How do you think I would look in all the feathers and sequins?" She struck her version of a Vegas showgirl pose for me.

My mouth opened, then it clicked shut. "Unbelievable," was all I could muster.

"Order for me, Noah?" Drink selector was just one of the tasks Sloane had assigned to me as boyfriend early on. Along with purse holder, shopping bag carrier, and doormat.

I flicked through Vesper's creative mixed drinks menu, trying to decide what was the most suitable drink for the occasion. Corpse Bride? Fear and Loathing? The Cyanara?

I leaned toward the bartender. "A Blue Blood. And another Hendertucky, please." I noticed my AmEx was no longer in the check holder. Jerking my head up, I saw Tim's back disappear into the crowd. *That crafty son of a bitch.*

Sloane's eyes surveyed me coolly, taking in my three-day scruff and rumpled suit. "You look like you've slept in your clothes."

"I sort of did. Big delay," I began. "I still haven't been reunited with my luggage."

I touched my tie defensively, and a jolt of adrenaline burst though me as the image of Brioni silk, sliding between Laney's breasts and down the rest of her gorgeous body, hit me.

"Oh, you poor thing!"

Sloane put on her concerned girlfriend actress mask for show and moved to embrace me, but I put a hand up between us. I didn't want her invading that sacred space or clouding my mind with her passive-aggressive tactics.

"Out of all the flights you could have taken, you chose a nondirect? What were you thinking?"

"I wasn't thinking," I said drily. *But I am now.*

Out of all the flights, how did I land on Laney's?

Luck? Fate?

My eyes focused in on the woman I had proposed to in front of Buckingham Fountain that Valentine's Day past. We had had the Initial Public Offering on our app stock . . . and I had gone into Insane Proposal Overdrive. *What had I been thinking?*

When Laney asked me back at O'Hare how I felt about pretending to be engaged to a total stranger, she had no idea its double meaning.

The bartender brought the fresh drinks. I swiftly moved Laney's drawing before Sloane could use it as a cocktail napkin. "I hear there's an Aureole here," she said breezily. "Their bar is supposed to put the one in New York to shame. We should have dinner there. And I want to try the Wicked Spoon, upstairs, for brunch. It's received amazing reviews."

"Sloane," I started. I didn't want to think about suffering through another dinner with her, or brunch, or anything in between. If I didn't say something now, my whole existence would be moving from one decadent feast to another, the experience meaningless, tasteless. Empty. I thought about Slim Jims and root beer floats and Laney.

"It's now or never," I heard an unfamiliar voice announce behind me.

It was raspy and robust but at the same time, diminutive. I swiveled my head the other way but was met with an empty bar stool. I dropped my gaze down a few inches.

Dressed in a small white outfit with a plunging V-neck and a high collar, a miniature version of Elvis stared up at me expectantly. His jumpsuit had a blue-and-gold peacock design embroidered on the front and along the wide pant legs, and probably all across the back as well.

A huge belt, covered in gold medallions and forming a design at the center that resembled the eye of a peacock feather, cinched his tiny waist. I thought about Laney's peacock feather tattoo and my insides turned to jelly. "For luck," she'd told me.

The mini Elvis's hair was a perfect black pompadour, and his sideburns were thicker than mine could ever grow. "Well?" He gestured. "A little help here? I got a show in twenty."

"Oh. Sure, man."

He put his shoe (not blue suede, I noted, but a classic white buck instead) on the rung of the bar stool and lifted an arm. I grabbed him near the elbow and in a swift heave-ho, he was up on the high white stool next to me.

"Thanks." He grinned.

Sloane, meanwhile, was growing impatient on the other side of me. She was the only person I knew over the age of four who needed constant entertaining and attention. It was exhausting and nowhere near as novel as during our initial courtship testing of the waters. I could only imagine it getting worse during the nuptial and newlywed phase. If only I had had the sense to put our relationship under the microscope like an alpha/beta trial years ago, I would've seen the glaring defects.

"Are you done playing tourist and hobnobbing with the locals?" she snarled, stabbing her ice with her stirrer.

I swiveled to look at her. I had been playing tourist all my life, apparently. Gawking at the glitz and giving much too much attention to the meaningless souvenirs along the way.

Now, Noah. Or never.

Or forever hold your peace.

"Sloane, you gave me a shot that day, because you said I made you laugh. But honestly, I don't think we've laughed together once since that day. I'm not happy in this relationship, and I can't imagine you are, either."

"I don't know why you are saying this." She haughtily sipped her drink. "We make a great couple. All my friends are jealous of us."

"Including Remy?"

She froze. "He's just the hired help," she said icily. *God, is she really that ruthless?* "He has nothing to do with us."

"There is no 'us,' Sloane! It stopped being about us soon after the wedding was announced. I want to be in a partnership, not an ownership."

"So I'll change," she said flippantly, as if she was talking about swapping her little black Helmut Lang dress for this season's Stella McCartney's.

"You've already been changing! And for all the wrong reasons. You've had all these surgeries, made all this fuss, just so you can get back at some guy who dumped you?"

Color drained from her perfectly made-up face. "I have no idea what you are talking about." Her voice shook as she tried to regain her composure. "You can go have dinner with the boys," she allowed, swinging her Tory Burch satchel bag onto her arm and almost knocking the peewee peacocked Elvis off his stool. "I've got the spa booked." She was off in a cloud of flowery perfume and the click-clack of her Louboutins.

"What. A. Royal. Bitch." Elvis used a dramatic pause between each word for emphasis, and all I could do was nod, shake my head, and nod again. "Not to stick my nose in or anything. But I was right here and couldn't help but witness it."

"Do you mind me asking . . . what's with the peacocks?"

"The King was fascinated by the symbol of the peacock as a good-luck charm," he rasped. "Sounds like you could use a roomful of them."

I wasn't religious, but if that was a sign from above, it couldn't have been any clearer than if the gargantuan chandelier were to come crashing down on my head.

Miniature Elvis drained his drink, hopped down, and swaggered off.

"Excuse me." I jogged after him. "But where can I find more of you?"

He looked taken aback. "People of very short stature?"

"No. More Elvii."

Set it Free

All You Had to Do

I'm in another time zone
I'm zoned out
I'm shut in.
My mind is reeling
I wish it'd shut up
What I'm feeling,
I wanna shut down.

All I have to do is
Forget you
Not say your name
Not take your call
It should be easy to
Hate you

'Cuz
All you had to do was,
All you had to do was tell me
After all.

It's not fair
It ain't right
I still want to hold you through the night
Want you to whisper all the things you never told me
In my ear

Now all you have to do is
Forgive me
Say my name
Will you take my call
It should be easy to
break me
'Cuz
All you ever did was
love me
After all.

(music and lyrics by Allen S. Burnside, copyright 2007 Laney Jane Hudson)

"Laney?"
   "Still alive, Mom."
   "Is your flight still on time?"
   "Yes."
   "Are you at the airport?"
   "No."

I stared across the Pacific, imagining the sigh she let go traveling from the Hawaiian islands, skimming the top of the water, and making landfall, blowing back my hair as it came ashore.

"The dress will get there in time for the wedding, Mom."

"I didn't just want the dress here, I wanted *you* here, too!"

I stood up and walked to the shoreline, the dress bag in my hand waving like a warning flag. "What about what *I* wanted, Mom? All those years ago! I wanted to go to California with Allen." The horizon blurred beneath my tears.

"It wouldn't have changed what happened to him, Laney."

"Who's to say?" I screamed. "Who's to say I shouldn't just put on this wedding dress and walk right into the ocean and join him?"

"Laney. I've got just one thing to say on the matter."

"What? A Veraism?"

"No, I didn't make this one up. And I don't want you to draw it. I want you to just listen. If you love something, you have to set it free."

"Oh, and if it comes back, you get to marry it a second time, like Ernie? And if it doesn't come back, it's died of cancer?"

"I should've told you about Ernie before this."

Allen's lyrics, penned just for me, were ricocheting through my skull like a pinball.

All you had to do was tell me.

"You should've told me a lot of things, Mom! You shopped at that King Kullen supermarket *every* week! You saw Allen's mom and she told you he was sick and you *never* told me! We could've had more time."

"I know you aren't going to believe me, but I loved Allen, too. Like he was my son. But you know my first marriage ended before it started. We were so, so young and we had to learn the hard way. I didn't want you and Allen making the same mistakes. I always had faith in Allen's talents; I had no doubt he would go far."

I stood frozen at the shore, phone pressed to my ear like it was a seashell sharing its most secret confessions.

"But I wanted you to find your own way. Not to just hitch yourself to Allen's star. I cannot begin to tell you the incredible guilt I've carried since Allen's death, honey. I was wrong about so much."

I was silent, letting it all sink in. Both for me, and for her.

"Deep down, I have always believed in you, Laney. And I'm so proud of your accomplishments. Now, please. Set him free."

I had my phone in one hand, and the bridal dress in the other. I had no free hands.

"Can you hold on a second, Mom?"

I set both down behind me, and with all my might and with all the love in my heart, I threw Allen's ring into the Pacific.

Then I picked up the phone and the dress bag. The heaviest thing to carry was a grudge. And I was starting to feel less burdened already.

"I'm back."

"Good. Now, go get on that plane. Because I'm not getting married without you here."

Noah

ONE MORE DAY

With a heavy heart, I walked past the Godzilla-sized red stiletto sculpture and found myself in front of the Cosmopolitan's glass-walled Pop-Up Wedding Chapel. *Commitment Ceremonies, Vow Renewals, and Faux Weddings,* the sign bragged. *Legally Binding Ceremonies* seemed to be added as an afterthought, in smaller font with an additional price tag. The thought of faking a wedding with Sloane, just to make her family happy, shot through one side of my brain and out the other. No, that wasn't fair to anyone, and that wasn't exactly solving any problems.

A space age–looking gumball machine caught my eye, filled with oversized novelty erasers shaped like diamond solitaire rings. "May I?" I mouthed to the woman working on the other side of the glass, pointing at the rings. She smiled and waved me in.

Tread lightly, I heard Laney's soft voice saying.

An eraser wasn't for the mistakes, just another tool to add to the arsenal.

"Do you need anything else?" The woman asked as she rang me up for the ring.

I heard Warren's words loud and clear: *You need to do what's best for you*, but they were all jumbled up with one of my favorite *Star Trek* quotes: "Logic clearly dictates that the needs of the many outweigh the needs of the few."

What Would Spock Do?

"Yes. I need to book a ceremony."

"*Bonjour*, this is Remy." Our wedding photographer's voice was higher than I expected, but loaded with all the impatience and irritation I would imagine from a French playboy who was probably breaking up his *ménage à trois* to take my phone call.

"Noah Ridgewood."

"Is this . . . Sloane's Noah?" His accent hit upon the vowels in our names, drawing them out.

"Yes. I'm calling to say your services are no longer needed."

"The wedding, then? Is it off?" That was when I heard it. There was no impatience and irritation. You'd think a guy who had just lost a huge money gig like the Bidwell wedding would be a bit put out. But no, what I heard in his voice was relief.

And hope.

"Her father found out she had hired you."

Remy dropped a few choice French curses. "He's a powerful man, her father," he said, his voice flat.

"That he is," I agreed.

"Do you love her, Noah?"

I contemplated his bold query. Most grooms would prepare for a cockfight, threatened by such a question. "I loved the idea of her," I finally said. "But I don't think she really ever wanted me to love her." It was true, looking back on her behavior. It was so obvious now.

Remy let out a sigh long enough for both of us.

"I loved her, Noah. From the moment I saw her through the lens of my camera in front of the Limelight. I was *paparazzi*, you see. Waiting at the nightclubs with the other vultures and their flashbulbs to catch the big money shot. But I didn't take any pictures that night. I knew the moment was captured forever, in my heart." His words, although cheesy, sounded strangely sincere. "Our love grew fast and intense. We were so happy. If I could hear the sweetness of her laughter every day, I needed nothing else in my life."

I couldn't control the snort that emanated from the back of my throat. Were we talking about the same girl here? As if he had read my thoughts, Remy added, "I know she's high maintenance, and the drama, *sacre bleu*, the drama! But I loved every bit of it. And more. You don't know the real Sloane. Trust me. Not the one I fell in love with."

"Then why did you break up with her?"

"Her father threatened to have my work visa pulled if I kept seeing her. *Mon Dieu*, it killed me to walk away from her! He sent her away to school, into the Midwest and away from me."

Enter the kid with the cheap suit and big dreams, I thought. Ripe for the picking. Just like that strawberry in her champagne glass. *Make me laugh*, she had said.

Sloane wasn't looking for revenge. She was looking for happiness. But she was making everyone around her miserable in the process.

"To photograph her on her wedding day would be a stab through my heart. But I couldn't say no. I said I would do it. It's my punishment for being weak, for letting her father win."

"Remy, you need to come to Vegas."

It was a gamble and the stakes were high, but he had nothing to lose. And neither did I.

Aloha, Mahalo

I moved through Lihue Airport, watching as people hugged hello and the occasional lei was thrown around a neck with fanfare.

Even after my mother's phone call, I still braced myself for the inevitable umbilical noose she was going to tighten around me when she caught sight of me. The very thought made me want to dive back into the safe, pressurized womb of the aircraft cabin. I didn't know how she'd done it, but Anita had pulled some strings with the other airline's flight attendants to make sure I had a hero's welcome.

A round of applause had greeted me as I boarded my flight without a minute to spare. *Oh, no, not again,* I had groaned inwardly. The flight attendant had given me a wink as she held open the first-class closet door for the dress. "Yes, here she is, folks!" Her voice was gravelly through the intercom. "The daughter of the bride has been traveling for three days trying to get her mother's dress to Hawaii—let's give her a hand."

My surprise had morphed into pride.

I was the dress bearer. It was my job to get it from point A to point B, and then the pressure was off.

Still, as I scanned the crowd for familiar faces, my doubts and nerves got the best of me. Vera was going to crucify me. There was still time to run. I pictured hopping onto the back of one of those slow-moving, beeping airport carts to stage my getaway. My mother chasing me through the airport, trying to get her clutches on the dress I dangled like a carrot on a stick.

Old habits died hard.

Maybe it was time to stop torturing my mother, and start talking to her.

"Laney! Laney!"

Dani was hopping up and down, curls bobbing. She already had an enviable tan and a cluster of guys watching as other things bounced under her coral-colored sundress.

I was enveloped in a hug that smelled of salt water and sunscreen, and it was as comforting as stepping into a warm house after a long day of stomping through snow. But it wasn't Dani who had grabbed me. My mother made sure she got the first honors.

"Oh, sweetheart! Thank goodness! We've been so worried. Are you okay? What an ordeal!" She pressed a kiss to my temple.

No berating? No interrogation about the dress?

"Paging the real Vera Hudson to gate 8," I joked. "Who are you and what have you done with my mother?"

"Helena."

She took my cheeks in both her hands, and now I knew she meant business. "If you think for one minute that I value that dress over my only daughter's well-being . . . perish the thought."

Dani's fingers danced around my shoulders, pulling my army coat off my back.

"No more need for this. You're here, you're finally friggin' here!"

I turned and hugged my best friend, tears welling as I whispered, "WWLD without you? Thank you."

She gave me a "you're crazy, but you're welcome" squeeze and murmured, "Oh, shut it. We'll talk later."

"Ernie's got the car waiting out front, chop chop!"

Vera was back in command. She plucked the garment bag out of my hands, and in that brief second, I saw time reverse for her. She was a bride, aglow with anticipation. Dani took my carry-on and we made our way out to ground transportation.

"Hiya, doll." Ernie greeted me with a hug. The customary Hawaiian shirts he loved to wear back in New York finally didn't look out of place here under the sun and gentle Pacific breeze. "Now we can officially start the party."

"Thanks, Ernie."

"You, curly doll"—he beckoned to Dani—"sit up front and make me look good, okay?"

He held open the door of the vintage red 1950s Thunderbird convertible he must've rented for the occasion.

"Yes, Mr. Crystal," Dani replied in mock coyness, complete with the champagne-pronunciation of his name my mother preferred.

Ever the gentleman, he ushered my mother and me in with a sweep of the door and clicked it closed with a wink. I think he was giving us some alone time.

As we wound through the lush landscape of Kauai, over one-lane bridges and past breathtaking waterfalls, my mother held tight to my hand.

"You look good," she started.

"Are you kidding? I'm a mess. The only thing fresh about me is my underwear."

"Good thing you packed three pairs. Right?" she said, egging me on.

"Yes," I admitted, laughing. "Your rule of three came in handy."

"Yes, three's a charm." She sniffed in satisfaction. "And I have Ernie to prove it." She must've noticed my skeptical look, because she added, "We just had to make a few wrong turns to find each other again."

"So who set who free in the first place?" I had to ask.

"Well." My mother reddened. "It's complicated. Let's just say we didn't have the luxury of planning a leisurely wedding the first time around."

"Mom!" I couldn't believe she never mentioned it once, after all these years. "A baby?"

She held out her hands in supplication, and raised her brows. I understood the wordlessness of such shock and heartache. After I slid my hand over hers, she continued. "We loved each other, but we lost . . . well, we lost direction after that. It was hard to find our way back to a good place, you know?"

I knew all too well. She squeezed my hand, but I squeezed back harder.

"You always were so much stronger than me, Laney."

She winced, and I suddenly understood the reasoning behind decades of minced words. And as her eyes channeled a hundred apologies, I realized her inability to support me, and my choices, hadn't come from disapproval, but rather from the unresolved pain of her past.

"Ernie wanted to go to school out west. He could've taken over my father's fur business once he retired, but he wanted to make something of himself, his own way, without my family's money. I didn't want to go out west, so that was that. We parted ways."

And here I thought my mother had been in the market for a sugar daddy. Turned out Ernie hadn't wanted her to be his sugar mama.

"Well, now that you're together, you're not going to change the business to Crystal Views or something, are you?"

My mother laughed. "Are you kidding? Ernie loves that I have my own interests and my own career. He's got his own kids, and I have you. We're not changing our wills or pooling our finances, sweetie. He's not looking to change up Hudson Views. But I am."

"What do you mean?"

We had arrived at our resort, and she whisked me through the property as she explained her latest idea.

"Honey, your dad started Hudson Views as an outlet for his cartooning. He had such a unique way of capturing the absurdities of life in a one-panel picture. Half the reason why I married him, I suppose; he could make me laugh at the darnedest things. You've got that gift, too. Anyone can write the one-liners . . ."

"But then they wouldn't be Veraisms," I told her.

"Well, true," my mother admitted without a hint of modesty. "But I want you to express yourself more. Do your own line. Anything goes."

"Anything?"

"Laneyisms!" She beamed. "I was talking to Ernie about it right before we left for Paris. I told him, if Laney can't be counted on to get the job done, then I just don't know if anyone can."

And here I thought I had eavesdropped on another one of her dressing-me-down sessions!

"Capture the attention of the twentysomething crowd," she continued. "They're all too busy with their screaming meemies to send an actual honest-to-goodness paper card."

I laughed. "You mean streaming memes, right? *Memes.*" I enunciated it for my mother, who was a hopeless Luddite when it came to any computer jargon.

If Noah was around, perhaps he could help me launch some sort of meme generator app using my drawings. Help me cure the world with laughter.

Then again, I could think of lots of other things to do with Noah if he were here.

I sighed, remembering our pillow talk back at the Drake. Noah wasn't really the type of guy to run from his problems. He was a logical, patient, step-by-step guy. Formulating a plan of action, and then coding it.

My mother sensed a shift in my mood. Taking my hand, she said, "Come see your dress."

"My dress?"

"Of course, silly. I had it custom-made. Remember all those torturous measurements I put you through?"

"Yes, but then you told me you didn't want me wearing the seafoam dress after all, because the color wasn't right for me."

"No, the color wasn't right for my *maid of honor.* I wanted you in something different." She threw open the closet door. "While you were carrying my dress cross-country, I was carrying yours. From France."

The dress was a halter-top style in a rich, iridescent blue silk that shone like the deepest color on the eyespot of a peacock's tail plume.

"Here's the best part."

Taking it down carefully by its hanger, she flipped it to show me the backless style. "Perfect to show off those tattoos of yours."

"I thought you meant the color would clash with my hair and skin tone, so I assumed you didn't want me in the bridal party," I mumbled, feeling stupid. "It's gorgeous. Thank you."

It really was. I could tell a lot of thought had gone into choosing something that was more my style rather than her own. And I realized the dresses I had halfheartedly thrown into my luggage to wear really weren't special enough for the occasion.

"Crap, I don't think I have nice enough shoes to do this dress justice."

My mom waved her hand. "Wear whatever is easy to walk on sand. Beach ceremony, remember?"

I looked down at my flip-flops. Thanks to Noah, I hadn't had to wear them in the Chicago winter, but they had, in fact, carried me the whole way here. Good enough.

Noah

LOVE REMOVAL MACHINE

I meandered through the Venetian on my way to Tim's texted rendez-vous point, letting the faux clouds of the blue sky lead me. Dusk was settling across Nevada, yet here I was in ever-sunny Italy. Laney had been right; what I had seen of Vegas so far was just a plastic mirage. Including the woman I once thought I wanted to spend my life with.

You don't know the real Sloane, Remy had said. And come to think of it, she really didn't know the real me. I had forgotten who that guy was. Until I had met Laney, I had forgotten he existed.

I came across one of my groomsmen, Jules, engaged in a staring contest with a powdery-faced mime in the middle of St. Mark's Square. Sidling up next to my friend of fourteen years, I murmured, "Is he supposed to be Dante?"

Jules didn't break eye contact, just squinted, hand stroking his blond goatee. "No, not Dante," he replied slowly. "I'm thinking . . . generic historical Italian figure."

I peered back up at the mime, frozen stiff on his small platform behind a curved balustrade. He was as white as a sheet personified.

"I know how you feel, man," I said, sympathizing with him under my breath, as the prospect of spending all of the next day with the Bidwells loomed large.

The dude was making bank—dollars of all denominations and many coins lined the railing. The only things whiter than his entire getup were the whites of his eyes.

"Never let them see the whites of your eyes," Jules said, squinting harder.

As a reference librarian at Evergreen State College, he had had a lot of practice mastering the steely stare.

"Aha! See that? He blinked. I win!" He slapped a ten-dollar bill down for the guy anyway, then turned to envelop me in a bear hug.

"Missed you, man! Just get here?"

"A couple of hours ago."

Strong, steady hands gripped my shoulders, and I knew they belonged to Mike, surgeon to the rich and famous in Reno. "Hey, now, the slacker has finally arrived!"

I felt knuckles dig into my skull, older-brother noogie style. Nate had arrived, too: the old man of the group. He was the only one married with a kid already. Yet he was still the most juvenile of the bunch.

"KISS minigolf!" Nate roared, throwing up the devil horns. "Are we there, or what?"

"Please," Mike scoffed. "I'm working on getting us some real tee time. Shadow Creek, homey."

He slung an arm over my shoulder, and one over Jules's. We started to walk and shoot the shit, with Nate bouncing to our left and our right like an excited puppy. It was as if we had never left the quad in the dorm, freshman year. All we needed was—

"Um, guys?" Jules pointed toward the indoor waterway winding through the "streets" of Venice.

Tim was floating by in a gondola, singing Styx's "Come Sail Away" in falsetto as the bored-looking gondolier steered the craft.

"Dude, what the hell is a pomander ball?" my best friend hollered, his voice carrying through the fake canal tunnel as he glided under the bridge.

I laughed, not wanting to get into the specifics of the sphere-shaped flower bouquets that Sloane insisted her bridesmaids needed to carry by loops of silk rope (probably spun by imported silkworms at nine dollars an inch).

"When she gets really excited, she calls them 'kissing balls,'" I informed him, following the boat from above, to where it eventually docked with little fanfare.

"Ha, you should be so lucky." Tim hopped out, and I swear there was a twinkle in his eye. "Come with me, lads. We're hitting old Vegas tonight," he said conspiratorially.

"Cheap tables and loose women?" Jules asked.

"Or loose tables and cheap women?" Mike countered.

"Affirmative." Tim clapped twice. "So let's get the lead out. Noah and I've got a mission to plan."

I had my credit card linked to my e-mail account, so anytime I made a purchase I would receive an electronic receipt. Charges started rolling in the next morning, and I just had to trust that Tim knew what he was doing: Cine-Prop Picture Cars, Inc.; Viva Vegas Theatrical Rental; Look-Alikes Party Starters, LLC; Samson's Surgical Supply. But when he called to casually inquire about my credit limit, I knew he was going for broke. Literally. "My pilot buddy's friend has a Hawker 800 on an empty leg to pick up some high-stakes gambler on the Big Island and bring him back here for the weekend. It's a one-way private charter at a third of the cost."

Slightly more expensive than lily of the valley imported from Holland off-season.

"Go for it," I commanded.

"Yes!" he hissed in victory. "Now *this* is the ultimate bachelor party! What's going to happen in Vegas later today . . . ain't going to stay in Vegas after all."

Warren was clicking in. "Hey, I have to take this call. Just don't get yourself court-martialed, okay?"

"You've been staring at those bananas all morning. I don't think they are going to ripen any faster on your watch," Sloane said.

I dragged my eyes away from the complimentary fruit basket that sat on the dining table of our sumptuous suite. Of course there was free fruit; there was complimentary everything when you shelled out the per-night charge on a suite of rooms like this. And it would sit untouched, because Sloane was a picky fruitophobe. And I would be gone.

"You should finish getting ready. We'll be late for brunch and the *Jubilee* tour."

Sloane was lounging on all the pillows of the bed, flipping through a trashy women's magazine.

"You should read this." She licked her finger and turned the page. "It'll teach you how to treat me better." She held it up so I could read the headline: *Understanding the Italian Man*.

"You're half an Italian man," she snorted, "so at least some of it should apply."

I thought back to Laney's question about the mysterious middle initial of my monogram. The name she had called melodic was one the Bidwell family would rather hide away as a dirty little secret. Luciano was just a little too ethnic for them even to list on the wedding invitation betrothing their WASPy daughter to me.

"Like?" I asked drily.

"It says that Italian men are very romantic and they should make their women feel really special when they are around them. Women are very important in Italian culture. That's why men always give them whatever they need and desire."

I stood up and wordlessly made my way into the bathroom. Everything was exactly where it had been the night before: my toothbrush, my toothpaste, my hairbrush. But none of it looked familiar.

"Oh, and that you are protective and possessive of who and what you love," she called after me.

I splashed water on my face, then slowly wiped it dry, watching my movements, dreamlike, in the mirror. Behind me, a new pair of pajamas, courtesy of Sloane, hung from the hook.

"Ha! Listen to this: 'Italian men can often be stubborn and unbending so make sure that you are ready to accept his decision or opinion. The only time they may change their minds is when their mother tells them to.' Maybe I *should* take your mother's calls more often."

I buttoned my shirt, fresh from the laundry service. I had taken Bidwell's advice and had had my suit pressed as well.

"I swear, you're worse than a girl! Hurry up in there."

My red Converse sneakers were waiting for me by the door. My computer was already over in Tim's room.

I was taking nothing else.

"Let's get out of this place," I said to my reflection.

The Wicked Spoon brunch put Laney's Eighteen-Wheeler breakfast to shame. Like most of Vegas, it was supersized, decadent, and completely over the top. Many items were miniature replicas of larger entrees, tempting you. *Try me! I'm so small. Just a bite. You can leave me behind if you want. It's all-you-can-eat buffet!*

Guests ladled plate after plate of the food, pacing themselves, strategizing, and wasting much too much. The servers were there to quickly whisk away any evidence of leftovers, your plated sins flying back to the kitchen to be scraped in the trash, sanitized back to white and sparkling clean, and stacked back on the buffet for you to start all over again.

I sipped my coffee and watched my soon-to-be-ex-future in-laws under the spell of the Wicked Spoon. Bidwell treated the place like he treated his business, acquiring load after heavy load. He'd pick and choose back at the table, give his approval of some items and utter dismissal of others. He pink-slipped the mashed potatoes but promoted the meat loaf to the center of his meal.

Anne brought everything back to the table sneakily, guiltily. Probably obsessed with body image and weight her whole life, Sloane's mother ate with no enjoyment. She tiptoed around the fatty skin of the fried chicken and made excuses for the five different desserts she sampled.

Sloane had begun with gusto, but quickly grew tired of it all. She had nibbled her way through every food group and meal—breakfast, brunch, lunch, dinner, and dessert—and seemed depressed she had no food prospects on the horizon to look forward to for a few hours. She moaned about fitting into her dress, rubbing her personally trained flat abs.

I had chosen wisely and partaken in moderation enough food to keep me moving through the day. I had tossed my white cloth napkin on the table a while back, indicating surrender. But my mind was already on freedom.

A tiny dollop of spun sugar from the dessert counter sat untouched on Sloane's plate as she chattered with her mother about the *Jubilee* backstage tour and the outfits we were about to see, and which of her bridesmaids had the body type to make her wedding wardrobe choice—Vera Wang silhouettes in the color "blush"—look as stunning as a showgirl. All talk always revolved around her and came back to: what else? The Wedding. It was loaded with all the anticipation that the ultimate reservation at a hot new restaurant held: coveted and bragged about, reserved months in advance, menu thoroughly researched. Yet Sloane was likely to be let down with the actual experience after all the hype leading up to it. Bored by the time the check came. And if I went through with it, I'd be left holding the bill for the rest of my miserable married life with her.

The spun sugar sat, pristine, in front of her. It was the perfect size for its pure sweetness, perched on a tiny silver paper cone. Unlike the bright pink candy floss of my memories from the fair, this was a pastel rainbow cloud, studded with small silver dragées.

I tasted Laney on my lips. I smelled her on my clothes. Her warm sugar scent hit my memory triggers.

If Laney was like the cotton candy at the fair, light and fun, Sloane was like the ridiculously huge stuffed prize that you wanted so, so bad the minute you laid eyes on it. The one you just *had* to win. So you played the game. All the other kids looked on, envious, as you lugged it around the fairgrounds with you all day. But soon you realized your folly; it slowed you down, and you were stuck with it.

"Noah!" Sloane had barely glanced at me through our entire meal, but now she was staring, wide-eyed. "I was going to eat that!"

Not today, I thought, as the last bit of cotton candy dissolved on my tongue. I felt lighter, less burdened, as we left our table, than I had when we arrived.

Our *Jubilee* tour guide was a fresh-faced girl from North Carolina named Mandy. She was still just "a bluebell," she confided, and hadn't been promoted to dancing topless just yet.

"I've been here five years, so here's to hoping!"

"Five years!" Sloane exclaimed. "I'd be lucky if I lasted a week!"

I was banking on lasting twenty minutes, tops. I had entered the VIN and license plate number of Tim's rental vehicle into GoToHail so I could track it, and it was about ten minutes out.

Mandy gave us a quick walk-through of the stage before we headed into the inner sanctum. The costume room was an explosion of colors. Shimmering outfits, sequined and encrusted with Swarovski crystals, abounded. "Feel this Bob Mackie," Mandy insisted, dropping a sparkling sapphire gown into my arms. And I had ribbed on Laney for having to carry her mother's heavy dress load.

"That baby weighs thirty pounds," she informed me. "Can you imagine carrying yourself up and down five hundred stairs on four-inch heels wearing that every night?"

"Nope."

Laney had told me I'd make a horrible drag queen. And she was right.

"Here's my very favorite costume—the bride," Mandy said.

Everyone oohed and aahed at the showstopping ensemble, which included rhinestones, white feathery wings, and a halo. "I think I need a halo, too," Sloane sighed.

I sneezed, and she shot me a wary look. "You're not getting sick, are you? It's probably the germs from all those planes you sat on. Disgusting."

"Now remember," Mandy tooted, "pictures are encouraged. The headdress room is next, and not to be believed!"

She led us into a small room that was like a Crayola box, stacked with feathers of every size and color imaginable.

"They use feathers from ostriches and vultures," she was saying, "dyed to order. Each headdress can take up to four weeks to assemble, as they wire each feather individually."

I had stopped listening. Taking a huge breath, I stepped up and willingly stuck my face into twenty pounds of bright yellow, dusty feathers.

"Oh, my God. Should I call security?" Mandy's voice wavered, betraying a little of that Carolina accent.

"Maybe 911 would be better, don't you think, dear?" Sloane's mom suggested, forever looking for approval from her husband. My eyes were quickly swelling, but I could feel Bidwell hovering, inspecting my transformation. I could smell the two screwdrivers he had had at brunch as he breathed over me.

"What is *wrong* with him?" Sloane wanted to know.

"Feathers," I croaked. "Allergic."

"Since when?" she demanded. "*I* never knew this."

"Since always. But you never bothered to listen, because everything has always been about you."

My ears felt host to a thousand angry bees, buzzing and stinging. I knew the feeling would move down my throat soon.

"But . . . but that's impossible," she sputtered. "The entire bottom of my gown is tulle and feathers. It's a chapel train!"

Talk about a straw breaking the camel's back. For me, it was a lone feather, slowly rocking back and forth in the air as it descended. It took its own sweet time to finally land, and it snapped me right in half.

"Sloane, I've been an afterthought in this entire relationship. Why should that change now?" I bellowed. Even Bidwell looked taken aback.

The itching had reached insane levels. I wanted to scratch my face off, tear my shirt off, and stick my head in a vat of ice water. Where was the Chicago snow when I needed it?

"I'm calling security." Mandy sounded more authoritative now.

"Air," I managed. "I just need. Room to breathe."

I felt my phone buzz in my pocket, indicating my GoToHail page was fulfilled and waiting at street level.

"Here, take the emergency exit."

I felt hands—Sloane's cool ones and Anne's bony ones—on my arms, leading me. I could hear the flat slap of Bidwell's soles leading the way.

"There's an ambulance now." My boss sounded eager to hand me off. "Not surprised; these casinos all must have in-house paramedics at the ready."

I heard the clanking of metal stretcher legs and someone say, "Whoa, lemme guess. All-you-can-eat crab leg buffet?" My eyes were swollen to slits, but I could make out the hazy forms of Jules and Mike standing beside a boxy white ambulance, dressed as paramedic and ride-along doctor, respectively. The ambulance had some red striping and a generic blue emergency medical care symbol on the side, the one that always reminded me of an asterisk with snakes on it. It even had its flashing lights going on top.

"He had this . . . this *gross* reaction to feathers. Will that scar?" Sloane wanted to know.

Mike was all business, snapping the gloves on, checking my pulse and blood pressure, while Jules rolled up my shirtsleeves and made sure the gurney straps were as tight as a straitjacket's.

"How long ago was the exposure?"

"It was, like, just now. We had barely even started the tour," Sloane complained. "Will it still be there by the weekend?"

"Sir," he said, addressing me, "have you had a history of similar reactions? And have you taken any new medications recently?"

"No medications at all, new or otherwise. And I haven't had a reaction like this since I was a little kid. I just try to avoid dusty, feather-filled rooms."

Sloane shrugged her shoulders defensively and made a clicking sound with her tongue as if to say, *So sue me.*

"Nausea?" he asked. I shook my head.

"How about cramping or diarrhea?" Jules chimed in. Oh, he was in his element.

"None of that," I said pointedly.

"Mild angioedema," Mike murmured, more to himself than to his supposed helper.

I felt the cool press of a stethoscope to my chest. "Deep breath, please."

I followed the good doctor's orders.

"Any tightness in your chest or shortness of breath?"

"Yeah, my chest feels . . . a little heavy." I tried to keep my breathing even as he did another go-round with the stethoscope. Sloane's parents gave each other a look. I wished Mike would pick up his pace. It had been a while since he had done an ER rotation as a resident, so he was probably a little rusty.

"He has a slight bronchoconstriction"—*boy, he's pulling out the old medical dictionary today*—"but vital signs are normal. Do you normally carry an EpiPen, sir?"

"No, never."

"Twenty-five milligrams of diphenhydramine," Mike said to Jules, who nodded and pulled a syringe from the medical kit in the back.

I hoped Mike wasn't going to let Jules play doctor with any needles.

"Grab the albuterol on the left." He turned to Sloane. "Miss, we need to start transport. If you'd like to accompany him to the hospital, you are welcome to ride in the back."

"Noah," she whined. "You know I get queasy if I'm not in a window seat."

I know it, all right. I huffed on the asthma inhaler and said nothing.

"We'll take a cab," her father announced. "After the tour. Assuming this isn't life or death?"

"No, sir, he'll be fine. I suspect he'll be released after a full workup. Just a precaution." Mike grinned his perfectly enhanced smile, and I saw Sloane's eyebrow go rogue, in that flirty way she had that had sucked me in at the Standard Club.

Gee, maybe I could've just introduced her to Doctor Love in the first place and avoided self-induced anaphylaxis, I thought wryly. Mike plunged the needle into my biceps.

"Sore spot?" Jules asked perversely as I winced. They lifted on Mike's count, and up I went into the back of the vehicle.

"Feel better, Ridgewood." It sounded more like a warning command than a well wish, coming from my boss.

"Honey," I heard Sloane's mother exclaim, just as the doors were closing, "is that an African American Elvis in the front seat?"

"Economy's tough, dear. Some of them have to moonlight."

Tim hooted a laugh as we careened down Las Vegas Boulevard. "Did you see the look on Sloane's face? She couldn't get rid of you fast enough!"

He had been hunched in the back of the ambulance the whole time, out of sight to avoid being recognized. Nate was behind the wheel, and, indeed, Black Elvis was riding shotgun. Minuscule Elvis, also known as Tommy, was perched in the middle, giving directions to McCarran Airport. "I don't blame her. You look like the Elephant Man."

"Shut it."

"Let's keep the patient calm, shall we?" Mike said, still insisting on checking my vitals every five minutes.

"You can quit playing doctor now," I told him.

He raised a brow of his own and shook his head with a slight smile.

"You're crazy, you know that? The Benadryl should kick in soon, though."

"Were you afraid of losing me back there?"

"No buddy dies on my watch," Mike vowed.

"And *nobody* ambushes the bachelor party on *my* watch," Tim declared, flipping his middle finger back in the direction of Bally's.

"Take that, you snobby motherfucker! And I'm maxing out your corporate card in the process." He high-fived Jules, who had buckled himself into the sideways seat. The satisfied grin on Jules's face told me playing doctor beat teaching college students how to use the card catalog by a long shot.

Tommy slid open the small window partition. "You guys okay with us making a couple stops along the way?" he asked, giving me a wink.

Tim gave him a salute, then turned back to me.

"When you shot me that coercion sign back at the bar, I knew it was going to be a delicate mission," he bragged.

"Most people would consider coercion by a rich blonde with tits the size of the Grand Tetons a first-world problem," Mike said, stripping off the white coat and scrubs. Like a superhero, he transformed back into Playboy Doc on His Day Off: crisp khaki linen trousers, white cotton shirt, and huaraches.

"Huaraches? What kind of doctor on call wears huaraches?"

"Asks the guy in the Italian bespoke suit and twenty-dollar Chucks," Mike retorted. "I'm beach ready. Too bad Grand Tetons turned down the ride in the ambulance after all. I bet she looks great frolicking in a bikini."

"Hey, I can give you her number. You and I, our paths never have to cross again." I laughed.

"You'd be dead to us, Mikey." Tim sounded like a character out of *The Godfather*. "You hear me?"

"Actually," I said, trying to smile through the swelling, "I think she has her eye on another man."

"Really?" Jules looked flabbergasted. "That was quick."

I thought back to my conversation with Remy. "More like a long time coming."

With that, I reached for my phone. This was going to be the easiest text I'd ever had to write Sloane.

Come to the Pop-Up Chapel in the lobby of the Cosmo tonight, 5 p.m. sharp. Alone. Bring your wedding dress.

Her reply was almost instantaneous, and understandably accusatory.

Why should I? I thought you were allergic to feathers.

I touched my cheeks. It felt like the swelling was starting to go down, thanks to that shot of prescription Benadryl. I always responded well to the over-the-counter version, which I'd pop after sleeping on a feather pillow by accident, so I was confident I'd look and feel normal again by the time we got to Kauai. Thinking about getting to the island and finding Laney made my heart drum double time.

I am. But Remy's not. He'll be there waiting for you.

I waited a beat before adding:

He never wanted to break up with you, Sloane. It was your father's doing.

It took her a while to text back. Maybe she was putting a lot of thought into what she wanted to say to me, for once.

OMG. U R Gr8!

Or . . . maybe not.

But another text quickly followed that one up, asking me not to hate her and wishing me well. That was all I needed.

"Enough," I said to Mike, as he came at me with the stethoscope one more time. "I'm fine. But I need to make a call."

Warren let out a long slow whistle. I had relayed the entire story to him, starting with Laney and ending with detailed instructions on how to wipe our computers clean. "So we've lost a few patents. And we're losing our funding and our distribution. But . . . we still have our integrity. It's okay, Scout. We've always landed on our feet, haven't we?"

"Yeah, we have," I said.

Tim had mentioned it was a skill he admired in me, but I had learned a lot from Warren over the years. More than I had previously owned up to. He had really taken over where my father had left off.

He had taken care of me, and now I was going to make sure he was taken care of. I reached for my laptop. Time to take Bidwell-Butler Solutions through a little "penetration testing," as we computer geeks called it.

"And, Scout?"

"Yeah, yeah, I know. My dad would've been proud."

"No, I was going to say your dad would've been laughing his ass off. Remember all his magic tricks? He always loved a good disappearing act."

Girl Talk

"Hit me."

Dani picked at the cucumber seaweed mask caking around her mouth. We had lost our spa house call, due to my tardy ETA, so we had decided to go the DIY route Friday afternoon: facials as we lounged in the hot tub behind our bedroom bungalow on the resort property.

"Favorite erogenous zone?"

Since meeting Noah?

"Pass."

Ankles.

Dani smacked me on the head with the Naughty Sleepover Q&A card.

"That's the third time you've passed, Laney. This is getting boring. If I didn't know better, I'd think you were passing just to get drunk."

I shrugged and took a swig of the mai tai she had strongly prepared.

"I might be trying to 'tai' one on. Get it?" My best friend groaned at my lame joke. "Actually, it's hard to drink with this junk hardening on our faces."

"Yeah, it gives a whole new meaning to trying to 'crack' a smile." She demonstrated, and a hunk of blue-green gook fell to the frothing water. We squealed with disgust. "What a glamorous night in, huh?""

"Just five more minutes, then we can wash it off."

Dani fanned the deck out in front of me. "There's got to be one question in here that you will answer. Pick. And answer."

I haphazardly pulled one out, sinking down in the Jacuzzi until the water was up to my neck. I breathed the steam in deeply before glancing at the card.

"Laney, jeez! What?" Dani looked alarmed as tears streamed down my green cheeks.

It was the "one that got away" question card.

I held it up for her to see.

"Oh, honey." Dani dog-paddled to my side. "Don't. You've wasted too much time on Allen Burnside. Not a minute more, do you hear me?"

"I'm not thinking about Allen," I sobbed. "It's Noah. I think he's the one that got away. Because I told him to stay away! I make a mess of everything and I . . . I was afraid of complicating his orderly, awesome life."

Love is wanting the best for someone, I heard Allen schooling me back at the Lake Shore Hotel. *Even if it makes you feel fucking awful.* I no longer heard the venom in his voice. Love and time had worn that away, leaving only truth.

"He's better off without me. And vice versa."

"Pfft, please," Dani razzed. "I bet Tech-Boy could use some upgrades to his life. Look at you! Laney 2.0, new and improved. With radiant skin."

I wiped the mask and the tears from my face with a washcloth.

"Believe me, I'm not compatible with the type of software he's used to . . . girls with tiny pores and big trust funds. Classy. The only way I land in first class is by lying."

We had weathered out a storm together, but the storm had passed. There was probably nothing but sunny skies ahead for Noah and his bride. And for my mother and Ernie's wedding.

And just a big shit cloud of nothing following me back to New York in a couple of days.

I climbed out of the hot tub and wrapped a towel around my bikini-clad body. The additional hours were catching up on me; the time change God's cruel joke. Giving me extra hours to rehash what I could've done differently when all I really wanted was to turn the clock back and forget.

"We need to get you a lei," Dani insisted, wiping the last bit of green from her temple and shaking out her damp curls behind her.

"Please. The last thing I need is to get laid."

I moved behind the bamboo half wall of the outdoor shower and stepped into the spray. The cool water soothed my skin made raw from the long hot tub soak.

"I said *lei*, you perv. As in flowers. Hawaii, remember? Let's throw on a dress and get in the spirit. There's got to be a luau happening somewhere. You know, where they dig up the pig that's been cooking all day under the sand?"

"That sounds kosher." I laughed.

The smell of hibiscus was all around me, and as I turned away from the spray, I realized there was one growing just three inches from my nose. Hawaii was real-deal beautiful. I needed to get my head out of the clouds . . . and my mind off the guy from seat 3A on Flight 1232.

Noah

T.C.B.

I didn't even have time to be nervous as the midsized, twin-engine aircraft came into view. "Move it out, men!" Tim was our fearless leader, doing head counts and getting us on board in an orderly fashion.

For once, I was filled with relief instead of dread as we roared down the runway and lifted, weightless, into the air, away from the strange land of Sin City. I watched as the landscape receded, everything shrinking into square patches of green, black, and terra-cotta. It looked exactly like the motherboard of a computer, with the roadways becoming a network of wires. I stared long after I could no longer see anything recognizable and my eyes had begun to water from the strain.

The clouds descended, then broke, and I gasped as mountains appeared, their faces striped like Indian war paint. Laney came to mind, sitting in the airport terminal and swiping wasabi over her sushi roll.

"I'm not running away."

I must've reminisced Laney's words out loud, because Tim replied, "Nope. You're running toward it. Five hours, as the crow flies."

Black Elvis, who was a real jazz cat named Stanley, turned in his chair. "You're taking care of business, man! Just like the King himself: T.C.B."

"How you doing, bro?" Tommy asked. He was in the seat across from me. Although his feet didn't even reach the ground, he threw his confidence around like a man twice his size.

"Better now," I said.

He held out his fist for a knuckle bump and almost broke my hand with his two huge gold rings: a big shiny lion head with glittery diamond eyes, and a sparkling horseshoe of stones.

I turned my attention to the photo gallery on my phone. I looked at the picture of Laney, working on her sketch by the dry fountain.

"This is nuts," I said. "No one falls in love in a span of four days."

"Romeo and Juliet did," Nate, our resident high school English teacher, supplied.

"There you go," Tim said.

I had a feeling he hadn't read the CliffsNotes to find out how that Happily Ever After had ended.

Full Circle

I was last in line for the bridesmaid processional, with Dani directly in front of me. We fiddled with our lone white orchids serving as bouquets and whispered like schoolgirls as we waited our turn.

"Think I'll get to walk with the Tight End?" Dani speculated, sneaking a peek at the rears of the groomsmen. Back in school, we would've passed a note back and forth with puffy bubble lettering to circle: *Yes or No*. Now, I used my pretty painted toe to trace a big *Y* in the sand.

Suddenly, we both froze and looked at each other.

Godzilla had spoken.

Or rather, he had roared from the beaded clamshell purse Dani had tucked under her arm. "Hurry, hurry!" I urged.

I had asked her to carry my phone and had forgotten to turn off the sound. She yanked it free and passed it to me.

Three o'clock, on the dot. He had set a task reminder.

A photo of me, clowning around in those shoes and wearing the dress, filled the screen. Tears filled my eyes.

Beneath it, his text read: *Has anyone told you today how incredible you are?*

I heard Dani's gasp. I hadn't told her about my little drunken fashion show.

"Your mom would completely *kill* you if she knew."

"Oh, Dani. If she even knew the half of it," I said, shaking my head with a smile. I touched my knuckles to my mascara-laden eyelashes, preventing the tears from forming inky rivulets down my perfectly made-up face.

Before I could even think of replying to his message, another one was delivered with a roar. Wedding guests turned in their seats to seek out the source.

"Laney," Dani hissed through gritted teeth, "we'd better put it away."

Or how beautiful you look?

It was the photo of me, eyes turned upward angelically, with a dreamy smile on my face. Clutched in my hands was that minibar bottle, empty of Jack, with Noah's remembrance poppy spryly poking out.

One of Ernie's groomsmen had taken the arm of my cousin Miriam, who was the bridesmaid in front of Dani. It was almost go time, but I couldn't bear to part with the phone, my only connection to those two magical days with Noah. I moved to hand it back, right as another photo popped up.

It was our selfie, cheeks pressed together. My eyes weren't closed, as I had claimed to him that night. They were wide and brightly shining. His were dark, warm, and sparkling. Maybe 90 percent due to the alcohol, but I knew there had been a tiny bit of both of us just being high on the moment, on the hopes of better things to come.

The delay had been an inconvenience, yes, but perhaps it had been the catalyst to jump-start each of our lives forward.

I wish I could tell you those things every day. I'm so glad I met you, Laney.

My tears were full-on faucet now. Dani went into defense mode and blocked the advance of her groomsman's arm.

"Hold your horses, buddy. The ocean isn't going anywhere. You okay, sweetie?"

She handed me a Kleenex. I quickly composed myself, setting the phone on vibrate and surrendering it. This was my mom's day. And I was truly happy for her and Ernie, for their chance together.

Dani tucked my phone back into her bag and kissed my cheek before heading down the sugary white sand strewn with red rose petals. She turned to give me one last wink before leaning into the crook of Tight End's arm and making her way down toward the water.

The chuppah could not have been any more beautiful: a simple bamboo structure with white sheer fabric twisting around it and billowing in the breeze. Ribbons as dark as my blue dress and as vibrant as the bridesmaid's seafoam hue wove through the white as contrast and looked stunning against the backdrop of the pristine sea.

In a few moments, my mother and her future husband would be underneath the peaceful canopy, uniting in marriage. But first I had to get down the aisle.

The string quartet, whose elegant sounds had blended in with the lapping sounds of the waves up until now, paused for a moment. Two of the women picked up ukuleles and began to play a song I knew, the Beatles' "Long and Winding Road," as my foot came down on the first cool, dewy rose petal. I couldn't help but think of Noah's red poppy, from where I found it in the snow.

I was vaguely aware of the smiling faces to my left and right and the whir and click of the photographer's camera.

But ahead of me was the limitless horizon of the blue Pacific. I was at the edge of an island, the place I had told Noah I liked best, back in Jughead's Diner.

You always know where you stand, I had told him.

I knew where I stood now. It was on my own two feet.

And perhaps good things came in threes:

I had a new starting point with my mother.

Allen was the wonderful part of my past that happened to include a killer soundtrack, as well as a song of my own that maybe I would let Three on a Match record someday.

And my future was like the favorite part of my sketchbook: a blank page.

A light ocean breeze blew against me, then it changed direction, pulling just a few strands of hair loose from my neat French twist.

Ernie smiled at me from under the chuppah. He looked like a million bucks in his white suit and traditional wedding lei of green maile leaves hanging around his shoulders like a vine. I kissed his cheek and moved to the other side of the chuppah to wait for the bride.

The ukuleles and strings began to play a beautiful rendition of the Beatles' "Two of Us" as my mother approached. It was a perfect song, given her and Ernie's history and memories. I don't know if it was Vera transforming the dress, or the dress transforming Vera, but my breath was taken away and my heart filled to bursting.

She looked as if she had just stepped out of her favorite fragrant garden. Around her neck was a triple-strand lei of tiny white flowers, and she carried a cascading bouquet of white orchids. Looped on each arm were three purple orchid leis. Ernie came halfway down the makeshift aisle of roses to meet her, grinning all the way, and they walked the last half together. They approached me, Miriam, and Dani first. My mother held out her arm and Ernie removed one orchid lei at a time. We each in turn bowed our heads to receive them.

"Good things come in threes, too," my mom whispered, her eyes lighting on mine. Now *that* was a Veraism I'd like to cross-stitch and hang on my wall.

They moved over to the groomsmen and bequeathed the remaining three leis before turning to the rabbi.

I tried to concentrate on the service itself, but my thoughts kept drifting, keeping time with the sound of the waves lapping at the shore behind me. Even with my toes gripping the warm sand, my mind was back in the snow.

With Noah at the fountain, the feel of his hands gripping my waist on the ice rink, and lying next to him on the freezing concrete under Cloud Gate. A delicious shiver of memory left me with goose bumps as I recalled our bodies crashing hot against each other in the hotel.

Enough. Back to reality, back to the present. My mother's day.

The rabbi was explaining the significance behind the Jewish tradition of breaking the glass. "But that's not exactly kosher, since we are on a public beach," he joked.

Indeed, the wedding site was open for all eyes to see, and the music and pageantry had attracted many beachgoers' attention. Some loitered at a respectful distance to watch the ceremony.

The rabbi went on to explain that in a new twist on the old tradition, Ernie and my mother would both don shoes and each break a glass wrapped in cloth on a wood platform. My mother had chosen a beautiful sea glass blue, while Ernie's was more of the green beer bottle variety. She would then add her colored glass to a vase of sand and he would add his to a separate vase, and finally they would combine the two colors, layer by layer, in one large vase to show the blending of their two lives.

I noticed a new spectator lingering on the sidelines, down the beach. He was tall, with chiseled features and shoe-polish black hair. Wearing white pants with a red-and-white Hawaiian shirt, he looked just like Elvis in *Blue Hawaii*. At any moment, I expected a big movie camera to roll up beside him and for someone to yell "Cut!" He looked that much the part.

But instead, another man stepped up, skin as cocoa dark as *Blue Hawaii* Elvis's was white. Either he was a pimp or he was crazy, decked out in a flamboyant white rhinestone jumpsuit and big dark shades.

And the unmistakable flip of a pompadour.

I turned to see if my mom or Ernie had noticed the uninvited guests in their strange choice of beach attire, but they were focused on pushing rings over each other's knuckles.

I glanced at Dani. Her eyes widened, and I traced her gaze. A G.I.-Era Elvis had joined the ranks.

Dani always did like a guy in uniform.

"Oh, my God," she mouthed at me.

I shrugged my shoulders, but my stomach was flipping like the pancakes from my Eighteen-Wheeler breakfast back in Chicago. I quickly glanced left and right.

"Why is there an army of Elvis impersonators at your mom's wedding?" Dani said in a hushed tone.

"I think . . ."

Out from behind the G.I. stepped a perfect miniature replica with a dazzling grin, decked out in Elvis's stunning peacock suit.

"I think they're here for me," I whispered.

A semicircle of Elvii was forming off to the far right. The wedding guests were beginning to take notice now. Vegas-Era Elvis, Gold Lamé Elvis—even a female Elvis in a sexy replica of the King's black jumpsuit was present and accounted for. I stood on my tiptoes and craned my neck, trying to see if anyone else was coming up the lone stretch of beach behind them.

My mom and Ernie stomped on the glasses. Dani gave a yelp. Her tiny purse, tucked under her armpit, was vibrating.

"Mazel tov!" everyone yelled, including a few of the Elvii. I got separated from Dani in the melee of mazel, everyone throwing arms up and kissing and hugging.

"Dani! What's it say?" I called, as the rabbi went in for the bear hug.

"Remind you!"

Her voice was drowned out when my cousin Miriam began singing a rousing rendition of the celebratory "Siman Tov," and was rallying everyone to join in and clap along.

"Remind me what?"

Dani pushed through the crowd, her hand catching mine. "*Behind* you! The text says 'Look behind you.'"

Behind me was the ocean.

And at the edge of it was a guy in a matchy-match suit.

"Laney, darling," my mother called out.

"Mom, I just . . . I gotta . . ." I pushed my flower into her hand, "I love you, congrats, hold that thought."

Noah had his suit jacket slung over one shoulder and his shirt-sleeves rolled up. But his tie was intact, and he was tracing on the dark flat sand with the toe of his red Converse high-top sneaker.

The wind teased his dark curls, and his hand held that ever-present phone. Stepping back, he admired his handiwork: a large heart etched in the sand. The bubbling surf flirted dangerously close to it.

I ran to him as fast as my long silk dress would allow, my bare heels digging down deep in the sand. He caught me up in his strong arms, pressing me to him.

Over his shoulder, I saw his phone impale the sand where it dropped, and I felt my feet leave the ground as he swung me.

"I see you picked up a couple of souvenirs in Vegas," I murmured. His neck smelled of limes and sunshine.

"Just a couple of good-luck charms," he replied. The Elvii were strutting down the beach toward us.

"Oh, so now you believe in luck?" I chided. "What happened to strategy? And product placement?"

"I still believe in all that, too," Noah said, gently setting me down. "And fate. And being in the right place at the right time."

Reaching into the pocket of his suit pants, he pulled out something round and pressed it into my palm, keeping his hands cupped over mine.

"Blow on it and make a wish."

"Another one of your magic tricks?"

"Go on."

I pursed my lips and blew lightly on our hands. He peeled his away from mine. Resting on my palm was a clear plastic bubble, and inside was the biggest diamond solitaire ring I had ever seen . . . faceted from a material I knew well.

"It's not for the mistakes," he said, dropping to his knees so he could pop open the plastic case and present the eraser ring to me. "I know we can't erase our pasts. But I thought it might come in handy when you start sketching the future. The highlights, the lowlights . . ."

The Elvii had gathered around the heart in the sand, surrounding us.

"I brought them all here as my witnesses—I'm not asking you to marry me just yet, Laney. But promise me you'll lay over with me somewhere, sometime soon?"

"Where to?" I asked.

"Anywhere you want. You did promise to kiss me on the return flight, and I'm going to hold you to that."

Noah

HOME

I twirled Laney around on the parquet dance floor under the huge tent overlooking the ocean to her guilty pleasure music: Billy Joel. "I picked this one," I murmured in her ear. "For both of us." The song was "You're My Home," and the lyrics were all that much sweeter as she sang them in my ear.

We continued slow dancing, long after the song had stopped and a rousing version of "Hot, Hot, Hot" began to play.

"Laney! Noah!" Dani squealed, "Conga line, come on!"

She had her fingers hooked into Tim's belt loops, and a long, hot pink feather boa around her neck. Apparently the DJ had brought a lot of props for the party. Laney's mom was leading the charge, with a sparkly tiara on her head, and Ernie was right behind, with huge plastic shades on.

The happy couple had been gracious enough to invite all of my bachelor party, the Elvii included, to join the merriment.

"*Ess, ess, kindela*," Laney's mom had said as the food came out. I assumed it was similar to my mother insisting "*Mangia, mangia,*" when I brought friends home.

"Because we don't have enough food . . . said no Jewish mom ever," Laney had teased, offering me a forkful of her mother and Ernie's red velvet wedding cake. Its icing was a cinnamon butter cream—a sweet, decadent, and hot combination, just like the girl from seat 3B on Flight 1232.

"No feathers near this guy," Laney called now.

She smiled up at me and added for my ears only, "Except my feathers, I hope?"

"Your feathers are perfect."

I touched her waist where I knew her peacock feather tattoo was hiding, and then spun her around. Her dress perfectly displayed her fierce, flaming phoenix feathers as well. "I can't believe you remembered that weird little fact about me."

She tapped the side of her head. "I've got your whole online dating profile right here. And I am keeping it all to myself. But perhaps a couple more rounds of Naughty Sleepover Q and A before I know everything . . . ?"

"I'm game," I said, giving her a squeeze.

"Is that your Bluetooth in your pocket, or are you happy to see me?" she teased, as my trouser pocket vibrated against her thigh.

It was Bidwell.

"I'm sorry," I said. "Do you mind if I take this? It's my final work call, promise."

Laney gave my cheek a kiss and went off to join the conga line.

"I told you it was a no-brainer, Ridgewood."

"Well, sir. Therein lies the problem, as I have a brain. And no one in his right mind would've accepted either choice. You should've picked some other two-bit Wop hack off the street to intimidate."

"You left my daughter at the altar!"

"Yes, sir. I did. At the altar, and in the arms of a capable man. Remy loves her far more than I ever could. And she loves him. I'd say it worked out well."

"Ambulance rentals, chartered planes . . . you've got a lot of nerve, Ridgewood," Bidwell sputtered. "Not to mention, you hacked administrator accounts that triggered automatic sell-offs of stocks?"

"It's called white hat hacking. Completely ethical. I exposed a weakness in your system. You should be thanking me. And Butler, too, while you're at it, as he was the one who wrote the code to stop it." Eventually.

"What do you want?"

"Give Butler a healthy severance package."

"And . . . ?"

"And I'll get out of your system." My choice of words wasn't lost on him.

I was done with his shady tactics and his marital manifestos. "I've dumped my Bidwell-Butler stocks and will use the profit to pay for the caterers and the reception hall. I take full responsibility for those June wedding incidentals . . . but I refuse to pay for her dress."

Bidwell heaved a gusty sigh. For a high roller, even he knew when to fold. "Good luck, son."

"I've got all the luck I need," I said, and I threw my phone as far into the Pacific as I could hurl it.

Bidwell would never have the chance to call me "son" again.

I shoved my hands in my pockets and stood staring out at the ocean for a very long time.

Until I had the feeling I was being watched.

No, not exactly watched. I was being sketched.

I turned around to find Laney, sitting in the sand. Her bare feet were tucked under her dress, and, sure enough, her sketchbook was in her lap.

"When we last left our intrepid hero . . ." she said, not so much as glancing up, her hands moving fluidly across the page. I noticed she was wearing her eraser ring.

Grinning, I dropped to the sand next to her. "He had a spine of steel grafted into his superhero bod and told the villainous boss to kiss his apps."

Laney applauded.

"But what happened to your 'live to work, work to live' motto?"

"Well, I think I'd like to help you out over at the Kitchen of Hope someday."

"I think that's a great idea," she said, flashing me that thousand-watt smile and making me feel like a million bucks.

"And I'm thinking of working on a new app, using QR codes with GPS tracking that you can attach to things, like a dress, so they can always be found." I winked. "Wanna be my beta?"

"Do you plan on losing me?" she asked, tossing her sketchpad into the sand. Reaching for my tie, she gently pulled me in for a kiss.

"Impossible," I replied, echoing my first word to her aboard the airplane when she claimed the seat in my row. And now she had claim to the first-class spot in my heart.

· ·

Noah and Laney
request the pleasure of your company
for the First Annual Celebration of Hope,
hosting deserving individuals and families
from Kitchen of Hope

· · ·

Six o'clock
Saturday, the eighth of June
Two thousand and thirteen

· · ·

The Altman Building
135 West Eighteenth Street, Manhattan
Dinner, with boogying down immediately following

· ·

Turn the page for a special preview of
Jessica Topper's next *Much "I Do" About Nothing* novel

Courtship of the Cake

Available June 2015 from Berkley Sensation!

"Winner, winner, chicken dinner! I don't know how do you do it, Danica James."

"Easy," I replied, handing the garment bag over the counter and into Bree's waiting arms. "I say yes, spend money I don't have on a dress I don't want, sashay down the aisle in it, and then I donate it to you."

"The only hard part to Dani being a bridesmaid," Laney added, "is not showing up the bride. Otherwise, it's a piece o' cake, right, Dani?"

I watched as my best friend selected M&M's from the candy dish Bree kept on the counter, using a vintage pewter salt spoon. Laney was just as picky about the brown M&M's as David Lee Roth backstage at a Van Halen concert.

She had to go and mention cake, didn't she?

I thumbed the tiny silver charm that hung at the hollow of my throat and wondered how the term *cake* came to mean "easy."

Bree laughed. "See? And the hard part for me is not showing up *as* the bride!" The shop owner held up her hand, fingers splayed to emphasize not only the number, but her latest rock as well. "Let's hope the fifth time's the charm, ladies."

Bree's habit of "falling in marriage" earned her spots on the local news and was the impetus behind the former fashion model falling into Diamonds & Fairy Dust, her bridal attire consignment business. The tiny Cornelia Street store carried everything from your suburban strip mall off-the-rack dress to the custom couture Vera Wang, which hadn't moved in the five years I'd known Bree. But once annually, she initiated Operation Fairy Dust, a dress drive for local high school girls in need, and accepted donations of gently used bridesmaid dresses to give away during prom season.

"It's gorgeous, Dani." She ran her hand over the ruched bodice and sweeping handkerchief skirt of the brilliant green gown. "We've still got a few schools in the area with prom approaching. You are going to make someone's dream come true."

Laney popped an M&M about the same hue as the dress in between my lips. "So what does she win?"

"Whatever it is, it had better be small enough to fit in my backpack. Unless it's a car, which I would totally accept." I laughed.

"According to my little black book of details, you have managed to donate a dress in every color of the rainbow. . . ."

"And don't forget the ones she brought in that *weren't* colors found in nature," Laney reminded, turning to me. "Like that Creature from the Seafoam-Blue Lagoon dress my mother made you wear at her wedding."

Bree laughed. "Earning the Rainbow Award is no easy feat. For that"—she rummaged under the counter and came up with the fluffiest rainbow Afro wig I had ever laid eyes on—"a picture on my Wall of Fame, if you will."

"You want me to wear *that*? I don't know where that thing's been!" It looked like a relic from New York's Studio 54 disco era.

"Trust me, it's new. No one but you has achieved rainbow status,"

Bree assured her with a grin. "You take 'always a bridesmaid' to a whole new level, Dani."

Always a bridesmaid and never a bride worked just fine for me; marriage required commitment. Of course, so did insanity. Coincidence? *I think not.*

Laney just about choked on her last M&M as I stuffed my mass of blond curls under the synthetic skullcap and mugged for Bree's Polaroid. Then she threw on a wig from the nearby display so I wouldn't have to go through the humiliation alone. Laney was good like that.

"How do I look?" she deadpanned. The long black Cleopatra wig was just shy of covering her poker-straight fiery red bangs.

"Ridiculous and lovely. Like Cher." I plopped a nearby tiara on the crown of her head and we pressed cheeks together for one last photo.

"Yeah, you should talk, Rainbow Brite. I think you used to have leg warmers that matched that hair."

Bree waved the developing print. "For your travels." She traded me the photo for the Afro, placing the small square into my hands as the image appeared; eighteen years of best friendship rising to the surface and solidifying like magic.

"I'm going to miss your visits, Dani. This one, though"—she reached to smooth Laney's fake bangs—"I have a feeling she'll be back. Just as soon as that new man of hers proposes."

"Hey, slow down there, Five Times' the Charm." Laney twined her own tresses with the long hanks of synthetic hair until it resembled a red-and-black candy cane. "Noah just finished paying off his non-wedding." The lovebirds had recently celebrated his near miss with Bridezilla by throwing a huge charity event in place of the already-booked reception, and were still recovering. "We're not in any hurry," she assured, but her mossy eyes blinked bright with the possibility.

Bree winked, more for my benefit. "Have fun. Be safe." Smiling, she moved on to help a customer.

Laney pouted and pulled off the wig. "I can't believe you're leaving, Dani—*again*. Just after I got you back. You tease."

"It's just for the summer, Hudson. Suck it up."

Despite all we had in common, Laney's homebody habits mostly confined her to the tristate area without complaint. My wanderlust since meeting Mick, on the other hand, had grown insatiable.

As had my sweet tooth.

"For someone who loves to live out of a duffel bag, you certainly held on to that dress from your sister's wedding for a record length of time. I was getting ready to call the Guinness Book," Laney ribbed knowingly.

Posy and Patrick were about to celebrate their first anniversary, and I was nowhere closer to figuring out just what the hell had happened to me that night of their wedding in New Orleans. Or why I couldn't let go of its memories . . .

I stole one last look at the dress as Bree hung it in the store window. Its opulently embellished halter and keyhole neckline had been perfect for the discreet touches and stolen kisses Mick had lavished upon me in public; its wisps of tiered chiffon held every whisper leading us out of the reception and back to my room.

"A wise woman once told me never to let a dress rule my life," Laney murmured.

The serene girl who stood before me was a far cry from the hot mess who'd been appointed dress bearer for her mother's cross-country nuptials this past winter. The one who had frantically texted, asking *WWDD—What Would Dani Do?*—every step of the way, until she had found her own footing. With a hand on my back, she pushed me over the threshold and out onto the quaint, one-block city street. "What would she tell you right about now?"

"I'm not as well-adjusted as you think I am," I mumbled.

"You are wonderful." Laney dropped a kiss on my cheek and an arm across my shoulder. "And I, for one, will always look up to you from my perch on your invisible psychiatrist's couch. As well as pay you in brunch food. What do you say?" She nodded toward the red-and-white-striped awning of the Cornelia Street Café. I knew tea and sympathy waited inside, as well as a willing ear if I was ready to talk about my rambling feet and broken heart.

"Sorry, girlie." I gave her a squeeze. "I can't stop; I've got to see a man about a car."

I was about to make my biggest commitment yet.

"So. How does zero interest for twelve months sound?"

My laughter reverberated off the chrome, steel, and safety glass surrounding me on the dealership floor. "Sounds a lot like my love life, actually."

I reaped the rewards of my own joke before the cavernous show-room quickly swallowed up the sound. It was fun while it lasted.

Kind of like my love life.

"Oh, please! I don't believe that for a second, Heartbreaker." Jax propped his feet up on the prime Manhattan real estate that was his desk and flashed me a grin. "And everyone says used car salesmen are the scammers and con artists?"

Jackson Davenport was not your typical used-car salesman; that was for sure. Upper East Side–born and summers in the Hamptons–bred. Valedictorian of our high school, Ivy League educated, and handsomeness so rugged, you'd think he stepped out of a Patagonia catalog. But he'd swapped his silver spoon long ago for a ballpoint pen, which he was now tapping against his teeth impatiently.

"Are you going to take the car or not, Dani?"

"Hell yeah."

Summer tour was calling, but it wasn't going to come to me.

Jax popped out of his chair. "Good. Then let's get this paperwork signed."

He spread a tree's worth of paper in front of me and pointed at the first X. "So what happened to that last guy, Marcus? He was cool."

"Firefighter Marcus . . ." I signed with a flourish, and relished the memory of those heated discussions we use to have, along with the slow burn of his lips. "He was a nice distraction."

"How about the bartender?" Jax flipped the page. "Here, here, and initial here."

"Sam? Arm candy." I tapped my temple, and then mimed cocking a gun. "Pretty empty upstairs." I lifted my pen to indicate I had signed, signed, and initialed.

"And Noah's friend . . . from Laney's mom's wedding? Soldier Boy?"

Tim had been a perfect partner in crime for the timeless, torturous bouquet and garter toss at the Hudson-Crystal wedding in Hawaii. After our respective best friends had snuck away from the reception together, Tim and I had been just about the only singles left on the dance floor to endure the humiliation. Tall and agile, he had barely needed to raise a hand to catch the lacy bit. And the flowers had landed right in my hands, despite Lady P, one of the many Elvis impersonators on site, and her valiant attempt to dive for it in her skintight black jumpsuit.

I let a wicked smile slip, remembering how Tim had eased that garter belt up my thigh, fingers climbing so high that I had to smack him with the bouquet to make him stop.

"Soldier Boy was fun," I admitted. He and I had both arrived in town last week to attend Laney and Noah's charity *soirée* for the Kitchen of Hope and had had even more fun. "But now he's back overseas."

"Pity. Mona and I really liked him."

While I had my dalliance du jour, Jax had long-term *relationships*. Mona—or Bitch'n'Mona, as Laney liked to call her—was his latest lady love. She had appeared on the scene after I'd moved out of state for my last job, so I didn't know her all that well. But if I knew Jax, it was serious . . . until the day it wasn't. My friend was an open and shut textbook case of serial monogamy.

Jax leaned over my shoulder and guided me through the last of the forms. His cologne had a hint of chilled cucumber with a citrus bite, and hung from his neck like a scrapbook for my senses. I was seventeen and running along the ocean shore again, not thirty-two and running away from my memories of Mick.

If that was even his real name in the first place.

"Tell me you're not still thinking about Mystery Man from a year ago?"

"Yep."

And I was still dreaming about him, too . . . especially on the nights when I ate dessert after eight o'clock. Mick had been just that sweet, just that sinful, and just that much of an indulgent fantasy.

I ran my fingers along the creamy silk ribbon at my throat, avoiding the charm tethered to it, and refrained from saying more.

While I sometimes found it easier to talk about it with Jax than Laney, I still hadn't been completely honest. The past year had hardly been a cakewalk.

"But you were the one who pulled the slutty Cinderella, right? Leaving him with a hard-on and a glass slipper at the end of the night?" Jax shuffled, collated, and stapled my paperwork while wearing a frown that indicated either intense concentration or massive disapproval.

Swallowing hard, I managed, "I just thought . . . he was different."

"No, you thought he was perfect. And he wasn't. So your playdar wasn't working that night? Time to forgive and forget."

I sighed. During the plane ride home from my sister's wedding in New Orleans, I had managed to work through all five of the Kübler-Ross stages of grief over Mick's deception: denial, anger, bargaining, depression, and acceptance. Forgiving was in there somewhere.

But forgetting? Kind of impossible. Not when those pale blue eyes haunted me every time I closed my own. His were icy like a husky's; mine were more of the Fiona Apple variety. Our gazes, made more electric and mysterious from behind the vintage masks Pat and Posy had insisted everyone wear during their reception, had locked in on each other the moment he'd stepped onto the dance floor.

I replayed his every move in stark, cinematic loops. And I heard his soft, sexy voice in stereo surround sound. I rewound my favorite parts and tortured myself by examining them in slow motion. Mick smiling. Tilting his head back in laughter. Touching my chin. Removing his black-and-gold scaramouche mask by its long-beaked nose as he moved to kiss me.

"I still can't believe I fell for a wedding crasher."

"You may just have met your match," Jax gently teased. "Funeral crasher."

I blushed at the title, thinking back to the day he and I met. I hadn't meant to attend the solemn graveside service for Jackson's family patriarch. But if I hadn't, this Townie never would've met the teen-tycoon-turned-used-car-salesman sitting across from her. Rolling his pen between his fingers in thought and absorbing everything around him, even though his imagination was light-years away.

Jax didn't need the job at the car dealership. But he took any opportunity to study the human condition as fodder to fuel his fiction.

"Maybe you'll write that story into one of your books someday."

"Maybe." Jax came back to earth and smiled at me. "But right now, I want to put you in the driver's seat. You ready?"

He grabbed my hand and we wound past the Bentleys and Lamborghinis smugly gracing Jax's uncle's showroom floor. The Davenport footprint was stamped all over Eleventh Avenue, where most of Manhattan's elite car dealerships sat. It had also worn a path down to Wall Street and back with its hard work and success.

Back in high school, hitching a ride with Jax meant showing up at the mall in a vintage Porsche Spyder, and posing for prom pictures in front of the Lotus used on the set of a James Bond movie. Until Laney and her high school sweetheart, Allen, had decided to reenact a Whitesnake video on the hood of Grandmother Davenport's Jaguar, resulting in a ban on young Jackson borrowing the keys to the family cars.

June heat rose from the city concrete and licked at my bare ankles as Jax pushed me gently through the automatic door and we left the air-conditioned building behind.

"You ready? No peeking, Danica James."

"How can I peek with your hands over my eyes?"

Jax knew me too well. I reached to pry his fingers apart to sneak a look, just like I'd do when he tried to protect me from the gory parts in a horror movie.

His hands dropped to my shoulders, mingling with my curls, and we both gazed upon the mustard-yellow Volkswagen bus baking in the midmorning sun of the back alley.

"You like?"

"Oh, my God. It's perfect." I gave his hands a squeeze, then shot forward to run my own down the VW's flat face. "How on earth did you get it?"

"Mugged a hippie." I threw him a look, and he laughed. "I put my feelers out. Auction in Michigan. It's a 1972 Westfalia. Fully restored, with a pop-up top."

"I see that." Teetering on the tiptoes of my sandals, I scoped out the camper's interior through the long side window. "A sink?"

"Yep, along with a few other upgrades. Built-in closet, icebox. Table folds out. Convertible bed, the works." Jax rocked back on his heels, pleased with himself. "Check out the seats. I think the upholstery is original."

"Avocado green. So sexy!" I reached through the open window and tentatively touched the wide steering wheel. The cogs in my head were already turning. "How many miles does it have on it?"

"Seventy-nine, five."

Not bad for a car ten years older than me. But still. I was going the distance. "Will it last me all summer?"

"It's going to get you where you need to go," Jax said.

I grimaced. That wasn't exactly the answer to my question.

"Treat you to lunch?" he asked. "We can hit the Rocking Horse."

"Depends. Where's your evil twin?"

Dexton Davenport hated me with the fiery passion of a thousand suns. And was often Jax's lunchtime companion if he roused himself out of bed early enough.

"Midtown. I think he was hitting Sam Ash and a few other guitar stores today. Come on," he coaxed. "Manhattan's big enough for the both of you."

"Dex despises me."

Jax rolled his eyes. He'd been stuck in the middle of this tug-of-war between me and his brother for years.

"No, Dex is just in a mood."

"He's been in a mood since your grandfather's funeral."

Jax laughed. It was a fairly accurate observation; what teenager wouldn't be grumpy upon learning of a deathbed confession that rocked his cushy little world, threw his family's inheritance into jeopardy, and forced him to slum it out in the suburbs for the rest of his high school career?

Jackson Davenport, for one. The good twin.

"So . . . carnitas and margaritas?"

His offer was poetic and tempting.

But I really needed to get going while I had the light.

"Rain check," I promised, throwing my arms around my friend. "How can I ever repay you for this?"

"Make good on the loan," he laughed. "Gypsy masseuse heartbreakers carry their checkbooks out on tour, right?"

"Always." My fingers performed a fluttering effleurage down his spine. "And maybe you'll take me up on that offer of a massage someday?"

"Rain check on your magic fingers," he managed, pulling away before he allowed himself to melt into me. "Oh, and I took the liberty . . . " He reached through the passenger window and pulled out a pair of custom vanity plates stamped with *WWDD*.

"Oh, Jax." Now it was my turn to melt as I watched my friend affix my favorite motto to my ride.

"Listen to that little voice inside your own head for once, will ya? WWDD?"

What Would Dani Do?

The phrase echoed as I navigated Mean Mistress Mustard, my new old van, through the snakes of traffic and into the Lincoln Tunnel with her headlights on.

It was true; my friends always looked to me for that voice of reason. My perfect mixture of level-headedness and levity. *Just walk away*, I had told Laney tenfold, guiding her through the land mines that came with loving a rock star like Allen Burnside. *Live a little*, I had urged her, when I knew all she wanted to do was die a little after losing him to cancer. And *be open to a grand adventure* were my words that helped get her on that plane to her mom's wedding and move her from heartache to happiness with Noah.

I needed to take my own advice, and taking the job as a backstage masseuse for the Minstrels & Mayhem Festival tour was certainly a start.

The tunnel rose, darkness dashed away by the unblinking eye of the summer sun.

I would forget Mick.

Starting with no dessert after eight o'clock at night.

Topper, Jessica,
Dictatorship of the dress /

Jan 2015